Prologue

Vatican City, Rome - October 1739

It was just after sunrise on a clear and unseasonably cold morning in the Holy City as Alessandro Morelli made his way through the east gate along the final stretch of Via Sant Anna to the Vatican Palace. As his feet patted on the flagstones and his breath condensed in the cold air in front of his face, he kept his hands buried deep inside his pockets and shivered. He was a short, middle-aged and slightly pudgy man with dark tousled hair wearing a long brown linen robe with a simple leather belt tied around his waist. A dark-grey hooded felt cape that partly obscured his face was draped over his shoulder.

As he hurried along the pavement, eager to get out of the cold whilst avoiding puddles of rainwater as he went, he glanced sideways along another street towards the enormous Piazza San Pietro. The largest square in the world, Saint Peter's Square was always packed full of worshippers whenever the pontiff held mass there. Above the square loomed the enormous

Basilica di San Pietro. Saint Peter's Basilica. One of mankind's most magnificent achievements and a true wonder of the world. Despite having worked in the Vatican for several years, the majesty of its architecture still managed to take Alessandro's breath away.

He entered the palace grounds and walked purposefully across the large courtyard of Cortile del Belvedere towards the Bibliotheca Apostolica Vaticana. The famous Vatican Library. In its earliest incarnation, the library dated all the way back to the 4th century when it was a mobile repository called the Chartarium that always travelled with the sitting Pope. In 1451, Pope Nicholas V decreed that all Greek, Latin and Hebrew codices should be gathered in one place and made available for scholars to study. This was partly done to consolidate all the written knowledge in the Vatican's possession, and partly in an explicit effort to create a repository of written texts to rival the ancient and now all but eviscerated Library of Alexandria in Egypt. Among the many thousands of documents were hundreds of ancient manuscripts from the Imperial Library of Constantinople, many of which had been stolen by Rome during the Fourth Crusade which resulted in the sacking of that city in 1204. The collection also included Greek classics translated into Latin and many obscure pagan texts. Now, more than three centuries after the construction of the Vatican Palace, the burgeoning library was home to tens of thousands of printed as well as handwritten books, manuscripts, ecclesiastical documents, scriptures and other texts covering theology, philosophy, history and law.

Alessandro had worked as a scribe in the library for three years. He was just one of many, transcribing original manuscripts from disparate sources into compendiums that could then be stored in an easily legible and accessible manner for use by the many scholars who congregated in Rome for this specific purpose. The work was referred to as *membra disiecta*, invoking the notion of 'dissected body parts', and its essence was the process of reusing fragments of one or more bodies of work to become another book. After hundreds of hours spent working in the library, Alessandro had become was exceptionally skilled at this work, and he had ended up as one of the most valued and trusted scribes working there.

One day, about four months ago, things had changed. Following a formal session with the chief librarian, the 73-year-old Vittorio Lombardo who was known by his official title *Bibliothecarius*, Alessandro had been brought before Cardinal Rossi, to whom the Pope had delegated ultimate responsibility for both the library and the church archives. The cardinal had given his approval, and Alessandro had then been inducted into an especially talented and trusted group of scribes who were allowed to work in the *Archivum Secretum Vaticanum* – the Vatican's Secret Archive. Here they would work for long hours every day and sometimes also during the night, painstakingly studying and transcribing the most sacred and important of the archive's texts, many of which were centuries old, and some of which were considered to be so dangerous that they were kept under lock and key in a separate section of the crypt deep beneath the Vatican Palace.

What chief librarian Lombardo and Cardinal Rossi could never have suspected, was that Alessandro was not at all what he appeared to be. His presence here was not accidental. His real name was not Alessandro, and his real purpose was much greater than simply toiling away as a lowly scribe. It was part of a grand design that had led him across the European continent for almost a decade in his search for the sacred book.

Never wavering from the duty that he had sworn to his brethren and to his masters to fulfil, he had offered his services as a scribe, first in the Eastern Orthodox capital of Constantinople where he worked for two years, eventually concluding that the book was not kept there. Then he had spent several years in Avignon in France where much of the Vatican Library's contents had been kept during the Avignon Papacy, which had followed from the death of Pope Boniface VIII after his arrest and maltreatment at the hands of the recently excommunicated King Philip IV of France. Ultimately though, this too had proven a fruitless endeavour, and after a time his masters had determined that the only place the sacred texts could be held was in the Archivum Secretum deep inside the vaults under the Vatican Palace in Rome, so that was where he had travelled. After a few weeks, and using his collection of references that were full of praise for his previous work, he had secured a position as a scribe in the service of the Holy See.

Today could end up being his last day in Vatican City. Today was when he would discover whether his years-long search had finally borne fruit. After many months of covert investigation and surreptitious late-night searches in the mile-long aisles of the secret archives, he now knew precisely where he needed to go and what to look for. All he had to do was get through the day and behave as he normally did, and then he would be able to put the final part of his plan into action. If successful, he would soon be in possession of an astonishing artefact. A prize more valuable than all the riches of the known world. His reward, which had been promised to him by his masters, would be bestowed upon him as soon as the book was delivered to its ultimate destination more than a thousand miles to the north along the pilgrimage route, the Via Francigena.

Alessandro proceeded through the main library's halls with their smooth marble floors, impressive high vaulted ceilings and long wide corridors. He exited the main building and walked across the smaller courtyard called Cortile della Bibliotheca to an entrance that was guarded by two intimidating soldiers from the *Guardia Svizzera Pontificia* – the Pope's Swiss Guard. It had been established by Pope Julian II in 1506 as a small private army of Swiss mercenaries, with the sole purpose of protecting him personally. Behind the two soldiers was a locked and sturdy-looking oak door through which Alessandro would be able to reach the Secret Archive.

The soldiers wore cuirass plate armour with chest plates decorated with an intricate and disturbing image of a fire-breathing devil, and around their necks, they sported white ruff collars. Covering their legs were baggy red and yellow breeches, and similarly coloured puffy sleeves extended out along their arms from the chest plates. On their heads, they wore their distinctive black-brimmed morion helmets, and in their hands, on which they wore black leather gloves, they held the fierce-looking part-spear and part-axe weapons called halberds.

The two men glowered at Alessandro as he approached, but they knew him by sight and allowed him to pass without unduly accosting him. Alessandro quickly inserted his key into the keyhole in the door, twisted it and then pushed the heavy door open. It squeaked on its rusty hinges as it swung aside.

Once inside, he shut the door behind him and pulled his hood back, rubbing his cold hands together. As usual, it was appreciably warmer inside the archive on account of the small wood burners placed throughout, and he proceeded through a long corridor to the scriptorium where he had his own desk amongst his colleagues. The room was rectangular and around twenty metres on either side, with a high wood-beamed ceiling overhead. About three metres above the flagstone floor were sets of lead-framed windows, intentionally placed up there to prevent anyone from looking in from the outside. The windows were small and let in less light than Alessandro would have liked, but he had eventually gotten used to them. There was a total of nine wooden desks arranged in a grid in the scriptorium, and all of the other eight were already occupied by other scribes, some of whom glanced up briefly to look at him as he entered. Unusually for Alessandro, he was the last person to arrive that morning. However, he had a very long day and night ahead of him, and if everything went according to plan, he would never need to come back to this place for the rest of his life.

He entered the room and walked silently to the back left corner where he took off his cape, sat down at his desk and began arranging his personal quills and inkwells just the way he liked to have them placed for his work. Once he was ready and everything was set, he bent forward slightly and continued where he had left off the evening before, transcribing a sheepskin manuscript from Tyre that had been written more than two centuries earlier.

The next twelve hours passed excruciatingly slowly, broken up only by a short lunch break. Later, at around four o'clock in the afternoon when the light coming in through the windows began to fade, chief librarian Vittorio Lombardo had arrived to light the candles on the walls as well as the small but effective oil lamps placed on each scribe's desk. Lombardo was an affable man in his seventies who was frail of body but bright in spirit. He was keen to make life in the scriptorium as agreeable as possible for his scribes, and he always had encouraging words and sage advice for them if they encountered difficulties in their work.

He was also a kind soul and was always close at hand to assist the scribes in any way he could. Yet, he never interfered, never told them how to do their jobs, and never stood watching over their shoulders to see if their work was of adequate quality. He understood that these men were in effect talented artists, and that he and the archive were best served by leaving them in peace to get on with their important work of ensuring the survival of the ancient texts for posterity.

Eventually, the Great Bell of the basilica, known as *il Campanone*, finally struck eight in the evening and all of the scribes began packing up their personal belongings and leaving the scriptorium. None of them took anything with them other than what they had brought in that morning. Taking written material out of the scriptorium, whether intentionally or by accident, would result in immediate dismissal by the cardinal, as well as a stint in the Vatican's prison.

Alessandro stayed behind and waited, pretending to be busy finishing a transcription of a section of text that required his full concentration. He had worked late into the evening on many previous occasions, so no one thought it unusual that he was the last of the scribes in the scriptorium that evening, least of all chief librarian Lombardo. As far as anyone was concerned, Alessandro was just a diligent and hard-working man, if sometimes a bit odd and reclusive.

After a few minutes, Lombardo emerged from the long corridor that connected the scriptorium to the administrative chambers of the archive. He was walking with the aid of his cane as usual, and he made his way calmly and unhurriedly towards Alessandro. As he walked, Alessandro could hear the gentle metallic clinking and rattling of the set of iron keys that was always attached to the chief librarian's belt. As had happened many times before, Lombardo slowly made his way to stand next to Alessandro, looking approvingly at the result of his day's work. The old man placed a frail but warm hand on the shoulder of what he considered one of his most talented scribes.

'Buona sera, Alessandro,' he said, his voice warm and empathetic.

Smiling as he spoke, Lombardo knew that he had made a good choice in picking Alessandro for this job. *'Come va, mio figlio?'*

''Not too bad,' replied Alessandro, sounding slightly subdued. 'I am just finishing up here.'

'It looks very good,' said Lombardo approvingly as he regarded the handwritten pages. 'I think you should go home for the evening. Get some rest.'

Alessandro nodded silently.

'Come now,' said Lombardo, and gave Alessandro's shoulder a gentle squeeze. 'This manuscript will be right here tomorrow morning.'

Alessandro rose, but then seemed to hesitate. He paused for a moment whilst looking down at the floor with a troubled expression on his face.

'Signore Lombardo,' he began, speaking in a hushed voice. 'May I speak with you privately? It is concerning… a personal matter.'

As he spoke, he glanced furtively towards the exit where the last of the other scribes was just in the process of leaving the scriptorium.

'Of course, my son,' replied Lombardo empathetically, his face immediately mirroring the obvious concern on Alessandro's. 'We will go to my chambers. Please come.'

Alessandro followed Lombardo silently along the low-ceilinged and vaulted limestone corridors towards the chief librarian's official chambers. After a couple of minutes, they stepped inside the office and Lombardo closed the door behind them. The décor was simple and ascetic, befitting of a pious man of the cloth, with a basic desk and a set of long wooden shelves mounted on the walls that were overflowing with stacks of books and piles of loose vellum pages.

'Please,' said the old man as he turned to make his way towards his desk. 'Tell me what is on your mind.'

What happened next came like a bolt of lightning from a clear blue sky. Before Lombardo even knew what was happening, Alessandro had placed a hand on his bony shoulder and pulled hard to turn him around. With the speed of a viper striking its prey, the usually mild-mannered scribe pulled out the short, curved silver blade that had been concealed inside the right sleeve of his robe and slashed violently across the chief librarian's throat. In the blink of an eye, the fiendish-looking and razor-sharp blade sliced open a long, deep gash across Vittorio Lombardo's throat. The weapon severed one carotid artery completely and cleaved his voice box in two, rendering him unable to cry out but allowing the air from his lungs to begin wheezing out. Blood immediately spurted from the open wound, and it sprayed the floor in front of him as he staggered backwards clutching desperately at his throat, trying desperately but in vain to call out for help. He was pressing his hands against his mutilated throat, but blood gushed out between his fingers and began soaking the front of his robe. His eyes were bulging as he tripped and fell against the wall behind him, and then he slid down to a sitting position with a stunned and crestfallen expression on his face, which conveyed the mixture of betrayal and surprise that he felt. As he looked up at Alessandro with tears in his eyes, he was unable to speak but simply mouthed the word '*Perché?*' Why?

Alessandro stood over him impassively and watched him, holding his gaze for several long moments as the blood drained from the old man's dying body. Then Lombardo seemed to sink into himself as the last gasp of air escaped from his lungs amid a gentle liquid gurgling sound, and then he slumped to one side and down onto the cold stone floor. His hands came away from his throat and fell limp onto the flagstones, and then he breathed no more. A large pool of dark red blood began to spread out onto the floor around him. Vittorio Lombardo was dead.

Alessandro wasted no time. He ignored the contents of the office, took a few quick steps forward to kneel beside his victim, and immediately unclipped the keys from Lombardo's belt. He then rose, opened the door a crack in order to look outside and make sure that there was no one else around, and then he slipped out into the corridor. Silently, he closed the door behind him and proceeded along a different set of corridors towards a winding stairwell that led down into the vaults under the library.

Where he was going now, no scribe had ever been before. Only the chief librarian, the cardinal and the Pope himself were allowed down there, and for good reason. At the very back of the crypt under the secret archive was a set of vaults that contained all the written material in the possession of the Vatican which could be conceived as inflammatory in some way, or which was perceived to undermine the Catholic Church. Most of it was simply heretical in one form or another. Other texts were more political and subversive in nature and were deemed to present an open challenge to the power of the Pope. However, there was another group of writings which were very different. On the extremely rare occasions when they were discussed or even mentioned inside the Vatican, they were referred to in hushed tones and variously described as 'pagan' or 'mystical', and sometimes 'evil'.

Alessandro knew that he had limited time to carry out his mission, so he hurried down the winding stairwell and arrived in an open space roughly four by four metres in size. Directly opposite and to either side of him were three large, solid-looking oak doors that were reinforced with hammered strips of flat iron bolted securely to them. Each one had a large keyhole next to the handle. Without a key, there was no way for anyone to enter this vault, and that was why Vittorio Lombardo had to die.

Alessandro hurried to the door on the left and fumbled with the bundle of keys until he found the right one. He inserted and twisted it, and then the lock clicked open, allowing him to push the door open. On the other side was a large room, perhaps twenty metres long and five metres wide, with a multi-vaulted ceiling that was roughly three metres high and supported by thick equidistantly placed stone pillars throughout. Placed lengthways in the room and stretching away from the oak door were three bookcases packed with hundreds, perhaps thousands of manuscripts, each one placed neatly in its designated spot on one of the four different levels of the bookcases. The air in the vault was dry and filled with the smell of parchment, leather and dust.

Even though he had never been inside the vault before, Alessandro had been able to uncover much of its contents and the order in which the texts were organised. This allowed him to move almost directly to the location where the sacred book was supposed to be kept. When he saw it sitting there on the shelf right in front of his eyes, he could barely believe it. Its plain exterior belied the immense power held within it, and when he spotted the emblem on its front, he instantly knew that his quest had finally come to an end. The book was large, roughly 40 by 50 centimetres and 15 centimetres thick, and when he picked it up it seemed unnaturally heavy, even given its size. He did not dare to open it. He had been given strict instructions not to do so by his masters, but even if he had been permitted to look inside, he would never have risked laying eyes on the words written there. Such was their rumoured potency that even a glance at them by an uninitiated like himself would render him insane.

Alessandro unfurled a set of leather strips that he had brought with him to strap the book to his back. He then donned his long dark cape and left the hood down so that it rested on top of the book to help conceal it. A few minutes later, he exited the archive and walked past two different sets of Swiss Guard soldiers, none of whom gave him a second look.

He then proceeded out of the Vatican Palace, through the gate and across the Piazza San Pietro, which was bathed in cold white light from the full moon above. Doing his utmost not to appear as if he was in a hurry, he continued along Via dei Penitenzieri down to a short pier by the Ponte Principe bridge across the river Tiber, where a small boat with a single occupant was waiting for him. Soon he was underway, sailing speedily downstream along the river towards the port city of Ostia which had been an important merchant harbour for the city of Rome since the days of the Roman Empire. By dawn, the small rivercraft had reached the mouth of the Tiber by the coast. Here it entered the main harbour and heaved to next to a large merchant vessel that was anchored there. Clutching the book, which Alessandro had now wrapped inside a large cloth, he climbed aboard the three-masted barque. He was then met by the captain who hurriedly showed him to his private quarters and then immediately ordered the crew to cast off and set sail for London.

★ ★ ★

London - November 1739

Archibald Valentine, the senior partner of the solicitors firm Valentine & Musgrave, closed the door to his expansive private study on the top floor of his grand Mayfair mansion and turned around to look at the package. It was sitting on his mahogany desk by the window overlooking the new and exclusive Cavendish Square. Until less than a decade ago, the area had been open fields and meadows. In 1686, King James II had first granted permission for a fair to be held in the first two weeks of the month of May, hence the name 'Mayfair'. In the early 18th century, King George I had then allowed for the expansion of the City of London beyond its walls, after which several new areas sprang up, Mayfair included.

Only the most wealthy and influential of the aristocracy and the country's political class, who were often one and the same, were given the opportunity to build here, and so almost the entirety of Cavendish Square was populated by Tory Party grandees. This was where Valentine, who was well-connected within political circles, had bought one of the most expensive plots and built himself a mansion on the north side of the square to envy all but the grandest of London residences.

He had just bid farewell to his unofficial business associate and general problem-solver, the burly and monosyllabic Cedric Barrow, who had taken the package off a recent arrival from Rome. Cedric had been a useful asset on many previous occasions when Valentine needed something done in the shadows, most often when pressure needed to be applied to someone in an 'extra-judicial' manner. The big man was loyal to a fault and made no secret of enjoying his work solving problems with brute force. None of what he did could ever be traced back to Valentine, but the unfortunate souls subjected to Cedric's powers of persuasion were always encouraged to put two and two together. And they were left in no doubt about what the incident related to or what was required to resolve the situation.

Having taken receipt of the precious cargo, Cedric had then ensured that the Italian scribe had met a swift but violent end. The scribe, a man by the name of Alessandro Morelli, had expected to be received in London with open arms and to have riches in the form of both wealth, knowledge and wisdom bestowed upon him. However, he was now floating languidly east in the cold and muddy waters of the Thames towards the estuary and eventually out to the open sea. Cedric himself had no idea who the man had been, and he did not care one bit. His master had given him a command, and he had simply obeyed.

Archibald Valentine was a short man who always wore round glasses and black braces. His attire, consisting of dark pinstriped trousers, a white linen shirt with puffy sleeves, a white cravat and a black silk vest under a grey waistcoat, was immaculate, as was the shine of his shoes. His dark but greying hair was brushed back and tied at the nape of his neck with a black silk ribbon, and his side whiskers were fashionably large and bushy yet perfectly trimmed. An impeccable appearance was one of the benefits of having a house full of live-in help, including maids and an ever-present manservant.

Keeping his eyes on the package, Valentine poured himself a large brandy from the expensive crystal carafe sitting on the console table next to the door and downed it in one gulp. Then he wiped his mouth with the back of his hand and burped. As he approached the package on the desk, walking across the polished but creaky dark wooden floorboards in his study, he could feel his heart beating in his chest. He could not remember the last time he had exerted himself to the point of having a pounding heart, but as he put his hands on the package and began to open it, he felt as if he had just finished running down to the river and back again. These days, not even the most riveting court appearances or the most bloodcurdling revelations during criminal trials could get him this stimulated and enthused. Next to the package was a large silver candelabra with six thick candles that bathed the desk in their warm yellow light. Off to his side, the fireplace crackled as the flames slowly consumed the heavy pieces of firewood he had placed there earlier in the evening.

He carefully cut the thin ropes that were wrapped around the fabric covering, and then pulled the fabric back to reveal a large leatherbound book. The candles flickered, and he leaned in over it to finally lay eyes on the prize he had been seeking for so long. It had taken years for Valentine to place his agents inside the Vatican. Finally, one of them had managed to obtain access to the library and then the archive, and he had then spent several years working to locate the fabled book. More than once, Valentine had wondered to himself whether it really existed or if it had never been anything more than a myth. But then one day Alessandro had located clues to its location inside the Vatican. It had been kept hidden in the vaults of the Secret Archive since the time of the Inquisition, specifically until the days just before Friday the 13th of October 1307 when scores of Knights Templar were arrested by King Philip IV of France and accused of heresy and even devil-worship. Many of them, including the order's grand master Jacques de Molay, were subsequently tried, found guilty and burned at the stake. In the aftermath, the sacred book had been taken from the crypts below a Templar castle in the south of France and brought to Rome, where it had been hidden away for more than four hundred years under lock and key in the vaults under the Vatican

Palace. Yet here it finally was. The key to untold power. A device to open the gates and forge a path to a whole new world.

Valentine had paid a king's ransom for it, but the money was immaterial, and it had not even been his own. His grand master possessed seemingly limitless wealth and would pay anything to get his hands on these texts. He was also certain to reward Valentine handsomely for his efforts. The grand master had only hinted at what was written on the parchment contained within the worn leather cover. But Valentine had never been in any doubt that these texts possessed power beyond imagining, and that only a small number of learned scholars would have the mental fortitude to read them and remain sane. He was also very familiar with the phrase *"The word is mightier than the sword"*, first attributed to an Assyrian sage by the name of Ahiqar who lived during the 7th century BCE. Never had truer words been spoken, and out of fear for his own sanity and out of respect and deference to his grand master, Valentine had promised not to read a single word or to even open the book. However, now that it lay here before him, he was unable to resist.

The dark leatherbound book looked even more ancient than it actually was, as if its pages had aged unnaturally rapidly due to the weight and power of the words and diagrams it contained. On its front cover was a strange symbol imprinted deep into the worn and scuffed leather. It was the patriarchal cross with its two distinct crossbars, which had been used extensively by the Knights Templar. The cross was sitting on top of what appeared to be a horizontal figure of eight, also known as the Ouroboros – the image of a serpent biting its own tail and an ancient symbol of continuity, infinity and immortality.

As he touched the sacred tome, Valentine felt a powerful and electrifying tremble ripple through his body, drawing him in and seemingly daring him to open it. It was as if it was calling out to him, urging him to come closer and read its hallowed contents. And Valentine, despite his promises to both the grand master and to himself, simply did not have the willpower to defy its command. He gently gripped the edge of the cover, feeling the weight and texture of the leather through his fingertips as he slowly lifted it and opened the ancient book to reveal an image that took his breath away. It was eminently familiar to him, yet it was as if he was seeing it now for the first time. It covered the entire first page of the book and was a detailed and magnificent depiction of Baphomet the horned and winged deity with the head of a goat and the body of a human hermaphrodite. The pagan idol, whose elements were originally sourced from ancient mystical Judaism, was sitting cross-legged with one hand raised pointing to a light crescent moon on its right, the other hand gesturing downward to a dark crescent moon on the left – the two celestial bodies signifying balance.

'As above, so below,' murmured Valentine quietly, invoking the well-known but ancient Hermetic axiom and the notion of the connection between the gods and the earthly existence, as well as the universal balance between light and dark, strong and weak, good and evil.

Rising from Baphomet's head between its two horns was a torch to signify wisdom, and on its forehead was an inverted pentagram to signify the challenge to the accepted order of the world. More than four centuries ago, men had been burned at the stake for their worship of this deity, but they had not died in vain. Their legacy was alive in the form of this text, and Valentine was almost overcome by its presence and palpable power. With it, he was sure that the grand master would be able to call forth the Legions and create a new dominion on Earth.

As Valentine turned over the page and looked at the exquisitely formed Latin text on the pages before him, a shiver ran down his spine. He knew that he should stop, but he was unable to do so. The horned creature had reached out to him across the centuries from the yellowed pages, and soon he was lost in its mystical words and incantations. Utterly entranced, he began to read, mouthing some words silently and whispering others with a quavering voice. Moments later, his eyes widened, the colour drained from his face, his hands began to tremble uncontrollably, and he felt his knees begin to buckle. He was not strong enough.

Squeezing his eyes shut, he quickly shut the book, removed his hands from it and took an unsteady step backwards, swaying slightly and breathing heavily. When he opened his eyes again, there was a sudden flicker of the candle flames. Then another. More powerful this time, threatening to blow some of them out. He turned his head towards the door, fully expecting it to have been opened somehow, but it was exactly the way he had left it. Shut and locked. Then he walked haltingly to the intricately lead-framed windows overlooking Cavendish Square outside. They were all closed tight. He looked over his shoulder towards the book. The candles were now burning gently and evenly again, and the fireplace bathed the room in a warm glow. Yet, when he looked closer, he realised that the bulky firewood logs had now been reduced to small glowing embers as if several hours had passed in just a few moments.

★ ★ ★

The following morning, after what had without comparison been the worst night's sleep Archibald Valentine had ever had, he asked for his breakfast to be brought to his bedroom. He spent most of the rest of the day pacing in his study and almost succumbing to the temptation of opening the book several times. He managed to resist the urge, and he instead busied himself with writing letters to a few of his clients and going for a long lunch by himself at his local members club. By late afternoon it was already rapidly getting dark again, and he hurried home along the snow-covered streets to his home where he then wrapped the heavy tome in a large black piece of silk and went downstairs to don his coat once more. He had already asked his manservant, Thomas Rhodes, to be ready to leave, and he was already waiting by the front door as Valentine came back down the stairs. The neatly dressed, tall and stoic-looking man in his mid-forties was muscular with a gaunt face, and he had short dark hair and green eyes and an air of aloofness about him that Valentine had always thought fitted his job rather well. He had come highly recommended by the grand master himself, having previously worked for him for almost a decade.

'Your carriage is ready,' said Rhodes evenly. 'Shall I carry your parcel?'

'No,' said Valentine as he hurried down the stairs to the lobby, clutching the silk-wrapped book. 'Just get me to Lambeth as quickly as you can.'

The two men put on their hats, flipped up their collars and stepped out into the street where Valentine's personal horse coach was waiting. It was a black closed-cabin carriage drawn by a single horse, and it had Valentine's family crest on the door. Rhodes hurried over to it, folded down the step, and opened the door to the cabin. Valentine shuffled down his mansion's wide stone steps to the street and climbed up into the cabin. As soon as he was inside, Rhodes closed the door and Valentine then locked it from the inside. You never knew when the riffraff of the city might suddenly attempt a robbery.

The coach tilted and shook slightly as Rhodes mounted it and climbed up into the exposed driver's seat at the front. On his command, the horse set into motion and within moments the coach was making its way south along Holles Street, across Hanover Square and then through the Burlington Estate where it seemed much of the respectable part of London was already out perusing the wares in the many shops.

Seventy-three years earlier, the Great Fire of London had decimated much of the city, but out here in the new West End, you could be forgiven for thinking that the fire had never happened. Mayfair was grand with its newly built Georgian mansions and townhouses. However, as the coach made its way southeast towards the river, there were an increasing number of houses that had survived the fire. Built during the reign of the Tudors, they had the characteristic oak beams inset into the brickwork, steeply pitched thatched roofing and multi-pane casement windows. High above the streets, smoke rose from thousands of chimney stacks servicing an even larger number of open fireplaces and cooking stoves inside thousands of small dwellings.

Leaving Mayfair, the streets turned from the recently laid cobblestone to the more traditional crushed pebble surface on the main thoroughfares and large flat stones in smaller alleys and side streets. All the trees in the squares and along the avenues were already bare, and even inside his comparatively warm cabin, Valentine shivered with cold.

As they turned the corner to head south along Whitehall, they slowed down as they passed a shop selling seasonal foods like meat pies and plum cakes. Valentine could smell them in the air as they went past. He even thought that he picked up the scent of Wassail, the punch prepared from sweetened and spiced brandy and wine garnished with apples and cinnamon.

They soon drove past the Palace of Whitehall, where 83 years previously, King Charles I had been beheaded on a cold December day, leading eventually to the rule of the Protectorate with Oliver Cromwell declared Lord Protector for life. As Valentine looked out of the window, he couldn't help musing sardonically over the fact that Christmas celebrations were banned during much of that time out of concern by the 'Godly' puritans that they were simply too closely associated with Catholicism. On top of that, there was no denying that the celebrations had become excessively drunken and debauched.

If only they knew, thought Valentine.

A few minutes later, the coach was making its way across Westminster Bridge, which had been finished and opened amidst much pomp and circumstance just over one year ago. It wasn't every year, or even every century, that a new bridge over the Thames was built. Valentine noted that whereas people in the streets of Mayfair had been well-dressed and were ambling along casually on the pavements, people in this part of the city appeared very different. They somehow seemed small and frail as they shuffled across the bridge, and most of them were woefully inadequately dressed for the cold weather.

Soon thereafter, Valentine was looking out at the borough of Lambeth, whose makeup was constituted of much smaller wooden houses in a generally poor state of repair. Many of these dwellings seemed more akin to tumbledown shacks than actual homes. It was a pitiful sight. When he had first been introduced to the grand master, Valentine could not for the life of him imagine why anyone would choose to live south of the river. Only later had he learned that Montague Manor was more than three hundred years old and that it had been built when there had been only one bridge across the Thames, namely London Bridge, and when the only houses south of the river had been in its immediate vicinity. Back then, the manor house had been sitting by itself on a large estate on the edge of the huge marsh and wetland area now called St George's Fields.

Rhodes made the horse take a left turn and proceed along Lambeth Marsh Road, where on the left Valentine could now see modest but neat dwellings, and on the right only the pitch black of the marshland. Soon thereafter, the coach turned abruptly right and began the dark half-mile, tree-lined approach to the manor house itself. The few times previously that Valentine had been here, he had marvelled at the ancient-looking gnarled trees with their enormously thick trunks and twisted branches. In all likelihood, they had been planted when the manor house was first built.

The coach finally arrived in the courtyard in front of the imposing Montague Manor, and Valentine exited the cabin as quickly as he could. Still clutching the silk-wrapped tome, he hurried up the thirteen steps to the massive oak front door. Rhodes had also dismounted and was already by his side, gripping the heavy brass doorknocker and knocking firmly three times. Almost immediately, the door swung open and they were ushered inside by the resident butler. He led them from the lobby, decorated opulently in the fashionable Baroque style, through two magnificent sitting rooms with ornately carved gilded furniture, cream-coloured wall panels and curtains, gilded mirrors and paintings, gold-embroidered fabrics and extensive use of the Rococo style, into an impressive high-ceilinged but much darker drawing room with large windows overlooking the grounds on one side and dark wood bookcases on the three remaining walls. He showed them inside, asked them to wait, and then closed the double doors behind them.

The drawing room, which was originally called a gentleman's withdrawing room, looked and felt more like a library than anything else. It smelled of old paper, leather and cigar smoke, and a bright warm glow emanated from the crackling logs in the huge fireplace. The heavy and richly decorated burgundy-coloured curtains in front of the tall windows had been drawn, and as Valentine and Rhodes stood there in silence, they both allowed themselves discreet glances around the room. The bookcases looked like they were threatening to burst with what Valentine estimated were easily several thousand volumes of old books and manuscripts, some looking eerily similar to the one he was holding in his hands.

Above the fireplace was a large oil painting that Montague had commissioned several years earlier from one of the most accomplished painters in the capital. It depicted the Great Fire of London, with roaring flames consuming house after house and the sky a rich orange from the glow of the conflagration below. In the centre of the painting was St Paul's Cathedral succumbing to the blaze and crumbling into the fiery inferno below. Valentine had seen it before, but he couldn't help but marvel at the skill and detail of the artist. In his mind, it conjured up notions of the fires of the mythical Greek underworld city of Hades.

After a few moments, a wall panel disguised as a bookcase opened and swung open next to an elaborately carved double pedestal partners desk made from richly veined rosewood. Valentine already knew of the secret passage down to the cellar beneath the manor house, but he had never been invited down there, and he would never dream of asking. Perhaps one day he would be allowed to enter. Surely, the fact that he had obtained the sacred book would be enough to ensure a promotion within the fraternity, and perhaps he would now be allowed to witness one of the spellbinding ceremonies.

When the bookcase slid back into place, leaving the secret passage entirely hidden from view of the uninitiated, grand master Godfrey Beresford Montague stood silently in front of them for a few moments before speaking. He cut an imposing figure. Tall and powerfully built, his face was staggeringly youthful despite his age. For some reason, his exact age was shrouded in mystery, but Valentine speculated that the grand master was at least a couple of decades his senior, although he did not look anything like it. He was dressed in a dark grey suit and carried a wooden cane with a large silver handle shaped like the head of a goat, and he rested his right hand on it with his index finger sitting between the two curving and twisting horns.

Montague was Deputy Treasurer of the City of London Corporation and also served as personal counsel to the Lord Mayor. In addition, he had recently been appointed to the newly established Privy Council to the King. As anyone in his wider circle knew, he owned one of the most extensive libraries in all of London, and he spent hours every day locked away inside it studying old manuscripts and religious texts.

He was believed by his peers to be a most learned scholar of Christianity because of his encyclopaedic knowledge of the scriptures, including all of their known sources brought before the two councils of Nicaea in 325 and 787 respectively. He was, however, also obsessed with money and status, and he had been fascinated by the occult from a young age. He had initially been enthralled by the German physician and demonologist Johann Weyer, who about two centuries earlier in 1577 had published the work *'De Praestigiis Daemonum'* – On the Illusions of the Demons. Later, his fascination had been directed at the French fortune teller, prolific poisoner and alleged sorceress Catherine Monvoisin who was said to have performed a black mass for Madame de Montespan, the mistress of King Louis XIV of France.

For many years now, Montague's main field of study had been the recently published 'Paradise Lost' by John Milton. He believed it to be a true account of how Lucifer and the other fallen angels had been defeated, banished from heaven and cast into hell, from where they eventually managed to escape to seduce and tempt God's most cherished creation – the humans. Much to the Grand master's chagrin, Milton had died before he had secured an opportunity to quiz him in person about precisely how the poem had come to be.

Montague had previously impressed upon Valentine that he had determined that the huge ten-volume poem could only have been revealed to Milton by Lucifer himself. Crucially, Montague was convinced that the notion of the Gates of hell, through which Lucifer escaped to the mortal plane of existence, should be taken literally. Even more astoundingly, the grand master postulated that those gates could be re-opened by the servants of Lucifer through rituals involving mystical incantations and blood sacrifice.

As unsettling and terrifying as this might sound to most simple folk, Montague was now pursuing the literal opening of the Gates of hell. To Valentine and the other members of the fraternity, however, it was anything but terrifying. It was exhilarating and awe-inspiring, and it represented a profound and exquisite opportunity to re-make the world in a more pure and righteous form. A world where the yoke of the church could finally be banished, where the shackles of Christianity were broken for eternity, and where the uncompromising and selfish individual could finally reign supreme in the Kingdom of the Dark Lord.

'Valentine,' said Montague in a low but powerfully baritone voice. 'Good to see you again.'

He took a few steps towards his guests and then stopped, pointing with his cane at the black silk wrapping in Valentine's arms.

'You have it?' he asked, his eyes gleaming as he looked first at the package and then at Valentine.

'I do, Grand Master,' replied Valentine breathlessly. 'We finally possess the codex. I am sure of it.'

Montague's head tilted slightly to one side and his keen pale blue eyes bored into Valentine's.

'I trust you did not open the book?' he asked suspiciously.

'No, Grand Master,' exclaimed Valentine, suddenly convinced that Montague was able to see right through his lie. 'I only laid eyes on the cover and the symbol imprinted on it. I never opened it.'

Montague regarded him silently for a moment and then nodded sagely.

'May I?' he asked, holding out his wrinkled old hands towards Valentine with his palms facing up.

'Of course,' said Valentine hurriedly and placed the hefty silk-wrapped tome in Montague's hands.

The weight of it did not seem to register in the Grand master's hands. Either the old man was strong as an ox, or Valentine had been mistaken when he had carried the book and felt it to be unnaturally heavy. Perhaps it only felt that way to the unworthy. Valentine began to sweat.

'I am grateful to have been given the chance to serve you,' he said. 'I should take my leave and allow you to commence your study of the codex.'

Montague looked once more at Valentine and nodded.

'Very well,' he said, returning his gaze to the wrapped package in his hands. 'If this really is what I think it is, it will take much of my time and all of my strength to compel it to do our bidding. I will send for you again once I have finished my work.'

'Thank you, Grand Master,' blurted Valentine, relief flooding through him. 'I shall continue to serve you.'

'You shall,' replied Montague and gave Rhodes an almost imperceptible nod. 'Good night.'

Valentine turned around and headed for the doors, and almost immediately they swung open as if the butler on the other side had known that his audience with the grand master had come to an end. The butler led Valentine and Rhodes back to the front door and opened it for them. The chilly air, damp and heavy with moisture from the surrounding marshland, was like a cold embrace after having just been inside the warm manor house. However, Valentine felt both thrilled and elated as he walked to the coach. This was his chance to finally enter the true circles of power in the world. Rhodes hurried ahead to the coach, lowered the step and opened the door for his master as he had done for years.

'Allow me,' he said, stretching out his left arm and offering Valentine a hand to get back into the cabin.

As he did so, Rhodes momentarily exposed the small tattoo on the inside of his wrist with the letters 'L.D.M.'. Rhodes had once confided in Valentine that he had acquired the tattoo as a young man when he had been badly smitten by a young lady by the name of Lily De Moulin. She was the daughter of a French accountant who had one day quite unexpectedly returned to Paris with his family, taking his daughter with him and thereby leaving Rhodes in despair. At least for a time.

'Oh, thank you,' said Valentine and took Rhodes' hand. 'I am quite exhausted, I must say.'

He clambered in and slumped heavily into the seat, expecting Rhodes to close the door as usual and mount the seat on the front of the carriage. Instead, his manservant climbed up into the cabin after him, placed a firm hand on his shoulder and used the other hand to pull out a long knife from under his coat. The murderous blade glinted briefly in the light from the manor house, and then Rhodes plunged it violently into Valentine's chest. With terrifying speed and power, Rhodes pulled out the blade and slammed it back into his master's chest three more times, sending spurts of warm blood flying inside the cabin. Valentine barely had time to react, and as his face contorted into shock and bewilderment, Rhodes brought the knife up towards his master's throat and sliced it open with one powerful scything blow. Deep red blood sprayed everywhere, and when Valentine finally attempted to scream, only a visceral gurgling noise came out. With his last ounce of strength, Valentine gazed up at Rhodes with a look of confusion and distress. Rhodes merely regarded him with a cold and detached glare – like a butcher bleeding an animal dry and watching its life ebb away before its slaughter.

When Rhodes was satisfied that Valentine was dead, he exited the cabin and wiped the blood from the blade, which now looked black in the pale moonlight. Then he climbed back up into the driver's seat and drove the coach around to the back of the stables and along a lane leading out into the marshland towards a group of small farm buildings owned by the estate but located half a mile from the manor house itself. Once there, he dragged Valentine out of the cabin, stripped him of his clothes and valuables and then dumped his naked lifeless corpse into a muddy pen full of large male pigs. They had not been fed for three days, and they immediately began feasting on the warm body. Within moments, steam from the corpse rose into the cold night air as it was ripped apart by the frenzied animals.

Rhodes returned to the coach and drove back towards the manor house. As he did so, he briefly glanced down at the tattoo on his wrist that was an ever-present reminder of whom he had sworn loyalty to.

L.D.M.

Lucifer Dominus Mundi.

Lucifer - Lord of the World.

★ ★ ★

Late the next evening, Cedric Barrow had gone to one of the ale houses near Borough Market just south of London Bridge. The tavern was called the Market Porter, and it was just a few minutes walk from his lodgings in Tooley Street near the Thames. Ordinarily, he would have made sure that he was asleep in his bed by this time, but quite unusually, Archibald Valentine had failed to send for him as he usually did on Monday mornings to hand him a list of his tasks for the week. In fact, Valentine had not been in touch for more than a week now, so Barrow had concluded that Valentine had most likely taken ill. As a result, he had decided to use the opportunity to get drunk in his local haunt and allow himself some much-needed female company and entertainment.

Things had gone precisely according to plan, and by midnight he had drunk somewhere in the region of eight pints of strong ale, lost several rounds of the dice game Hazard resulting in both an argument and a punch-up, and he had enjoyed a liaison with a lady of the night in a dark and damp alleyway nearby. All in all, a good night. At twelve o'clock, as the bells of St Paul's Cathedral chimed midnight less than half a mile away across the river to the north, Barrow had staggered unsteadily out of the Market Porter and begun to make his way home.

As he left the ale house, a tall man wearing a long black cape slipped out of the shadows and began following him silently. He kept his distance as Barrow threaded his way through the warren of dark and narrow streets and alleys towards the river. When Barrow turned down an almost deserted side street, the man picked up the pace and caught up with him. Just as he was passing Barrow, who was now ambling along slowly and drunkenly, the tall man feigned tripping and bumping into him. It felt like there were two short sharp impacts, but then the man apologised loudly and profusely and peeled off down an alley where he disappeared into the foggy darkness. Only then did Barrow notice that the piercing pain he had felt in his side as the clumsy man had stumbled into him was in fact not a side stitch that had resulted from excessive alcohol consumption and too much walking. He reached inside under his jacket to place his hand on the area from where the piercing pain emanated. When he pulled it back out to inspect it, he was shocked to see that it was completely covered in blood. Swerving to one side, he attempted to support himself against a cold and clammy brick wall whilst panting and looking back towards where the man had disappeared. He suddenly felt fear. He felt vulnerable. The street was now empty and silent. He called out.

'Help!'

He had never called for help before in his life, but he somehow knew instinctively that he was now in serious trouble. The pain that was blooming out through the left side of his abdomen was now becoming excruciating despite the dulling effect of the alcohol. He coughed and spat out something thick and red. Then he retched from the pain. As his left lung filled up with blood and his ruptured kidneys began to fail, he sank to his knees and then toppled over on his side onto the wet cobbled street, panting and wheezing while a dark pool of blood slowly began to spread around him. He suddenly no longer possessed the power of speech, and his limbs began to refuse his commands. Had the blade also been laced with poison?

Soon thereafter, Cedric Barrow was lying dead next to the brick wall on the dark cobbled street, reduced in just a few minutes from a strong man in the prime of his life to a lifeless corpse. Just a loose end that had now been neatly tied up by Thomas Rhodes.

★ ★ ★

LONDON - DECEMBER 21ST, 1741

Christmas had come to London once more. It was almost 11 p.m. and just below freezing. There was a thin layer of powdery snow covering every rooftop, and the parks and squares looked pristine in their crisp whiteness. On the doors of houses were holly wreaths with green leaves and red berries. However, the deep-seated scepticism about all things continental and possibly also Catholic, meant that the centuries-old German tradition of bringing conifer trees decorated with gingerbread, apples and small coloured glass ornaments had yet to make it to London. However, Christmas carols could be heard emanating from the churches and the public houses where the citizens of the metropolis were taking the opportunity to celebrate with a drink or two.

Inside the imposing colonnade-fronted temple-like building belonging to the fraternity on Upper Thames Street right next to London Bridge in the City of London, Grand Master Godfrey Montague was standing by the fireplace in one of his private rooms. As in previous years on this day of the winter solstice, which again marked the shortest day of the year, he had called together the *Filii Luciferi* – the Sons of Lucifer. The solstice was an age-old pagan tradition now usurped by the relatively new custom of Christmas. However, this was not the reason for the gathering that evening. Having spent several months investigating the contents of the codex brought to him from the Vatican, Montague had finally arrived at an appropriate way to commence the long sequence of sacrifices that he deemed would be required to break through the divine veil and communicate with the Dark Lord.

Outside the grand building were parked a handful of horse-drawn coaches, each with their dedicated driver patiently waiting for their respective masters to finish their business inside the building. Officially it was known as the home of the Worshipful Company of Jurists, one of the City of London's esteemed guilds and trade associations known as the Livery companies. However, amongst the select members of the fraternity that had converged in the opulent interior that evening, it was simply called the Temple.

One of the drivers waiting outside was Thomas Rhodes, who had arrived several hours before the others, and who was now parked off to one side near a narrow alleyway with a side entrance into the building. Earlier in the evening, after dropping off Montague at the Temple and temporarily removing the Montague crest from the doors of the gleaming jet-black coach, he had driven it about a mile east to the deprived area of Whitechapel where groups of harlots were huddled around wrought iron fire baskets waiting for the next customer to come along. As they plied their age-old trade, small groups of puritans were ineffectually harassing them with the prospects of eternal damnation and hellfire, but neither the harlots nor their patrons paid their zealous harriers any notice.

Wearing a long black coat and a black tricorn hat pulled down low, Rhodes came walking out of a courtyard with a young woman in tow. He had carefully selected one of the many ladies of the night that were offering their services to the well-to-do clientele frequenting this part of town late in the evening. The pretty, young and buxom redhead had enticing blue eyes and rosy cheeks, and she had said that her name was Lydia.

After agreeing on a price, Rhodes had led her to his coach and helped her climb up into the cabin. Offering her a bottle of brandy to keep her company until they arrived at their destination, Rhodes had then driven a short distance north to a small deserted alley where he had suddenly stopped the coach, jumped down onto the cobbles and climbed in the back with her. Before she realised what was happening, he had pushed her violently back against the seat. He then extracted a recent European invention from his coat pocket, a small metal syringe with a hypodermic needle, which had been provided to him by his master for this purpose. Pinning the young woman in place, he pressed the short stubby needle through the skin on her neck and injected her with a powerful dose of opium directly into her bloodstream. Within seconds, her pupils had dilated to large black voids and the muscles in her body had relaxed as the drug flooded through her veins and sent her into a stupor of drowsiness and lethargy. Twenty minutes later, Rhodes had bundled her through the side entrance to the Temple on Upper Thames Street.

About five metres below street level, the congregation had gathered in the Temple's candlelit *Sanctum Sanctorum* – The Holy of Holies. The room was circular, roughly eight metres in diameter, and it contained a circular stone platform placed in its centre. On one side of the room was a doorway to a long corridor leading to a winding stone staircase that extended up into the Temple. On the far edge of the platform opposite the doorway was a patriarchal cross made from polished silvery metal. It was about two metres tall and sitting on an Ouroboros – the ancient horizontal figure-of-eight infinity sign that had originally been conceived as an image of a snake biting its own tail. The entire human-sized symbol was known as the brimstone symbol.

The platform, which was in fact a type of altar, was made from perfectly smooth stone. Into its surface had been carved neat grooves roughly one inch deep and one inch wide. Together they formed the shape of a pentagram covering the entire altar, with each of the five points of the star-shape reaching the edge of the platform. The lower point of the pentagram was pointing directly towards the doorway and the corridor, with the other four points placed along the curved edges of the platform, two on either side.

In front of each of the four lateral points stood four men dressed in long black flowing silk robes with red hoods which blocked the candlelight and obscured their faces in the dimly lit room. Around their necks hanging on long thick silver chains, they each wore a silver brimstone symbol. Together, the four men uttered an incantation in unison, after which the fifth and final member of the gathering, the officiant known as 'The Ancient One' and the most senior member of the fraternity, appeared from the corridor and moved to stand directly in front of the fifth point of the pentagram. His name was Godfrey Montague, and he was wearing a black silk robe identical to those of the other four men, but instead of a red hood, he wore a chilling full-face mask in the shape of the head of a goat. Only his mouth and jaw were visible. On its forehead, the mask had two horns twisting up into sharp points, and between them was a small lit torch. On the forehead of the goat head was a silver pentagram.

This was now the third time the five men, representing the very pinnacle of the fraternity, had met for this ceremony on this, the shortest day of the year. Each of the two previous attempts had proven fruitless. Failures. But Montague was undeterred, believing that they need only persevere until their reward was finally released to them. He was convinced that it was only a question of time and sacrifice before they were heard.

He reached inside his robe and extracted a small wooden box, which he opened. From it, he lifted what appeared to be a walnut-sized piece of rock crystal with a rich yellow colour similar to that of a lemon. It was a piece of sulphur that he had personally mined during one of his sojourns to Italy. It was from inside a mine near the city of Catania in Sicily, less than ten kilometres from Mount Etna whose magma conduit reached deep into the fiery Earth.

Depositing the sulphur crystal in a small polished silver tray that was placed just inside the fifth point of the pentagram, he then used a candle to ignite the crystal. The candle quickly set it aflame, and as it burned, it emitted a rich blue flame that shone its eerie light up onto Montague's terrifying horned mask. Amid the continued chanting, and as the fire continued to slowly consume the crystal, the sulphur produced its characteristic acrid brimstone smell. The heat of the combustion gradually transformed, as if by magic, the yellow crystal into a blood-red liquid in the bottom of the silver tray.

At Montague's signal, the four men ceased their incantation after which the grand master called out a plea in Latin, asking their Lord to accept their offering.

'Accipe sacrificium nostrum!'
Accept our sacrifice!

'Mundus flammae!'
The world aflame!

At that, a large man who was clad entirely in black appeared from behind the tall silver brimstone symbol mounted on the other side of the platform. He was wearing a frightening black executioner's hood over his head with only two narrow slits for his eyes, and with his powerful gloved hands, he was holding the arms of a young redheaded woman who was wearing only a white partly see-through satin négligée which accentuated her figure. She seemed to have been heavily drugged, and she was staggering unsteadily along next to and slightly in front of the man.

As he pushed her up the five steps and onto the raised platform, she glanced bleary-eyed around the room with a perplexed yet detached look on her face. With the swift efficiency of someone who had performed this task before, the hooded man quickly tied her arms tightly to each side of the patriarchal cross with a rope and then did the same with her feet at the base of the brimstone symbol. She winced slightly at the pain as the ropes cut into her wrists, but the drugs quickly made the discomfort fade. Before stepping down and disappearing behind the brimstone symbol, the hooded man gripped the top of the négligée and ripped downwards, stripping it violently off her body and leaving her completely naked. She twitched nervously as it happened, but upon seeing the five robed figures standing in front and below her, one of them with a bizarre horned mask on his head, an almost coy and coquettish smile spread across her face, as if to say that she had never been involved in a séance like this before, but that she was intrigued to find out what would happen next.

Suddenly, the entire brimstone symbol rotated counter-clockwise 180 degrees, leaving her strapped upside down to the contraption. As it did so, she produced a small yelp and then a detached and drunken-sounding giggle as it stopped. After a couple of seconds, the hooded man reached around from behind the symbol with a curved silver blade and slit her throat wide open with one quick swipe. The young woman instantly panicked, writhing frantically in her restraints and attempting to scream but producing only a blood-choked gurgling splutter as the blood gushed from her neck down across her face and onto the platform.

The five participants in the ceremony stood motionless and watched as the warm blood kept pouring from the open gash in the young woman's throat and began to pool in a small basin cut into the platform directly below her. From there, it immediately began to flow along the grooves in the platform's surface, gradually creating the gruesome shape of a crimson pentagram as it moved. Soon, the woman's struggle abated, and within less than a minute she hung motionless – the last of her blood trickling into the basin. By now the pentagram of blood was fully formed, and the red liquid began to spill over the small cuts in the platform's edge where the five points of the pentagram were located. It then flowed languidly into five small silver goblets, one for each of the ceremony's participants.

Emulating The Ancient One, the four other participants picked up their drinking vessels and brought them up to their lips. Performing the ritual in perfect unison, they each drank greedily from the warm blood in their silver vessels, and then they raised them up high. Still, with blood on his lips, The Ancient One then proceeded to utter two Latin phrases repeatedly.

'Aperite portas inferi!'
'Open the gates of hell.'

'Sit mundus ardeat!'
'Let the world burn.'

The other four participants joined in so that the dimly lit underground sacrificial chamber was filled with the reverberating sounds of the diabolical incantations growing ever louder. The energy flowing through the five men felt electrifying and transcendental as if the very air in the chamber burned and glowed with the power of the gory demonic ritual.

Finally, amid the crescendo of the chanting and the final spasms of the dying woman, Grand Master Montague called out to Lucifer once more, this time at the top of his voice, urging him to open the gates of hell and release his hoards upon the world. And in that moment it finally happened. Montague felt it. He was sure of it.

The Dark Lord answered.

ONE

LONDON – EARLY JUNE, PRESENT DAY

Andrew Sterling was in the basement underneath the HQ of the low-profile SAS sub-unit where he had been working for the past five years. The unit was focused exclusively on combatting threats from biological, chemical and nuclear terrorism, both through intelligence gathering and direct action when necessary. The basement level was divided into several separate sections, one of them being a 30-metre-long firing range. It was early in the morning and Andrew had the entire range to himself. At sunrise around 4:45 a.m. he had slid out of the bed he shared with his girlfriend Fiona Keane, donned his running clothes and trainers and gone for a morning run on Hampstead Heath. Fiona was a historian and archaeologist at the British Museum in Bloomsbury in the West End of London, and since she did not have to show up for work until 9 a.m., Andrew was keen to let her get as much sleep as she needed.

The heath was a few hundred metres from the large house he and Fiona now lived in together after he had inherited it following the death of his parents just over a decade ago. Running on the virtually deserted heath as the sun came up over London was the best way for him to wake up, clear his head, and obtain a focused frame of mind for the day ahead. It was also an excellent way for him to stay physically fit, and combined with his regular stints in the gym, he was probably in better shape than 99% of other men in their late thirties.

By the time he got back to the house, sweating and panting but feeling invigorated and ready for the day, Fiona was in the shower. He made them both a cup of coffee and wolfed down a plateful of waffles laced with maple syrup – something he had come to appreciate after several visits to the US.

After a leisurely breakfast with Fiona, chatting and marvelling together at the latest sensationalist yet vacuous headlines on the morning news, Andrew took a shower and put on a casual suit which Fiona said made him look like an accountant. He then kissed her goodbye, left the house and got in behind the wheel of his forest-green metallic-effect Aston Martin DB9 and drove to the office on Sheldrake Place near Holland Park in Kensington.

Now by himself inside the underground shooting range and wearing dark blue jeans, a black shirt with the sleeves rolled up and yellow ear muffs, Andrew looked down at the Glock 17 in his hand, flicked the magazine release catch and popped out the magazine.

This was a fourth-generation version of the weapon, which had been a favourite of special forces units across the world since its introduction in the 1980s when it had replaced many older types of weapons, including the Beretta Px4 and the Heckler & Koch P30, both of which had previously been used by the British armed forces.

Quickly inspecting the magazine to make sure it was full and that the bullets were perfectly aligned and ready to be fed into the chamber of the gun, Andrew slapped the 17-round magazine into the grip and pulled back the slide to chamber the first round. He adjusted his feet to enter the so-called Isosceles stance. Facing forward and placing his feet about half a metre apart and bending his knees slightly, he held the gun out in front of himself with his arms straight and looked down its iron sights. He then took a quick breath, inhaled and then exhaled halfway and held it, squeezing the trigger whilst keeping the weapon trained at the target 30 metres away.

The dry crack of the unsuppressed pistol inside the confined concrete shooting range was surprisingly loud, and the first bullet slammed into the centre mass of the human-shaped paper target at the other end of his lane. So did the next two rounds. He adjusted his aim slightly and fired three more rounds, all of which found their mark in a tight grouping in the face of the target.

He glanced to his right to see a live image of the target on a small monitor next to him. Content with his result, he hit the button to swap out the target for a fresh one, and then shifted his body into the Weaver stance. Placing his right foot back about thirty centimetres and pointing out to the right, shifting his left foot forward slightly and pointing straight ahead, he once again bent his knees, brought up the gun and aimed down the sights. This time he fired three rounds in quick succession, lowered the gun, and then brought it up to re-aim and fire three more. Once again, he checked the monitor and was gratified to see that all six of the 9mm Parabellum bullets had found their marks very near where he had been aiming.

During his time in the SAS, Andrew had fired hundreds of thousands of rounds, the vast majority of which had been on shooting ranges and in so-called 'kill houses' where he and his platoon mates had practised breaching and clearing buildings to the point where they not only felt that they could do it in their sleep but where they knew exactly where their comrades were, what they were about to do and how they would do it. These exercises were always carried out with live ammunition, which carried with it inherent risks, but it was the only way to properly simulate an anti-terrorist operation and ensure that everyone was as switched on as they needed to be in case they were called out to the real thing. And invariably, the real thing always happened eventually, although mostly in the shadows and out of the media spotlight. The vast majority of their operations were never reported or even acknowledged publicly, especially if they had been carried out abroad, which was most often the case.

Being part of a tight-knit, well-oiled machine like a platoon of highly trained special forces operators was something only a tiny fraction of the armed forces ever got to experience, and it was something Andrew was not afraid to admit he sorely missed from time to time. However, the work he did now was immensely gratifying in its own right, and now that he was a bit older and hopefully slightly more mature than when he had first gone through selection and joined 22 SAS, he was in no doubt that this was all part of a natural and healthy progression.

Andrew never brought his phone down to the firing range. He did not want to be distracted, and he also did not want to ruin the concentration of anyone else who might be down there honing their firearms skills, just in case the phone suddenly rang or an email or a text message pinged in. Having completed his session, he exited the firing range, taking off the earmuffs as he walked back up the stairs to the ground floor. He then proceeded up to his office on the 2nd floor where he discovered that there was a voice message on his phone from Fiona. She usually preferred writing text messages, and it was unlike her to leave a voicemail unless there was something urgent that she needed to discuss with him.

The message was brief, but Andrew could hear quite clearly from the tone of her voice that she was worried about something. She did not explain what exactly but instead asked if she could come by and see him immediately. Without hesitating, Andrew sent her a message asking her to come straight to the office as soon as she could, and only ten minutes later he got a call from the receptionist to say that Fiona was waiting in the lobby. She had correctly assumed what he would decide to do and had left their home immediately after leaving the voice message. Andrew asked for her to be allowed upstairs.

'Come and sit,' he said as she entered his office, motioning to the two-person Chesterfield leather sofa across from his desk. 'What's happened?'

Fiona had deep concern written all over her face, and as she sat down she was wringing her hands and looking fleetingly at Andrew as if trying to decide how to begin.

'It's my little sister, Caitlin,' she said, the timbre of her voice betraying real unease.

Andrew had met Caitlin on a number of occasions. She was five years Fiona's junior if he remembered correctly, and a happy and gregarious redhead. He liked her a lot but considered her somewhat flighty and a bit of a hippie. An aspiring earth mother who was into transcendental meditation and alternative pacifist anarchic lifestyles, whatever that meant exactly. In any case, it was something he considered to belong in the distant past of the 1960s and 70s. In other words, Caitlin was nothing like her older sister, although he knew that the two of them had been like twins when they were growing up in central Dublin. They were inseparable, boundlessly loyal to each other and always looking out for one another.

'Is she all right?' asked Andrew.

'Well,' said Fiona anxiously. 'That's the thing. I received a message from her just after you left this morning, which suddenly has me really worried.'

'Where is she?' asked Andrew as he sat down next to Fiona and took her hand in his.

'I don't know,' continued Fiona. 'I just have a really bad feeling about this. I think something might have happened to her. Something bad.'

'What did the message say?' Andrew probed gently.

'Something very cryptic,' replied Fiona, 'but let me just tell you about something else first. Remember how she asked to see me a few weeks ago, and she and I then went for lunch together?'

'Sure,' said Andrew. 'You guys went to the Coffee Cup in Hampstead, didn't you?'

'That's right,' said Fiona. 'A few days before that, she had sent me a message. Let me just find it.'

She extracted her phone from her handbag and tapped and swiped a few times.

'Here it is,' she said. 'This is what she wrote to me a few weeks ago. "If you truly love someone, should forgiveness be without bounds?".'

'What does that mean?' asked Andrew with a perplexed look on his face. 'Was she in some sort of abusive relationship?'

'No,' replied Fiona, shaking her head but looking concerned. 'At least, not that I know of. She had just met some French guy here in London, and I am sure she would have told me if there was a problem. In fact, during our lunch, she kept going on about him, and she brushed it aside when I tried to ask if everything was ok with him. She seemed quite smitten, actually. She said she had just been back to Dublin to see some of her old friends, and that she was thinking about introducing him to them.'

'What do you know about this guy,' asked Andrew. 'Does he have a name?'

'His name is Antoine,' replied Fiona. 'She met him in the commune where she is living.'

'The one near Portobello Road?' he asked.

'That's right,' said Fiona. 'Whirlwind romance, apparently. I asked her if I could see a picture of him, but she didn't have one because she said he doesn't like having his picture taken, which I thought was a bit odd. Anyway, she took one of him later when he was asleep. I've got it here.'

Fiona showed Andrew her phone. On the screen was an image of a bed in a small and messy bedroom with sunlight coming in through a window that was out of shot. On the bed, lying on his back with one hand under the back of his head, was a young man with longish blond hair who looked to be in his early thirties. He was attractive with the physique of a swimmer and a face that would not have been out of place in a fashion magazine, and he appeared to be fast asleep.

'Good looking chap,' said Andrew. 'Is he Caitlin's type?'

'I honestly don't know these days,' replied Fiona and shrugged. 'I mean, he's in her bed half-naked, so I guess so.'

'What's that?' asked Andrew focusing in on Antoine's arm. 'Just there by his wrist. Looks like a tattoo.'

'It is,' said Fiona. 'Caitlin told me about it because she thought it was the most boring tattoo she had ever seen.'

'Are those letters?' asked Andrew.

'Yes,' replied Fiona. 'It's an acronym. L.D.M. Supposedly, it is the name of a lake and a hard-drinking rowing club that he used to be a member of when he was younger. Lac de Montriond in the French Alps. It's apparently a very picturesque lake that is very close to the Swiss border where he used to live. Caitlin said he was planning to take her there someday.'

'Could the two of them have gone there?' asked Andrew.

'Your guess is as good as mine,' shrugged Fiona, studying the photo on her phone. 'The truth is, I know next to nothing about this guy.'

'I feel like a voyeur,' said Andrew pulling back again after having seen the photo.

'Me too,' said Fiona. 'Anyway, as I said to you, this morning Caitlin sent me another message. Let me just read that to you as well. "If you don't hear from me for a while, then don't worry. Remember that the truth is rarely pure and never simple, and you cannot shake hands with a clenched fist."'

'Crikey,' said Andrew, raising his eyebrows. "That's deep. Sounds like poetry. Is she quoting someone?'

'That's exactly what I thought too,' said Fiona. 'It seems familiar, but I can't for the life of me remember where it might be from.'

'Could it have anything to do with her... lifestyle?' asked Andrew hesitantly. 'I mean, she's a bit out there sometimes, right? Has she been involved with anything or anyone that could have caused her to disappear like this? Aside from this Antoine character?'

'Well,' sighed Fiona. 'Over the past couple of years, she has been into Wicca in a big way.'

'Wicca,' repeated Andrew. 'As in, witchcraft?'

'No, not exactly,' replied Fiona. 'Wicca isn't really witchcraft, although some practitioners call themselves witches. It is more of a spiritual thing. A sort of pre-Christian pagan religion which is based around things like harmony with nature, meditation, feminism, ethics and apparently also various rituals. I think they believe in reincarnation as well. I'm not exactly an expert, but that was the sense I was getting from Caitlin. And all of those things are definitely right up her street.'

'I see,' said Andrew. 'Interesting. I had been under the impression that Wicca was all about medieval witchcraft or even devil worship.'

'What – like Satanism?' asked Fiona. 'No, not at all. Satanism is completely different. That has always been centred around the explicit worship of Satan. Although, lately, I get the sense that it mainly revolves around Satan as an icon of rebellion against religious dogma and conformism in general. But again, the Wicca that Caitlin was fascinated by was just about spiritualism, respect for Mother Earth and an attempt to commune with nature as far as I understood it. She told me she had been reading books by its modern founder Gerald Gardner, who was a bit of an eccentric, to say the least.'

'So, if it is a religion,' interjected Andrew, 'do they have a god?'

'I guess you could say they have two,' replied Fiona, 'although I am not actually sure the term 'god' is appropriate here. At least not in the conventional omnipotent sense that Christianity and Islam use. They are more like minor deities. One of them is a female archetype goddess called The Lady, and the other is a horned male god referred to as the Lord. They are meant to represent balance in nature, which is a general theme that runs through all of this stuff.'

'Sounds fairly harmless,' said Andrew. 'Like a bunch of New Age hippies. Except perhaps for the bit about the horns. You could be forgiven for thinking that had something to do with Satanism.'

'Yes,' said Fiona. 'Caitlin once told me that it was probably one of the reasons why these sorts of pagan beliefs were driven underground during the time of the Inquisition in the middle-ages. I can certainly see why they were confused with devil worshippers. But she assured me that it had nothing to do with Satan, and I don't think she would ever have got involved in anything like that.'

'I am sure she wouldn't have,' said Andrew, who despite his reservations about Caitlin's unorthodox lifestyle knew her as a kind and gentle soul.

'Anyway,' said Fiona, wringing her hands. 'When I got that message, I initially dismissed it as more earth mother nonsense, to be honest, but then I suddenly got really worried about her. I am not sure why. Something just doesn't feel right. I tried to call her about an hour later, but I got an automated message telling me that the number has been disconnected. Caitlin would never do that. It's just so out of character.'

'That does sound strange,' said Andrew. 'Have you thought about contacting the police?'

'Fat chance,' scoffed Fiona. 'They're understaffed as it is. There is no way they would allocate resources to some flighty hippie who hasn't been in touch for a couple of days.'

'Listen,' said Andrew, placing a hand gently on Fiona's shoulder. 'Let's go down to her commune together. I'll drive us there. There is bound to be something the other residents can tell us about Caitlin and Antoine. I would bet anything that this whole thing has to do with him. Who knows. Perhaps they eloped to a cottage in the French Alps and forgot to tell anyone?'

'I wouldn't put it past her,' smiled Fiona, 'but I still think she would have told me.'

'Well, let's find out,' said Andrew, picking up his jacket from the back of the chair he had slung it over before going down to the shooting range. 'It is the only thing we have to go on for now. Come on.'

Two

The drive to Notting Hill took only a few minutes, and when the Aston Martin DB9 pulled up and parked opposite the handsome Georgian townhouse on Arundel Gardens that had been converted into a commune, it earned Andrew and Fiona a few looks from a small group of people who were just entering the building. Expensive cars were probably anathema to most of the people living there, even if communes like these often had their fair share of residents who came from highly privileged backgrounds but would do anything to hide it. The entire ethos was one of collectivism, which carried with it an inherent opposition to concepts like materialism and capitalism.

As they walked up the steps to the front door, they could hear reggae music coming from inside and in the windows were various flags and banners with 'No to Nuclear Power' and declaring the building a 'Prejudice-Free House'.

'I feel like I have stepped into a time machine and gone back to the 1970s,' whispered Andrew as he momentarily leaned closer to Fiona.

'Well,' she smiled. 'I believe that is the general idea around here.'

'How do these people afford a townhouse like this?' asked Andrew quietly. 'It must be well out of their budget.'

'I reckon they are mostly arty types from well-off families,' replied Fiona. 'Caitlin told me that several of the twenty-something people living here are the children of city bankers and lawyers. I guess this is their way of rebelling, even if their parents actually pay all the bills.'

The door was unlocked and left on the latch, so they simply pushed it open and entered to be greeted by the unmistakable smell of cannabis. A young couple brushed past them from one of the untidy-looking common spaces, which would once upon a time have been an elegant living room belonging to much more gentrified residents than the current occupants. The two youngsters were giggling as they went, but then the young woman turned around when she and her companion were halfway up the stairs to the first floor.

'Can I help you,' she asked with a smile and in a clipped middle-class accent.

'We're looking for Caitlin,' said Fiona. 'I'm her sister Fiona.'

'Oh. Hello,' she said, her face lighting up. 'Caitlin has mentioned you from time to time. I'm Izzy. No, I haven't seen her for a few days. I think she left with Antoine.'

'Do you know where they went?' asked Fiona.

'I am afraid not,' replied Izzy, whose name was probably short for Isabella, and whose surname was possibly quite lengthy, hyphenated and related to a geographical part of the country. 'She mostly kept to herself after she met Antoine. I think they are very much in love.'

'I see,' replied Fiona. 'I'd like to see her room. Could you show me?'

'Of course,' replied Izzy, and began walking up the stairs, the young man following her silently and looking slightly put out at being interrupted by the unexpected visitors. 'Please come with me.'

Izzy showed them along a corridor to a room at the end with two windows overlooking the neatly manicured private garden at the back, which the property shared with all the other residents on that street.

'Who did Caitlin mostly hang out with here?' asked Fiona, as Izzy was about to disappear into what was presumably her own bedroom.

'That would be Maggie,' replied Izzy. 'She's downstairs. She's the one with the guitar.'

At that, Izzy allowed herself to be pulled into her bedroom, and then the door was shut and locked amidst much giggling from both her and the young man.

'Kids these days,' smiled Andrew and shrugged as they entered Caitlin's bedroom.

The room was roughly four by four metres in size, and aside from the exterior wall with the two windows, it had one wall covered with bookcases and various pieces of colourful abstract art on the others, along with a full-length mirror leaning against the wall next to the door. In the corner of the room next to the bed was a small desk with an office chair. There was no PC or laptop.

'This is the room in the photo that Caitlin sent me,' said Fiona, and pointed to a low bed with a pink velvet headboard. 'This was where Antoine was sleeping.'

'I think you're right,' said Andrew. 'Pretty small place, especially for two people. Or maybe he didn't actually live here. Let's look around and see if we can find any clues as to where they might have gone. Actually, why don't you go through drawers and closets? I feel a bit weird rummaging through her things.'

'Fine,' said Fiona, methodically beginning to pull out drawers and searching them. 'I don't really know what we're looking for, but we might know when we find it.'

Andrew walked over to the bookcase and tilted his head to be able to read the titles on the spines.

'Lots of pretty serious literature,' he said. 'Your sister is very well-read.'

'She has a degree in Philosophy and Sociology from Trinity College in Dublin,' said Fiona. 'She was always lost in some book or other when we were growing up.'

'I see,' said Andrew. 'There is quite a bit of poetry and some heavyweight authors as well. Edgar Allan Poe. Oscar Wilde. Mary Shelley, Dickens, Shakespeare. Seems like she read all the greats. And there are also several here about the Knights Templar.'

He pulled one of them down from the shelf and opened it. The front cover was emblazoned with the red Templar Cross on a white background.

'This looks like it was a gift from Antoine,' he said. 'It's signed by him with a personal message. "For my Lily". Does that mean anything to you?'

'No,' replied Fiona as she was rummaging through Caitlin's knicker drawer. 'Not a thing.'

In between some of the other books was a large picture frame, which Andrew pulled out and placed upright on the shelf in front of himself.

'What am I looking at here?' he said, taking a step back to get a better view.

Fiona came over to stand next to him.

'I am pretty sure that is a reproduction of a very well-known oil painting called 'Pandemonium' by the 18th-century painter John Martin.'

'Do you actually have an eidetic memory?' asked Andrew glancing at her and smiling.

'As good as,' said Fiona. 'It comes in handy from time to time.'

'It's a pretty disturbing painting,' said Andrew, studying the image.

It depicted a hellish scene of what looked like fiery lava flows inside fissures in black rock, and in the distance was an enormous palatial fortress of some kind, its towers with battlements extending up into a murky darkness above. In the foreground was a solitary figure standing on a rocky outcropping. He was armed with a lance and a golden shield and wearing a bright red flowing cape, and he had his arms raised up high. Next to the warrior-like person was a smaller figure who seemed to be cowering in the darkness nearby.

'It is quite famous,' said Fiona. 'It is on display in the Louvre Museum in Paris if I am not mistaken. But what on earth is it doing here? This is very unlike Caitlin. We were brought up as Catholics, loosely anyway, so this is pretty off-piste for her.'

'So, it is called Pandemonium?' mused Andrew. 'As in *chaos*?'

'Well, that's what the word has come to mean more recently,' replied Fiona, 'but in the 1840s when this painting was created, it had a somewhat different meaning. Listen to the syllables. Pan-demon-ium. In John Milton's epic poem 'Paradise Lost', it is the capital city in hell. The name is Greek and means 'All the Demons', and it is the city in hell where the fallen angels converge in a great council to plan their assault on the Kingdom of God.'

'Right,' said Andrew slowly, glancing at her sceptically and raising one eyebrow.

'It is actually a very famous story,' insisted Fiona. 'Have you never heard of it?'

'I might have heard the title at some point,' replied Andrew, 'but I can't say that poetry has ever managed to captivate me.'

'Fair enough,' said Fiona. 'It isn't really what most people would think of if you asked them about poems either. It is more like a dramatization of the expulsion of the archangel Lucifer from heaven, and of his imprisonment and eventual escape from hell along with his horde of lesser fallen angels.'

'Sorry, what was the name of the poem again?' said Andrew, glancing up at the bookshelf next to him. 'Paradise Lost?'

'That's right,' replied Fiona, still captivated by the print of the painting hanging on the wall.

'You mean this one?' said Andrew, extracting a meaty black hardcover book from a shelf and showing it to her.

'Uhm… yes,' said Fiona hesitantly and took a couple of steps towards him. 'Yes. That's it. Why has Caitlin been reading this? It is nothing like what she would normally be interested in.'

'I think the answer is here,' said Andrew, having flicked through the first few pages. 'There is another short handwritten note on this page at the front. It says, "From Antoine. Let the light shine".'

'What?' said Fiona, now beginning to sound slightly agitated and reaching for the book to see for herself. 'Who the hell *is* this guy? He is beginning to give me the creeps.'

'I agree, it is a little bit of an unusual present,' said Andrew and pointed up towards the top of the shelves. 'Look. That's got to be him, right?'

In a small silver frame on the top shelf was a picture of a raven-head Caitlin and a handsome young man in his early thirties. He had model features with high cheekbones, piercing blue-green eyes, perfect white teeth and an easy smile. His longish blond hair was swept back with a side parting, and a half-day stubble made him look relaxed and unpretentious.

'Yes, that looks like him,' said Fiona.

'Ok,' said Andrew, and took out his phone to take a picture. 'Let's keep this for future reference.'

'What is that over here?' said Fiona, taking a step towards a bookcase where there was a small ornately carved whitewashed wooden picture frame with a reproduction of an oil painting of a red-haired woman wearing a flowing white gown who was reclining in a chair.

There was nothing on the painting to indicate who the woman was, but attached to the bottom of the frame itself was a tiny brass plaque with the name 'Lilith'.

'Who is she?' asked Andrew. 'And is it me or does she look a bit like Caitlin?'

'Someone named Lilith,' said Fiona and picked up the framed picture. 'No idea who that is.'

She turned it over and read the text on the small paper label stuck to the back of it.

'Dante Gabriel Rossetti,' she read. 'Lilith – 1866'.

'Never heard of him,' said Andrew, 'Or her for that matter. But then I am not really into art.'

'And look at this,' said Fiona, and picked up a sheet of paper that lay in front of the picture frame. 'Two printed tickets to the British Museum from about six weeks ago. I guess she and Antoine might have gone together. Odd…'

'Did she not tell you?' asked Andrew. 'I mean – you work there. Would she not let you know if she was coming for a visit?'

'She might not have if she was going with Antoine,' replied Fiona.

'I wonder why they went,' said Andrew.

'Me too,' said Fiona and shook her head. 'It's odd.'

She walked over next to the bed and knelt down by a bedside table with a shaded lamp on it. Next to the lamp was a small, cheap-looking glass-fronted photo frame. Inside it was an intricate arrangement of six small straight twigs that had been painted black and laced together with black sewing string to form a pentagram. Next to each of the five points of the star were symbols. The top one was a circle, signifying the spirit. Next to the top left point was a triangle pointing up with a line through the middle, which signifies air. Below that was the same triangle pointing down, signifying earth. The top right symbol was a simple triangle pointing down. Water. Below that was a similar triangle pointing up. Fire.

'Look,' said Fiona quietly and pointing to the symbols as Andrew came over and stood next to her. 'Spirit. Air. Earth. Water. Fire. The Wicca Pentagram. She is into Wicca, I knew that already. But somehow this pentagram gives me the chills now.'

'Let's just keep looking,' said Andrew. 'There might be more like this.'

Fifteen minutes later, they were standing in the middle of the room with their hands on their hips and looking around to see if they had missed anything.

'I think that's all of it,' said Fiona. 'There doesn't seem to be anything missing, except for some clothes and her money. And I imagine she has her passport with her.'

'I agree,' said Andrew. 'I don't think there is anything more to find here. Let's go downstairs and talk to this Maggie person that Izzy mentioned. She might have something for us.'

Descending the stairs back down to the ground floor, Andrew and Fiona could hear the faint strumming of a guitar coming from the back of the house.

'That has to be Maggie playing,' said Fiona. 'I am guessing her real name is Margaret. Not a bad guitar player, by the sounds of it.'

As the two of them emerged into the large common space towards the back of the house, no one paid them any attention. It was clear that the commune was a revolving door of temporary residents, friends and acquaintances, and that anyone could walk in or out as they pleased.

Sitting in an old burgundy-coloured and almost threadbare armchair was a woman with a guitar. She had green eyes, high cheekbones and long flowing blonde hair, and she appeared to be in her early forties, perhaps slightly older. Compared with most of the other people in the commune, she certainly stood out for that reason alone. Next to her, lying on an ashtray that was balancing on the armrest, was a joint from which a small light grey column of aromatic smoke rose. This was clearly where the smell of cannabis came from.

'Maggie?' asked Fiona as she and Andrew stopped in front of her. 'Sorry. I am Caitlin's sister Fiona. I am trying to find her.'

'Well, of course you are,' said Maggie, smiling at her coyly and completely ignoring Andrew. 'I have heard a fair bit about you. Beauty clearly runs in the family.'

'I am trying to find her,' repeated Fiona. 'She hasn't been in touch for a while, and I am worried that something might have happened to her.'

'You and me both,' said Maggie, placing the guitar against the wall next to her. 'I haven't seen her for more than a week. We were supposed to go shopping for a new sofa for this place near Portobello Road, but she just seems to have left. It's very unlike her.'

'Any idea where she went?' asked Fiona.

'No,' replied Maggie, 'but I bet it has to do with her new flame. A Frenchman named Antoine something or other. Or perhaps he never gave his surname. I can't remember now.'

'How long do you think their relationship has been going on for?' asked Fiona.

'Antoine has only been on the scene for a couple of months,' said Maggie, putting the joint to her lips and inhaling. 'Caitlin was never short of young men interested in her. Can't say I am surprised. She's gorgeous – much like her sister, I can see.'

She shot Fiona a flirtatious look and smiled, making Fiona blush before clearing her voice.

'What did you make of him?' she asked Maggie, her tone even.

'Honestly?' said Maggie. 'I didn't like him much. He was always really sweet and attentive to Caitlin, but whenever she was out and he was here by himself, he seemed completely disinterested in the rest of us. It was like we were all just beneath him. His only focus was Caitlin, which I suppose was nice for her, but none of the rest of us ever warmed to him. I actually found him a bit creepy myself, but then I find most men creepy.'

As she finished her sentence she glanced at Andrew and held his gaze for a few seconds, during which time Andrew simply regarded her impassively, unwilling to be dragged into her personal issues with men or gender or her father or whatever her problem was. The tension in the air was suddenly palpable, but then Maggie broke into a disarming smile.

'Anyway,' she said. 'I really like Caitlin a lot, and not just because she is drop-dead gorgeous. She's a lovely person with a good heart, so I've been a bit worried about her too, to be honest. I am glad to see that her sister is here and looking out for her.'

'I'd like to ask you,' said Fiona. 'As you might know, Caitlin has always been a free spirit, and she has been very interested in Wicca lately.'

'I know,' nodded Maggie. 'She was really captivated by it. Read everything she could get her hands on. Such a head on that girl. Made the rest of us look like chimpanzees. And I really think she embraced the whole thing. Reincarnation. Cosmic Energy. Karma. The Wiccan Rede. The Rule of Three.'

'Sorry, what are those?' asked Andrew, which earned him a slightly stand-offish glance, as if Maggie had been surprised that he actually spoke.

'It's very straightforward,' said Maggie, returning her gaze to Fiona. 'The Wiccan Rede simply says "Do as you will, so long as you do no harm.". And the Rule of Three is a cornerstone of the Wicca tradition. Sort of a cosmic balance thing which states that the energy you put into the universe, either positive or negative, will come back to you threefold.'

'Sounds very sensible,' observed Fiona, 'whether you're into Wicca or not.'

'That's what I always thought,' smiled Maggie and nodded again.

'And what about Antoine?' asked Fiona. 'Is he also into those sorts of things?'

'It certainly appeared that way,' replied Maggie. 'Caitlin seems to have found a kindred spirit in him. He appeared to be as much into it as she was, and he said he had lived for a while as part of a Wicca community in the south of France. I personally didn't believe him. I am sure he just said all those things to get into bed with her. Sorry if that seems cynical.'

Fiona decided to ignore her last comment and instead pressed on.

'Do you remember seeing or hearing anything regarding either Caitlin or Antoine that you thought was strange or that seemed odd or out of place?'

Andrew had now decided to simply stand back and listen to Fiona's line of questioning. She was extremely adept at covering lots of ground whilst not coming across as intrusive or overbearing.

Maggie took a deep breath and lifted her head to look up at the elaborately corniced ceiling of the common room. Then she tilted her head slightly to one side and gave a quick half-shake of the head before stopping herself.

'Not really,' she said, 'except for one time when I was walking in the back garden. We share it with about ten other properties, so it is quite big, but there's hardly ever anyone out there, especially late at night. I like to walk barefoot on the grass out there. It makes me feel connected to nature. Anyway, I guess it also makes me difficult to hear because one evening a few weeks ago after most people had gone to bed, including Caitlin if I remember correctly, I was walking out there, and suddenly I almost bumped into Antoine who was standing halfway inside a bush talking quietly on his phone. As soon as he saw me, he seemed to abruptly end the call and shove the phone into his pocket, as if he was trying to hide something.'

'Do you think he was cheating on her?' asked Fiona.

'I don't know,' replied Maggie, 'but I wouldn't put it past him. On the other hand, thinking back to that moment, the tone of his voice as he spoke on the phone seemed tense and not like someone talking to a girlfriend or a lover. It was like he was telling someone something secret and important. Anyway, it could have been nothing or it might have been something. I really don't know. All I know is that he has kept his distance from me ever since, and now both of them seem to have disappeared. So, I frankly wonder if something fishy is going on. But then again, I can be a bit paranoid. I do know that about myself.'

Maggie glanced at Andrew again.

'Are you a copper?' she asked.

'No,' replied Andrew. 'I am just Fiona's partner.'

'So, you're not married then?' asked Maggie hopefully and shot Fiona a mischievous smile.

'No,' replied Fiona, taking Andrew's hand in hers. 'Not yet anyway.'

Maggie shrugged and inhaled another lungful of smoke imbued with the scent of marijuana.

'Is Sean a friend of yours?' she asked nonchalantly after exhaling a cloud of smoke.

'Who?' asked Fiona.

'Sean...' Maggie repeated with one eyebrow raised.

She paused, and her eyes darted up and to the left as if she was trying to recall something. She eventually shook her head and returned her gaze to Fiona.

'I don't actually think he gave me his last name,' she said. 'Anyway, he was here yesterday asking questions about Caitlin.'

'I don't know anyone named Sean,' said Fiona sounding perplexed and looking at Andrew who shook his head. 'What did he ask you?'

'Same sort of things you have just asked,' replied Maggie. 'Also wanted to know if Caitlin had been involved in occult activities. I don't think he knew about Antoine, and I didn't tell him. He seemed a bit shifty to me, to be honest. Or perhaps he was just nervous. He almost came across as if he thought someone was about to barge in and arrest him.'

'Strange,' said Fiona and frowned. 'I have no idea who that could be.'

'Well,' said Maggie. 'If you find him, tell him not to come back here. I will make an exception for you, but I don't want to sit here every other day and answer questions from strangers about a missing friend of mine.'

'We will,' said Fiona, still looking perturbed and worried. 'Anyway, Maggie. We really appreciate your time. It's been very helpful.'

'No problem,' nodded Maggie. 'I hope you find her. I haven't known her for that long, but I like to think of her as a good friend nonetheless.'

Very nice to meet you,' said Andrew as the two of them turned and left the room.

They left the townhouse in silence and exited onto the pavement, where the sun was shining and the birds were chirping merrily in the trees that lined the road. As they stopped on the pavement, Andrew turned to Fiona.

'Could someone like Antoine have manipulated Caitlin?' he asked. 'Using Wicca as a way in and then introducing more sinister things.'

Fiona sighed and stared off into the distance. Then she looked down at the ground.

'I can't imagine why someone would do that,' she said. 'But to answer your question, then yes. Caitlin was always very impressionable. A dreamer. Always looking towards the horizon. Always searching for a deeper meaning. If this Antoine is as smooth an operator as he appears to be, then I guess it is possible that Caitlin might have bought into whatever he was telling her. Even if it was much darker than anything else she had delved into.'

'Such as biblical characters like Lucifer?' asked Andrew.

'Yes,' said Fiona reluctantly. 'I would hope not, but I can't rule it out.'

★ ★ ★

From inside the silver Audi TT that was parked across the street about thirty metres to the west, it looked through the dark tinted windows as if the man and the woman who had just come out through the front door of the commune were having a brief conversation. It was definitely the same couple that had entered less than an hour earlier.

The woman, whose features somehow looked vaguely familiar, stood with her hands on her hips and her head down absentmindedly toeing something on the pavement with her right shoe. After a few moments, the tall and powerfully built man by her side put his right arm around her and the two of them crossed the street and got into a green Aston Martin.

Three

For several minutes, Andrew and Fiona sat in silence inside the DB9, both pondering what they had just discovered and trying to come up with a way forward that might lead them closer to finding Caitlin.

'Well,' said Andrew scratching his chin. 'That was certainly interesting. Paradise Lost, Pandemonium, Lilith and a chap named Sean. I am not sure what to make of it all.'

At first, Fiona said nothing but just stared vacantly out of the windshield. Then she took a deep breath and exhaled slowly with her eyes closed.

'I think I was wrong,' she said.

'About what?' asked Andrew.

'About Caitlin,' she replied. 'I think she was into more than just this Wicca stuff. I am starting to worry that she might have been involved in something much more sinister.'

'Or perhaps this Antoine character is not what he seems,' suggested Andrew. 'I didn't like Maggie much, but I think she might be on to something as far as he is concerned. I really doubt Caitlin would be into anything as dark as devil worship. And I say this as someone who is in no doubt that gods and demons are nothing more than the collective figments of the human imagination.'

'Perhaps,' shrugged Fiona. 'I hope so. But what about the copy of Paradise Lost and the Pandemonium painting? I still can't believe Caitlin would be attracted to any of it. It is really confusing, but then so were her text messages. Asking me if forgiveness should be boundless. She was clearly referring to Antoine, right? So, what was he involved in, and who was he talking to late at night in the garden?'

'The truth is rarely pure and never simple,' mused Andrew, repeating part of the message Caitlin had sent to Fiona, whilst idly observing a hippie couple entering the commune. 'I wonder what she meant.'

Suddenly Fiona sat bolt upright in her seat next to him.

'Oh shit!' she exclaimed. 'I think I know where that quote is from.'

'Really?' said Andrew and turned to face her. 'Who?'

'It's Oscar Wilde,' she said excitedly.

'Ok…,' said Andrew. 'So?'

'You said you saw some of his writings on Caitlin's bookcase, right?' said Fiona. 'Oscar Wilde. The poet and playwright. He is probably the most famous of all the Irish poets.'

'I still don't understand where this is going,' said Andrew looking perplexed. 'What does Oscar Wilde have to do with any of this?'

'Caitlin and I grew up on Merrion Square in Dublin, and Oscar Wilde was born on Westland Row in 1882, about a two-minute walk from there. We used to practically walk past his childhood home on our way to Trinity College.'

'Where you studied History and Archaeology and she studied... what was it again?' asked Andrew.

'Philosophy and Sociology,' replied Fiona. 'Anyway. Later on, Wilde's family actually moved to Number 1 Merrion Square, just a few houses down from ours. There is a sculpture of him in the northwest corner of Merrion Square just across from his family home. It is quite an unusual statue too. It is a life-sized stone sculpture of him reclining on a rock with a rather whimsical look on his face. But guess what - his right hand is resting on his chest, and his hand is clenched.'

It took Andrew a couple of seconds to connect the dots.

'You cannot shake hands with a clenched fist,' he said, repeating the short second sentence from Caitlin's message, suddenly realising what Fiona was talking about. 'When Caitlin sent you that strange message, she wasn't just reciting random quotes. She was literally referring to that particular sculpture.'

'That's right,' said Fiona, frantically swiping and tapping on her phone. 'It is the only logical explanation. And look at this. That part of her message was a quote from Indira Gandhi. Caitlin always really admired her.'

'But why be so cryptic?' asked Andrew.

'I am not sure,' replied Fiona. 'I think maybe Caitlin was worried that Antoine was monitoring her phone, so she sent me a message within a message. Quotes that only I would understand the meaning of.'

'It would certainly fit with what Maggie told us about him,' said Andrew. 'But what does it all mean?'

Fiona clenched her jaw and hesitated for a moment, and Andrew could practically hear the gears turning inside her head. Then she turned to him.

'I need to get to Dublin,' she said resolutely. 'Caitlin was trying to tell me something about that statue, and I need to find out what it was. Will you come with me?'

'Absolutely,' replied Andrew without a moment's hesitation. 'Whatever this is, it is clearly important to you, so that means it is important to me too.'

'Thank you,' said Fiona and leaned over to kiss him gently on the cheek.

'We might as well get moving,' said Andrew. 'I can drive us to an airport right now if you'd like.'

'Great,' said Fiona. 'Let me just hop online and see if I can get us on a flight to Dublin today.'

A few minutes later, Andrew started the engine of the DB9, and then they raced east through the capital towards London City Airport, where an Aer Lingus flight to Dublin was scheduled to depart less than two hours later. Once there, they parked up in the long-stay car park and ran into the small but efficient terminal building where they rushed up the escalators and hurried through the departure lounge and out to the gate which was just closing. Ten minutes later they were seated in the small turboprop aircraft that would take them northwest over much of the south of England, Wales and then the Irish Sea to Dublin.

In the final minutes before takeoff, Andrew sent a message to his boss, Colonel Strickland, the head of the specialist SAS anti-terror unit that Andrew was attached to, letting him know that he was taking several days off to attend to urgent personal matters. Andrew and Strickland had worked together for long enough for them to trust each other implicitly, and Strickland would not question why Andrew needed the time off. And because of the mutual respect between them, Andrew also had no reservations about asking Strickland for a favour. He sent the colonel the picture he had taken of Caitlin and Antoine together and requested that Strickland pull whatever strings he could with the Metropolitan Police to acquire any CCTV footage from around the Commune on Arundel Gardens in Notting Hill. Specifically, he wanted to attempt to get a positive ID on Antoine, and perhaps even discover more about his movements around London. With the Met's advanced facial recognition software at their disposal, they might be able to come up with something. Andrew knew next to nothing about the man, but what he felt he knew for certain was that the Frenchman was not what he seemed.

★   ★   ★

'Oscar Fingal O'Flahertie Wills Wilde,' said Andrew and smiled. 'Quite a mouthful. My name is positively boring compared with that.'

They were standing in the northwest corner of Merrion Park in central Dublin, a stone's throw from the enormous Georgian square that was surrounded by grand colonnade-fronted buildings comprising the National Museum of Ireland, the Irish National Gallery, and the Irish Parliament – Leinster House. In front of them was the life-sized Oscar Wilde Memorial Sculpture, with the stone sculpture of the poet reclining on a huge boulder.

A few metres away was a small playground where children were running, laughing and squealing in the universal language of play. It was a warm late afternoon in the Irish capital, and the sun was getting lower in the sky. However, with sunset being close to 10 p.m. at this time of year, they had several hours of daylight left.

'You said he had a whimsical smile on his face,' observed Andrew, 'but it looks a lot more like a sarcastic sneer to me.'

'It actually depends on which angle you look at it from,' said Fiona. 'Wilde was a multifaceted person who was both celebrated and reviled during his lifetime, and that was deliberately incorporated into the sculpture.'

'So, what are we looking for?' asked Andrew, turning his body and glancing over his shoulder towards the entrance to the playground, where a small group of parents were chatting whilst monitoring their offspring playing on the equipment.

'I am not sure,' said Fiona, moving towards the two-metre-tall boulder the sculpture was sitting on whilst looking up at it. 'But it must have something to do with the clenched right hand resting on his chest.'

'Any idea what that is supposed to signify?' asked Andrew.

'No,' replied Fiona, 'but I am going to take a closer look. I just hope there aren't going to be any Garda units passing by. Keep a lookout for me?'

She walked up to the boulder, took a quick look to her left and to her right to make sure no one was watching, and then she placed one foot on a small ledge near the bottom of the boulder and climbed up onto it. Andrew said nothing but turned around to scan the pavement of Merrion Square North on the other side of the park fence just a few metres away. Anyone walking or driving past would have been able to see Fiona climb onto the memorial. She adeptly scaled the boulder and crouched down next to the sculpture, holding onto the shoulder of Oscar Wilde for balance as she inspected his right hand.

'There's something here,' she said, quickly turning her head slightly to speak to Andrew over her shoulder. 'Something tucked into his fist. It looks like a small plastic bag.'

'Well, pull it out and let's get going,' said Andrew with a mixture of impatience and amusement at seeing the normally well-behaved Fiona Keane looking like she was about to vandalise a treasured monument.

She extracted a sealed clear plastic bag about the size of a credit card and jumped down to rejoin Andrew.

'Well done,' he smiled. 'And you didn't even get us arrested. What's inside there?'

Fiona held the plastic bag in the palm of her hand, and the two of them huddled around to inspect it. Inside was a tiny black piece of plastic with one corner cut at an angle and a small sticker attached on its side.

'It's a micro-SD card for a phone or a camera,' said Fiona, looking up at Andrew. 'We need to see what is on there. There might be images that Caitlin wanted me to see.'

'All right,' said Andrew, taking her other hand. 'Let's find a quiet place to sit.'

The two of them walked past the playground and into the small park in the middle of Merrion Square, where they found a wooden bench under a couple of birch trees overlooking the open oval-shaped lawn. The lawn was neat and well-maintained with small flowerbeds dotted here and there. Fiona carefully extracted the micro-SD card from the plastic bag and inserted it into a slot in her own phone. A few taps and swipes later, she had opened a file manager that showed them the card's contents.

'There's just one file here,' she said. 'It's a video.'

'Ok,' said Andrew. 'Do you want to watch it here or go somewhere else?'

'Here's fine,' replied Fiona, quickly glancing left and right along the virtually deserted path. 'I need to see what this is.'

She tapped on the file, and it immediately opened up in a video player. In the middle of the screen was Caitlin's face looking into the camera from an angle suggesting that she had been sitting down with her phone in her hands when she made the recording. She was outside somewhere, and there were a couple of birch trees behind her and the sound of children playing in the background. Fiona drew a quick breath.

'She was sitting right here on this bench,' she said, not taking her eyes off the screen.

Caitlin appeared distressed. She had rings under her eyes and a generally haggard look on her face. Her voice was weak and slightly high-pitched, betraying distress and hinting that she might have been crying.

'Shit,' breathed Fiona. 'This is bad.'

Caitlin sniffed a couple of times, and then she began to speak.

Hello Sis. If you're watching this, you're in Dublin and you've solved my little riddle. I always knew I could count on you. I am recording this message onto a memory card because I don't want to send it to you. I think Antoine is reading my messages somehow even though I delete them after I send them, and I just don't want him to know.

Anyway - remember when we met up for lunch in Hampstead? I told you everything was fine, and I really wanted to believe that myself. But it's not true. It's not fine. Not now.

Antoine is behaving really strangely lately. I caught him sitting in our room quietly mouthing some weird incantations or something when he thought I was out. It almost sounded like prayer, but it was like nothing I have ever heard before. It was sinister somehow, and he became furious with me when he realised that I had been watching him. He has also been speaking to strange people on the phone and refusing to tell me who it was. It has been really upsetting, so one day I decided to start the voice recorder on my phone and leave it in the room. Then I told him I was going to go and meet a friend for a couple of hours. When I came back, I listened to the whole thing, and he turned out to have had another phone conversation with someone. The phone was tucked behind a pillow, so I could barely hear what he was saying, but he definitely mentioned my name, and I am sure I heard the name Baphomet. You know, that horned occult guy?

At this, Caitlin seemed to choke up, shaking her head slightly as if she couldn't quite believe what she was saying. Then she continued.

Anyway, he was all lovely and attentive after that, and he told me he wanted to take me on a secret trip at the end of June, but he refused to say where. And when I told him I had plans to go to a music festival then, he got really angry and said I would choose him over my friends if I really loved him. So, I guess I have to. He says he has something really special planned for me, but I am not sure if I want to go now. It's all becoming really weird and creepy.

Caitlin took a deep breath and paused as if trying to find a way to say what was on her mind.

> *I went to see Friar Cormac just now. He was always a good listener, but there's obviously nothing he can do. He's an old man, and I am not sure he's quite with it anymore.*
>
> *Anyway, I really don't want you to worry about me, but the fact that you are watching this means that I am in real trouble and I need you. Please look for me. Please find me. I love you. Bye.*

The recording ended, and Fiona immediately burst into tears, hiding her face in her hands.

'What the hell is going on?' she said. 'Where is she? What's happened to her?'

Andrew placed an arm around her shoulders and gently pulled her towards himself.

'This Antoine sounds like a certifiable sociopath,' he said. 'This is classic manipulation and coercive control.'

'We need to find her and get her away from him as soon as possible,' said Fiona, regaining some of her composure.

'I agree,' said Andrew. 'But we have no clue where she might be. Do you have any ideas at all?'

Fiona shook her head and sniffed.

'No,' she said. 'They could be anywhere by now.'

'Who is Friar Cormac?' asked Andrew. 'Catholic, I presume?'

'Yes,' replied Fiona. 'He's an old family friend. Retired now, but he used to be the chaplain at the Trinity College Chapel when both I and then later Caitlin studied at Trinity. He knew us for most of our childhoods. Lovely man. Always a shoulder to cry on.'

'We need to go and see him,' said Andrew resolutely. 'He is one of the last people to have spoken to Caitlin before she disappeared. It is possible he remembers things she said that could help us find her, so he just might be able to help. We don't have any other leads.'

'You're right,' nodded Fiona. 'Even back when we knew him mainly as the chaplain of the College Chapel, he was known as a pretty serious scholar of history and religion. I am sure his knowledge has only grown since then, so I suspect he might help us clarify some of those things that Caitlin seems to have become involved with.'

'A friar and a scholar,' nodded Andrew. 'Very good. Do you know where he lives?'

'Yes, if he hasn't moved,' nodded Fiona. 'And I really doubt that. He is not the sort of person to move around unless he really has to.'

She rose and Andrew followed suit.

'He is probably at home with his books,' she said. 'Both Caitlin and I owe much of our love of reading to him.'

'So, where to?' asked Andrew.

'This way,' said Fiona, gesturing towards the southeast exit of Merrion Square Park. 'He still lives in a little townhouse on Pembrooke Street. It's only about a 10-minute walk from here.'

'All right,' said Andrew, giving her a hug and then taking her hand and giving it a gentle squeeze. 'We'll figure this out together. Ok? Try not to worry. Come on.'

Four

When they arrived at Friar Cormac's handsome end-of-terrace Georgian house, Fiona stepped up to the oak front door that was painted a glossy dark green and gripped the polished brass door knocker shaped like a lion's head. She knocked twice and took a step back, glancing at Andrew with a nervous smile. For several moments, nothing happened.

'He's probably in his library at the back,' she said. 'I hope he remembers me. It has been a long time since I last saw him.'

There was the sound of shuffling feet on the other side of the door followed by silence for several seconds as if someone was taking a moment to observe them through the door spy. Then there was the metallic noise of a heavy bolt being slid aside, the door being unlocked. Finally, the door opened and swung aside. The appearance of the man opening the door initially surprised Fiona, despite her recognising him instantly. Unlike how Fiona remembered seeing him, he was not wearing the simple hemp rope around a mid-grey hooded robe known as a cowl. He looked to be about seventy-five years old, but he had a round youthful face and keen blue eyes looking out through small oval rimless glasses with black sidearms. His medium-length side-parted grey hair was receding slightly, but it was combed neatly. He was wearing a red and green checkered dressing gown over a pair of dark green pyjamas and a pair of fluffy brown slippers. In his right hand was a tea mug.

'Friar Cormac,' said Fiona uncertainly. 'I am not sure if you remember me, but I am…'

Before Fiona could finish her sentence, the man's face lit up, he hurriedly put down his tea mug on a small mahogany console table by the wall and came towards her with open arms.

'Fiona Keane!' he exclaimed with a wide beaming smile. 'How wonderful to see you again. How long has it been? Fifteen years? Of course I remember you! And I had a visit from your little sister Caitlin not long ago. How are you, my dear?'

'Not too bad,' said Fiona uncomfortably. 'It is actually Caitlin I am here to talk to you about. Anyway, this is my partner, Andrew.'

'Partner,' repeated Cormac with a smile and a faint wink as he shook Andrew's hand. 'Don't worry. I won't judge you, even if the Lord might have misgivings.'

'Nice to meet you,' said Andrew, shaking the old man's surprisingly strong hand.

'Come in. Come in.' said Cormac and beckoned them inside with his hands.

They stepped through the front door and into a hallway with large black and white checkered floor tiles and an elaborate crystal chandelier hanging from the ceiling. Cormac then led them through a living room to his study at the back, where he gestured to an old Victorian blue velvet sofa in the bay window. As they walked, Fiona noticed that there was not a single sign of a woman's touch anywhere in the house.

'Would you like something to drink?' asked Cormac.

'No thanks,' replied Fiona, looking at Andrew who shook his head. 'We don't want to take up too much of your time.'

'Oh, it's no trouble at all,' said Cormac and settled into what was clearly his usual spot – a plush but worn armchair near the fireplace. 'It's lovely to see you.'

The study was more akin to a library than anything else. It had books everywhere, dark polished wood floors and an elaborate cornice on the ceiling. As Andrew and Fiona made themselves comfortable, they looked around and both noticed the beautifully carved wooden bookcases and the desk at the far end of the room, where several old tomes appeared to be lying open.

Suddenly, Fiona spotted something hanging over the fireplace, and it took a few moments for her brain to register what she was looking at. It was a heavily ornate metal crucifix with a *fleur de lis* at each of its four ends. But what took Fiona aback was that it was upside down.

'An inverted cross?' gasped Fiona and looked at Cormac. 'That's… a Satanic symbol.'

'Oh, don't worry my child,' he said disarmingly, smiling as he turned in his chair to look at it himself, almost as if he had forgotten that it was there. 'That is the Cross of Saint Peter. I know that these days it is perceived as something nefarious, but it was not always so. Peter the Apostle, or Simon Peter the Rock, was the first pope of the holy Roman Church. And as you might remember, he was martyred in Rome. Crucified by Emperor Nero in the year 64 AD at what is now the site of Saint Peter's Basilica. But because he felt unworthy of being put to death in the same manner as Jesus Christ, he asked to be crucified upside down.'

'Oh, right,' said Fiona and sat back on the sofa. 'I remember the story of his death, but not that his cross was actually inverted.'

'Don't judge too hastily, my dear,' smiled Cormac, a hint of disappointment in his eyes.

'Sorry,' smiled Fiona. 'You always did tell us to be open-minded.'

'Anyway,' said Cormac. 'Please tell me what troubles you. It is about Caitlin, you said?'

'It is,' replied Fiona. 'Did she seem upset or concerned when she came to see you?'

'I didn't think so,' said Cormac, spreading out his hands as he lifted his eyebrows and shook his head. 'She seemed perfectly happy. I got the impression she was just taking the opportunity to see an old man again before he joins the Choir Invincible, as they say. What has happened?'

'Well. I'd rather not go into too much detail,' replied Fiona, 'except to say that I am worried Fiona has become involved with people who engage in some disturbing activities. Rituals. Devil worship, to be precise. And now she has just simply disappeared. We went to her commune in London, and we found several things there that we felt were quite disturbing, including a painting by John Martin. Pandemonium. You are probably familiar with it.'

Cormac nodded sagely. He was now leaning forward in his armchair, his hands folded in front of him and a grave look on his face.

'She has also been reading Paradise Lost,' said Fiona, 'which is such a long way from anything she has previously taken an interest in, so I am concerned that someone is trying to lead her down a dark path. We know that she has referred to Baphomet.'

At the mention of the name of the centuries-old deity, Cormac's face visibly tightened around his eyes and he pressed his lips together slightly.

'I see,' he said, not taking his eyes off Fiona.

'Now that she has vanished,' Fiona continued, 'I really don't know what to make of it all. What do you think? Should I be worried about her reading that sort of literature?'

Cormac bowed his head looking down at the floor for a few moments as if gathering his thoughts before speaking. Then he glanced up at Fiona again with an empathetic look on his face.

'Why don't we just back up and start at the beginning,' he said. 'How familiar are you with the story behind Paradise Lost? It is quite a well-known literary work within Christian theology, although of course, it is a version of events that the Catholic Church would never officially endorse as actual gospel. And nor would the Church of England for that matter.'

Andrew and Fiona looked at each other and Andrew shrugged.

'I could do with a slightly better understanding of this if I am going to be any help here,' said Andrew.

'If you wouldn't mind explaining,' said Fiona. 'That would be really helpful.'

'Certainly,' said Cormac, shifting in his chair to make himself more comfortable. 'Fiona, I am sure you'll be familiar with this, but let's start with the basics of the scriptures and then move on to Paradise Lost.'

'Sounds good,' said Fiona looking at Andrew who nodded.

'Ok. Let's begin,' said Cormac. 'The Old Testament teaches us that on the second day of the world's creation, God created heaven and Earth, as well as the angels and the archangels. And importantly, all of the angels were created to have free will, so any sin or act of defiance against God was always going to be a conscious choice of theirs. They all resided in heaven, and the most well-known are of course the archangels Gabriel and Michael. But alongside them was Lucifer, who was imbued with beauty and wisdom beyond those of the other angels. He was the highest being God had created, and because of this he succumbed to pride and vanity, and he wanted to create his own throne above that of God. In order to achieve this, he gathered other angels around him, supposedly one-third of God's host of angels, and he lied to them to rally them to his cause, declaring that he would rather be a king in hell than a servant in Paradise. This is, incidentally, why he is also known as the Father of Lies.'

Cormac paused to reach out for the tea mug he had set down on a small table next to the armchair. He took a sip and then continued.

'The Book of Revelations tells us that together, Lucifer and his host of angels rose up against God and a huge battle commenced – one that shook the earth and in which the archangel Michael led the heavenly host wielding a flaming sword. After a terrible battle, Lucifer and his armies were defeated, and they were cast out from heaven, known from that day forward as the Fallen Angels. For three days they fell until they reached the underworld of hell, where they were trapped. But Lucifer also suffered the additional punishment of being disfigured into the hideous form of Satan. His anger, however, was unabated, and Paradise Lost then recounts how he and the other fallen angels gathered in their new capital in hell, which they called Pandemonium. Here they debated what to do next, and after hearing various suggestions of outright war against heaven, repentance and patience in the hope of being forgiven by God, and desires to build a city to rival heaven, Lucifer finally decided to follow the advice of the fallen angel Beelzebub and resolved to focus all of their collective efforts on exacting revenge on God by corrupting his most favourite creation – Man. Lucifer arrived at the Nine Gates of hell, where he tricked his way past the gatekeepers Death and Sin, who were actually his own children. He then managed to sneak unseen out of hell and into the Garden of Eden, where he took the form of a serpent and tempted Eve to eat the forbidden fruit from the tree of knowledge. This was yet another act of defiance in that Lucifer wanted Man to have free will and possess agency and wisdom, which God had denied his creations. Ever since then, and following the eviction of Adam and Eve from the Garden of Eden, Lucifer and his legions have attempted to continue to corrupt humans, tempting them to sin and thereby barring them from entering heaven and leading them away from God. There is a lot more to the poem, but I think those were the most relevant parts.'

'Heady stuff,' said Fiona, straightening her back after sitting hunched forward and listening intently to the friar. 'If nothing else, it is a great story.'

'I think we are more or less familiar with that,' said Andrew. 'But Paradise Lost is not scripture, right? It is just a poem.'

'Yes,' replied Cormac, 'It is. But arguably it is a very influential one, and many believe that the story as it was laid out in Paradise Lost is essentially a true account.'

'I once read a very small part of it,' said Fiona. 'I remember it being quite unsettling and wondering how Milton came up with the whole thing.'

'Oh, but Paradise Lost was not just a work of fiction on the part of John Milton,' said Cormac. 'Paradise Lost is largely based on a text called Genesis B, which was a poetic rewriting of much of the Book of Genesis. It is believed to have been written around 880 AD. So, whereas Paradise Lost is about 350 years old, Genesis B is more than a thousand years old. And there are scholars who are convinced that Genesis B was based on even earlier texts, which could conceivably have been original biblical texts that were later expunged from the official canon after the two Councils of Nicaea.'

Andrew looked uncertainly from Cormac to Fiona and back again. 'The council of Nicaea?'

'Oh,' said Cormac apologetically. 'In 325 CE, the newly converted Roman emperor Constantine I decided to convene a council of scholars in Nicaea in present-day Turkey. The problem he wanted addressed was that there were so many different types of Christianity and dozens of different scriptures being followed by many disparate groups of people all throughout the Roman Empire. In his efforts to consolidate his own power in Rome, Constantine I decided to appoint himself Pope of the Christian church and to make sure that there was only one *correct* form of Christianity with him at the top. So, at the first council of Nicaea, it was decided which texts should be considered canonical scripture and be included in the Bible and which should be considered apocryphal. Ultimately, it ended with the decision that only the scriptures Matthew, Mark, Luke and John were to be accepted as scripture and that everything else was therefore by definition heretical. This later resulted in any non-canonical scriptures being hunted down and destroyed across the empire because they represented a rallying point of potential adversaries to the new pope and emperor. For that reason, most of those scriptures were either destroyed for good or lost to history for centuries.'

'Right,' said Andrew. 'What exactly is meant by *apocryphal?*'

'Well,' said Cormac, sipping his tea. 'The term comes from the Greek words *apó* which means 'from', and *krúptō* which means 'I hide', and it just means secret or hidden away or obscured. In this context, it essentially means that a text is not recognised as being part of the canonical writings in the Bible, even though it might be older than other texts that are included, and despite it often covering certain topics in much more detail than the canonical texts. Because of these councils, the Christian orthodoxy is often called the Nicene orthodoxy.'

'I see,' said Andrew. 'Regarding these councils. Was it just a simple vote?'

'It was,' replied Cormac. 'I will be the first to admit that the whole thing was a somewhat arbitrary affair. It was also no doubt highly political because the whole purpose of the council was to concentrate power in the hands of Constantine I, using the burgeoning new Christian religion as a tool to do so. But anyway, I guess at some point they simply had to try to amalgamate all the different versions of the gospels into one book and get rid of anything that didn't fit with the accepted scripture.'

'So, this means that there are many different versions of the gospel,' interjected Fiona, 'including some that go against the Nicene orthodoxy or official gospel.'

'Sounds messy,' said Andrew.

'It certainly can be,' said Cormac with a wry smile. 'Anyway, let's get back to Lucifer, and let's do that through one of the most important apocryphal texts. It is called The First Book of Enoch, and it has proven extremely controversial for reasons I will come to in a minute. By the way, Enoch was the great-grandfather of Noah, just to place him in the biblical lineage.'

'Noah, as in Noah's Ark?' observed Andrew.

'Correct,' replied Cormac. 'Anyway, you might be familiar with the huge find of religious manuscripts discovered hidden in the Qumran caves just after the Second World War. The Dead Sea Scrolls?'

Both Fiona and Andrew nodded.

'Good,' said Cormac. 'Now, among the thousands of fragments of texts recovered from those scrolls are some that are unequivocally determined to be parts of the First Book of Enoch, and these fragments are from around 300 to 200 BCE. Close to two-and-a-half-thousand years old, several centuries before the birth of Jesus Christ.'

'An amazing find,' said Fiona and looked at Andrew, who was beginning to look impatient.

'I am sorry,' smiled Cormac. 'I get carried away. Anyway, the First Book of Enoch tells the story of the Watchers who were angels created to watch over and guide humanity, and it takes place hundreds of years after creation but before the Great Flood. Enoch writes that some of the Watchers lusted after human women, and that two hundred of them took human wives and had children with them. They also shared some of their secret heavenly knowledge with them. Forbidden knowledge, as it is known, which related to astrology, metallurgy, sorcery, magic spells and even the true divine origin of man. Those pregnant women gave birth to the so-called Nephilim, who grew to become monstrous giants some four hundred feet tall.'

Andrew's face was now a picture of scepticism. As he and Fiona listened to Cormac, Andrew watched Fiona out of the corner of his eye. She was sitting forward on the edge of the sofa, wringing her hands, and as the old man spoke, he could practically hear the cogs in her brain moving as they analysed every word trying to decide what it might mean for Caitlin.

'I do understand that all of this sounds somewhat outlandish to a lot of people,' said Cormac almost apologetically, 'but that is nevertheless what the First Book of Enoch says. It proceeds to tell us that the Nephilim were possessed of insatiable hunger and that they consumed everything. Humans, animals and ultimately each other. And they engaged in the worst sin of all, which was to drink blood. Because of their unholy conception, God said that in death these Nephilim should dwell on Earth and suffer endless hunger to torment them. And they would become what we know as demons, their fury directed toward humans. In the end, God decided that the Watchers and their offspring had so corrupted the Earth that he saw only one remedy. The Great Flood. A deluge to cleanse the Earth, but one where only Noah and the Ark survived and where countless innocents perished. A clean slate, as it were.'

'The god of the Old Testament really did not mess around, did he?' said Andrew.

'Well. What the Watchers did,' said Cormac, 'was, according to Enoch, the Original Sin. This is obviously in contrast to what the Bible says was the first sin, namely Eve eating the apple. That specific part in itself made the Book of Enoch controversial, and it probably caused it to be excluded from the Bible as we know it.'

'I never knew any of this,' said Fiona, 'but I guess it makes sense.'

'However,' said Cormac, holding up an admonishing index finger. 'There is actually more to it than just that. In Jewish folklore, which can be said to be where the Book of Enoch ultimately stems from, long before the story of the Watchers and before Eve was created from Adam in the Garden of Eden, Adam had a different wife. She was moulded from the same clay as Adam, and she was created at the same time. So, she was specifically not created using a rib from Adams's body the way Eve subsequently was, but in exactly the same way as Adam. As an equal. And unlike Eve, she was not a submissive woman. She was strong and independent, and she refused to submit to Adam and instead went out and seduced the archangel Samael, producing demons as offspring. I am sure you can see why this was both controversial and also incompatible with what is now the accepted version of the Old Testament.'

'Yes. A non-subservient woman,' scoffed Fiona sarcastically. 'What a scandal. What was her name?'

'She was called Lilith,' replied Cormac.

At that, Fiona suddenly froze and looked at Andrew.

'The framed picture in Cailin's room,' she whispered. 'The plaque underneath it had the name Lilith written on it.'

Then she looked at Cormac.

'What do you suppose that means?' she asked apprehensively. 'Why would Caitlin have a picture of someone like Lilith in her bedroom?'

Cormac shifted uncomfortably in his armchair.

'I am not sure,' he said haltingly. 'I wouldn't necessarily read too much into that. I believe Lilith has been used by feminists as a sort of icon for the fight against the religious patriarchy, and I can certainly see why. The Lilith in the Book of Enoch would not conform to her husband's expectations, and so she chose to become an outcast and decide her own fate.'

'I suppose it makes a certain kind of sense,' said Fiona reluctantly. 'But I guess I am just disturbed by these very dark stories and themes that Caitlin seemed to have been drawn into.'

'I understand that,' said Cormac empathetically. 'This is not for the faint of heart, and for a gentle soul like Caitlin it does seem quite uncharacteristic, I must say.'

'Can I ask something?' said Andrew. 'If it is true that Paradise Lost was derived from Genesis B, and if Genesis B was derived from much earlier texts written around the same time as the First Book of Enoch, then you could say that the entire story of Paradise Lost is a good proxy for original pre-Christian scripture.'

'You could probably say that,' nodded Cormac. 'And many serious scholars would agree.'

'And if someone was looking to learn about or get closer to or possibly even worship Lucifer,' continued Andrew, 'then Paradise Lost would not be a bad place to start.'

'Probably true as well,' said Cormac.

'And taking that point even further,' said Andrew. 'Is it possible that someone might read Paradise Lost as fundamentally a literal and true account of historical events?'

'I have no doubt of that being a possibility,' replied Cormac. 'What is certainly true is that Milton's account of Lucifer is strangely sympathetic compared with how Lucifer is most often depicted, and it paints a picture of someone whom most of us probably share character traits with. On the face of it, this account may appear to be just a 17th-century poem, but it is perfectly possible that precisely because of Genesis B it should at least indirectly be regarded as founded in ancient scripture on par with the First Book of Enoch and perhaps even the canonical biblical scriptures.'

'That's quite a statement from a catholic man of the cloth,' observed Fiona with a cautious smile. 'There is a lot more to you than meets the eye, Friar Cormac.'

'There is indeed,' nodded Cormac with a wry smile. 'I have spent many years ensconced in these matters, and they are endlessly fascinating to me.'

'If we could,' said Andrew. 'I think we would appreciate it if we could have your thoughts on this Baphomet character. As Fiona mentioned, his name came up when we were looking through Caitlin's things back in London.'

'I can certainly try,' said Cormac uncertainly, 'but this is by no means my area of expertise. It falls much more within what one might call occult or pagan beliefs, although these things often define themselves relative to religions such as Christianity, so there is a sort of overlap I suppose. Anyway, Baphomet is a rather obscure minor deity that I believe is closely associated with the Knights Templar.'

'Really?' said Fiona, exchanging a quick glance with Andrew.

'Indeed,' said Cormac. 'To be specific, when the Templars were accused of heresy by King Philip IV of France, they were accused of worshipping this being among other things. It is an ancient horned pagan idol that has the body of a hermaphrodite and the head of a goat.'

'And this is what led the Templars to be burned at the stake by the Catholic Inquisition, right?' asked Andrew.

'Yes,' replied Cormac hesitantly. 'That and many other charges. I think it is fair to say that this was not our finest hour.'

'By which you mean the Catholic Church,' said Fiona.

'Correct,' replied Cormac.

'But all of that is a long time ago now.' observed Fiona. 'Hundreds of years.'

'Yes,' responded Cormac hesitatingly. 'In some ways, it is now all assigned to the history books. In other ways, perhaps not so much. Anyway, I am not sure exactly when and where Baphomet actually originated, but it was always a fairly common character in pagan worship. My impression is that even today it is widely employed in occult contexts and even devil worship. But I am no expert on this. Far from it. If you want to understand this in-depth, you should probably find an authority on the Knights Templar, and that certainly isn't me.'

'Caitlin was involved with someone who she believed was worshipping Baphomet,' said Fiona. 'It obviously came as a shock to her when she found out about it, and we are wondering whether that means that somehow there is something nefarious involved in Caitlin's disappearance.'

Cormac looked pained as he once again shifted in his armchair and seemed to wince at the thought of someone he had known since she was a small child possibly being involved in occult practices.

'I am as disturbed by this as you are,' he said. 'I can't honestly tell you not to worry about this. The worship of these sorts of deities is obviously unsettling to someone like me, but then I may well be biased. What concerns me the most is that it appears to be so far removed from what any of us would ever have expected Caitlin to become involved with. I take it there are other people involved?'

'One in particular,' replied Fiona. 'A man she met not that long ago. We think he has introduced her to this and perhaps convinced her to leave with him. Or perhaps something much worse has happened.'

As she finished her sentence, Fiona choked up, causing Andrew to reach out and take her hand, giving it a gentle squeeze.

'I am afraid I can't think of anything more to say that might help,' said Cormac, 'but rest assured that if I think of anything I will be in touch. And please don't hesitate to call me if there is anything else you think I can assist you with. Both of you.'

Cormac looked from Fiona to Andrew, and Andrew nodded in acknowledgement.

'Thank you,' he said. 'We intend to do whatever it takes to find Caitlin.'

'I am very sorry,' said Cormac, slowly getting up from his armchair. 'I don't mean to be rude, but I have an appointment very shortly, so I must prepare for that. But once again, please do get in touch if you think I can be of help.'

'We will,' said Fiona. 'And thank you very much for your time.'

Cormac escorted them back out to the front door where he stepped forward and gave Fiona a brief hug, and then he shook hands with Andrew.

'Don't let it be another fifteen years before you come and see me,' he smiled as the two of them were leaving.

'I will try not to,' said Fiona.

After his visitors had left and begun making their way back along Pembrooke Street towards the city centre, Cormac closed the door and engaged the bolt. He paused for a moment, allowing his head to rest gently against the door with his eyes closed. Then he turned around and walked back to his study and the desk with the old books lying open.

Five

Christopher Haywood was standing by the three-metre-tall floor-to-ceiling windows of his large 28th-floor office in the Shard tower in London's financial district, the City of London. Tall, athletic and remarkably youthful despite his advanced years, he was the CEO and senior partner of the old and highly respected law firm Montague Solicitors. His face was chiselled and his straight and neatly trimmed black hair had streaks of grey at the temples, giving him a distinguished look. He could easily have passed for someone in his late forties, and to his amusement, he had become aware that behind his back amongst his acquaintances in the City, none of whom knew his exact age, people would often refer to him as 'Dorian Gray' – the character in the Oscar Wilde novel published in 1890 who sells his soul to the Devil in exchange for eternal youth. Dorian Gray's age only manifested in an ever-degrading portrait of him that he kept locked away in an attic, leaving the man himself seemingly unaffected by the passage of time.

Haywood's pinstriped suit, crisp white shirt, silver tie and cufflinks completed the impeccable ensemble that projected the very image of success and respectability in the upper echelons of London society. The added pedigree of his family's history and its legacy of philanthropy ensured that there was virtually no door that was not open to him anywhere in this city or the country for that matter.

Montague Solicitors had taken out a 99-year lease on the entire 28th floor soon after the completion of the 310-metre-tall Shard – the only firm that had been offered a contract of that length. Most other firms used rolling 10-year leaseholds, but Haywood had good reason to believe that Montague Solicitors would be around for a very long time. In fact, if it came to a bet between who was more likely to still be standing after 99 years, the Shard or Montague Solicitors, he was in no doubt who he would put his money on. Much like the needle-like tower with its apartments, offices and restaurants that seemed to stretch up and reach for the sky, Montague Solicitors had long been at the pinnacle of London's thriving corporate sector. Operating with legendary discretion, yet able to pull off wins in the most unlikely legal cases, its name was spoken with reverence and admiration, sometimes even dread.

The home that Haywood shared with his wife Felicity in one of the eye-wateringly expensive apartments on the 66th floor was where he spent most of his time. However, he made sure to make an appearance down in the law firm's offices at least a couple of times every week just to show his face and keep the troops in line. Not that they really needed it. They only hired the most capable and driven young lawyers, and as far as anyone knew, no one had ever quit the firm.

Officially, the Shard only had residential apartments on floors 53 to 65, but by pulling the right strings and greasing the wheels with the required amounts of cash, Haywood had secured for himself a private residence on the 66th floor that was suitably obscured from the rest of the world. Overlooking most of central London from a height of around 230 metres, the enormous apartment which had its own private elevator down to the parking garage was around two thousand square feet in size, and it was a paragon of modern metropolitan interior design. However, his personal drawing room and office was decorated like something out of the 18th century, with much of the furniture passed down to him by his various illustrious ancestors.

Haywood's two grown-up children had both gone off to university several years ago. The eldest, Edward, was doing his PhD in ancient history at Oxford, and Charlotte was in the process of completing her Master's degree in Biochemistry at the Sorbonne University in Paris. Haywood had never been very interested in having children, and he had taken a decidedly hands-off approach to raising them. Felicity, the nannies and the boarding schools had taken care of that. Only when they had become teenagers had Haywood taken an interest in them, although mainly in Edward, who one day many years from now would end up carrying the mantle if all went according to plan. Of course, it might not all go according to plan, but Haywood had a contingency lined up for that eventuality.

As he stood there facing north and looking out across London, he turned his head slowly from right to left, taking in the view. To his right, a couple of kilometres away was Canary Wharf with its ever-increasing number of office towers and residential blocks. Around it, the river snaked its way south past the Isle of Dogs and the Millennium Dome, past Greenwich and back north towards the site of London City Airport, after which it broadened and continued out towards the English Channel and the North Sea. On a clear day, he was usually able to see all the way out to the Thames Estuary, some 60 kilometres away. Directly across the river from where he stood was the bustling City of London, where trillions of Pounds in securities were changing hands every day, many of which were influenced by his firm in one form or another.

Further to the left towards the west was St Paul's Cathedral, which he couldn't help but find amusing had burned down in the year 1666 of all years. It had been a beastly conflagration, and it was difficult to believe that such an event had not somehow been ordained by a higher power in order to send a message. It also happened to have been the year the founder of Montague Solicitors had been born. Once again, not something that should be assigned to mere chance. After everything Haywood had seen in all his long years of life, it was clear to him that there was no such thing as coincidence, but that there was most certainly something very real called providence.

As he gazed further west, he could see the London Eye and Big Ben behind it by the Houses of Parliament, and if he turned his head slightly further and looked south-west, he could see the area just north of the Imperial War Museum which had once been known as St George's Fields. It was there, just on the edge of what had at that time been marshland, that Montague Manor had once stood. The place where it had all begun almost three centuries ago. Montague Manor had eventually been sold by the family, but the ancient secrets that had been uncovered within it by his ancestor had been carried forward through time and through many generations to now be in his sole possession. As he turned his head to face forward again, his eye caught what appeared to be an Aer Lingus flight with its characteristic green and white livery coming in low over central London on its final approach from the west to the east towards London City Airport.

Haywood took a deep breath through his mouth and exhaled slowly through his nose. There was something inspiring about being this high up and being able to see this much of the world all at one time. It filled him with the sense of agency and power that all humans subconsciously crave. The power to mould the world to one's own designs. The power to be the master of one's own destiny. Haywood, employing shrewdness, cunning, a razor-sharp intellect, and with the help of his powerful family and its countless connections, had more than achieved this goal for himself.

As he looked down at the tiny ant-like people walking across London Bridge below him, he was very much both literally and figuratively above them all. Observing the small shapes below him as they scurried along going who-knew-where, he reflected on what it might be like to be one of them. Existing only in the limited world that they could see and feel for themselves, no doubt believing in the myth of their own agency and their own ability to decide the course of their lives. They appeared to him like a shoal of dim-witted fish swimming against the current, never realising that every day of their lives the water – reality itself – was working against them and holding them back because they had not been given the gift of knowledge. Deep and profound knowledge about how the world really worked and what could be achieved with the right tools and the right conduit to power. If they understood how their realities were defined by forces unseen and unknowable to them – mechanisms to which only a small group of people were ever afforded access – they would surely collapse to their knees out of sheer shock and debilitating despondency.

Invariably his eyes drifted down to the large and imposing temple-like building immediately to the west of London Bridge. It sat on the wharf next to the river on the north bank, almost directly opposite the Shard. With its towering colonnades and spiralling volutes, its Greek-style slanted pediments and its detailed balustrades wrapping around the top of its roof, it looked like it had been transplanted from the top of the Parthenon in Athens to the edge of the Thames in central London. This was the home of the livery company carrying the name the Worshipful Company of Jurists, whose board of directors Haywood had headed up since the death of his father several decades earlier. Since its inception centuries ago, the livery company had effectively been under the control of the Montague family. It might seem unorthodox to most people, but in the end, there was nothing solicitors liked more than tradition and stability – or at least the appearance thereof. It also meant that the fraternity could operate freely from within the temple.

As he stood there gazing down at the Temple, a short electronic buzz suddenly brought Haywood back from his reverie. He walked over to his desk and pressed the button on the intercom panel embedded in the polished mahogany desk.

'Sir,' said the soft and pleasant-sounding female voice, which sounded like it belonged to a woman in her thirties from an upper-middle-class family. 'Your visitor is here.'

'Thank you, Victoria,' said Haywood, his rich baritone voice sounding calm and authoritative as always. 'Send him in.'

As a favour to a friend who headed up a major investment bank in Canary Wharf, Haywood had agreed to meet a young man in his early thirties who had just been promoted to Executive Director, and who Haywood had been told might eventually become a prospect for the fraternity. Based on his CV and the glowing recommendation from his friend, Haywood had even begun to wonder if he might possibly be a useful replacement for his young protégé, Tristan Maxwell. Haywood had invested fully in young Maxwell, who was now a junior partner in the firm, partly because of his pedigree and family connections but mainly because of his sheer force of will and his absolute and unquestioning loyalty to Haywood personally. However, Haywood had on several occasions become concerned that the young man might not possess the strength of character necessary to stay the course and ultimately fulfil his role within the fraternity. The same ferocity with which he supported Haywood in all his endeavours, regardless of their moral implications, no doubt also had the potential to ultimately culminate in a direct challenge to Haywood's authority. But time would tell. He was still young, relatively speaking.

Twenty minutes later, the rather disappointing meeting had come to an end and Haywood was sitting at his desk in his soft black leather office chair. The young man had all the required pedigree, but he clearly lacked the mindset necessary to completely submit to something much bigger than himself.

Haywood recalled how he had been 12 years old when his own father Cyril had taken him aside to have 'the talk'. Back then, most things in the world had been very different, but the fraternity had remained the same since its inception, and at that time his father deemed it the right moment for the young Christopher to be inducted. Cyril had sat him down inside his office in the family's country estate near the village of Albury in the rolling hills of west Surrey. Christopher had grown up there before being sent off to boarding school, and his childhood had been a happy one as far as he could recall. A couple of years before he had been born, his father had married his French mother Genevieve, who was from old Languedoc nobility. She had been kind and loving as well as beautiful, but she suffered from bouts of depression and was absent for long stretches of time. Back then, Christopher did not understand why, but it eventually became clear. It was yet another lesson demonstrating that everything has a price.

When Cyril had sat his son down for what would turn out to be the most consequential conversation so far in his young life, it had been a warm summer's day, and he had just come back from the estate's small lake where he had been fishing whilst being watched over by one of the estate's groundsmen.

'Chris,' his father had said solemnly. 'You have reached an age where I am finally able to pass on to you a great gift which I myself received from my father many years ago, and he from his father before him. Not money, not property, but the power to affect the world around you. Power through deep and ageless wisdom. The ability to harness ancient forces that can help you create great wealth, but more importantly, powers that will give you influence over others throughout the rest of your life. And perhaps one day you will succeed where we your ancestors have so far failed.'

The mystified young Christopher had then been taken on the train to London where they had been met by a man whom he had never seen before, but who showed his father deep deference, even fear. He led them down through a locked door to the underground system near Monument Station. They then proceeded through a warren of tunnels past several disused and abandoned tube stations that his father said had been used as bomb shelters during World War Two. Finally, they had arrived at a rusty but locked metal door, which the man opened with a key. Inside was a small room with no other exits and nothing on the walls except for peeling paint. There was no furniture, except for a table and two chairs in the middle of a room and a single buzzing tube of fluorescent light suspended above it. The chairs were placed on opposite sides of the table, and on the chair furthest from the door sat a blindfolded man who had his arms tied behind his back and his ankles laced to the metal legs of the chair. He was wearing what appeared to be an expensive but dirty suit, he looked like he had fallen over in the dirt and his body jerked nervously as the heavy door was yanked open noisily.

Christopher's father had placed a hand firmly on his son's shoulder and led him through to stand next to the table, one step behind and to the right of the empty chair. What followed next was something Christopher had never imagined he would experience, and something that at the time had shaken him to the core. However, now, many years later, he was thankful that it had happened because it showed him his true path forward through life.

His father had sat down opposite the man while their escort walked behind him and untied his hands and removed the blindfold. Blinking nervously and with a quavering voice the man had then proceeded to tearfully beg for mercy and forgiveness. It was not entirely clear to the young Christopher what his transgression had been, although it seemed to have something to do with a fraternity and with keeping secrets. However, what had been abundantly clear was that his father was there to decide the man's fate. He spoke to him in hushed, menacing tones, revealing a side of himself that Christopher had never seen before and presenting the bound man with his choices. Cyril also laid out the consequences to the man's family of him making the wrong choice. As his father spoke, the man whimpered, but his head nodded in abject resignation. Christopher had sensed that his father was manipulating him through sheer force of will, pulling him along a train of thought that he did not want to follow, but that he clearly nevertheless felt powerless to resist.

Then unfolded the most shocking scene that Christopher had ever witnessed. His father had extracted a revolver from his coat pocket, inserted a single bullet in the empty drum, flicked the drum into place and put the gun on the table in front of the suited man. He then nodded at him, but the man now shook his head – his lips pressed together, tears streaming down his face and snot dripping from his nose. It was a pathetic sight, and at that moment Christopher had shifted slightly on his feet as he felt a small ember of empathy for the poor man. His father had instantly sensed the burgeoning weakness in his son and had turned his head swiftly to fix him with a brief but hard stare. At that moment, Christopher had realised that in some respects the person on trial was not the man in the chair. It was him. This was a test. He mustered all of his mental strength and clamped down hard on the nascent emotion of compassion, throttling it before it could fully emerge, and leaving it dead inside himself like a stillborn child never given the chance to live. He suddenly grasped that this was all part of what was required to access the powers his father had spoken of. The ability to transcend his basic impulses. From that day forward, he had become the master of his own emotions, allowing him to do things that most people would instinctively recoil from and thereby placing himself outside of the norms of society and gaining an immeasurable advantage over others.

Seeing the welcome sight of his son taking control and detaching himself from his baser emotional impulses, his father had then turned back to face the man in the chair. He looked straight at him, and in a strangely melodic yet ominous-sounding tone of voice he had begun an incantation in Latin that Christopher did not understand but which seemed to completely change the demeanour of the man sitting bound in front of them. It was as if somehow the mesmerising voice and the strange incantations were reaching inside his mind and forcing him to obey. His face, having previously been contorted in a mask of pain and despair, gradually began to relax as an apparent acceptance of what was to come seemed to wash over him. He looked down at the revolver and picked it up. Only much later did it occur to Christopher that at that moment he could have turned the gun on his father and given himself a chance to escape, but such was the power of his father's words that he instead closed his eyes, cocked the gun's hammer and without hesitation brought it up to his right temple and pulled the trigger.

In the confined space of the small concrete-walled room, the gun sounded to Christopher like the deck cannon on a warship firing when it went off. As the dry crack of the weapon instantly reverberated around the room, the bullet tore up through the man's head at an angle, exploding out of the top of the other side taking blood, brains and bits of skull with it and flinging them through the air and onto the wall and the floor next to him. As soon as it happened, his entire body went limp, and he lost his grip on the revolver, which began falling to the floor as his body slumped forward.

Throughout the whole thing, Christopher's father had not seemed to move a muscle. He simply sat immovable and watched as the man's ruined skull smacked down onto the table with a loud wet thud and a pool of blood began to form around it, threatening to spill over the edge and onto his clothes. Only then did he stand up and take a step back, once again placing his hand on his son's shoulder. No words were spoken as the two of them left their escort to clean up the room. They ascended back up to the world of apparent normalcy above, where throngs of people went about their business, oblivious to what had just transpired nearby.

When they re-emerged into the light, he distinctly remembered feeling taller and strangely also much older. And when he looked at other people around him, they appeared to him to be smaller, almost as if he was now looking down at them. But if there was one thing that he took away from that harrowing yet formative experience deep underneath the apparently civilised world of central London, it was that words matter. Words hold power. And that power was a real thing. A weapon that he could learn to wield.

Half an hour later they had exited his father's chauffeur-driven car in front of a huge grey temple-like building near the Thames. His father had then taken him through the lobby of the building where two guards had immediately stood to attention as they spotted them enter. They ascended the enormous sweeping staircase up to the first floor and along a long corridor where oil painting portraits of old men in dark suits were arranged side by side, each one with a brass plaque bearing the name of each subject. The first one read 'Godfrey Beresford Montague'. At the end of the long row of paintings was a portrait of his father Cyril, and next to that was a blank space with a plaque that already read 'Christopher Beresford Haywood Montague'. This was where his portrait would one day be, should he choose to follow in his father's footsteps.

The two of them had entered Grand Master Cyril Montague's private chambers, where Christopher had been presented with a small silver brimstone symbol. After that, his father had sat him down to what he later found out was called his Day of Revelation. His father spent the next many hours pulling back the veil from his young eyes and allowing him to suddenly see the world the way it really was. Gone was the naivety of childhood, and in its place was a hard and unfeeling cynicism, what he would later come to think of as simple pragmatism that let him see the world and his life in an entirely new light.

About a year later, after coming back from boarding school at half-term, his Day of Ascent arrived. He had been raised to worship his father but also to crave his own power and wealth and to ultimately succeed his father in every respect. Now that the great day was here, he was never in any doubt that he was making the right choice. He had been led by his father into the same temple building by the edge of the Thames. However, this time he had been taken down deep inside the bowels of the building and into the ceremonial chamber. Here, like all of his male ancestors going back to Godfrey Montague, he had committed himself during a special ceremony to devote himself to helping Lucifer emerge through the Gates of hell and cross over into this world in physical form. He swore to continue the work and assist him in his inexorable rise to take the false God's place and change the world forever. It was only a question of time before the key to unlocking the gates was found, and when that happened he wanted to be on the winning side.

After the ceremony, which constituted his official induction into the fraternity called the Sons of Lucifer, his father had commanded the other members to leave the ceremonial chamber. He had then, in a reasonable and rational fashion, explained to Christopher how lesser people would consider the ceremony barbaric and sick, but that it was really no different from the way people consume the flesh of other living beings simply for the furtherance of their own survival, aims and desires. Consuming the meat from a cow, said his father, was the same as consuming the energies and the life of all other living things.

'Each one of us is ultimately here on our own,' Cyril had said, 'and the consumption of the assets of the world around us is an integral part of our very nature. It always has been. Every second, thousands of people are born and thousands of people die. It is simply part of how the world works, and no one has the right to deny those of us who have received the gift of knowledge our rightful place in that world.'

Even back then, during his very first ceremony, Haywood had felt the palpable power of it as it unfolded. With its visceral nature and its incantations directed at Lucifer himself, it seemed to him that the air itself was seething with barely contained energy that was on the cusp of splitting open reality as he knew it and open a way for the Dark Lord to come through. But so far, every single one of the two annual attempts during summer and winter solstice had failed. Year after year the failures kept mounting, and every time, even though he intuitively felt that they were close, he had also sensed that somehow there was something missing. Some hidden knowledge. Some secret to the whole thing which was as yet undiscovered. Now, however, he felt convinced that he had finally uncovered the nature of the key that would unlock the gates and discovered where after many centuries it might be found.

Six

When Andrew and Fiona landed back at London City Airport, they quickly made their way through passport control and down the escalator to the outside where Andrew's Aston Martin was parked less than 50 metres away. As they left the on-site parking area and headed west towards central London, a silver Audi TT slipped in behind them – the driver making sure to keep at least one car between himself and their vehicle.

Just before taking off from Dublin Airport, Fiona had sent a message to someone she had once met very briefly at a drinks reception that had been arranged by a history society whose name she had forgotten. But she had remembered him clearly because he had been impressive in his knowledge of all things medieval, including the Knights Templar.

By the time they landed in London, the professor had responded, so Fiona turned to Andrew as they began their drive from the airport towards central London. She showed him an address on her phone and quickly entered it into the car's satellite navigation system.

'I've managed to set up a meeting with a Professor Malcolm Kersley,' she said. 'It was pretty short notice, but he happens to be free for the next few hours, so I think we should pay him a visit.'

'All right,' said Andrew and glanced at the route to the address. 'Which university is it?'

'Oh, he's retired now,' replied Fiona, 'but he was a professor of history at University College London for a couple of decades, specialising in the late medieval period and the Knights Templar. I once met him briefly a long time ago, but I've seen him several times on TV over the years. It turns out that he lives in Islington by Finsbury Park, so it is not too far.'

'Ok,' nodded Andrew. 'Anything in particular you want to talk to him about?'

'Well, given what we've discovered so far,' said Fiona, 'I simply thought that we really need to understand what we are dealing with here, and that means getting a much better understanding of the Knights Templar and this Baphomet character. If anyone is able to tell us about that, it would probably be Kersley. And he very kindly agreed to see us.'

'Okay,' said Andrew. 'We've got plenty of time.'

Just under half an hour later they parked in front of a neat and well-maintained Victorian terraced house on the north side of Endymion Road, just across from Finsbury Park. The front of the house faced south and sat at the end of the terrace next to the New River, which meanders slowly south through the park towards central London.

'Cute house,' said Fiona as they stepped out of the car into the warm evening air.

The sun was now low in the sky, and it bathed the park and the entire street in a pleasant golden light that gave the trees and bushes which lined the road a particularly bright green and vibrant patina. They walked up the gravel path through the modest front garden and stepped up to the dark grey front door. Fiona gripped the heavy brass knocker shaped like a lion's head and knocked firmly twice. Within seconds, they could see movement through the door's frosted glass side panels. When the door opened they were greeted by a short bookish-looking man who appeared to be in his mid-sixties. He had a serious but friendly face and sported a side parting of his grey and severely receded hair which gave the impression of a particularly large forehead. He was wearing reading glasses with amber-coloured plastic frames, a beige suit jacket over a light blue shirt with a green bowtie, and tucked into his hand was a small wooden pipe which he held in front of his chest as he regarded his two visitors over the top of his glasses.

'Ms Keane?' he asked inquisitively.

'Yes,' said Fiona with a smile. 'Thank you so much for taking the time to meet us. This is my partner, Andrew. We really appreciate this.'

'Very nice to meet you,' said Andrew and extended his hand. 'Thanks for seeing us.'

'That's quite all right,' said Kersley, shaking both of their hands and then gesturing for them to enter. 'Come through. We'll sit in my study at the back.'

They followed him into a small room with an almost threadbare grey rug that looked like it had been laid down several decades earlier. Above their heads was an ornate white corniced ceiling with a silver chandelier, and around them the walls were impossible to see because they were entirely covered by bookcases from floor to ceiling and wrapped around the entire room. In the centre of the study was an old wooden desk with piles of yet more books on it. Next to it was a simple but well-worn leather office chair that could probably be acquired in upmarket central London furniture shops in the 'retro' section, but which had almost certainly been here for at least as long as the rug. It was everything one might expect from a retired history professor.

They made themselves comfortable near the bay windows facing the immaculately kept back garden that had the New River on one side and a similarly neat garden on the other.

'So,' smiled Professor Kersley, making it sound like a question. 'The Knights Templar.'

'Yes,' said Fiona. 'As I mentioned in my email, I am a historian and archaeologist with the British Museum, and I was wondering if you might be able to enlighten us on the Templars, specifically with regard to the idea that they worshipped something called Baphomet.'

'Fiona knows much more about this than I do,' interjected Andrew. 'In fact, I am a complete novice, so please assume that we are starting from scratch.'

'Right,' smiled Kersley, puffing gently on his pipe a couple of times whilst seemingly pondering how to begin for a moment. 'Certainly. I can do that. May I ask what this is all about? It's just that you came here on such short notice, and I sensed a certain amount of urgency in your email.'

Fiona glanced briefly at Andrew who sat immobile with a neutral expression waiting for her to respond. As a rule, Fiona did not like to keep things hidden from people she was asking favours from, but she was not inclined to tell Kersley anything about her sister or what they had discovered about Antoine.

'It is just a project I am working on at the Museum,' she lied. 'We are discussing possibly creating a special Templar exhibition later this year.'

'I see,' nodded Kersley slowly with a quizzical expression whilst giving Andrew a quick glance before returning his gaze to Fiona. 'Well, let's get started then. And let's begin with their name. They are commonly known as the Knights Templar or simply the Templars, but their full name at their inception was actually *Pauperes commilitones Christi Templique Salomonici* in Latin, which means 'The Poor Fellow-Soldiers of Christ and of the Temple of Solomon'. Quite a mouthful. They were founded by a man named Hugues de Payens, who also became the first grand master, along with eight other French knights. This happened in Jerusalem a couple of decades after the First Crusade had conquered that city in 1099. The whole thing started because large numbers of pilgrims from Europe, France especially, began converging on what became known as the Kingdom of Jerusalem after its capture, and many of them were robbed or killed on the way there. So, there was a dire need for some sort of military force to protect those pilgrims. And this was where Hugues de Payens stepped in after arriving in the city around the year 1115. He approached the King of Jerusalem, Baldwin II, who had recently been installed by the Catholic pope in Rome, and he asked him for permission to create a monastic military order for this express purpose. With the added support of the Catholic patriarch of Jerusalem, the permission was eventually granted and this small band of French knights were then given a wing of the palace on the Temple Mount in the recently captured Al-Aqsa Mosque. This, of course, was where the Temple of Solomon had once stood until the 6th century BCE, almost two millennia before the Templar Order was founded. And that is how they acquired their name.'

'So, the Templars were an exclusively French endeavour?' asked Fiona.

'It was,' replied Kersley. 'At least in the beginning. All of the members were from the French aristocracy, and throughout their entire history, they only accepted new members who were already knights of some renown. And the Templars seemed to do a rather good job of it, because, in 1129 at the Council of Troyes, they received an official endorsement from the Catholic Church in Rome after committing to the monastic tenets of poverty and chastity, as well as a vow to defend the Holy Land on behalf of the Church. And this is really where things start to accelerate for the Templars, both in terms of their influence and their wealth, and as I am sure you know they eventually became extremely powerful and wealthy.'

'Didn't their wealth then fly in the face of their poverty vows?' asked Andrew.

'The individual knights themselves were committed to poverty,' said Kersley, 'and that poverty vow is symbolised on their seal, which is an image of two knights riding on a single horse. However, the Templar Order amassed huge wealth, partly because they received enormous amounts of donations from all over Europe to further their work in protecting pilgrims and defending Jerusalem from the Muslims, and partly because they began to engage in what can best be described as international banking. It was also the case that any knight who joined the Templars and then fell in battle would forfeit all of their land and wealth to the Order. But perhaps an even more important factor was that they were exempt from paying taxes because of their status as a monastic order serving directly under the papacy in Rome. In fact, in 1139 Pope Innocent II issued a papal bull – which is an official proclamation by the Vatican – which stipulated that they were to be exempt from any and all local laws in any country or jurisdiction. They were also exempt from the influence of any Church authority except that of the pope himself. This was obviously an extremely important development, and because of the power of the Church at that time, no monarch anywhere in Europe dared to go against that proclamation. At least not for a very long time after the Templars were established.'

As he spoke, Kersley puffed on his pipe ever more vigorously as he began to enter his stride, seemingly oblivious to the way the smoke languidly swirled up and into the rest of the room, making Fiona cough every few minutes.

'So, they effectively dispensed with their tenets when it suited them?' said Andrew.

'You could certainly argue that point,' said Kersley hesitantly. 'But it has always been the case that money can bend laws, even if it doesn't make them break. And the Templars were no exception. The more power and wealth they accumulated, the more feared and influential they became, which in turn made them even more powerful and wealthy. And so it continued for the next century and a bit.'

'That sounds like a recipe for disaster if you ask me,' observed Andrew.

'Well put,' said Kersley, removing his pipe from his mouth and pointing it at Andrew with an appreciative smile. 'You've hit the nail on the head. This was indeed what eventually sowed the seeds of the downfall of the Templars.'

'What did you mean by saying they engaged in international banking?' asked Fiona.

'Oh,' said Kersley. 'That is just shorthand for a system they set up to protect the wealth of pilgrims, and it was simple enough but actually quite ingenious. Essentially, it involved promissory notes that the Templars issued to pilgrims before they set out from Europe. A pilgrim would hand in a certain amount of money to the Templars near where they lived, and in return, they would receive an encrypted note which they could then carry to Jerusalem where they could cash it in at the Temple Mount. This removed the risk of carrying gold or silver coins on the roads, and it was so effective that it quickly spread throughout Europe and into other areas where the Templars had established local chapters. And of course, the Order always took a fee for their services in the form of a percentage of the value concerned. For these reasons, the Templars have often been called the world's first multinational corporation.'

'It definitely sounds like banking to me,' observed Andrew dryly.

'Anyway,' continued Kersley. 'Over time the Order became ever more powerful, and at its peak, it is estimated that the total number of members was between fifteen and twenty thousand. However, only around two thousand of those were actual knights. The rest served in non-combat support roles as well as clerical and administrative roles and so on. But all in all, it eventually became a truly enormous organisation, especially for its time. And I think most people today are familiar with the uniforms of the knights, which were white tunics with a red cross emblazoned on the front typically worn over chain mail.'

'But it didn't last,' said Fiona, already knowing the rough outline of what happened next.

'That is correct,' said Kersley, shifting slightly in his seat to make himself more comfortable. 'I think it is useful to think of the Templars at that time as the beneficiaries of an extremely powerful brand. It was in many ways the coolest company to work for. A bit like the leading-edge technology companies of today. Many young French nobles aspired to join the Order, and this played a big role in their continued ability to amass wealth and power. However, the whole point of the Templars was that they were seen as guardians of the Holy Land and of Jerusalem in particular, so when that city fell to the Muslim forces of Sultan Saladin in

1187 and all of the various French knights, organisations and citizens were kicked out, a large part of what you might call the *raison d'etre* of the Order fell away. The Templars retreated north to the city of Acre and eventually across the seas to Cyprus. This was in the early 13th century. Now, at this point, Europe began to come under threat from the Mongols under Genghis Khan, so in the minds of many European rulers the Holy Land became less and less important, and that directly began to translate into less influence for the Templars. However, they still retained huge wealth, they still controlled a huge part of the money lending market, and they still had the autonomy that had originally been bestowed on them by Pope Innocent II. For these reasons, the Templars hung onto much of their power and independence throughout Europe until the end of the 13th century when things finally came to a head. You see, the French monarch at that time, King Philip IV, had more or less exhausted the wealth of his nation in endless wars with the Kingdom of England and also the Kingdom of Aragon in what we now call north-eastern Spain. And whatever money he still had was most likely borrowed from the Templars. The Catholic Church in Rome through Pope Boniface VIII condemned the king for his lavish spending on the wars, and Philip responded by levying a tax on the Church, demanding half of its income. Pope Boniface then forbade any transfer of funds to Philip, so at this point, there was a standoff between the two. In response, Philip established his own competing clerical authority in Avignon with loyal French bishops and nobility supporting him, and they eventually denounced the sitting pope. Boniface attempted to draw a line under the whole thing by issuing a papal bull in 1302 stating that Rome possessed absolute papal supremacy. In other words, he attempted to subdue both Philip IV and the French church using the innate authority of the Catholic Church. However, Philip completely ignored this and actually had Boniface detained during which time he was apparently mistreated, and he died shortly thereafter. Philip immediately seized the opportunity, and his council of clerics elected their own pope in 1305, a bishop by the name of Raymond Bertrand de Got who then took the name Pope Clement V thereby effectively hijacking the papacy from Rome and placing it in Avignon.'

'Crikey,' said Andrew and raised his eyebrows. 'Papal piracy. I never knew about any of this.'

'Well, it was certainly a bold move, to put it mildly,' said Kersley. 'But it was plain that the French had had quite enough of the Catholic Church's authority at that point in time, and of course, there was the issue of the money which clearly dictated a lot of these events. Anyway, it is probably fair to say that this shift in power within the Catholic Church invalidated the special position that the Templars had enjoyed since their founding. It also allowed the new Pope Clement V, who was of course doing the bidding of Philip IV, to bring the Templars to their knees by accusing them of heresy, blasphemy and all sorts of other crimes. But in the end, it was really only about the money. King Philip simply wanted to get his hands on their vast wealth.'

'And I guess this is where Baphomet comes in,' said Fiona.

'Precisely,' replied Kersley. 'But there was a whole list of charges levelled against the Templars, including spitting on the cross and even denying Christ. And there is good reason to believe that this was actually true.'

'How so?' asked Fiona, looking perplexed. 'That would seem completely out of character for these men who were essentially Christian warrior monks.'

'It is quite simple,' said Kersley. 'For generations, the Templars were in battle against Muslims in the Holy Land, so the idea was that if they were ever captured they expected to be forced to perform those precise acts. Spitting on the cross might simply have been a form of conditioning that would allow them to potentially do it for real one day if need be.'

'That sounds like a bit of an apologist reason, doesn't it?' said Andrew.

At that, Professor Kersley frowned and regarded Andrew for a brief moment whilst looking slightly defensive, even offended. But then his demeanour softened again and he continued.

'Well, you might say that, I suppose. But I happen to think it is quite likely to have happened. At any rate, there were also other charges, including the notion that they venerated a severed head. It is not exactly clear whose head that might have been, although there are theories that it might have been the head of John the Baptist.'

'Really?' asked Fiona. 'What's the connection?'

'My own theory,' said Kersley, 'is that from the outset the Templars among others saw themselves as guardians of ancient secrets that had been passed down from John the Baptist. The initiates of this ancient wisdom were known as Johannites, and as you may know, each grand master of the Templar Order was given the honorary title of 'John'.'

'I have never heard of this,' said Fiona.

'Well, there's no proof one way or another of whose head it really was,' said Kersley, 'but I think there might be some truth to this as well, simply because of the idea of *Memento Mori*.'

'That's Latin, right?' said Fiona. 'Something along the lines of remembering death.'

'Yes,' nodded Kersley, 'Or more precisely, remembering that one day you will have to die. I think it is very likely that this was deeply embedded in the Templar creed, given that they were a military order who had sworn to never retreat from the battlefield unless their banner had fallen. Naturally, this meant that death was always a very real thing for these men, and getting used to the idea through some sort of regular ritual would have made eminent sense.'

Kersley shifted his gaze to Andrew and regarded him once more across the top of his glasses in what almost seemed like a challenge. Andrew simply held up his hands and tilted his head slightly to one side.

'I am a military man,' he said, 'so no argument from me there.'

As he put his hands back down, Andrew glanced briefly at Fiona, who was looking at him with a nervous expression. She seemed uncomfortable with the somewhat confrontational turn their meeting had suddenly taken. Then she returned her gaze to Professor Kersley and smiled.

'So, after these trials, the Templars were put to death, right?' asked Fiona.

'That is correct, said Kersley. 'Almost all of them were killed over the next several years, most notably the grand master Jacques de Molay who was burned at the stake on the island of Ile des Javiaux in the Seine in Paris.'

'And presumably, Philip IV stole all of their wealth?' asked Andrew.

'Almost certainly,' said Kersley, 'although there are persistent rumours that it was spirited away to some as yet undiscovered location. Who knows…'

'So, what can you tell us about Baphomet?' asked Fiona. 'This mysterious creature that they seemed to have worshipped.'

'Well, as I assume you are aware,' said Kersley, 'Baphomet is a pagan deity that is actually much older than Christianity and perhaps even Judaism. And the Templars were indeed accused of worshipping him. This was obviously seen as heretical at the time, but I think there is good reason to believe that this really happened.'

'Really?' asked Andrew. 'But Baphomet was a sort of demon, right?'

Once again, Kersley frowned. He clearly held a deep affection for his subject matter, and he obviously did not appreciate anyone taking liberties with it, or worse still, being ignorant of it.

'No,' he said, now sounding slightly exasperated. 'That is just tosh that has been peddled by the Church for centuries. Baphomet was a deeply venerated being that conveyed the notion of balance, both within the world and within each individual.'

'So why was it seen as heretical?' asked Andrew.

'Well, quite clearly anything that isn't strictly in accordance with the prevailing religious dogma is by definition heretical,' shrugged Kersley.

'But how and why did the Templars incorporate the idea of Baphomet into their beliefs,' asked Fiona. 'Especially given their sworn religious tenets of service to the Church.'

'That is indeed a very good question,' replied Kersley. 'Let me explain by way of an example. The Templars are known to have employed something called the Atbash Cypher. It is a simple substitution cypher used to encode and decode messages. You simply swap the first letter in the alphabet for the last. You then swap the second for the second to last and so on. If you do that with how Baphomet is written in Hebrew, you get the Greek word 'Sofia', which means wisdom. This is indicative of the connection between the Templars and the early Christian Gnostics who valued knowledge above all else – especially deep insights or spiritual knowledge about the world.'

'That sounds more like philosophy than religion,' observed Fiona.

'That's right,' said Kersley. 'The Gnostics of early Christianity were devoted to this sort of deep knowledge and understanding. And it is not difficult to see why. Knowledge is the gift that has allowed humans to rise above all other creatures on this Earth. The Gnostics were prepared to deviate and even go against the Nicene orthodoxy and the religious dogma of the Church of Rome in their pursuit of it. And I happen to think that was a very admirable thing.'

'So, what is the essence of Gnostic teachings?' asked Andrew.

'Well,' said Kersley, 'Gnosticism relates to *gnōsis*, which is the Greek noun for knowledge. But, similarly to what we see in French, the word 'knowledge' can take on two meanings. There is the French word '*savoir*', which simply means to know or be aware of, and then there is also the word '*connaître*' which holds a much deeper meaning of knowing something by personal acquaintance or experience. In other words, it is a form of experientialism that isn't purely about what can be reasoned or deducted. And it is the latter form of knowledge that Gnosticism revolves around. It most likely originated in the non-rabbinical Jewish and early Christian sects of the 1st century CE, although it draws on elements from much earlier Persian teachings. The endpoint for this philosophy is to acquire divine insights through one's own experiences, and this is held as being much more important than doctrinal faith as presented by dogmatic religious teachings. The emphasis is on the individual and its own deep understanding of the world, rather than the collective passive worship of some deity or other.'

'That sounds almost like Protestantism,' said Fiona.

'In a way, yes,' nodded Kersley, 'But some elements of Gnosticism were quite radical and were considered heretical after the First Council of Nicaea in 325 CE, and afterwards their books were either hidden or destroyed. You see, in the early days Christianity was fragmented along many theological fissures, and many different sects were pursuing different directions of faith within the same framework using different gospels and incorporating varying levels of heretical ancient mysticism. For example, the Gnostics often tended to praise the serpent in the Garden of Eden for bringing knowledge to Adam and Eve and thereby freeing them from the slavery of existing without free will. Some might say that this urge for free will is a deeply held desire in all human beings that we in our modern world celebrate practically above all else. Conversely, the unyielding dogma of the major Abrahamic religions is increasingly seen as being in opposition to the individual's ability to express itself and seek its own truth. The clear implication here is that the individual, through personal experience, reflection and especially rituals, can obtain divine insights and come to know and understand everything there is, including both God and Satan. I am sure you know that Satan was first called Lucifer, the Light Bringer. The fallen angel who brought the light of knowledge to Adam and Eve.'

'You seem to have studied the Gnostics quite deeply,' said Andrew.

'I have,' replied Kersley. 'They are an integral part of the Templars as far as I am concerned. I spent six months at the Coptic Museum in Cairo researching Gnostic texts from the Nag Hammadi Library, and it is quite obvious that there is a clear line between the Gnostics and the Templars. You even see it in some of their official regional seals which include images of various gnostic deities such as Abraxas which is a being with the body of a man and the head of a cockerel.'

'I think I have heard of the Nag Hammadi Library,' said Fiona. 'It was a huge cache of ancient apocryphal gospels, right?'

'That is correct,' said Kersley. 'It was found in the Egyptian desert in 1945, and it contains 2nd and 3rd-century apocryphal gospels along with a number of other gnostic texts. It was an amazing discovery, and I think it is fair to say that it ended up challenging the Nicene orthodoxy in quite a major way. Some of those texts cast the life and death of Jesus Christ in a starkly different light compared with what you will find in the Bible.'

'It seems to me that there was a veritable buffet of different belief systems back then rather than a small number of major dogmatic religions,' observed Fiona. 'People seemed to shop around for whatever deity they thought they needed.'

'Yes, that's quite accurate,' said Kersley and puffed on his pipe again. 'Of course, this was all prior to the modern age of science with its emphasis on empirical evidence. In fact, back then, science was referred to as philosophy because, loosely speaking, my thoughts about the underlying reasons for a natural phenomenon would have been as good as yours or anyone else's. People simply didn't have the insistence of evidence that we in the modern world have. This obviously extended to beliefs about religion, magic, demons and everything else people could imagine. And in some ways, you could argue that all of this was just an attempt to understand and explain the world around us, but without the scientific methods and tools that we have available today. Many centuries earlier, the ancient Greeks like Aristotle had done a decent job of attempting to emphasise things like the experimental approach and empirical evidence. But ultimately the world at that time was so enmeshed in what we today would call mysticism and superstition, not to mention a whole tapestry of various gods and religions, that it was impossible to study any topic without also having faith entering into the equation in some form. And because no self-respecting would-be ruler would even consider taking power without a credible claim to divine backing, religion and faith became an integral part of how people understood the world and how power was wielded in those days.'

'Sounds very messy,' said Andrew. 'All of these different gods and minor deities.'

'You could call it that,' said Kersley, 'but for most of human existence this was the norm. In today's world, we tend to think of religion in terms of monotheism. In other words, we are conditioned to think in terms of just one god that heads up everything, but that is a fairly new phenomenon. For the vast majority of human history, there have been a huge number of different major and minor gods and spirits, some good and some bad. Just look at the Greek pantheon of gods, for example. Until science as we know it arrived, conjecture was really all people had to work with, and if an assertion about something appeared persuasive, then there was little reason to doubt it being true. An interesting example of this is King James I of England, who of course lived before the Enlightenment. He is the author of the King James Bible, which is the standard Church of England Bible. But what most people don't know is that several years prior to its publication, King James also wrote *'Daemonologie'*, which is a comprehensive dissertation on demons, black magic, witches and even necromancy. So, in many ways, it was mainstream theology until quite recently.'

'Amazing,' said Fiona. 'I guess what you're saying, is that people lived in a very different world in the past. A world where belief trumped evidence and where people's minds were susceptible to what we would probably consider pretty outlandish ideas.'

'Yes and no,' replied Kersley. 'It is important to realise that there are plenty of people today who subscribe to the same ideas that were prevalent back then – belief in Baphomet and Lucifer included. As an example, the Vatican to this day still operates a large group of dedicated exorcists who travel the world to vanquish demons from people who are believed to have been possessed.'

'Wow,' said Fiona. 'My head is beginning to spin. I had no idea of the complexity of all this. Anyway, if I may, I assume that you are familiar with John Milton's 'Paradise Lost'?'

'Of course,' replied Kersley, sounding surprised that she might think he wasn't.

'What do you make of that particular work of literature?' she asked.

'I think it is quite a magnificent piece of poetry,' Kersley replied. 'And I am aware that it has spawned things like Luciferianism, which I gather venerates the characteristics of Lucifer as an enlightened rebel. But as to whether Paradise Lost should be taken literally, that is up to each person to decide for themselves. And the same could be said for the Bible and every other religious text. In my view, people should be free to decide for themselves.'

'Can I ask one question about something slightly different?' said Andrew. 'I am just curious about your research when you still worked as a professor at UCL. I think it is fair to say that much of what we have talked about today would be considered quite esoteric by most people. How did you secure funding for your work?'

'Like any other researcher,' shrugged Kersley. 'Despite how it might seem to you, there are lots of people who consider it an important field of study, both for religious and non-religious people. The university obviously provides a basic platform, but I have always had a small number of generous donors who have provided funding for things like research trips, assistants and so on.'

'Interesting,' said Fiona and glanced at Andrew. 'Right, I think that covers everything we needed to know. Thank you very much for your time. We really appreciate this.'

'You're welcome,' said Kersley, getting up from his chair, smoothing down his jacket and adjusting his bowtie. 'I hope it was useful.'

'Very,' said Andrew. 'Thank you.'

The two of them rose and thanked Professor Kersley once more, and then he escorted them back out to the front door and bid them farewell.

'Wow, that was quite a lot to take in,' said Fiona quietly as the two of them walked along the path through Kersley's front garden and back out to the street. 'And that is coming from someone like me who is used to some pretty heavy research.'

'Yes, but what did we actually learn that we can use?' asked Andrew, 'except that Kersley is a big fan of the Templars, and apparently that a bit of casual worship of Baphomet isn't such a big deal.'

'I guess that was the main thing that struck me too,' said Fiona. 'He seemed pretty blasé about that aspect of Templar history. He clearly admires them. But I guess what we did learn from him was that the Templars did worship Baphomet and that they were a much more complex entity than most people think. This gnostic belief system of theirs seems to reach back through time to ancient Judaic mysticism. So, to call them Christians actually seems like a bit of a stretch. And perhaps they never saw themselves that way, and it was just a convenient façade they established to gain the approval of Rome. For all we know, the founding knights could have been Gnostics before they ever went to the Holy Land. They could even have been part of what he described as Luciferianism.'

'I guess that is all speculation, but it sounds reasonable enough,' said Andrew, 'But where does that leave us?'

'Well, I still can't say I feel any better about the idea of Caitlin being involved in anything to do with the worship of Baphomet,' said Fiona. 'There's just something quite dark and creepy about that whole thing, regardless of what Kersley thinks. Especially after what we have learned about Antoine.'

'I agree,' said Andrew. 'Anyway, let's get back to the house and rest our brains. Mine feels like it is about to explode.'

Seven

Christopher Haywood left his private office inside the sumptuous 66th-floor apartment and stepped into the elevator to the parking garage underneath the Shard. Waiting there was his personal driver wearing his standard black suit, white shirt and black tie. The always polite and perfectly presentable Tom stood by the open passenger door of the six-and-a-half-metre-long Mercedes-Maybach S 600 Pullman Guard, waiting for Haywood to enter.

Officially, Tom had worked as Haywood's driver for almost a decade, but his skill set extended well beyond his capabilities behind the wheel. After a military career that included a stint in the SBS, which he later had to give up because of a knee injury, he had joined the Metropolitan Police's Protection Command, one of the commands within the force's Specialist Operations directorate. As a close protection officer responsible for ensuring the physical safety of government ministers and diplomats both in the UK and abroad, he had received extensive weapons training and had taken part in a long series of advanced driving courses offered by elite instructors who also worked with the UK's various special forces units. It was in this capacity that he had been approached by a Home Office mandarin. This official, whose name Tom never discovered, had access to all of the Protection Command's evaluation results, and he had offered him what he described as a once-in-a-lifetime opportunity to work for a truly exceptional individual. He then had a long personal meeting with Haywood that was significantly more in-depth than his interview when joining the Met. His personal life, past relationships, finances and employment history had been dissected in considerable detail, and by the end of it, Tom had been offered the position as Haywood's new driver after his predecessor had retired. The job came with a pay package that was multiples of what he could ever have achieved even as a senior officer inside the Special Operations directorate. It came only with one condition – that he never ever, under any circumstances, divulge anything Haywood said or did, or any information about where he had been or might be in the future. Tom did not hesitate in signing up, and since that day he had never once wavered from his duties.

The black armoured limousine that Tom drove for Haywood was always polished to a high sheen, and it weighed more than five tonnes. Its six-litre twin-turbo V12 engine produced 630 brake horsepower, which was about twice that of a standard Porsche 911, and despite its massive weight, it could propel the vehicle from 0 to 60 mph in just over six seconds. If ever Haywood needed to be whisked away from a potential threat, this vehicle would be able to do the job very well indeed.

Haywood ducked slightly and climbed into the huge passenger compartment, sat down in the plush reclining leather seats made bespoke in black with burgundy trim to accentuate the edges of the seat and armrests. He adjusted his tailor-made suit and his silver cufflinks and then pressed the button for the armoured door, which quickly swung shut with a soft yet meaty thud betraying its hefty weight. In fact, the entire limousine was armoured and certified for blast resistance, making it capable of absorbing both small and large calibre gunfire, as well as a 15kg TNT blast at a distance of just two metres.

He looked up and the muscle memory in his index finger found and flicked the switch for the panoramic sunroof, which slid open. He always liked being able to see up and out, even during nighttime. The 3D surround sound system was already filling the spacious interior with classical music. Today he had pre-selected the dulcet piano tones of the French composer Maurice Ravel, about whom it had been said that "he was only teachable on his own terms". In other words, he was a maverick who did not play by the rules laid down by other people. Haywood identified with that more than he could put into words.

He activated the electrochromic glass privacy screen to the driver's seat, instantly turning it from clear to opaque. He then flicked the switch for the same to happen to the side windows, and also for the drapes to be pulled closed, thereby giving him a complete sense of privacy and separation from the world outside. Finally, as Tom started the engine and the car began moving slowly up and out of the parking garage under the Shard, he reached down to the central console to make sure the driver intercom was switched off. Then he selected the comms menu and tapped on the number for Tristan Maxwell. When Maxwell picked up, there was a slight rustling sound on the line, mixed with the sound of voices and phones ringing.

'I am very sorry, Sir,' said Maxwell in a clipped accent. 'I am just out on the floor. I am moving into my office now. One moment please.'

Haywood did not respond but simply waited as the long and bulky Maybach exited the parking garage and turned out onto St Thomas Street, driving slowly west towards Borough High Street and London Bridge. Soon there was the sound of a glass office door being closed, and immediately the low-level murmur of voices and office noise in the background disappeared.

'There,' came Maxwell's voice again. 'Finally free of the great unwashed. How may I help?'

'I need an update on the dig site,' said Haywood. 'What's the latest from our team in France?'

'Everything is going according to plan,' said Maxwell. 'We believe we're close. We have been able to rule out two locations under the inner walls by the portcullis, and we are close to dismissing another by the west tower. That leaves only the main site under the chapel. If what they think they have discovered holds true, then it simply has to be there.'

'Very good,' said Haywood. 'We don't have much time.'

'I know, Sir,' said Maxwell. 'The team is working flat out.'

'Very good. Now, I also need an update on our girl,' said Haywood evenly. 'How is she doing?'

'She's doing well, Sir,' replied Maxwell matter-of-factly. 'Already in place and ready. She fits the bill very nicely, I must say.'

'Any issues?' asked Haywood.

'Oh, just the usual,' said Maxwell casually. 'Not particularly enthusiastic about things, but then she obviously won't be feeling like that for too long now.'

'Excellent,' said Haywood. 'Tristan, I don't need to tell you how important this is. We can't have any screwups, do you understand?'

'Yes, Sir,' said Maxwell. 'Absolutely. Don't worry. There won't be any issues. The situation is secure.'

'Good,' said Haywood. 'And Tristan, I think it is time to remove a certain piece from the board. A rather obnoxious locust that just won't seem to go away.'

'The reporter,' said Maxwell.

'Indeed,' replied Maxwell. 'He has proven extremely tenacious, and he is clearly not going to back off. At the moment, he doesn't represent a major threat, but that could change if he gets lucky and stumbles across something sensitive. It is becoming quite clear to me that he is simply not susceptible to our attempt at... persuasion. So, I need you to solve that problem. Permanently.'

'I understand completely, Sir,' responded Maxwell, a hard edge now entering his voice. 'I will take care of it immediately.'

'Very well,' said Haywood. 'That is all. Check in with me tomorrow. I need twice-daily updates from now on, is that clear.'

'Certainly, Sir,' said Maxwell. 'Understood.'

Haywood disconnected the call and leaned back in his seat feeling vaguely reassured by what he had heard. Perhaps Maxwell was a serious prospect for full membership of the fraternity after all.

As he looked out through the window at the pedestrians walking across London Bridge, he managed to catch a glimpse over the railing towards the west along the Thames to the area of London called Temple – so named because of the Temple Church built by the Knights Templar after their supposed dissolution in 1312. He only caught a brief glimpse of it, and then it was gone behind the buildings once more.

Driving in an armoured limousine to get across a distance that could have been covered by foot in ten minutes might seem like overkill, but Haywood had learned from bitter experience to eliminate all possible risks. Not only was he immensely wealthy, which always carried with it certain obvious risks, but with the history of his family being what it was, he could never be too careful.

★   ★   ★

On the way back home from visiting Professor Kersley, Fiona was in the passenger seat deeply engrossed in something on her phone. She tapped and swiped with the expression of someone who was trying to recall something she had forgotten. As they were approaching Hampstead she suddenly brought her right hand up to pat her jacket pocket and then looked up and turned to face Andrew.

'Turn around,' she said.

'What? Why?' said Andrew perplexed.

'I will explain later,' she replied. 'Just take us to the British Museum. There is something I need to show you.'

'You want me to take you to work?' asked Andrew, looking at her sideways with a dubious look on his face. 'It's the end of the day. Don't they close right about now?'

'Please just do it,' she insisted. 'It will all make sense when we get there.'

Twenty minutes later, they had parked on Bedford Square and walked the rest of the way to the British Museum on Great Russell Street.

'We'll go in through the front entrance,' said Fiona. 'I'll take us inside and get you a quick visitor's badge from one of the attendants there. They all know me.'

They walked through the tall black-painted wrought-iron gates with their gilded *fleur-de-lis* spikes running along the top, and approached the woman in the high-visibility vest standing just on the other side with a clipboard and a tablet.

'Hi Anna,' said Fiona cheerfully. 'I know we're closing soon, but I am just bringing in a friend for a quick visit today.'

'Oh, hey Fiona,' said the woman. 'No problem. Have fun.'

'Come on,' said Fiona, turning to Andrew and taking his hand.

The two of them walked across the small exterior courtyard and entered through the main entrance just behind the colonnade that fronted the Greek temple-like façade. The museum was as busy as ever. The almost one million square foot treasure trove of ancient artefacts from around the world possesses around 8 million objects, of which roughly eighty thousand are on display at any given time. Because the museum was approaching closing time, Andrew and Fiona were moving against the general current of visitors as they made their way into the enormous building, which accommodates almost six million visitors every year.

Soon they emerged into the largest covered square in Europe, the Queen Elizabeth II Great Court, whose roof is a torus-like shape made up of 1656 large and uniquely shaped panes of glass, bathing the entire vast central courtyard in natural light. Placed in the middle of it was the large circular Reading Room, so named because it used to be just that for the British Library. Each side of the courtyard was constructed to resemble a Greek temple, and the floor was off-white and polished to the point of being moderately reflective. The soft muffled echoes of the voices of the many visitors reverberated endlessly around the cavernous space in an almost uniform white noise reminiscent of the sound of waves from a distant beach.

'We just need to walk to the other side,' said Fiona and pointed past the reading room to the far left corner. 'Then we'll take the stairs up to the upper floor. It's up there.'

'What is?' asked Andrew.

'All good things…' smiled Fiona.

Andrew armed himself with patience and followed her. He was just pleased to see her smile again after what had undoubtedly been a very difficult day. They ascended the stairs in the wide northwest stairwell next to the corner of what had once upon a time been a large open-air quadrangle before the courtyard was covered by the glass torus. Walking up the stairs and making their way into the museum proper, they then proceeded under the high semi-vaulted ceilings of Rooms 59, 58 and 57, all of which contained artefacts from the ancient Levant, to emerge into Room 56 which held items from ancient Mesopotamia. Just inside the room on the right-hand side of the eggshell-coloured room was a large white glass Display Box with the number '23' on it.

'Here it is,' said Fiona, pointing to a stone relief about 50 centimetres tall and 35 centimetres wide hanging inside the display box and bathed in a soft neutral light.

'This is the Burney Relief,' she said. 'Also known as the Queen of the Night Relief.'

Andrew stepped closer and leaned forward slightly to peer at it. The artefact was made of baked clay, and the relief itself was protruding several centimetres from the base. The naked female figure in the middle of it was curvaceous, and she wore a horned headdress characteristic of Mesopotamian deities. In her hands, she held a rod and a ring of justice, which were symbols of her divinity. Stretching downward along her back were long feathered wings, indicating that she was a goddess of the Underworld. Her legs ended in sharp talons that completed the bird-like appearance and invoked notions of sirens or harpies. On both sides, she was flanked by owls and lions.

'What is this?' asked Andrew. 'Or perhaps I should ask, *who* is this?'

'This is Lilith,' replied Fiona. 'At least according to some interpretations.'

'Lilith?' said Andrew, straightening up and turning to look at Fiona. 'The Lilith that Caitlin had a picture of in her room?'

'Yes,' replied Fiona. 'Or possibly her mythological progenitor. What you are looking at here is more than three-thousand eight-hundred years old. Its exact provenance is a bit murky, having initially emerged through a Syrian antique dealer in the 1930s. But there is no debate about it originating in southern Mesopotamia around the year 1800 BCE.'

'But how can this be Lilith from the Book of Enoch if she was from Mesopotamia hundreds or thousands of years before the Bible was even conceived?' asked Andrew.

'Because the world back then was not as simple as it later became,' replied Fiona. 'At least not in terms of deities. Many of the characters in the Bible, whether we are talking about the Jewish or the Christian version, are amalgamations of much older characters from a whole range of ancient belief systems. Unlike all of the main characters of the cast in the Bible such as Yahweh a.k.a. 'God', Jesus, Satan, Adam and Eve, Noah and so on, who all came from Jewish Abrahamic mythology, Lilith is thought to be much older. She existed before there were angels and demons. Before messiahs and floods. Perhaps she is older even than the notion of Yahweh itself.'

'Wow,' said Andrew, and glanced at the relief again, marvelling both at how well preserved it was given its age, and also at what the relief represented.

'Imagine you had a time machine,' continued Fiona, 'and imagine that you could go back to the streets of ancient Babylon around the year 1800 BCE during the Bronze Age. Then imagine that you were able to ask the locals about Yahweh, the archangel Michael or even Lucifer, you would have been met with a blank stare. There simply were no such things at that time, and there wouldn't be for several more centuries or even millennia. However, if you were to ask about Lilith, or *Lilitu* as she would have been known, you might have watched the blood drain from their faces and been left standing by yourself fairly quickly. At that time, she was very real and very much someone people wanted to protect themselves against.'

'She sounds intimidating,' said Andrew.

'Oh, she terrified people,' said Fiona. 'People wore amulets during the night to ward her off since this was when she was thought to be active.'

'Like a demon,' observed Andrew.

'Precisely,' nodded Fiona. 'She originated in the ancient Sumerian and Babylonian culture, probably along with Zoroastrianism, actually.'

'Which is what exactly?' asked Andrew.

'In a nutshell,' said Fiona, 'Zoroastrianism is a truly ancient Persian religion founded by the prophet Zoroaster. It is in many ways the progenitor religion to Christianity. It is where the notions of a balance between good and evil came from, which then is believed to have eventually fed into the new monotheistic Abrahamic religions like Judaism, Christianity and Islam more than a thousand years later. Before that, pretty much all of the ancient belief systems were made up of dozens of major and minor deities who were believed to govern individual aspects of life, and who required their own type of worship and sacrificial offerings. And Lilith was one of them. Over the centuries, she seems to have morphed into several different types of beings as the first strands of Judaic mythology began to form and coalesce into what we know as the Jewish scripture, including the Christian Old Testament. But she is also credited with lots of other unsavoury things, like being a succubus and giving birth to hundreds of demons.'

Andrew raised his eyebrows with a sceptical and slightly confused look on his face.

'Busy lady,' he observed dryly. 'And quite the character. But how is that relevant now?'

'Well,' said Fiona. 'What matters here is that as Jewish mythology formed, she finally begins to take shape as Adam's first wife, made from the same clay and imbued with the same rights and mental faculties as him. And as Friar Cormac explained, this didn't go down well with Adam, and she eventually left the Garden of Eden, after which God created the more compliant Eve from Adam's rib. And as Cormac said, this is why feminists love Lilith so much. What they tend to conveniently forget is that she was also viewed for centuries as a determined murderer of infants, causing new mothers to use those amulets I just mentioned to attempt to prevent her from showing up during the night and killing their babies.'

'Crikey,' said Andrew. 'I like her less every minute. Anyway, I guess what you are getting at here is that for anyone taking the mythical parts of Abrahamic religious scripture literally, like our friend Antoine might be doing, Lilith is a major character connected to the Garden of Eden, Adam, and then Lucifer in the form of the serpent.'

'Exactly right,' nodded Fiona affirmatively. 'So, if Antoine was trying to transition Caitlin from fairly innocuous things like Wicca towards more sinister occult beliefs, then he could do a lot worse than to introduce the feminist icon, Lilith. She is an incredibly old and hugely complex deity, which would provide someone like Antoine with lots of different hooks. Lilith offers something for everyone, but especially someone like Caitlin, and that might have been why he brought her here to the British Museum. To get her interested.'

'All right,' said Andrew, shrugging but nodding reluctantly. 'Ok. Let's say you're right. But why did we need to come here if you could just have shown me a picture of Lilith online?'

'Come with me,' said Fiona, and held up the two tickets for the British Museum that they had found in Caitlin's room at the commune. 'When I saw these tickets for the museum in Caitlin's room, I suddenly had an idea. We obviously can't tell from the tickets if Caitlin and Antoine actually ever came here and what they might have looked at, but I know someone who can help us figure that out. We're going to visit a friend of mine in the CCTV room.'

As they turned and walked back out of Room 56 and through Room 57 towards the stairs down to the ground level, Andrew walked past a young man who somehow seemed familiar. He was wearing a light grey sweatshirt, light blue jeans and a black linen ball cap.

Had it not been for Andrew's sharp senses and observational skills developed over many years as a special forces soldier, he might not have noticed. However, he was trained to register the small but important things in the surrounding environment, and there was something about this young man that registered somewhere in his brain. As he and Fiona walked past him and continued on towards the stairwell, Andrew's mind was racing, subconsciously scouring his memories for a match. A couple of seconds later and almost at the doorway into Room 58 he finally had it. It was the blond hair sticking out from under the ball cap near the back of the man's head that did it. Without turning around, Andrew stopped and quickly reached out to grab Fiona by the arm.

'Fiona,' he said calmly. 'Turn left and pretend to be looking at this display box.'

She did as he asked, and he then stepped over to stand next to her whilst leaning in slightly and whispering.

'Don't look behind us,' he said, 'but I think Antoine is here. He's the guy with the black ball cap in the far corner.'

Fiona was struggling to resist the impulse to look, but managed to stare straight ahead into the display box, never registering what she was actually looking at there.

'Are you sure?' she whispered.

'Positive,' replied Andrew. 'He must have been tracking us somehow.'

'From Dublin?' asked Fiona sounding incredulous.

'Unlikely,' said Andrew. 'But he could have been waiting for us at the airport. I am sure it is him, and he definitely isn't here by accident. He seems to be by himself. I didn't spot Caitlin.'

At the mention of her sister, Fiona involuntarily turned her head and glanced in the man's direction.

'Oh shit,' she muttered quickly. 'He's looking at me.'

Andrew decided to turn and look for himself, and there was Antoine clearly looking straight at the two of them, his athletic body frozen in place but with the demeanour of a coiled spring ready to be released. An instant later, he spun around and bolted for the doorway in the opposite direction, back into Room 56 towards the stairwell in the northeast corner of the gigantic museum building.

Taking a moment to register what was happening, Andrew quickly glanced at Fiona as he took a step back and began moving behind her.

'I'm not letting him get away,' said Andrew hurriedly and set off in a sprint, turning his head to call to Fiona over his shoulder. 'Stay here!'

Making the most of his head start, Antoine had now reached the wide stairwell and was bounding down the first section to the first of three landings on the way down to the ground level. Andrew was in mid-sprint through Room 53 which was the last room before reaching the stairs when he heard the scream of a woman echoing up through the stairwell followed by the noise of thudding and clattering. Antoine had apparently barged into a pair of young women who had been on the way up to the upper floor, and he had knocked one of them over, leaving her sprawled on the granite stairs as Andrew reached the top step.

'What the hell!' shouted her companion angrily, and when she saw Andrew come barrelling down towards her, she looked for a moment as if she was about to take her anger out on him. However, when she saw his physique and the hard determined look on his face she quickly seemed to change her mind and stepped aside to make way for him.

Upon finally reaching the ground level, Andrew emerged into the Great Court and headed straight for the exit, even though he could not at first see Antoine. However, after a few seconds, he spotted him, and as expected he was heading for the exit as well. Andrew was in excellent physical shape, but he was surprised to find that he had only gained marginally on the Frenchman. He considered shouting out for a security guard to assist him, but they were as likely to try to detain him as they were to obstruct Antoine, so instead, he pushed harder – his arms pumping at his sides, his legs burning with lactic acid from the explosive exertion and his lungs tingling with the constant pushing of fresh air in and out in rapid succession. He felt his right hand involuntarily moving up towards the left side of his chest where he would have had a Glock 17 strapped in a holster if this had been an operation run by 'the Firm'. Then he checked himself. This wasn't a war zone. Even if he did catch the Frenchman, there was a limit to what he could do to him. But he wanted answers, and he was going to get them.

Antoine was about thirty metres ahead of him, and although Andrew could not see him clearly between the throngs of other visitors, he thought he spotted the Frenchman pulling out a phone in mid-sprint across the courtyard and holding it up to his head for about five seconds.

Is he calling in the cavalry? thought Andrew.

While still running at full tilt, Antoine adeptly sidestepped a woman with a pram, burst outside the museum building and headed straight for the main gate where Andrew and Fiona had come in half an hour earlier. As he exited out onto the street he stopped briefly looking first to the right and then to the left, after which he bolted left. Andrew could still track him through the tall black wrought iron fence, and as he exited the museum grounds and sprinted along the pavement, he was now less than twenty metres behind him. He clearly had the upper hand on Antoine when it came to stamina, so he was already thinking ahead how to overpower and restrain him when the Frenchman suddenly swerved into the street and yanked open the passenger side door of a silver Audi TT that had suddenly come to a stop in the middle of the road. He launched himself inside, and before the door had closed properly the Audi's engine roared and the car's tyres spun on the road surface, creating a small black cloud of burnt rubber and producing a characteristic screeching sound. Within seconds, the Audi had accelerated away along Great Russell Street and past Bloomsbury Square towards the east.

Exhausted and out of breath, Andrew slowed to a jog and then came to a stop, bending over with his hands on his knees, his eyes closed and his face in a grimace as he panted hard trying to re-oxygenate his blood. After a few seconds, he stood back up and placed his hand on his hips whilst looking into the distance. The Audi had sped away and was now nowhere to be seen.

'Well played,' he grumbled reluctantly. 'You little shit.'

He quickly glanced at his wristwatch, reached into the back pocket of his trousers and extracted his phone, placing another call to Colonel Strickland. He detailed what had just transpired and provided the exact time and the make and a description of the Audi TT, and then he requested that this information be included in the Met's efforts both to identify the man calling himself Antoine and an attempt to determine his recent whereabouts.

A couple of minutes later he was back inside the Great Court where he was met by Fiona, who clearly had not been content with simply waiting for him to come back upstairs.

'What happened?' she asked as she rushed towards him. 'Are you all right.'

'I'm fine,' said Andrew, still breathing heavily. 'I almost had the bastard, but he had help. Someone picked him up in a silver Audi and raced off.'

Fiona pressed her lips together and began pacing back and forth in front of Andrew whilst wringing her hands.

'What the hell is going on here?' she said, clearly without expecting an answer but getting increasingly agitated as she spoke. 'Who is this Antoine really, and what on earth does he want with my sister? And where the bloody hell is she anyway? And why would he follow us here?'

'Fiona,' said Andrew, reaching out to take her hand and gently guide her around to face him. He then took her other hand in his. 'Fiona. Please try to calm down. We'll figure this out together. Ok? Now, who was it you wanted to take us to? Someone in the CCTV room?'

'Oh, yes,' replied Fiona, having seemingly forgotten her earlier plan. 'Right. Ok. Yes. Let's go. His name is Rob. I've known him for a couple of years. He and I trade mock insults when we bump into each other, but he is a really nice guy. Come on. I will take us to him.'

She led them back out through the lobby and left towards a set of stairs leading down. On the wall above the stairs was a sign that read 'Staff Only.' Down on the sublevel, they walked along a short corridor to a set of double doors where Fiona swiped her electronic employee keycard, after which the lock snapped open, and she pushed the doors open. On the other side was a small seating area with a comfortable-looking sofa, and further along was a door with a sign saying 'CCTV Ops'. Fiona pressed a small button next to the door and waited. After a couple of seconds, a male voice came through a small speaker.

'Yes,' it said, sounding bored.

'Hey Rob,' said Fiona. 'It's me. Fiona.'

'Oh. Hi Fiona,' replied Rob, now sounding more cheerful. 'Come on in.'

The door buzzed and Fiona pushed it open, revealing a dark room roughly five by five metres in size with an entire wall full of monitors, each of which showed a live black-and-white feed from the multitude of CCTV cameras keeping a watchful eye on every room of the museum. In an office chair by a desk in front of the enormous bank of monitors was a man who swivelled around 180 degrees as they entered.

'Hey,' he smiled. 'How's it going? Is this my new replacement? Have I finally been fired and released from this hellhole?'

'Sorry,' said Fiona. 'I am afraid I don't have that kind of clout around here. You know I would if I could.'

Rob grinned good-naturedly and got up from his chair.

'What a shame,' he shrugged. 'I guess I really will end up dying down here.'

'This is my partner, Andrew,' continued Fiona, gesturing. 'He's helping me look into something.'

'Nice to meet you, ' nodded Rob.

'You too,' replied Andrew stepping forward and shaking Rob's hand.

'But then I already know you,' said Rob, raising his eyebrows.

'Excuse me?' said Andrew and looked at Rob with a slightly confused look on his face, but then it dawned on him. 'Oh. Right. The chase. Yes, that was me. I guess you saw that.'

'Sure did,' said Rob. 'I was about to call security, but the two of you were out of the building and off the premises before I had time, so I figured there would be no point. Who was that guy anyway?'

Fiona proceeded to tell Rob about Caitlin's disappearance and Antoine's suspected involvement, leaving out the most personal details.

'So, if you wouldn't mind helping us,' said Fiona, 'we would really like to see the footage from twelve days ago if you still have it.'

'Of course,' said Rob. 'Everything is stored digitally, and we compress the footage first so there is really no need to ever delete any of it. We just load it onto some large drives and keep it just in case something happens and the police come knocking.'

'Great,' said Fiona, and handed Rob the printed tickets that she had taken from Caitlin's room in the commune. 'If you punch in this ticket number, can you see when it was registered at the front gate?'

'Absolutely,' said Rob, taking the ticket and sitting down at his terminal, where his right hand flew across the numpad section of his keyboard, hitting the Enter key with a flourish.

He inspected the results on his main monitor and then typed in a couple of commands and used the mouse to select the footage from the date and time of Caitlin and Antoine's visit. Within a few seconds, recorded footage of the outside of the building was displayed on a large central monitor on the wall in front of them.

'There they are,' said Andrew. 'Just coming through the gate now. And now going to have their tickets inspected. And in they go…'

The three of them watched as the monitor showed the feed from several cameras consecutively as Rob tracked Caitlin and Antoine walking into the building, through the lobby and into the Great Court. They were holding hands and looking relaxed and cheerful.

'He's wearing the same clothes as today,' said Fiona. 'Black cap, grey jumper and blue jeans. Weird. Doesn't he ever change?'

'I could make a joke about the French and personal hygiene here,' said Rob, 'but I won't do that since it is your sister's boyfriend.'

'Hmm,' grumbled Fiona. 'I have a feeling his personal hygiene is going to be the least of our problems. Can we fast-forward a bit and see where they go.'

'Sure,' replied Rob and pushed forward on a red plastic ball embedded in his terminal.

They watched as Caitlin and Antoine walked at an unnaturally fast pace across the Great Court to the northeast corner. Rob swapped cameras as they went, tracking them entering the stairwell, exiting onto the landing on the upper level and proceeding through Room 53, 54, and 55 without making a single stop to look at anything. Upon entering Room 56 they made a beeline for Display Box 23.

'Bloody hell,' whispered Andrew. 'You were right. Antoine took her here specifically to look at Lilith.'

'Ah,' said Rob. 'Lilith in 56. The one with the nice rack.'

Fiona looked down at him and frowned.

'Rob,' she said, shaking her head. 'You're a creep, you know that?'

'I know,' said Rob and sighed. 'It's one of my best qualities.'

Andrew ignored the two of them and studied the image which Rob was now playing at normal speed, as Caitlin and Antoine stood in front of the display box, Antoine seemingly explaining something to Caitlin who was nodding and smiling. At one point, Antoine reached up to place his hand on the back of Caitlin's head. He then drew it gently towards himself and kissed her on the forehead.

'Stop there,' said Andrew.

Rob immediately paused the recording.

'Who is that?' mused Andrew, taking a step closer to the large monitor and studying the image closely.

He pointed to a tall young man behind the couple who was wearing an expensive-looking dark suit and a navy-blue newsboy cap pulled down low over his forehead as if trying to obscure his face. He had short black hair and carried himself with the self-assuredness of someone who believes they are in control of what is going on around them, and he seemed to be walking past Caitlin and Antoine, but he was clearly looking directly at them.

'Do you have this from another angle?' asked Andrew.

Rob quickly swapped to a different camera that was slightly closer to the trio.

'Could you run that again slowly?' asked Andrew.

Rob backed up and ran it again at half speed. The man walked behind and past the couple, clearly looking at them as he passed. Then he turned and walked back, once again with his eyes locked on the two of them. To Fiona, he suddenly seemed disconcertingly like a shark circling its prey.

'What is he doing?' she asked.

'Did you see that?' said Andrew, turning to the two others.

'Shit,' said Fiona, sounding disturbed. 'That guy just nodded at Antoine.'

'They are communicating,' said Andrew, his eyes still locked onto the image on the large monitor in front of them. 'Some sort of signal.'

'Ok, what the hell is going on?' said Fiona, fear now creeping into her voice.

'I don't know,' said Andrew, wincing slightly as if uncomfortable with what he was about to say. 'But if I had to guess, I would say that Antoine brought her here, not just to look at Lilith, but for her to be inspected by this man. Whoever he is.'

Fiona was too stunned to say anything, but a deep chill ran down her spine.

'Can you copy that section onto a file and dump it on a memory stick for us?' asked Andrew. 'I would like to keep it.'

Rob glanced at Fiona who nodded silently.

'Sure,' said Rob and created the file in just a couple of seconds.

'Let's see what happens next,' said Andrew, pointing at the monitor.

Rob continued the playback, and the three of them watched as the tall man in the suit drifted off into the adjacent room, after which he picked up the pace and walked downstairs, across the Great Court and out of the building. Caitlin and Antoine remained at the display box for another few minutes, and then they also left the museum.

'I don't know what to say,' said Fiona with a slight tremble in her voice. 'This is the creepiest thing I have ever seen. And it's my sister.'

'Can you go forward to today so we can see what happened?' asked Andrew.

Within a few seconds, Rob had conjured up the recording from half an hour earlier, showing Andrew and Fiona entering the museum from Great Russell Street. Less than a minute later, Antoine walked through the front gate and proceeded to follow them inside the building.

'How the hell did he know?' asked Fiona.

'Can you fast forward a bit?' asked Andrew.

Rob did as he was asked and the monitor above them on the wall showed a speeded-up version of Andrew and Fiona arriving, standing by the display box, and then of Antoine filing into the room behind a group of three other visitors. He turned his back to them, seemingly looking at a different display box near the other end of Room 56. Then followed the chase, the cameras capturing Antoine knocking over the woman on the stairs and Andrew in close pursuit.

'Let's see what he did in the courtyard,' said Andrew.

They watched as the footage from one of the cameras there showed Antoine reaching inside his jacket pocket as he ran, bringing a phone up to his head – his lips moving as he spoke a few words.

'So, he did actually call for backup,' said Andrew. 'He was working with someone else. Possibly the tall guy in the suit.'

Fiona was too stunned and disturbed to speak.

'Ok,' said Andrew. 'I think we've seen enough. Could we also have that last bit on the memory stick?'

'Of course,' said Rob and loaded the file onto the memory stick.

'Thank you very much, Rob,' said Fiona, looking both bewildered and worried by what she had just witnessed. 'I really appreciate this.'

'No problem,' replied Rob, his lighthearted demeanour from earlier now having evaporated entirely as the seriousness of the situation became apparent. 'Anything else I can do, just let me know.'

Andrew and Rob shook hands again, and then Andrew and Fiona left the CCTV Ops room, returned to the ground level above and exited the museum. They barely spoke as they drove back to Hampstead.

Eight

The Maybach pulled up and parked by the side of the road on Upper Thames Street after which Haywood got out and hurried up to the front door of the fraternity's home that he had just been observing from his 66th-floor office across the river. Once inside the large, high-ceilinged lobby, he headed straight to the tall glass-fronted security gate that stretched across the entire lobby and prevented unauthorised access from the lobby into the building proper. The entire thing was constructed from thick bullet-proof glass, and the only access point was a single compartment similar to an airlock. The compartment was fitted with a suite of scanners and sensors that not only prevented anyone from carrying concealed items inside but which also required a keycard and the successful completion of a biometric ID check in the form of a retinal scan before someone would be let inside.

The biometric check allowed for the members of the fraternity to enter anonymously whilst wearing face masks or hoods, which was now a requirement for moving around inside the Temple. In fact, there were strict rules stipulating that any member wishing to enter the temple had to wear the full gold-embroidered facemask issued to them by the grand master himself. Not only did it enforce visual uniformity among the members of the fraternity, but it meant that only the grand master knew who the members of the fraternity actually were. Each individual member knew only the grand master by sight and was unaware of the true identities of any of the other members. This was all to prevent rivalry and scheming against the grand master, and to ensure that one weak link in the fraternity could not result in the entire organisation potentially being exposed to the public. This almost happened in the 1830s when one of Haywood's forefathers had first taken over the reins from his own father. One of the lesser members at that time who was a top civil servant in the Bank of England was manoeuvring to obtain as much information about the fraternity as possible and then blackmailing the grand master with the threat of going to the newspapers with the story. The member eventually ended up dead and floating in the Thames, and it was after that episode that the anonymity requirement was instituted.

However, since there was no scheduled gathering today Haywood was not wearing his mask, and he walked into the airlock compartment, strode briskly to the opposite end of it and inserted his golden but otherwise unmarked keycard into the reader and let the red light from the retinal scanner sweep across his eyes. Almost immediately, the light on the card reader went from blue to green, and the retinal scanner produced a quick double-beep to indicate that it had successfully completed its ID check.

The glass double doors on the far side of the compartment opened and Haywood walked up the wide sweeping staircase to the first floor and proceeded along a long, wide wood-panelled corridor. This was where he had first laid eyes on the complete collection of oil portraits of previous grand masters when he was a weedy 12-year-old. The most impressive painting remained that of Godfrey Montague painted in 1734, but the lineage of successors that had remained unbroken since then was filled with illustrious names, many of whom had been prominent members of the government, the civil service, the military top brass and the London establishment through that extended time period. At the end of the line of portraits hung his own, and next to it was an empty space with a small polished brass plaque underneath bearing the name of his son Edward.

At the end of the corridor was the solid oak door that led to his personal quarters inside the temple. He swiped his keycard again, after which the lock clicked and he was able to push the door open. As he walked to his desk inside what looked like an office that had not changed its appearance for centuries, the door closed and re-locked behind him. With dark ornate wood panelling stretching from floor to ceiling, intricate cornice above and paintings, bookcases and the family coat of arms on the walls, it exuded history.

It also functioned as a reminder of the prominence and status of his lineage.

He took off his coat, placed it over the back of a chair and poured himself a glass of whiskey from the large silver drinks tray that lived permanently on an ancient-looking varnished mahogany console table. The console was next to a tall bookcase filled with several dozens of thick volumes of dusty-looking leatherbound books. He downed the drink in one gulp and replaced the glass on the tray. Then he walked to his mahogany desk and sat down in the cushy brown leather Chesterfield office chair and slid the Samsung tablet that was lying on the desk over in front of himself. The tablet had the largest screen available since much of his time researching was spent reading scans of ancient occult texts and studying in great detail photos of various pieces of art produced throughout the past several millennia.

Looked at on that timescale, the Sons of Lucifer were a relatively new fraternity, but it traced its roots all the way back through various secret brotherhoods to the time before there was even such a thing as the Bible. Its more modern incarnation had been a splinter group within the Knights Templar, which, following the official dissolution of the Order by the Catholic Church, would not lie down and accept defeat. After all, how could it, given the profound and deeply consequential mystical knowledge it had accumulated through the centuries? And this was not simply a question of beliefs and principles. This was a direct function of observed results during ceremonies that attempted to use ancient incantations to address deities such as Baphomet and, with the help of

Godfrey Montague's extensive work, also Lucifer himself. Taken together, the work of the Sons of Lucifer held the promise of untapped power on an almost unimaginable scale. Something that would turn the world upside down – or perhaps more accurately, inside out. All they needed was the missing text. The hidden key to open the gate. But they were close now. Haywood could feel it in his bones.

The fraternity had only ever had two purposes. Firstly, to serve Lucifer and to work tirelessly towards helping him materialise once again and take his rightful place in the world. Secondly, at all costs to preserve itself until the re-emergence of the Lord. Always hidden yet always working towards its ultimate ends. From its inception, it had in effect only ever been the private organ of the Montague family. All other members, none of whom knew each other's true identities, were only ever selected and groomed to ensure the continued functioning and absolute secrecy of the Sons of Lucifer within society at large. And the phrase 'at all costs' had always been taken literally. Nothing could be allowed to stand in their way, and many men had paid with their lives to ensure that this had remained so.

Haywood swiped across the tablet, entered his access code and opened the secure email with the attachment detailing the latest progress report from the dig site in southern France. It had been expertly annotated by Tristan Maxwell, and after reading it Haywood leaned back in his chair having acquired yet another layer of confidence in his project. It really did finally seem like he, unlike all of his predecessors going back almost three centuries, would be the one to finally achieve their ultimate goal.

He switched off the tablet, rose and walked over to a section of wall with a roughly two-metre-tall oil painting. It was a full-scale portrait of Godfrey Montague, and it was sitting inside an ornately carved gilded wooden frame. Pressing a small button on the outside edge of the frame, the entire painting slid aside to reveal a small open elevator which he stepped into. A couple of seconds later, it descended roughly ten metres into the bowels of the temple. Haywood emerged into a large circular antechamber, which was also accessible from the ground floor via a narrow set of winding stairs with a thin metal railing attached to the stone wall. This was what the lower-ranking members of the fraternity would use to access the crypt during ceremonies. However, this access was blocked by heavy metal gates both at the top and at the bottom of the stairwell.

The antechamber had been constructed more than two centuries ago from light-coloured granite, and its marble floor was a large inverted pentagram mosaic. The walls were draped in a plethora of mystical and occult items and artwork depicting ancient religious and alchemical symbols. Had it not been for a set of seven small oil lamps that were lit automatically when someone entered, the chamber would have been pitch black. However, the gently flickering flames inside the oil lamps cast a warm glow inside the chamber, and Haywood always felt it as a warm embrace whenever he descended to this place on his own. A doorway led to a long corridor which extended deeper into the underground complex and ended in the ceremonial chamber, where very soon the final ritual would be carried out.

On the lintel above the doorway was a brimstone symbol, and next to the doorway was a small alcove with an altar to their deity. All of the highest-ranking members of the fraternity had something similar secreted away somewhere in their private homes. On the other side of the alcove was a heavy, black-painted oak door leading to a room that only he had access to.

As he had grown up, Haywood had discovered that in popular culture there was such a thing as occultism and satanism. It seemed to have always been fairly widespread, especially recently when it had received much attention on social media and from various conspiracy theorists on TV. He was aware of the major characters in the almost comical cavalcade of crackpots that had pushed these laughably simplistic ideas since the mid-19th century, and he held nothing but disdain for people like Helena Blavatsky, Aleister Crowley and Anton LaVey whom he considered snake-oil salesmen and self-aggrandising charlatans and conmen. To Haywood, their various endeavours were on the same childlike level as those of the people using tarot cards or spotting the face of Jesus on a piece of burnt toast. In fact, he couldn't quite decide which one of them was more ridiculous. Between them, they did not possess the faintest trace of the deep understanding of the ancient texts that formed the foundation of his fraternity. And they could not begin to fathom the enormity of the quest for its ultimate goal – the release and deliverance of Lucifer to the Earthly realm on his Day of Emancipation. However, they, and people like them, did serve one very useful purpose. They focused public attention onto the loony fringes of so-called modern satanism, thereby deflecting it away from the true servants of Lucifer who possessed real power and influence that the little people could never imagine and would never understand.

Haywood walked to the heavy black oak door and inserted his key into the lock. He turned it counter-clockwise, at which point it clicked and the door swung open. Beyond was a carefully temperature-controlled room which, like his private quarters upstairs, appeared exactly the way it had done since the temple was built. This was the grand master's private study, completely isolated and away from even the faintest noise from the modern world above. This was where all of the original ancient texts were kept, and here he could immerse himself in his research entirely, as all of the previous grand masters had done before him. From the oak door to the other end of the room stretched a roughly one-metre-wide deep red carpet that lay across the wooden floorboards, and all along the walls on both sides were old tomes, several of which were lying open on pages that he had recently been studying. Sometimes it was better to work with the original texts, although he tried his best to use digital scans whenever possible. These texts were mostly very well preserved, but they would not last forever.

He closed the door behind him and walked along the rug whilst glancing at the ancient tomes, many of which were completely unique as far as he knew. It was an extensive and utterly priceless collection gathered through generations of his family for over three hundred years. To his right was a centuries-old copy of the Zohar, the pre-Christian mystical text that was in many ways the foundation of the Judaic religion, which then itself became the basis for Christianity. Next to it were stacks of many more similarly influential books concerning Jewish mysticism.

The next one along was a Gnostic text from the 6th century. Being one of the first factions within early Christianity, the Gnostics were effectively stamped out after the Councils of Nicaea after which they were considered heretics. They did not subscribe to what they considered a simplistic and limited version of Christianity, but they instead incorporated mystical and other ritualistic elements into their beliefs, including many that had been formed several millennia earlier in Persia and Mesopotamia. And as Haywood and his team of French archaeologists had now found physical proof of, Gnosticism had also been at the core of the beliefs and practises of the Knights Templar.

Further along was an original copy of what was known as the Codex Tchacos, which contained the apocryphal Gospel of Judas from El Minya in Egypt. It was discovered in the 1970s, and it detailed how Jesus, three days before his death, shared secrets with Judas about what will happen during the End Times. According to the codex, he also asserted that the god of the Old Testament was evil. He accused his disciples of worshipping a god of the underworld, and he told them that because of this their fates were sealed and that they were beyond redemption. The codex also describes how Jesus took Judas on a journey into an infinite realm, where, among other things, he showed him an angel called the God of Light. This text in particular had been a rich source for Haywood in his research. The gospel had originally been written in Greek and then later translated into Coptic Egyptian, and Haywood could read both of these languages as well as Latin and Aramaic. He he still remembered the surge of excitement he had felt when he had first studied this ancient heretical text and had discovered that in fact Jesus and Lucifer might be one and the same.

On the other tables in the room were many more similar texts such as the Secret Book of John and the Secret book of James, both of which were Gnostic texts written around 100 to 200 CE, and both of which claimed to contain the secret teachings of Jesus, including that he was, in fact, the serpent in the Garden of Eden.

There were also a number of volumes written by several Zoroastrian magi from ancient Mesopotamia. Being the mystical state religion of ancient Persia, Zoroastrianism included the clearly defined duality between good and evil. Darkness and light. This was then woven into the pre-Christian Judaic belief systems during the so-called Babylonian Exile that followed the fall of Jerusalem in 586 BCE when the Jews were forcibly taken as slaves by King Nebuchadnezzar II. Zoroastrianism also included the ancient philosophy and practice of alchemy. These metallurgical methods, which could easily be seen at the time as barely understood magical or esoteric rituals that were capable of transforming one type of metal into another, were closely guarded secrets amongst the Zoroastrian magi and tightly intertwined with the idea of gnosis. Once again, much of this was pursued during the Middle Ages by various groups in Europe, including the Knights Templar.

The most recent text in the room was a first print edition of Paradise Lost from 1667, the year after the Great Fire of London. Haywood had spent thousands of hours down here in this unique library studying that particular book in great detail as well as all of the other ancient tomes, and in all of his research, he had found nothing to suggest that Paradise Lost was not essentially a true account. First revealed in Genesis B by Lucifer himself, it had then later been clarified by John Milton in his seminal poetic work. In addition, everything that his forefathers had discovered during three centuries of research since Godfrey Montague had first acquired the Lucifer Codex from the Secret Archives at the Vatican, indicated that the codex was exactly what it claimed itself to be. There was no doubt in Haywood's mind that it was a very real mechanism that would allow for the opening of the literal gates of hell and for the appearance in physical form of Lord Lucifer. But he was now convinced that it was missing one crucial element. One final lost chapter that would unlock the gates. This was what had formed the foundation for his work over the past two decades, assisted by the man he referred to only as 'the Scholar'. And in particular, it had been the impetus behind his recent archaeological efforts in the south of France.

When he reached the end of the red carpet, Haywood stopped in front of another solid oak door, which he opened with his keycard. As it swung open amid a faint hiss of air, it revealed a separate room which was visually the antithesis of the secret library. It was small, only three by three metres, and the walls were made of metal and polished to a matt sheen that sent heavily diffused reflections of the soft yellow ceiling spotlights bouncing around inside it. The temperature was noticeably lower than in the library, but the air inside was as dry as that of a desert. The door quickly swung shut behind him, and once again the only sound he could hear was the faint hiss of the air as the door's hermetic seals engaged.

In the middle of the room where a number of overhead spotlights were grouped together was a pedestal made from the same metal as the walls. On top of it rested what appeared to be a large glass display box. As Haywood stepped up to it, the ceiling lights automatically sensed his presence and increased their output noticeably, making the light from the display box's contents bloom out into the otherwise dark room. Despite having laid eyes on this many times before, it still almost took his breath away.

Inside the display box lay the Lucifer Codex. Written on vellum an unknown number of centuries earlier, its thick leather cover had a clearly discernible dark brown thumbprint. It had been created by the blood of the Secret Archive's chief librarian and planted there when the scribe took it from the shelf in the crypt under the Vatican almost 300 years ago. It had been just one of many necessary sacrifices made along the way to gather the ancient sources the fraternity required.

Haywood pressed a button, and the thick glass lid of the display box slowly flipped open. Then he picked up a pair of thin black silk gloves and put them on. Placing his hands gently on the codex, he clearly felt the energy emanating from it like faint heat or electricity, hinting at its potency and making a shiver run down the length of his spine. As he stood there, he could have sworn that he heard a deep but faint warbling noise at the very limits of his perception.

Once my work is complete, he thought, *the world will finally be transformed. Turned inside out and reordered according to the principles of man's baser instincts. And only the strongest and most faithful will survive.*

NINE

Having returned to their house in Hampstead, Andrew and Fiona were now in the living room slumped on the sofa and looking out of the window to the garden where the last golden sunlight of the day was caressing the green leaves on the trees as they rustled gently in the warm summer breeze.

'I really don't like the feeling of being watched,' said Fiona, 'but someone is clearly monitoring us. And Antoine was not working alone.'

'I agree,' said Andrew. 'I must admit that when you first told me about Caitlin having gone missing, I thought she had probably eloped to some tropical island with her French beau, but that is obviously not what has happened.'

'The very fact that Antoine is still here in London and that Caitlin is gone tells me that something is very wrong,' said Fiona with a pained expression. 'And sneaking around trying to observe the two of us in the

British Museum is just plain creepy. What could possibly justify that? And who was that tall guy in the Museum?'

Fiona closed her eyes, let her head drop and sighed heavily. After a moment, she opened her eyes again and turned to face Andrew.

'I am really worried now,' she said. 'None of this is remotely normal. It's sinister, I can feel it. Antoine is really bad news. I just know it.'

'I think you're right,' said Andrew. 'There is something very disturbing about this whole thing.'

At that moment, Andrew's phone rang so he picked it up and looked at the screen.

'It's Strickland,' he said. 'Let's hear what he's got for us.'

He put the phone on speaker and placed it on the coffee table in front of them.

'Colonel,' said Andrew. 'Thank you for coming back to us so soon. I have Fiona here with me.'

'Very good,' said Strickland, his clipped but calm voice giving Fiona a welcome sense of reassurance. 'How are you holding up, Fiona?'

'I've been better,' said Fiona, trying to put a brave face on it despite Strickland not being able to see her. 'I am just desperate to find out where Caitlin is.'

'I understand,' said Strickland empathetically. 'Well, I've got some news for you. I asked the Met to run the photo of your French chap through their facial recognition systems, and they came up with a couple of interesting tidbits. Firstly, they managed to match his face to some CCTV footage they have of him and Caitlin walking along Arundel Road where I believe she lives. So that confirmed for us that the system works and is able to identify him, at least some of the time. We obviously also gathered the available footage from around the British Museum after your little run-in with him there, and we managed to track the silver Audi TT to the area near Tower Bridge where it disappeared into a parking garage. The garage's own CCTV systems seem to be out of order, so we have been unable to find out anything more at this stage. And so far we have nothing on the driver of the vehicle. The car's windows were heavily tinted so we couldn't see who was at the wheel. However, we were also able to track Antoine to a few other locations in London. That was mainly around the Tower Bridge area, and only because he was wearing the same cap he had been wearing at the museum. I am afraid that's all it takes to negate the CCTV cameras. No face, no ID. That's just how it is. Anyway, none of the limited footage we have obtained implies anything untoward or provides us with any clues as to where he actually lives.'

'That's disappointing,' said Andrew with a slight grimace. 'I had hoped we would be able to discover where he might be holed up.'

'Well, hang on. There's more,' said Strickland. 'On the occasions where the facial recognition systems did manage to track him, he was observed entering the underpass beneath Tower Hill just outside the tube station and directly opposite the Tower of London. However, he never came out again. The chaps in the CCTV control room at the Met watched the footage for the next hour, and they are adamant that he entered the underpass but never exited again.'

Andrew and Fiona looked at each other and exchanged bemused glances.

'What does that mean?' asked Fiona.

'Well,' said Strickland. 'Either he stayed in there for hours, or he somehow managed to change his appearance to such an extent that he was unrecognisable when he re-emerged. There were a couple of people emerging during the subsequent minutes that could possibly have been him, and they both made their way along Tower Hill towards Saint Kathrine Docks just a stone's throw from the Tower of London. That is where roadside CCTV lost coverage. But anyway, hundreds of people pass through there every day during rush hour, so there is a possibility that he somehow managed to evade both the facial recognition systems and the officers watching the footage.'

'There is one more possibility,' said Andrew. 'There might be a passage into the old disused tube tunnels from the underpass. Do we know if that is the case?'

'I am not sure,' said Strickland. 'You would have to go and look for yourself. It is not something I can ask the Met to do. I have already pulled a few favours on this.'

'We understand,' said Andrew.

'Anyway,' continued Strickland. 'The Met also ran the photo of his face through various databases, and they initially identified him as one *Antoine Reynard*. However, with the help of our international partners, it quickly turned out that this is a false identity. The real Antoine Reynard died seven years ago in a road accident in the Alsace, but your chap seems to have successfully stolen the dead man's identity and lived under that name here in the UK for at least the past four years.'

'So, who the hell is he then?' asked Fiona, now beginning to sound agitated. 'And how can someone just steal someone else's identity like that and not be found out?'

'The answer to your first question,' said Strickland,' is that we simply don't know at this stage, but we will keep digging. As for how this type of identity theft is possible, it all comes down to a few simple things. Firstly, the two men bear a striking resemblance to each other. Any border official at a port or an airport would look at those photos and probably be unable to tell the difference, which I suspect is why the identity of Antoine Reynard was chosen for your chap, to begin with. In addition, if you have sufficient resources and the right connections, then it is absolutely within the realms of possibility to fabricate an entire suite of official documents that all marry up and that taken together would fool anyone into believing that this person really is who he says he is. Especially here in the UK, where we don't have direct access to French personal identification records and systems.'

'In other words,' observed Andrew. 'He would have to have had some pretty powerful friends in order to pull this off. Whoever created the fake ID for our friend was very particular about picking one that actually matched his looks very closely.'

'But who could do such a thing?' asked Fiona. 'Who has that sort of power?'

'Perhaps it is more about who has the money to make it happen,' replied Andrew. 'Enough money will grease any wheel, in my experience.'

'You are probably correct,' said Strickland.

'But then what the hell are we up against here?' said Fiona, looking both perplexed and concerned. 'Who are these people?'

'It would be virtually impossible for us to find out who is pulling the strings on something like this,' said Strickland. 'All we can do is look at what we can actually see here on our side of the border, and sometimes that just isn't very much. Especially when we are dealing with people who seem to possess very significant resources and influence. But I agree that it all seems very murky. And I do understand how this must be very frustrating for you.'

'Thank you, 'said Fiona. 'We really appreciate your help.'

'There's one last thing,' said Strickland. 'It's about the man whom you felt was interacting surreptitiously with Antoine at the British Museum. We managed to identify him without too much trouble. His name is Tristan Maxwell, and he is a junior partner at something called Montague Solicitors Limited. I am told it is one of the oldest and most prestigious law firms in London, although I must admit that I have never heard of them before today. Anyway, he has no criminal record. Never even had a parking ticket or been involved in anything untoward, financial or otherwise. He is squeaky clean, as they say.'

'So, what are we going to do about it?' said Fiona and looked at Andrew. 'Are we just going to sit on our hands?'

Andrew sighed and his face took on a slightly strained look, but before he could say anything Strickland spoke and articulated almost exactly what he was thinking.

'There's really nothing we can do at this point,' said Strickland, sounding as if it pained him to be the bearer of unwelcome news. 'The reality is that he was a visitor at the British Museum and happened to glance at another visitor for a moment – at least that is how he is bound to present it. And there is no way for us to argue differently. He was perfectly entitled to be there, and nothing he did even remotely warrants the involvement of the police.'

Fiona looked taken aback, turning to face Andrew.

'He's right,' said Andrew placatingly. 'I agree that the encounter looked odd, but there is nowhere near enough there for us to do anything about it.'

Fiona's expression hardened, but she did not speak. She knew that they were right, but the frustration at seeing what she regarded as an accomplice being left alone was almost too much for her to bear.

'I am sorry,' said Strickland, seemingly sensing the tension in the room. 'I wish there was something more we could do, but even if we managed to persuade the Met to haul him in for questioning, the reality is that they would get sued to hell and back for unlawful detention, and they would most assuredly lose. I don't like it any more than you do, but if you want to find out what happened to Caitlin, you'll have to find another way of doing it. And I really should tell you that whatever you decide to do, I don't want to know about it.'

There was a brief pause.

'Do we understand each other?' asked Strickland in a tone of voice that hinted at some deeper meaning.

Andrew and Fiona glanced at each other. They both understood quite clearly the implications of Strickland's words. If they were planning to employ unorthodox, possibly even illegal methods in order to find Fiona's sister, then Strickland would not stand in their way as long as they did not tell him precisely what they got up to.

'Absolutely, Sir,' said Andrew.

'We do,' said Fiona. 'And thank you again. We realise that you probably have much more important things to focus on right now, so we really appreciate your time and effort here.'

'You are very welcome,' said Strickland. 'Good luck to you both. I hope to hear from you soon.'

* * *

When she came to, her eyelids felt as heavy as lead. After taking her first conscious but laboured breath, it required a determined effort to open them. When she finally managed it, she wasn't sure what she was looking at. It appeared to be some sort of masonry. A stone block wall stretched up next to her towards a ceiling several metres above. She turned her head slowly to one side to look around, but her vision was blurry and she felt decidedly odd. Like she had been drinking.

Where was she? All she could make out was that she was in a small room, perhaps three by four metres, and the only sound she could hear was that of her own breathing. She managed to lift her head and place an elbow underneath herself, which allowed her to then sit up and swing her legs out onto the cold flagstone floor. She looked down and realised that her feet were bare, and only then did she notice that she was wearing something she didn't remember ever wearing before. It was a long garment like a robe made from coarse grey linen. It looked like something out of the Middle Ages. She felt hungry. So very hungry.

She put her head in her hands, took a couple of deep breaths and then rubbed her eyes. They felt puffy, and small amounts of rheum were making her eyelids stick together. Had she been crying? She couldn't remember. She rubbed again to clear them and then lifted her head to look around.

She was sitting on a small narrow wood-framed bed with a basic grey blanket made of a rough, prickly fabric. The floor was made of large dark grey flagstones and was covered with a fine layer of dust. The walls were neat stone masonry constructed from large square granite blocks that had been polished smooth and cut to fit together so tightly that the crevasses between them did not appear to contain any mortar. Above her head was a vaulted ceiling with low gothic arches emanating from the four corners and then sweeping upwards to meet at the apex directly above the centre of the room where a single lamp cast a weak yellow light across the interior.

On the opposite side of the room from the bed there was a metal door inset into the wall by a couple of inches. It was a dull gunmetal grey colour, and it had no handle on the inside and its surface was smooth with rivets all around the edges. It looked like a bulkhead door on a ship or submarine. Next to the bed along another wall was a small wooden table and a bench made from two pieces of railway sleepers cut to around one metre in length and bolted together with two long metal rods with large nuts screwed onto the ends. On the wall opposite were two rusty metal chains bolted to the wall, each with what appeared to be metal restraints at the ends. The chains were covered in dust and cobwebs.

Still feeling groggy and disorientated, she staggered to her feet and took a couple of unsteady steps away from the bed to stand in the middle of the room. She looked up and stretched for the light above her. It was just too high for her to be able to reach. Then she slowly did a full turn, looking at her surroundings and trying to remember how she had got there, but her memory produced nothing. Her mind felt strangely fragmented. Like a puzzle where only a few separate sections had been completed, but where the complete image was still disjointed and unknown.

Directly above the bed was something she had not noticed before. A small window. Or rather, a brick that seemed to have been made from opaque glass. It let in a small amount of light from the outside, wherever that was. There was daylight out there, or more precisely, the golden light of what she assumed was either sunset or sunrise. However, she was unable to discern any details or any movement out there. All she was able to see what that it was daytime.

She looked down and turned her wrist to see that she was still wearing her watch, but somehow it had stopped working. Slowly, she brought it up to her face and looked at her own reflection in the glass pane behind which the watch's hands sat immobile – locked into their positions at seventeen minutes past two. The person looking back at her seemed vaguely familiar, like an acquaintance whose name she had temporarily forgotten. She looked intently at the red-haired girl in the watch face and blinked a couple of times. She could not even remember her own name. What was happening to her?

Suddenly filled with anxiety, she began frantically patting down her own body, feeling through the coarse fabric for injuries and pulling away the linen methodically to inspect her limbs. To her intense relief, she eventually assured herself that she had no cuts or bruises, and she did not have any sensation of pain anywhere in her body.

She glanced again at the door and then at the metal restraints bolted to the wall. What on earth were they for? Then she noticed that a wooden box was sitting on the bench, and that next to it on the floor was a metal jug with a metal beaker next to it. She slowly walked over to it, sat down on the bench and flipped open the lid of the box. It contained a piece of bread and an apple. Lifting the jug, she discovered that it was full of cool fresh water. She immediately began eating the bread. It was very basic, but it tasted divine to her, and as soon as she began eating it her body let her know just how famished she really was. She began wolfing down the food faster and faster, gorging on the bread, then biting off a big piece of the apple, pouring herself some water and drinking it greedily. Soon all of the food was gone, and she then sat silently looking at the empty box and slightly out of breath from the effort of eating. Where had the food come from? Who was keeping her here?

She then spotted something that had been there all along, but that was easily missed because of its small size. Directly above the metal door was a small black circular thing, seemingly inset into the masonry. Looking at it closely, she noticed a faint reflection of the light in the ceiling. It was a camera. She got back onto her feet and began walking towards the door, suddenly feeling very tired. She was halfway to the door when she was overcome with drowsiness and almost fell over. She staggered back to the bed and fell onto it. The room was suddenly spinning, and her vision gradually constricted into a black tunnel with an ever-smaller light at the end of it.

Something in the water, she managed to think before the darkness swallowed her and she fell asleep again.

TEN

The next day, Andrew and Fiona had decided to take action. They had once again discussed speaking to the police but decided against it. Not only was the basic issue of a young woman and her boyfriend not being in touch for a couple of days unchanged. But now they realised that the people responsible for Caitlin's disappearance were most likely in possession of considerable resources. This meant that those people would likely be able to compromise any police investigation. So, at least for the moment, they had decided to work on their own initiative, and that involved a very simple plan. A stakeout.

In the early afternoon, they made their way by the London Underground from Hampstead to Tower Hill. They walked out of the station building and up the steps to the large elevated circular platform directly in front of the station exit, where a roughly four-metre-tall sundial was placed. Standing by the platform's railing they could look directly across to the Tower of London with its outer defences, inner walls, battlements and small towers with cupolas near the centre of the castle. Since its foundation in the late 11th century following the Battle of Hastings and the subsequent initiative on the part of the victorious William the Conqueror to build fortifications across his new territory, the castle had served as a treasury and the home of the Royal Mint, an office for public record, and lately the home of a major tourist attraction – the kingdom's Crown Jewels. Behind it on the other side of the Thames at a distance of roughly half a mile was the Shard stretching up into the clear blue sky, seemingly reaching for the heavens.

Off to the left from where they stood they could also see the underpass going beneath the busy Tower Hill thoroughfare where cars, buses and taxis were driving along as they did at all hours of the day virtually every single day of the year.

'I think you were right,' said Andrew. 'If Antoine was picked up on CCTV in this area on multiple occasions, then he must live somewhere nearby.'

'Yes, but where?' said Fiona. 'It could be anywhere around here. Where do you think might be a good place to sit and watch?'

'Strickland mentioned Saint Kathrine Docks,' said Andrew and pointed southeast to an area immediately next to the castle a couple of hundred metres away, 'so I say we just go and plant ourselves at one of the restaurants there. It is a perfectly pleasant area to be in if you absolutely have to sit down for a few hours. It certainly beats lying in a ditch in a desert without being able to move for days. If nothing happens, we'll have a nice afternoon in the sunshine, and if he does turn up... well, then I guess we will have to take it from there.'

'All right,' said Fiona, and then she gestured to Andrew's chest. 'You know I don't like those things, but I assume you're armed?'

Andrew patted the left side of his light black leather jacket where a Glock 17 sat securely strapped to his chest in a shoulder holster.

'It's one of the advantages of being part of an anti-terrorism unit,' he said. 'I can carry a licensed firearm when I think it is needed.'

'We need to check out the underpass on the way over there,' said Fiona, taking the lead down the stairs on the eastern side of the sundial platform. 'That's where Antoine seemed to disappear from CCTV coverage.'

They walked past a life-sized bronze statue of Roman emperor Trajan, which had been placed in front of one of the last surviving sections of the original Roman walls of what was once called Londinium. After another ten metres, they descended the two sections of concrete steps to the underpass. The five-metre-wide passage was dark and plastered with a dozen adverts behind reflective plexiglass covers along both sides, tempting pedestrians to purchase food from nearby restaurants, tickets for riverboats and a special discount on a visit to see the Crown Jewels just on the other side of Tower Hill.

The bright sunlight pouring in from the other end of the underpass to the south made them squint as they entered, and it had the effect of placing the passage in a stark silhouette. This in turn meant that as they walked through it, they almost missed the narrow door on their right. It had been covered with one of the adverts, whose black-framed plastic housing exactly matched the dimensions of the door. But the hinges of the door protruded noticeably on the left-hand side of it.

'What have we here?' said Andrew. 'Some sort of door.'

'I would never have spotted that,' said Fiona. 'I wonder where it leads. Are you able to open it?'

Andrew examined its edge on the opposite side from the hinges. As he did so, Fiona did her best to screen him off from other pedestrians, but several of them looked suspiciously in their direction. Stopping for any reason in the middle of an underpass in London was an unspoken pedestrian *faux pas* that was bound to get people's attention.

'If there is a way to open it, I can't see it,' he said quietly. 'And I am not sure ripping off the placards and trying to force our way through is a good idea. At least not at this time of day.'

'We might have to come back later,' said Fiona.

'Yes,' said Andrew. 'Perhaps when it is dark and there are fewer people. I am going to need a crowbar for this anyway. Let's get over to the docks.'

The two of them continued through the underpass and out into the sunshine, where they found themselves in what used to be the moat around the Tower of London. They continued along the footpath, back up a set of steps to cross over the two-lane approach to Tower Bridge and then across the small parallel road called Tower Hill Way from which there was access down to Saint Kathrine Docks.

It had been many decades since the docks had served their original purpose. They were now a marina surrounded by residential blocks, and there was a plethora of restaurants and cafes wrapping around most of it. The marina itself seemed almost full to capacity with a wide range of boats of different shapes and sizes. There were a large number of small pleasure boats, but also two yachts that could just barely fit through the locks leading out to the Thames. There were even a few houseboats moored along the quayside.

The two of them descended the steps to the marina and walked along for another thirty metres before Andrew motioned to a set of tables and chairs that had been arranged on the wide promenade-like stretch between the buildings and the quay. They belonged to a pizza restaurant, and they were partly enclosed by tall movable planters with small green hedges. It looked very inviting in the sunshine.

'How about this?' he said. 'It looks pleasant enough, and we can see the whole marina from here, including the steps leading back out.'

'Sure,' said Fiona. 'Fine by me.'

They selected a table that was partly obscured from the entry points to the marina, but which allowed them to look out nonetheless. Soon, a waiter appeared and Fiona ordered a latte, whilst Andrew asked for a small beer and some salted peanuts. They then began what was without a doubt the most overrated activity of any investigation. The completely open-ended and very often fruitless stakeout. After an hour, they ordered the same again.

'This could end up being a long afternoon,' observed Andrew sipping his beer.

'I don't mind at all,' said Fiona evenly. 'It's the only lead we have, so we are following it.'

'That's my girl,' smiled Andrew.

Fiona got out her phone and sat back staring intently at it and swiping and tapping every once in a while. Without having to ask, Andrew already knew that she was not just idly killing time but busy looking into something.

'This is interesting,' she eventually said. 'There used to be a tube station on Byward Street just a couple of hundred metres west of Tower Hill tube station. It was called Mark Lane and it opened in 1884 when the Metropolitan Railway and the District Railway were merged to become part of the Circle Line. And now listen to this. The station was closed in 1967 because it had reached its capacity, and a new station, today's Tower Hill Station, was opened to service the Circle and District Lines instead.'

'I think I see where this is going,' said Andrew, leaning forward, folding his hands and placing his elbows on the table. 'You're saying that there is a passage from that underpass towards the west to the abandoned station.'

'That's right,' said Fiona. 'Mark Lane Station is still very much there, and so are the tunnels that used to service it. And I have no doubt that there would have been an underground connection from it to Tower Hill station, even if the two were not open to the public at the same time.'

'And that is where you think Antoine went when he disappeared?' said Andrew.

'Exactly,' replied Fiona. 'That's why the Met's CCTV footage saw him walk in but never out again.'

'But there is nothing down there in those tunnels,' said Andrew, 'except for several decades' worth of dust and dirt. He couldn't possibly live down there.'

'No,' nodded Fiona, 'but he could probably use them fairly consistently to disappear if he thought he was being watched or followed.'

'Right,' said Andrew pensively, and turned his head to look out across the marina. 'So, I guess the idea that Antoine might turn up here in this marina is suddenly looking pretty unlikely.'

'Possibly,' said Fiona, taking a sip of her latte. 'If he can move around this area unseen using those tunnels, then I am not sure why he would come here. Unless he lives in one of these buildings.'

'If he does, it is probably under a false name,' said Andrew, looking around at the various apartment blocks surrounding the marina. 'With his connections, that should be pretty easy to pull off, so running a check on all the residents here won't turn up anything.'

'This is all so weird,' sighed Fiona. 'What the hell are these people up to? And what have they done with Caitlin?'

'There seems to be an awful lot of skulduggery going on,' said Andrew. 'The only thing I feel confident about is that whatever it is that is going on is important enough for them to go to extraordinary lengths to keep it a secret.'

'But why get my sister involved?' said Fiona exasperated. 'My sister is a gentle soul with a harmless hobby. What could they possibly want with her?'

'Your guess is as good as mine,' said Andrew, shaking his head. 'But I am afraid we have to assume the worst. This whole thing with Antoine and his involvement with Caitlin, his fake identity, the tunnels, and his bizarre connections to a major law firm. All of it smacks of something pretty nefarious, as much as I hate to say it.'

'The bottom line is that we can't rely on help from anyone,' said Fiona steely-eyed. 'We have to play hardball from now on, and if I ever get my hands on that bastard…'

She trailed off as her gaze hardened even further and her jaw muscles clenched.

'If we find Antoine,' said Andrew, 'I am going to put the thumbscrews on him until he tells us everything there is to know about this whole thing. No more walking around asking people nicely.'

'Oh shit,' said Fiona suddenly, her eyes locked on something behind Andrew. 'I think that's him. He's coming down the steps.'

Calmly, Andrew picked up his beer and took a sip whilst twisting his upper body slightly to the side, just enough for him to be able to see the steps leading up to Saint Kathrine's Way. She was right. It was Antoine. He was wearing black jeans, white trainers, a light blue jumper and what appeared to be the same black linen ball cap he had been wearing at the British Museum. Andrew took a long time to finish what was left of his beer, holding the glass up in front of his face to obscure it whilst at the same time observing the Frenchman as he approached them. He was now only around twenty metres away and walking calmly along with a self-assured stride. As Andrew studied him, it was obvious that the man kept himself in shape. He had the athletic demeanour of someone who probably went to the gym several times every week and who took pride in his physical appearance.

Andrew turned back to face Fiona and put the beer glass down on the table.

'Make sure he doesn't spot you,' he said, reaching inside his jacket, ready to unclip the quick release on his pistol's shoulder holster. 'We need him to come closer.'

Fiona shrank back in her seat and attempted to hide her face behind Andrew.

'Not a care in the world,' she said quietly but disdainfully as the Frenchman approached, clearly with a spring in his step and appearing not to sense any threat to himself. 'Where is my sister, you piece of shit.'

'Fiona,' said Andrew. 'Please stay calm. We need this guy to talk, and that means we need to grab him and restrain him.'

Fiona's eyes flashed as she tracked Antoine with her eyes. Fifteen metres now.

Whether it was some sort of sixth sense or whether Fiona's tense body language and narrowing eyes somehow caught Antoine's attention, the end result was the same. From one moment to the next, his demeanour changed completely. His head swivelled to the side as he locked eyes with her. His body immediately cancelled its forward momentum, and he stopped dead in his tracks, seemingly frozen to the spot like the pillar of salt into which Lot's wife Edith was transformed as punishment for looking back at the destruction of the city of Sodom.

'Oh shit,' she whispered. 'He has seen me.'

Immediately, Andrew jumped up from his chair causing it to fly backwards as he spun around reaching inside his jacket for his pistol. In that same moment, Antoine spun on his heels and bolted for the steps leading back up to Saint Kathrine's Way.

'He's going for the tunnels!' shouted Fiona as she jumped to her feet.

Andrew vaulted over the planter with the small hedge that was between him and the Frenchman, landed adeptly on his feet and immediately transitioned into a run.

'Stay here!' he shouted as he began to give chase.

'Hell no!' replied Fiona, moving swiftly around the table to follow suit.

'It's not safe for you!' Andrew shouted over his shoulder as Fiona was doing her best to keep up with him.

Fiona hesitated and then stopped, watching Andrew as he bounded with incredible agility up the two long sets of steps from the marina and up to Saint Kathrine's Way in pursuit of his quarry. Then she grimaced and shook her head.

'Screw this,' she grumbled to herself and set off after him.

About thirty metres ahead of her, Andrew had now just reached the top of the steps. He sprinted across Saint Kathrine's Way and out into the busy traffic of the Tower Bridge approach. Antoine was already safely across and heading for the steps down into the former castle moat. A white van braked hard to avoid hitting Andrew. He leapt out of the way and continued forward, and he was about to cross the second lane of traffic when a red vintage Lamborghini Diablo that had been hidden behind the van suddenly appeared less than five metres away. The driver immediately spotted him and slammed on the brakes causing all four of the performance car's wide tyres to lock up and screech across the tarmac leaving a cloud of smoke from the burnt rubber behind it. It was almost enough to stop the car, but not quite. Had it been another van or a bus, Andrew might have ended up in an intensive care unit or worse, but because it was a low-profile performance car with a long sloping bonnet and windshield he was able to leap up into the air and allow the car to partially pass underneath him and shunt him up into the air as its forward momentum was converted into his upwards motion. He felt a sharp pain in the right side of his chest but was otherwise able to maintain his orientation as he spun in the air. As the car passed underneath him and came to a screeching stop a couple of metres further along, he somehow miraculously managed to land more or less on his feet suffering only a few scrapes on his left elbow and knee and feeling winded. The driver emerged from the Lamborghini with a furious look on his face and came towards Andrew looking like he was ready for a fight, but as soon as he saw Andrew's Glock 17 he quickly lifted his hands up and out to his sides and backed off silently.

The traffic had now come to a complete stop in both directions and Andrew grimaced as he resumed his pursuit. He vaulted down the steps into the castle moat where he could see Antoine running along the gravel path towards the underpass by Tower Hill tube station. Attempting to ignore the pain in his ribs on the right-hand side of his chest, Andrew bounded down into the grass-covered moat and began running along the path to where Antoine had now disappeared around the corner into the underpass. He picked up the pace. He knew he only had about twenty seconds to catch up with the Frenchman before he would disappear into the abandoned tunnel systems.

As he turned the corner to the underpass, he spotted the Frenchman in the middle of opening the metal door into the tunnel system. They were the only two people there.

'Stop!' shouted Andrew, coming to a halt and pointing his pistol at the Frenchman. 'Don't move!'

Antoine glared at him without moving a muscle, seemingly assessing his options. Just then a young woman with a black goth outfit, pink spiky hair and wearing headphones came down the steps from the platform with the sundial where Andrew and Fiona had been standing just a few hours earlier. She seemed to be in a hurry and was taking two steps at a time as she descended. When she saw Antoine and then noticed Andrew behind him at the far end of the underpass holding a gun, she instantly froze.

Andrew had spotted her coming down the steps, and he already knew what was about to happen. Antoine had turned his head at the sound of the woman skipping down the stairs, and he now turned back to look at Andrew. A contemptuous, mocking leer spread across his face. He knew that he was between the woman and Andrew and that she was now directly in Andrew's line of fire. He ripped the metal door fully open and bolted through it, slamming it shut behind him.

'Shit,' exclaimed Andrew and sprinted for the door.

When he reached it he realised that it had closed but that the lock had not engaged. Only the door's latch bolt maintained a weak grip on the aluminium doorframe, so he stepped up to the door, placed his hands on its edge and squeezed his fingers into the narrow gap between it and the doorframe. Lifting one foot off the ground and placing it against the wall, he then pulled as hard as he could, even though the metal was cutting painfully into his fingers. Within a couple of seconds, the doorframe had been bent out of shape to such an extent that the latch bolt finally popped free and the whole door swung open, almost causing Andrew to lose his balance. He stood in front of the gaping black hole for a second. There seemed to be no illumination inside whatsoever, and he suddenly felt the sense of a strange vertical abyss staring back at him. He shook his head. There was no backing out now. This was his chance at getting his hands on Antoine and finding Caitlin. With his gun ready, he stepped inside.

He found himself in a narrow service tunnel that had clearly never been intended for use by commuters. It was no doubt a relic from the time immediately before passengers were re-directed from Mark Lane to Tower Hill, and it now looked severely run down. The ceiling was only just high enough to allow him to stand up straight, and the walls were rendered with simple smooth concrete. They might once have been painted a matt grey, but any paint had peeled off long ago, leaving only the dry and dusty concrete. Clipped onto the walls with rusty metal brackets and seemingly running the length of the tunnel were what appeared to be several thick black electrical cables. The air was cool and dry, and it had a mouldy quality to it that stuck in his throat. The dark floor was covered by a thin layer of powdery dust, but he could distinctly see a set of footprints leading away from the door.

Andrew gripped the front of his Glock 17 and switched on the attached tactical light. It immediately produced a cone of white light that swept forward and illuminated the tunnel for at least twenty metres ahead of him. He also engaged the inbuilt laser light which instantly shot out a narrow but powerful stream of photons that emitted light in the green spectrum. This would allow him to simply place the bright green marker on a target and squeeze the trigger, safe in the knowledge that the bullet would hit that spot every single time.

He flicked the Glock's safety to Off, brought the weapon up and advanced down the tunnel. Within a few moments, he was enveloped by the darkness with all of his attention directed ahead of him, the light and sounds of the world above having now effectively ceased to exit. Gradually, his eyes began to adjust to the relative darkness, and he suddenly thought he heard the faint sound of footsteps on metal in the distance.

He picked up the pace and walked quickly along the narrow tunnel until he arrived at a ninety-degree turn. Clearing the corner in textbook tactical fashion, he then proceeded another five metres until he came to a metal concertina grille that had been pulled halfway across, partly blocking his way. Clearly, Antoine had passed through here and had made a half-hearted attempt to prevent his pursuer from following him. This meant that he was scared. And so he should be. Andrew had already resolved to fire at anything that moved, not necessarily to kill, but certainly to wound and to immobilise.

He squeezed through the half-open barrier as quietly as he could. Any sound down here would instantly give his position away. He found himself in a large lobby with a wider tunnel leading to a set of stairs going up to his right and another tunnel to his left stretching about ten metres further along where it made a ninety-degree turn to the right. All the walls were covered by high-gloss white tiles, and above the stairs going up was a faded old sign saying 'Exit'.

He was now inside the abandoned Mark Lane Station. It was strikingly similar to the familiar interiors of most central London tube stations, many of which dated back to Victorian times. Like most of those stations that were still in use, this one would now have been nowhere near able to deal with the commuter numbers of a city whose population had more than doubled since the late 19th century.

He turned to the left and advanced toward the ninety-degree turn whilst listening out for the sound of movement. There was none. The only thing he could hear was the sound of his own heartbeat and the rush of blood through his veins. He had switched into the hunter mode that he had employed in the past on active duty in the SAS, and despite the unfamiliar environment, he felt confident in his ability to hunt down and defeat the Frenchman.

As he approached the corner up ahead, it occurred to him that there was a reason why Antoine had sprinted all the way back to this place instead of trying to hail a cab or simply attempting to disappear in the throngs of tourists around the Tower of London nearby. That reason was simple. This dark and treacherous place was his home turf. He had probably been here dozens of times, and he likely knew every nook and cranny in this sprawling and dilapidated underground complex. That clearly gave him the tactical advantage, and for all Andrew knew he could have stashed weapons down here for this precise scenario.

He pressed forward undeterred, the green laser light occasionally reflecting on the surface of the glossy white tiles and sending random streaks of faint green light bouncing around the dimly lit space. When he turned the corner, he was surprised to find that what had once been a set of steps leading down to the train platform was now a large open drop to the floor several metres below. To his left, a bulky staircase had been constructed from wide beams of riveted steel. It had once been painted a dull green colour, but most of the paint was now seemingly in a race to see which parts could peel and shed themselves from the metal structure first.

Andrew advanced towards the staircase and stopped briefly to inspect it in an attempt to ascertain whether it was safe to use, or whether he would be better off with the much noisier option of jumping down onto the platform from the ledge where the stairs had once begun. He decided to use the stairs and managed to move down to the platform almost completely silently when he suddenly thought he heard a faint brief scraping sound as if someone had dragged something across the floor up ahead. He stopped, but the sound had now ceased. Continuing to move forward along the platform, he became increasingly aware that he and Antoine were playing this game on the Frenchman's terms.

The platform itself was as dilapidated as everything else Andrew had seen so far. However, the space was unusual in that unlike other tube stations he had seen, it had a row of wide tiled pillars lining the edge of the platform. On the opposite side of it near the wall were benches bolted into the concrete floor, as well as several narrow side passages which would have once allowed the flow of commuters to move off the platform and connect either to the opposite platform or another tube line. As he proceeded, still gripping his pistol and sweeping it smoothly from side to side in order to illuminate and map out his surroundings, he felt certain that if Antoine was to lie in wait and attempt an ambush, one of the side passages would be where he would do it.

Andrew moved up to the corner of the first passage and swept around it, prepared to fire, but the passage was empty. As effective as the weapon-mounted tactical light and the laser pointer were, at that moment he would have given anything for a set of night vision goggles.

As he walked along the abandoned platform that was covered in a thin layer of dust, he could see multiple sets of footprints. Either there were several people down here, or this was a well-trodden path for Antoine. Andrew hoped for the latter but mentally prepared himself for the alternative. Suddenly, another thought formed in his mind. If Caitlin was being held captive somewhere by Antoine and his accomplices, then there was every reason to think that she might be held somewhere down in this underground complex. Not only did that make sense because it was so hidden away, but it also added an extra layer of complexity to what he was in the middle of doing. He was almost certainly one of the most proficient weapons handlers and hand combat fighters in the country, but even he could conceivably end up accidentally injuring or even killing an innocent person in the middle of a firefight. If it came to it, he had to make absolutely sure that Caitlin was nowhere nearby if he ended up having to use his weapon.

He advanced further and had almost drawn level with the platform's second connecting passage when he ended up placing his right foot on what must have been a small shard of glass that had been covered in dust. It produced a faint but distinct grinding and crackling noise as it splintered under his shoe. Realising that it would have given his position away to anyone nearby, he rushed forward and cleared the corner. Once again he was half-expecting Antoine to be there, but once again it was empty.

However, between the distraction caused by the shattering piece of glass and the urgency to move up and clear the next corner, Andrew had left himself vulnerable to the one place where Antoine had decided to lie in wait. Andrew sensed movement behind him and spun around to see the Frenchman emerge from behind one of the platform's pillars less than two metres away. His face was locked in a frenzied grimace, and in his hands he held a rusty old metal pipe about a metre long. Andrew swung the pistol around, but he was not fast enough to prevent Antoine from bringing the metal pipe down and across in front of himself, striking Andrew's wrist and knocking the pistol out of his hand. It flew a couple of metres through the air and clattered to the floor, finally sliding to a stop under one of the benches but still shining the light from its small barrel-mounted torch back towards the two men.

Completely caught off guard by the ferocious attack, Andrew staggered back whilst gripping his wrist and grimacing from the pain. Immediately, the Frenchman came at him again, swinging the metal pipe wildly. Andrew drew back his upper body and turned his head just in time for the sharp end of the rusty metal to merely swipe viciously through the air an inch from his throat. He felt the faint rush of air against his skin and knew that Antoine had both missed and would now be off balance because his powerful blow had failed to connect.

Keeping low and spreading out his arms to his side, Andrew spun to face Antoine and then launched himself into a rugby tackle that caught the Frenchman in the abdomen before he could reorientate himself and bring the pipe to bear once again. As Andrew barged into him, he was only too aware that what he had collided with was pure lean muscle. Antoine was clearly even more powerful and athletic than he appeared. The force of the impact knocked him over and the two of them crashed heavily onto the dusty concrete platform. As they fell, Andrew saw Antoine's hand scrabbling for something in his back pocket. A second later, there was a brief glint of a blade as Antoine raised it above his head and prepared to bring it down into Andrew's exposed neck. Andrew let go and rolled to one side just as the knife scythed down viciously through the air, very nearly burying itself in his shoulder. He punched Antoine in the gut as hard as he could and then used his elbow to take a powerful swipe at the young man's face. The elbow connected with the bridge of Antoine's nose amid the sickening crunching noise of bones and cartilage being crushed. Blood instantly spurted out, and the Frenchman involuntarily raised both hands to his face and staggered backwards a couple of steps.

Released from the mélange of fists, arms and a deadly blade, Andrew spun away and immediately launched himself through the air towards the Glock 17 that still lay under the bench a couple of metres away, shining its light at the frenzied fight. He landed heavily on the platform, but his momentum carried him forward and made him slide the last short distance to the bench. He quickly reached underneath it and gripped the pistol just as he heard the sound of footsteps rapidly coming towards him. Twisting onto his back, he raised the pistol to see the crazed Frenchman tearing towards him with the knife held high in one hand and the metal pipe in the other. His previously handsome face was a bloody mess with his nose clearly broken and slightly askew, and blood was pouring down onto his light blue jumper which was now also covered in dust and black dirt.

At this point, Andrew's instincts had taken over, and he brought the pistol up to aim squarely at Antoine's forehead. In any other situation, this would have been the right decision, and his muscle memory had already made that choice for him. However, if he wanted answers from Antoine, he could not afford to kill him. In the final split second before the charging Frenchman reached him, and just as he was about to launch himself into a frenzied last attack using the knife and the metal pipe, Andrew adjusted the aim slightly down so that the green laser dot was on Antoine's chest. Had he had more time, Andrew would have aimed for his shoulder or even his legs, but as it was, time had run out. Either he fired now or he would be overwhelmed by his attacker. All he could do was hope for the best.

The Glock barked angrily twice in quick succession, tearing open the relative silence of the large open platform, and the bullets instantly punched into Antoine's chest. One of them went straight through, puncturing a lung on the way and exiting his back to slam up into the ceiling. The other smacked into a rib on the left side of his chest, splintering it and continuing on to travel clean through his heart's left ventricle chamber before finally ending up lodged in his spine.

The loud cracks from the shots reverberated around the platform, and they were still in the process of dying down as Antoine staggered forward and fell onto his front right next to Andrew. The Frenchman's face smacked forcefully into the dusty concrete floor, and Andrew could hear cranial bones breaking. Andrew quickly spun away and jumped to his feet, gun still pointing at his attacker. Antoine's left eye twitched once, and then he let out a long, slow breath as his final lungful of air abandoned his body. Then he lay still on the cold platform floor. Antoine was dead.

'Shit,' whispered Andrew to himself.

Antoine had been their best hope of finding a clue to where Caitlin might be. Regardless of her exact current location, Andrew now felt more convinced than ever that she was being held against her will. And now the only person they knew for a fact was involved in her disappearance had expired right here in front of him. An expanding pool of blood was spreading out from his corpse. It looked like black oil as it slowly crept across the floor, slowly reaching out in all directions.

'Why did you have to be so stupid?' winced Andrew as he lowered himself to rest on one knee next to the dead Frenchman.

He rolled Antoine over onto his back and began methodically searching his pockets. In the left front pocket of his black jeans was a wallet. Andrew quickly flicked it open and saw that it contained several debit and credit cards, as well as a couple of twenty-pound notes. There were a few other items in there, but he did not have time to examine them all right there and then. With the Frenchman now lying on his back, his right arm had flopped out to the side, exposing the three-letter tattoo that Andrew and Fiona had first spotted in the photo Caitlin had sent to her sister.

'L.D.M.' muttered Andrew to himself.

At that moment, he heard footsteps coming from behind and above him. He instantly swung around and raised the gun. On the other side of the gun sight standing at the top of the steel staircase was a figure holding some sort of torch that was bright enough to obscure the person. Andrew aimed and placed the green laser dot where he thought the figure's chest might be.

'Andrew, it's me!' shrieked Fiona in a panicked voice.

Her arms flew up, and she stood there trembling for a moment as the laser dot danced over the front of her white blouse and the light from her phone illuminated the ceiling above her. Then the green dot disappeared as Andrew lowered first the gun and then his head, breathing a sigh of relief at not having fired. Had Fiona waited just a couple of seconds longer before identifying herself, he could have shot her. He looked up at her again as she descended the stairs and hurried towards him.

'What the hell are you doing here?' he said sounding frustrated. 'I told you to...'

'Yes, you did,' countered Fiona, 'but I don't have to do as you ask.'

'Fair enough,' sighed Andrew and stood, taking a step back to put his free arm around her shoulders. 'Sorry, but I could have shot you.'

'Is he dead?' asked Fiona, pointing weakly to Antoine even though the answer was quite obvious.

'Very,' replied Andrew. 'Unfortunately. I tried to take him alive, but he was like a man possessed. It was almost as if he didn't care whether he lived or died. He just kept coming at me like some sort of deranged zombie.'

'What could make him do that?' asked Fiona with a dismayed look whilst studying the dead Frenchman who was now lying face up in a large pool of his own blood. 'What was he protecting?'

'I don't know,' said Andrew. 'What I *do* know is that we need to get out of here. I have seen no sign of anyone being kept down here, but we need to check the other end of the platform and the passages down there.'

He gestured towards the far end of the platform and the two remaining passages that he had not yet had time to clear before Antoine had attacked him.

'Being kept?' repeated Fiona incredulously. 'You mean Caitlin? Kept prisoner down here?'

A visible shudder ran through her body as she hugged herself, contemplating the idea and looking around the cold, dilapidated space.

'It was just a thought,' said Andrew. 'I think it is very unlikely, to be honest. But we need to make sure. Let's do a quick sweep.'

It took them just a few minutes to reassure themselves that there were no hidden spaces where Caitlin could have been kept prisoner, and as they were about to walk back along the platform towards the staircase, Andrew suddenly stopped dead in his tracks.

'Don't move,' he whispered.

Fiona looked at him with a confused expression on her face as she mouthed the word *'what?'*

Andrew pointed to his ear and nodded in the direction of the staircase, and then Fiona was able to hear it too. Voices. Movement. It was faint and clearly not close by, but there was a distinct sense that it was getting closer with every second. Then they heard the unmistakable sound of a bark.

'Fuck,' grimaced Andrew, realising that the young woman in the goth outfit had probably called the police after seeing a man with a gun. 'A canine unit. We need to get the hell out of here right now.'

The Metropolitan Police's contingent of Dog Support Units, a.k.a. DSUs could be deployed for any number of reasons, including in forensics roles as well as suspected drugs, firearms or explosives-related offences. If one of their highly trained German Shepherds got the scent of either one of them, it would be almost impossible to shake it.

'Are you sure?' asked Fiona hesitantly. 'Can't we talk to them? We didn't do anything?'

'Well, not aside from killing a French national,' he said. 'I agree that we don't have anything to hide, but we can't afford to sit in a police station for the next twelve hours while this whole thing gets sorted out. We need to find Caitlin, and she might not have a lot of time. Let's go.'

Fiona nodded her acceptance and the two of them hurried quietly back to the far end of the platform, where they slipped into one of the four passages. It took them to a larger open space with a metal staircase similar to the one they had descended at the other end of the platform. They ascended as fast as they could whilst trying to make as little noise as possible. They reached a landing where a set of regular steps led up through a stairwell to a large lobby that was blocked on the far side by an enormous wooden door. Inset into it on one side was a standard-sized door with a handle.

'I think I know where we are,' said Fiona and hurried up to the smaller door, putting her ear to it. 'Traffic noise. This is the exit to Byward Street. We're in the old lobby of Mark Lane Station.'

Andrew tried the door handle but the door didn't budge.

'Locked,' he said and looked around. 'This might work.'

He walked over to a metal rod that was lying on the floor next to one of the walls. Picking it up, he returned to the door and quickly managed to wrench open the lock. He then opened the door, at which point it turned out that Fiona had been right. Outside was Byward Street with cars racing back and forth, and in through the opening poured the orange light from the sun that was now hanging low in the sky over the south of London. However, they were still unable to get out. Pulled across the large door was an equally large metal concertina grille similar to the one they had passed on the way into Mark Lane Station.

'That's not good,' observed Andrew deadpan.

'Wait,' said Fiona and pointed. 'The key is in the lock. It can't be operated from the outside, so whoever closed this up just left it in.'

'You're right,' said Andrew, and reached across to the key that was sticking out from the lock on the inside of the grille. 'Let's see. Moment of truth.'

He turned the key, and it moved surprisingly smoothly in the lock, rewarding him with an audible click as it opened. As soon as he heard it, he reached in with both hands, grabbed the handle on the concertina grille and hauled it across far enough for the two of them to be able to squeeze through. Less than a minute later, they were through and walking west along the pavement on Byward Street.

'What now?' asked Fiona.

'We find a hotel,' said Andrew.

'What?' asked Fiona. 'Why?'

'Because we have to assume that we have been caught on CCTV somewhere around the Tower of London,' he replied. 'I was running around in public with a gun. There's bound to be questions to answer, and we don't have time for that.'

'Fine,' said Fiona and tugged at his sleeve, guiding him around the corner and north along Seething Lane. 'There happens to be a very nice one right here.'

She pointed up at an enormous five-storey building constructed in a sumptuous Greco-Roman style with enormous colonnades, tall multi-paned windows and smooth limestone exterior walls. It looked more like a palace than a hotel.

'The Four Seasons Hotel,' said Andrew. 'Looks expensive.'

'It is,' said Fiona, 'but I think we deserve it after today.'

Eleven

Wearing his expensive navy-blue tailor-made suit, a crisp white Zegna shirt and a silver Gucci tie, Tristan Maxwell left the offices of Montague Solicitors in the Shard and made his way north across Tower Bridge. As he reached the north bank of the river, he glanced over at the temple-like building that was the home of the Sons of Lucifer. His initiation into that fraternity had without question been the highlight of his life so far, but he intuitively knew that he was only scratching the surface of what was possible as a member of that fraternity. Haywood had shown great faith in him by allowing him to join at such a relatively young age, and Maxwell was grateful for that. Since his induction a couple of years earlier, Maxwell had worked tirelessly as Haywood's confidential fixer, and he would stop at nothing to please his master and thereby elevate himself within the fraternity. However, in the quiet and private recesses of his own mind, he had long ago resolved to play the long game and attempt to one day take over Haywood's position as head of the brotherhood. He had seen enough to know that the Sons of Lucifer, despite being entirely hidden from public view wielded astonishing influence in the City, and with himself at the helm, he saw virtually no limit to his own power. All he had to do was remain loyal to Haywood, and then patiently await the opportunity that would one day surely come.

So far as a junior member he had not yet been invited to any of the sacrificial ceremonies that took place twice a year. However, he had been involved in procuring several of the offerings, and Haywood had recently also revealed the nature of some of the archaeological work that the Sons of Lucifer were carrying out in a number of different locations in the south of France. Maxwell had not yet witnessed any rituals that could demonstrate whether any of the occult elements of the fraternity's activities actually had a real effect and whether the underlying theological foundations were true. But that was almost irrelevant to him. What mattered was that it was real in the minds of the senior leadership and in the minds of all the people who were carefully being cultivated to do the bidding of the fraternity. This faith manifested itself in powerful leverage over people, and that leverage could in turn be translated into very real influence over their decisions. With a carefully designed and perfectly calibrated personal influence campaign focusing on the basic levers of greed and fear, each individual was eventually tempted to cross the proverbial Rubicon and support the efforts of the Sons of Lucifer, even if they were not yet allowed to join the fraternity itself, and even if they did not understand its true nature. Even Maxwell was sometimes amazed at how easy it was to make other people do exactly what they were told, almost regardless of what that was.

Early on in life, his well-meaning but emotionally distant parents had carted him off to a so-called therapist who had diagnosed him with a borderline personality disorder. As a young boy, he had initially felt ashamed of what was made out to be a serious medical condition that required some form of intervention or treatment, but as he grew older he realised that his ability to detach himself emotionally from other people around him was, in fact, his personal superpower. It allowed him free rein across the whole spectrum of human social interactions without ever being burdened by notions of morality or guilt. In that respect too, he had obtained freedom.

His parents had put him into therapy for years, but he had eventually concluded that they themselves were all utterly deluded. They lived in the imaginary world of morality, and they clung to it like drowning sailors clinging to the wreckage of a sinking ship. If only they would let go and just swim.

Eventually, he had finally broken free of the suffocating societal tyranny and refused to be treated as if he was the one who was ill. As the years passed after that, he had developed ways of navigating the world without other people noticing his superpower, and he only deployed it very selectively when a significant opportunity revealed itself. At boarding school, he had been made head boy. Simultaneously loved by both the teachers and the other students, despite constantly manipulating the two against each other for his own entertainment, and managing to secure better grades for himself than he otherwise would have. The same pattern had repeated itself at Oxford where it became second nature to such an extent that he no longer had to put in any effort. Later, when he joined his first law firm, he had skilfully played the game of office politics and consistently outmanoeuvred all of his equally ambitious young colleagues. Eventually headhunted for the position at Montague Solicitors, he had finally reached a place in life where he could allow his talents to truly shine. Haywood's mentorship and subsequent offer of junior membership in the fraternity had been an added bonus that had suddenly opened up the door to a whole new reality that he was determined to exploit to its fullest. However, all of those things were goals beckoning to him from the far future. For now, though, he needed to focus on the present, which involved ensuring that the upcoming ceremony went smoothly for Haywood and the senior members of the fraternity. And he was determined to do what he could to ensure that the work currently being conducted in France bore fruit.

Maxwell did not have a wife or partner or girlfriend. He simply saw no point. He had never even considered having children, and as far as he was concerned, women were temporary distractions that could be both spectacularly good entertainment if kept at arm's length or an insufferable ball and chain that would ultimately end up weighing him down and trapping him in a joyless existence without the freedom to do as he pleased. And he was quite happy to be called a nihilist. After all, what else was there in life other than the pleasure and satisfaction of the moment? Above all else, he craved power, especially power over others, simply because it was the tool through which he could attain unrestrained freedom. And any kind of partner would invariably scupper that ideal.

He proceeded onto King William Street and then turned east towards Great Tower Street. He preferred walking to taking a taxi, even in bad weather, and he had yet to obtain a position within the firm that would allow him his own chauffeur-driven car. After another five minutes of brisk walking, he entered the pub called The Hung Drawn & Quartered on Great Tower Street, a stone's throw from the Tower of London. The interior had recently been refurbished and looked nothing like what most people would think of as a pub, except perhaps for the bar, which offered a large selection of ales. The high-ceilinged open space had several tall Greek-style columns reaching up towards the ceiling that was framed by an intricate gilded cornice. The walls were painted a dark teal colour and the leather furniture along with the golden chandeliers and the wall-mounted vintage lamps with their gold-trimmed black fabric shades almost gave the interior the feel of a West End gentleman's club.

Maxwell did not particularly like pubs or the ale they served, but on this occasion, he was prepared to make an exception. He was meeting a junior solicitor from another City law firm to have a drink. He could think of a million other things he would rather be doing, but the fact remained that this particular acquaintance was on a fast track to the board of directors in the rival firm, and Maxwell wanted to make sure he had the man's career trajectory mapped out so that he would know when to step in and make sure that the rival firm remained a minor rival. Something was bound to arise from the conversation that would be useful as leverage at a much later stage.

They greeted each other with a handshake and made themselves comfortable in a booth with chesterfield-style leather seats, after which the younger man fetched them drinks at the bar. For the next hour or so, Maxwell was being his usual charming self with his winning smile and his good looks and middle-class deportment. Throughout the meeting where the two of them talked shop and exchanged amusing personal anecdotes, during which time Maxwell felt excruciatingly bored, his eyes were fixed on the other man boring into him without a shred of warmth or empathy and searching for some weakness or leverage that could be exploited later. Put simply, he was as always looking for a way to dominate.

After an hour of having almost brought his own mind to the point of spontaneous combustion with the sheer dreariness of listening to the other man prattle on about nothing that was even remotely interesting, Maxwell let it be known that he had a date with a young woman who worked as a secretary at one of the big accountancy firms. Seeming cheerful and friendly and sad to have to leave so soon, he made his excuses and left the pub. Once he was back out on the pavement, his demeanour changed in an instant.

Fucking muppet, he thought to himself. *I can't believe I have to waste time on lightweights like him.*

He made his way east past the Tower of London and then cut north into the borough of Tower Hamlets and the area of Whitechapel. The borough was both one of the wealthiest areas in London, comprising Canary Wharf with its many financial institutions and the thousands of people working there, and also some of the most deprived areas with council estates and the small badly maintained homes of people working for minimum wage or less. The stark contrast between the two had remained almost the same for centuries, and it was no accident that this was the area where Jack the Ripper had once plied his gruesome trade.

Maxwell walked for about half an hour until he arrived at a small disused warehouse behind a chain link fence. It had once been a car mechanic's shop, but it had gone out of business many years ago. Maxwell had purchased it recently as a way to obtain some privacy when he felt the urge to meet with one of his female acquaintances. He unlocked the gate and then used a different key to open the warehouse itself. It was virtually empty, and a thick layer of dust covered the entire concrete floor. The only windows in the building were placed a couple of metres off the floor. This meant that the interior received plenty of sunlight, yet no one on the outside could see in. In the middle of the open space was a strange collection of furniture. There was a large Persian rug on which was placed a three-seater leather sofa, a small table next to it with a couple of bottles of whiskey and a set of overturned shot glasses. There was also a tall metal coat stand with nothing on it.

Maxwell walked to the coat stand, took off his suit jacket and placed it on the top hook. Then he removed his tie and looped it over the hook underneath. Finally, he removed his cufflinks and slipped them into the inside pocket of his jacket. He glanced at his Philip Patek wristwatch, which had cost what most people earn in a year, making a sullen face. She was late again. He walked to the small table, picked up a bottle and poured himself a glass of single malt which he downed in one. Then he wiped his mouth with the back of his hand and poured himself another.

Just then, there was the sound of the door opening, and a woman in her mid-twenties walked in. She was petite with straight shoulder-length hair, and she was dressed in a short black crushed velvet dress with black stockings underneath. On her feet were high-heeled suede shoes that gave her an elegant posture as she entered. All of her clothes had been hand-picked and paid for by Maxwell via the monthly clothes allowance that he funded on top of her regular retainer.

Her face was pretty despite her eyes looking slightly sunken, but her make-up was perfectly applied. If she were to stroll through the City of London, people would assume that she was working as support staff for a major international bank or asset manager. However, that was not at all what she did for a living, and her purpose here had nothing to do with finance, except in the sense that she was paid extremely well for her time. As she approached Maxwell she appeared timid as if waiting for him to take the initiative, and he duly did so.

Reaching into his trouser pocket, he extracted a small bundle of something that looked like thin blue rubber, which he unfolded and shook. They were disposable surgical gloves that he had ordered online. He slipped them on and waited for the woman to stand close to him. He gently brushed her hair aside and leaned down to kiss her as she looked up and met his gaze. There was no fear in her eyes. Only acceptance.

In the next instant, he slapped her hard across the face. Then he headbutted her and punched her hard in the stomach, causing her to cry out and double over. Grabbing her roughly by the arm, Maxwell kept her upright and punched her again, this time in the face. Her lip split open and blood was dripping down onto her dress. He then slapped her as hard as he could across the face once, twice and then a third time at which he lost his grip on her, and she staggered to one side struggling to remain upright on her high heels. During the entire ordeal, she made virtually no sound. This was part of the deal and a pre-requisite for being paid.

Maxwell panted hard and looked at her with a leer. This was exactly what he needed after having spent that excruciating time with the dweeb at the pub. He changed his stance and his weight from the left to the right foot the way he often did when sparing with his personal Taekwondo instructor. Channelling the force all the way from his shoulder through his arm and into his fist, he punched her as hard as he could, wincing at the stab of pain in his knuckles. She fell over onto the dirty concrete floor with a heavy thud. He then kicked her several times in the stomach and once in the head, and then he finally relented, standing over her and watching her curled up in the foetal position – a weak whimper escaping her bruised and bleeding lips.

He straightened up and rose to his full height, lifting his face towards the ceiling and taking a deep breath. He let a huge lungful of fresh air rush into him whilst a ripple of satisfaction moved through his entire body. Finally, he adjusted his clothes, walked to the coat stand and put his shirt, tie and cufflinks back on. He then returned to the prone woman and dropped a money clip full of £20 notes on the floor next to her bleeding face.

'Thank you,' he breathed softly but without a trace of empathy in his voice. 'See you next week.'

Then he walked out, leaving the young woman sobbing quietly on the cold floor.

★   ★   ★

Andrew had been right in saying the Four Seasons Hotel was expensive, but having spent a few hours in the executive suite getting showered and ordering a fortifying room service dinner with a bottle of vintage wine, it almost began to feel worth the money. About an hour after arriving, he had then received a message from Colonel Strickland letting him know that the Metropolitan Police had contacted the SAS after identifying Andrew as the gunman chasing another pedestrian near the Tower of London. Strickland had put his neck on the line by concocting a story about how Andrew was working covertly on a classified case involving a possible terrorist threat to another country. He had told the Met about how that country's government had requested absolute secrecy for the moment, and how as a result, Strickland was unable to divulge the exact nature of the operation. This had halted the Met's desire to put out a notice on him and Fiona, and Strickland's story was probably enough to hold off further questions for a while longer. However, the colonel had also requested that they wrap up whatever they were doing as soon as possible. Once again, he had declined to seek more information from the two of them. He simply did not want to know.

The colour scheme of the Four Seasons' executive suite was soft and calming, with most of the walls covered in elegant contemporary wallpaper. The remaining walls and the ceiling were partially clad in walnut wood panels. There were gold-framed paintings, large mirrors and pieces of art tastefully placed everywhere, and the whole space was delicately lit using concealed LED strips connected to dimmers. All of the furniture was upholstered in cream-coloured fabric, and the sofas were practically calling out to be sat on with their smooth plush velvet seat coverings and soft silvery cushions with gold thread piping around the edges.

'I could get used to this,' smiled Fiona half-heartedly.

Andrew knew that she was trying to lighten the mood after a very heavy couple of days, but he also sensed that she was failing miserably to make herself feel better. After all, they were no nearer to discovering what had happened to Caitlin or where she might be, and she had just witnessed Antoine dead in a pool of blood. She understood as well as Andrew that he had been their best bet to find her sister.

'I am glad you haven't lost your appetite,' said Andrew.

'Unlikely to ever happen,' she replied.

As they finished their meal, Andrew cleared a small space on the table and began laying out the contents of the wallet he had taken off Antoine's dead body. Aside from a few notes of cash, there were two credit cards and one debit card, an EHIC European health insurance card and a UK National Insurance card. All of them were issued in the name of Antoine Reynard. In a separate slot was another plastic card, but it was of a type that neither Andrew nor Fiona had seen before. It was white with a blue twisted rope around the edges, and in the top right corners was a golden anchor with a number on it.

'What's that?' asked Fiona, leaning closer to inspect the card.

'It seems to be a mooring license,' said Andrew. 'Antoine had a mooring spot inside Saint Katherine Marina. Berth number 16. This permit allows him to moor a vessel there that is up to fifteen metres long and four metres wide. Pretty big. Looks like a rolling 18-month contract.'

'A boat?' said Fiona, frowning for a brief moment, but then the penny suddenly dropped. 'A houseboat. I'll bet you anything he had a houseboat there.'

'You might be right,' said Andrew. 'It would give him a nice off-the-grid place to live. He might have another place somewhere in London, but a houseboat in that marina would give him a secluded spot where he could spend time practically anonymously and lie low if he needed to.'

'Is there a vessel name on the card?' asked Fiona.

'No,' replied Andrew, and glanced at his wristwatch. 'There's only one way to find out more. We need to go over there and have a look for ourselves. But not right now. It's only 9 pm. I say we make our way over there after midnight. If there is a houseboat at Berth 16, then we need to get inside. And since we don't have the keys, we will need to break in, so the last thing we need is a busy marina with restaurants and bars still open.'

'That's another three hours,' Fiona. 'Any suggestions about what to do until then?'

'Absolutely,' replied Andrew and rose. 'Follow me.'

A couple of minutes later they were sitting in the aptly named Rotunda Bar just off the hotel's lobby and reception area. It was an expansive circular space with a large lit-up cupola overhead at its centre. The walls were rendered in white plaster with reliefs of mountains and forest motifs, and on a raised area on the far side was a long bar with a grand piano next to it, where a young woman in a black dress was playing the dulcet tones of a delicate classical piece.

After they had received their drinks and found a relatively private table near one of the walls, Fiona took the opportunity to call the marina's managing agent and inquire about a berthing spot, making it known that she was particularly interested in acquiring Berth 16 because of its relatively secluded location within the marina at the end of a floating pier and away from most bars and restaurants. The female agent had explained that this particular berth was unlikely to come on the market any time soon since the current license holder had been renting that particular spot continuously for the past six years. In addition, he had never missed a payment or presented any problem for the agent or the marina. Asked for the name of the license holder, the agent had declined, citing strict privacy policies. Fiona thanked her and put down the phone.

'So, Antoine has been there for as much as six years,' she said. 'Or rather, he has owned the license for that long, but who knows where he has been and what he has been up to during that period.'

'But Strickland told us that Antoine Reynard had lived in the UK for only four years,' said Andrew. 'So, who was there before him? Or did he live there under a different identity for the first two years?'

'Every time we uncover something new about him, he seems even dodgier than before,' observed Fiona. 'I can't believe Caitlin got involved with someone like that.'

'Maybe he was just an excellent actor,' said Andrew. 'The most successful psychopaths usually are. But at least he is no longer around to cause trouble any more. I am guessing he is in a morgue right now being examined by a coroner.'

A dark cloud seemed to fall across Fiona's face as she recalled the sight of the recently expired Frenchman on the dusty abandoned platform just a few hundred metres away from the elegant and civilised venue where they were sitting.

'I will never get used to seeing dead people,' she mused quietly, with a thousand-yard stare across the rotunda.

'Good,' said Andrew grimly. 'You don't want that to happen. Trust me.'

'I can't stop thinking about why Antoine and whoever he is working with would go after someone like my sister?' asked Fiona, almost rhetorically.

'Hard to know,' said Andrew. 'But if they are involved in some sort of occult activity, they probably needed someone who was already attuned to this type of thinking. And perhaps they thought that if she suddenly disappeared, then no one would notice or care. That's how these things often play out. I bet Antoine, or whatever his real name was, had done this more than once before.'

'Well, that's a big fucking mistake,' said Fiona bitterly. 'I am going to find those bastards and rip their heads off. And what about that guy from the British Museum? Maxwell. Can't we just find out where he is and then put the thumbscrews on him ourselves? He is clearly involved somehow.'

'I agree that it certainly looks that way,' said Andrew. 'And I am also sure that if I got my hands on him, I would be able to make him tell us everything he knows. The problem is that we have no hard evidence. What if he is innocent? What if what we thought was some sort of interaction between him and Antoine was just a random glance? We can't just engage in vigilantism, no matter how strong a hunch we both have. We need proof.'

'I know,' Fiona sighed, sounding dejected. 'I guess I am just desperate for anything that can help us.'

'I understand,' said Andrew, reaching across the table and taking her hand gently. 'I am right there with you. I want to find her as much as you do. But if we behave recklessly and do something stupid, there then is every possibility that the chances of finding Caitlin go down, not up. For now, at least, we have to operate in the shadows. And getting inside that houseboat is a good place to start.'

The next few hours in the Rotunda Bar went by quickly. They ordered another round of cocktails and snacked on a shared platter of garlic bread and olives. When they finally rose from their chairs at just after midnight, the Rotunda Bar was still busy and the female piano player had been relieved by a middle-aged man in a dark tuxedo playing modern jazz.

'Grab that cushion, please,' said Andrew and pointed at a small emerald velour cushion on the chair next to Fiona's. 'We're going to need it.'

Fiona did as he asked, compressed it as much as she could and only just managed to stuff the whole thing into her bag. The two of them then exited the hotel and walked east past the Tower of London back down the stairs into Saint Katherine Marina. Berth 16 was on the far side, and as they proceeded along the quayside, most of the bars were in the process of closing and the restaurants had already shut their doors several hours ago. The marina was now relatively quiet, except for one pub where a group of loud punters were spilling out onto the quayside seemingly having a good-natured argument about football.

Andrew and Fiona kept walking on for another couple of minutes until they reached the eastern edge of the marina. Here, a floating pier about two metres wide extended out from the quayside, and having assured themselves that no one was nearby, the two of them hopped over the gate and walked out towards the end of the pier. Directly in front and above them, the full moon low hung in the black night sky partly illuminating even this dark section of the marina. Just below it, they could see the top third of the Shard poking up behind the residential blocks that surrounded the marina.

On both sides of the floating pier were moored a number of small pleasure crafts, and at the very end was an approximately twelve-metre-long houseboat that was painted dark green and looked to be relatively new. It had a row of long rectangular metal-framed windows along its sides, and near its stern was a narrow articulated gangway that was folded up onto the pier. When they reached the end of the pier, Andrew turned casually towards Fiona.

'Don't stop,' he said calmly as he approached the small gantry and began unfolding it. 'Just behave as if this is our boat.'

He lowered the end of the folding gantry onto the houseboat, and the two of them swiftly stepped across and proceeded down into a small area in front of the houseboat's main entry. It consisted of a set of small double doors that were locked with what looked to be a heavy-duty mortice lock. Andrew knelt next to the doors and motioned for Fiona to join him. As she did so, a helicopter flew across the sky to the north, the characteristic sound of its rotor blades filling the air.

'Let me have the cushion,' he said, so Fiona extracted it from her bag and gave it to him.

'What are you going to do?' she asked, craning her neck up and around to look and make sure no one was watching them.

'I don't carry a suppressor,' he said, extracting the Glock 17 from his shoulder holster and placing the cushion directly in front of the lock. 'Probably best to move back a bit.'

Fiona did as he asked, and then Andrew shoved the muzzle of the pistol deep into the cushion, adjusted his aim slightly and fired the weapon once. The cushion was surprisingly effective at dampening the noise from the gun. A muffled crack did escape from the cushion's fluffy wadding, but to anyone in the vicinity of the marina and unaccustomed to the sound of firearms it would have sounded like a chair being knocked over or someone clapping their hands loudly.

As it turned out, Andrew's aim had been almost perfect. The 9 mm bullet tore through the cushion and then punched straight through the metal lock, causing it to instantly disintegrate and be ripped out of its housing inside the thin wooden door. As the two of them sat still listening out for anyone that might have heard the shot, they instead heard the faint metallic noise of the lock's components clattering onto the floor inside the houseboat.

Andrew immediately thumped his shoulder heavily into the doors, finally causing the lock to break completely and the doors to swing open.

'Get inside,' he said quietly, and within seconds the two of them had entered the houseboat and shut the doors behind them.

The boat's interior was dark, except for the pale moonlight coming in through the windows on the side that was facing south. It looked neat and tidy with a small but modern kitchen island in the middle and a seating area beyond it towards the front of the boat on one side of the space. Directly opposite the sofas was a desk with stacks of books and a laptop. At the far end of the room was a closed door to another compartment.

'Let's draw all the curtains before we hit the lights,' said Andrew, and the two of them went along the two walls methodically pulling all the thick black linen curtains across the windows, thereby making it impossible for anyone on the pier to look inside.

Andrew then returned to the doors and found the light switch. When he flicked it, a series of LED strip lights that were concealed inside narrow recesses running the length of the space on both sides came on. They bathed the interior in a pleasant, soft light. The walls were painted a rich dark grey, the frames around the windows had a high-gloss chrome finish, and the floor was light-coloured polished wooden planks. Over the kitchen island was a metal extractor fan, and on either side of it were two expensive-looking glass pendant lights. The whole space gave the appearance of being an upmarket bachelor pad.

'Oh shit,' Fiona suddenly breathed, standing immobile and looking through the large open space.

'What?' said Andrew, turning to face her.

'I'm just thinking that maybe Caitlin was here at some point,' she replied. 'That thought gives me the chills.'

'I guess it's possible,' said Andrew, walking to the middle of the space near the kitchen island. 'Although, I think that it is probably unlikely. I reckon this was Antoine's secret bolthole that he could escape to if he thought he was under pressure somehow. It was clearly where he was headed when we first spotted him this afternoon.'

'Right,' nodded Fiona, shaking her head slightly as if to attempt to extract herself from her moment of contemplation.

'Let's start looking around,' said Andrew, and began walking past the kitchen island towards the comfortable-looking seating area at the front of the boat. 'Antoine clearly isn't working alone, so I am sure it is a matter of time before his accomplices turn up here. I want to see what is behind this door.'

The door near the seating area and next to the desk had dimly lit bookcases on either side. It was made from dark wood and it had a shiny brass handle. Andrew gripped it, opened the door and entered with his weapon out in front of himself. As it turned out, the room beyond was a bedroom. However, instead of having one large double bed in the centre of the room which the space would easily have accommodated, there were two single beds on either side. Directly opposite was a set of double doors made from the same wood as the door to the bedroom. Fiona followed him inside.

'That's odd,' she said. 'Two beds. Who else lived here?'

'Two separate wardrobes as well,' said Andrew, opening the one on the left side of the room next to one of the beds.

Fiona opened the other and looked inside.

'Whoever they are, they are both men,' she said. 'At least judging by their clothes.'

'Let's see what's behind here,' said Andrew and moved towards the double doors which he figured led to the last room at the very front of the boat.

He tucked the pistol back into his shoulder holster, gripped the two handles on the double doors and pulled them open. Immediately, a soft red automatic light came on inside the tiny space, and Fiona gasped as she saw what was inside.

Twelve

When Tristan Maxwell returned to his office at Montague Solicitors in the Shard, all of his colleagues had already gone home for the day, many hours ago. The sky outside the floor-to-ceiling windows was black, but the thousands of lights of central London gleamed far below him.

The city that never sleeps, he thought. *Or was that New York?*

After his weekly encounter in the warehouse in Whitechapel, which never failed to give him the release of pent-up frustration that he required on a regular basis, he had felt clear-headed and ready for another multi-hour stint at the office. Sleep was for losers and old people, and he had never been shy about doing a line of coke if he felt like he needed it. And all that bullshit about the drugs being in control of you rather than the other way around was just nanny state propaganda. *He* was in control. Completely.

He had just sat down at his desk preparing to go over some contracts involving the ownership transfer of an Angolan petrochemicals plant between a Russian oligarch and a local general when he received a text message on his encrypted app. It was from a man named Laurent, and it was unusually curt. However, once he had read it, he understood why. Antoine was dead. Apparently killed by an unknown assailant inside one of the abandoned tube stations that they liked to use.

'Shit,' winced Maxwell. 'That's all I bloody need.'

He rose from his chair again, walked over to the window and looked down at Saint Katherine Marina just across the river to the northeast. Then he shook his head.

I fucking knew that guy was useless, he thought to himself.

All that French idiot had to do was to procure another ditsy redhead that looked vaguely like the biblical Lilith for the ceremony. And then the bastard goes and gets himself killed, the stupid moron. And not only that, but he does it in a way that attracts the police and leaves the entire enterprise open to unwelcome scrutiny. But quite clearly, that was what happened when family connections were allowed to determine hiring policies.

Inbred frogs, he thought.

Then another thought occurred to him. Eventually, he would almost certainly need to remove young Edward Haywood from circulation, especially if it began to look as if he might take over from Haywood

Senior. In that event, Maxwell felt confident that some unfortunate but lethal freak accident could be arranged for Edward. After all, despite his family pedigree, his clean-cut looks and his impeccable manners, Maxwell had friends in low places that could be called upon to help solve otherwise unsolvable problems.

'One problem at a time,' he muttered to himself. 'If you want something done properly, you have to do it yourself.'

He picked up his gold-plated phone and speed-dialled Christopher Haywood's number. The CEO was not going to be happy, especially not by being interrupted at this time of night – even if the grand master never did seem to sleep. However, this was sufficiently important for him to be contacted directly at this hour. The potential fallout if this issue was not handled correctly could end up being severe.

A brief and unpleasant conversation later, Maxwell then called a clean-up team which he directed to the location in the marina. He needed the houseboat cleaned out, burned and sunk before sunrise.

Finally, he dialled the number of a mobile phone registered in France. A couple of seconds later, the phone rang inside a campervan near a small town in the south of the country. He informed the person on the other end of the line of the change of circumstance and delivered a quick broadside of instructions to speed things up and ensure that everyone was working flat out from now on. With only a few days left until the summer solstice, time was of the essence. Finally, Maxwell announced that he would be visiting the dig site in person very shortly.

After he had disconnected the call, he pondered possibly paying a visit to the latest 'Lilith' before heading off to France. After all, he had himself played a role in acquiring her by supplying Antoine with the intravenous midazolam that had been used to induce her short-term memory loss. Contained inside a jet injector the size of a pen, it had allowed Antoine to pacify her at a time and place of his choosing, and it ensured that she would have no memory of the event afterwards. As long as she remained drugged up the way she had been so far, she would present no further problems until the ceremony.

Deciding against paying her a personal visit, he instead logged into the encrypted feed from the CCTV system that was monitoring her twenty-four-seven. Gazing intently at his PC monitor, he leaned forward to get a better look at the solitary figure currently lying on the bed in the medieval holding cell. She was pretty. It was a shame, really, because very soon she would be dead.

★ ★ ★

Neither Andrew nor Fiona could have prepared themselves for what they saw. The small compartment at the front of the houseboat was only about two metres wide and about one metre deep. The red light that was mounted in the low ceiling illuminated what appeared to be a small stone altar, and placed on top of it was a roughly fifty-centimetre-tall metal sculpture of a horned creature sitting cross-legged with one hand held out to the right indicating up, and the other hand held out to the left indicating down. It had the body of a hermaphrodite, its face was that of a goat, and on its forehead was an inverted pentagram.

'Baphomet,' whispered Fiona breathlessly, her voice trembling as her hands instinctively found their way up to her mouth.

'Bloody hell,' said Andrew quietly. 'We were right all along. Antoine was deep into some seriously occult beliefs.'

The sculpture was a dark greenish brown and looked like it had been made from bronze a very long time ago. The pentagram on its forehead was significantly lighter in colour and appeared more polished, giving the impression of it having been touched often, possibly as part of some sort of ritual. The whole wall behind it was covered with a shiny silvery wallpaper and from a small hook hung an inverted crucifix. On the two walls on either side of the small altar compartment was a metal gilded *fleur-de-lis*, the stylised image of a lily often associated with French royalty.

'Fleur-de-lis,' said Fiona slowly as a train of thought developed in her mind. 'French lilies. Lilith.'

'Yes,' said Andrew, inspecting the two metal ornaments. 'This can't be a coincidence.'

'And the inverted cross,' said Fiona, shuddering as she thought of Friar Cormac and the inverted crucifix she had seen in his home a couple of days earlier. 'I suddenly can't help but think of Cormac.'

'Same here,' said Andrew. 'I know this isn't easy for you to contemplate, but is there any way at all that Cormac could be implicated in any of this?'

'I can't believe that,' she replied, shaking her head. 'I just can't. He has known us since we were small children. If he is involved, then I don't know who or what to trust anymore.'

'All right,' said Andrew, getting out his phone and taking several pictures of the altar compartment. 'I think we have seen enough of this. Let's move on. I want to have a look at Antoine's desk.'

He closed the doors to the altar and the two of them returned to the houseboat's main room. The sturdy wooden desk next to one of the bookcases was made from mahogany, and it had a dark green leather top with studs around the entire circumference. On the right side was a banker's desk lamp with a green glass shade and a polished brass stand. Next to it were two stacks of old books, and lying in a pile next to them was a collection of maps.

Andrew leafed through the maps while Fiona picked up each of the books and inspected them one by one.

'Paradise Lost,' observed Fiona evenly. 'No surprise there. An English translation of the ancient Jewish mystical text the Zohar. Copies of the bible in English and in Greek. A large volume containing all of the apocryphal biblical texts. Sticky notes attached to pages with references to Lucifer. Several other books on the occult. And a couple more on the Templars. It seems like he might have been researching something to do with Baphomet and Lucifer.'

'All of these maps cover a small area in the south of France,' said Andrew. 'Just outside a town called Roquefort-sur-Garonne. Some of them seem to be copies of very old maps. We need to take all of this stuff with us. We don't have time to study it all right now.'

'I will see if I can find us a bag,' said Fiona and walked to the kitchen island where she began rummaging through cupboards and drawers.

As she did so, Andrew opened a small wooden chest slightly larger than a cigar case that was sitting on the desk next to the banker's lamp. It was exquisite craftsmanship, and neatly inlaid into the lid was a shiny brass fleur-de-lis.

'Well, have a look at this,' he said, looking inside just as Fiona returned with a large sturdy holdall made from black polyester fabric and sealable with a zip and large Velcro patches.

'Multiple IDs, passports, driver's licenses,' said Andrew. 'Some of them French. Some English. Seems Antoine really was an international man of mystery.'

'I knew it,' said Fiona.

'Let's grab all of it,' said Andrew, shutting the chest's lid and shoving it in the holdall. 'Now, let's have a look at this computer.'

The laptop was flipped open, and when Andrew tapped the space bar the screen instantly came to life, which meant that the laptop had been in sleep mode. However, it immediately produced a prompt on the screen with an input box requesting a password.

'Shit,' said Andrew. 'I was hoping we would get lucky.'

'See if "Lilith" does the trick,' said Fiona.

Andrew typed in the name and hit the enter key, but it turned out to be invalid.

'How about "Baphomet" instead?' she said.

'Nope,' said Andrew after typing in it.

'What about the name "Sofia"?' said Fiona.

Andrew looked at her quizzically, but then shrugged and typed in the name. When he hit the enter key, the screen immediately revealed the computer's desktop image, which was a photo of what looked like a medieval castle in a landscape of rolling forested hills.

'Well done,' he said, sounding impressed. 'What would I do without you and your eidetic memory? Anyway - let's see what we have here.'

He opened a file manager and selected the Documents folder. Inside were reams of documents, which according to the meta-information, had been written by Antoine himself. They were more akin to scholarly research pieces than anything else.

'Wow,' said Fiona. 'They almost look like dissertations. But there are dozens of them.'

'He was busy boy,' said Andrew. 'I wonder who commissioned all of this work. Or perhaps he was doing this on his own initiative.'

'I very much doubt that,' said Fiona. 'Anyway, let's just get out of here. This place gives me the creeps. We can look at all of this stuff later after we get home. We *can* go home, right?'

'Yes, we probably can,' replied Andrew. 'Now that Strickland has got the police off our backs, we should be safe to head back to the house.'

They did a quick sweep of the houseboat but found nothing else of interest, so they packed up everything they had discovered and exited the boat. They then made their way quietly back across the gangway to the floating pier and exited the marina.

★ ★ ★

Fabrice Benoit opened the door of the large and comfortable campervan that had been his temporary home for the past several weeks. It was a far cry from the elegant and high-ceilinged apartment in the 16th arrondissement of Paris where he had lived since his teaching days.

Benoit was barrel-chested, built like a tank, and still strong as an ox despite his age of 57. He had short but thick tousled dark hair with a bit of greying at the temples, and he sported a neatly-trimmed short dark beard. The skin on his handsome face was olive-toned, and he had a distinctive slightly aquiline nose, which together with his genteel accent gave him an air of aristocracy, which he never failed to exploit whenever possible. He was wearing a cream-coloured shirt with the three top buttons undone, and as always his sleeves were rolled up, exposing his log-like lower arms and large hands. On his legs, he wore dark beige trousers and black wellingtons.

Benoit had never been shy to admit that he had always been the consummate ladies' man. He had never married, but not for lack of potential candidates. He simply preferred the freedom of being an eternal bachelor, and he had acquired a reputation for being 'handsy' with his female assistants. However, at this point in his life, he was too much of an old dog to be learning new politically correct tricks. If they didn't like it, they could just quit. So far, the latest incarnation in the form of a 28-year-old brunette named Gabrielle had put up with what he merely considered compliments.

He had always regarded himself as a bit of a maverick and a rogue, and that was also how he had been viewed by most of his peers in academia before he turned to private enterprise. As far as he was concerned, there was nothing wrong with taking a shortcut to get to where he wanted to go, even if that had landed him in trouble on several occasions. Most notably, he had been dogged by persistent allegations of fraud and plagiarism after his doctorate thesis in archaeology was accused of presenting himself as having discovered new types of artefacts that were already known to archaeology. There had also been the unfortunate incident of him passing off a fake cuneiform tablet as genuine and attempting to sell it to a Paris dealer. In the end, through a series of overly ambitious decisions, he had ended up with an unrecoverable reputation, after which he had entered into private business. A couple of decades ago after a number of lean years, he had hit the jackpot when he had been contacted out of the blue by a certain English aristocrat by the name of Cyril Montague, and he had been working for the family on a generous retainer ever since. When Cyril had died, the retainer had continued and the project had been taken over by Cyril's son Christopher who had inherited both the family business and his father's penchant for the occult. Whether there was any truth to what the Montagues seemed to believe about the various artefacts Benoit had been tasked with recovering was immaterial to him. He fancied himself a treasure hunter. A Parisian Indiana Jones. And he was enjoying life and was perfectly happy to keep his thoughts to himself and continue to be paid handsomely for his services.

Over the course of the past many years, they had carried out several different digs at both this and a handful of other castles in the Languedoc, but they had always come up empty-handed. However, with Christopher Haywood now at the helm their efforts seemed to have become significantly more focused, especially after the recruitment of two of Benoit's countrymen who apparently had some sort of distant personal connection to this particular château.

Looking out at the castle's inner courtyard, Benoit winced at the weather, as he had done several times over the past week. Yet another day of unseasonable rain during what ought to have been a dry and balmy late June. The sun was about to slip beneath the horizon, and the darkness was closing in rapidly because of the heavy cloud cover. However, that would make no difference now that the excavations had moved from the grounds near one of the towers to instead take place inside the chapel.

He placed the lit cigar in his mouth, inhaled a lungful of acrid but gratifying smoke and then blew it out into the evening air where it was immediately peppered with dozens of large raindrops and carried off by the wind. Reaching over to a console table that sat along the wall next to the campervan's door, he picked up a large wineglass full of local red wine and downed half of it in one gulp. This was one of the benefits of working on home turf as opposed to in one of those godforsaken countries in the Middle East where alcohol was not only frowned-upon but outright illegal. He still remembered his first archaeological jaunt to eastern Libya, where his assistant at the time had arrived in his tent beaming from ear to ear at having found him a bottle of non-alcoholic red wine. Needless to say, she had been on the first flight back to France the next morning.

'*Magnifique!*', he mumbled to himself in a baritone voice, smacking his lips and wiping his mouth with the back of his hand.

Replacing the wineglass on the console table, he folded up his shirt collar, took his light beige Panama hat off the coat stand next to the door and placed it on his head. Then he stepped out of the campervan, closed the door behind him and began jogging across the neat but soggy grounds of the castle's inner courtyard. Ahead of him was the open door to the chapel, and the light was spilling out from the large pole-mounted floodlights that had been set up inside the medieval building. Off to his right about fifty metres away was a veritable swimming pool where their previous efforts had been concentrated. Large piles of soaked brown soil lay next to the excavation pit where they had spent almost a week before realising that what they had found was not the entrance to a hidden crypt but simply the foundations of a much earlier defensive structure.

When he was almost at the chapel entrance, a brilliant streak of horizontal white lightning ripped across the sky in an instant. Less than a second later, there was an ear-splitting crack as the soundwaves from the air molecules that had been turned into white-hot plasma slammed into the courtyard. Benoit could feel the energy of the thunder in his chest as it hit him, and he felt a rush of exhilaration at the power that was on display, and a natural high from the instinctive realisation of the danger it brought with it. It felt as if the gods were angry.

It must be a sign, he mused to himself with a grin.

He entered the chapel, took off his hat and slapped it on his thigh to get the water off. Then he ran his fingers through his thick mop of hair. Seeing him enter, Gabrielle, who had blond hair and was wearing a khaki shirt and a black skirt, immediately approached him to take the hat. She smiled obsequiously at him, and he gave her a pat on her *derrière*.

Benoit strode purposefully up the centre aisle of the chapel towards the altar, where two of his crew were waiting for him. They had finished drilling the series of holes in a neat line across the several-tonnes heavy marble altar in preparation for cracking it open. Ultrasound scans had revealed that it was hollow, and Benoit had instructed his workers to break it open carefully. Not because he wanted to limit the damage to the centuries-old altar, but because he was concerned about potentially damaging what he hoped would be inside.

At his signal, the workers hacked out the marble around a section of holes on the altar's side, and then they placed a large metal wedge in the gap. One of the workers then took a heavy-looking sledgehammer and held it with both hands. Drawing it back along his side, he then swung it forcefully forward. When the hammerhead connected with the wedge, the altar immediately split in two with a dry crack. Soon there were two more workers attaching straps to the two halves and dragging them away from each other amid a loud grinding noise.

As the two sections separated, a small wooden chest fell out onto the floor and Benoit immediately rushed to it and fell to his knees. It looked very old, but it was an impressive piece of craftsmanship nonetheless. He opened the lid and looked inside to see a handful of very large, thick gold coins.

'*Merde!*' he said with a frown.

This was a disappointment. Having discovered that the altar was hollow, he had hoped to get lucky and discover the artefact. However, that was not to be. There would have been a time when finding gold coins would have been a source of excitement, but not this time. Benoit was now looking for something very different. Something that would trigger a bonus which would make this tiny haul look like charity. He tossed the coins back into the chest and rose. Then he spun on his heels and headed towards the exit to return to his campervan and his wine. He was almost at the door when one of his workers called out to him.

'Monsieur Benoit!' he said. 'Look at this.'

Benoit stopped and turned around to see Maurice resting on one knee on the spot where the altar had stood. He was holding the sledgehammer in his right hand just below the hammerhead, and his other hand was placed flat with its palm down onto the marble floor. Lowering the sledgehammer, Maurice gently tapped the marble next to his knee, and it produced an unmistakable sound. There was no doubt in Benoit's mind. There was a hidden cavity underneath the floor, and it was clear that the altar had been protecting it ever since the chapel's construction several centuries earlier. He walked back to stand next to where the altar had been, his hands on his hips and a wide grin slowly spreading across his face.

'*Cassez-la!*' he said. 'Break it.'

Thirteen

Just over an hour after leaving the marina, Andrew and Fiona were back in their living room in Hampstead. Andrew had spread all the different maps taken from Antoine's houseboat out onto the floor, and he was busy studying them when Fiona suddenly sat up in the sofa.

'Oh wow. Look at this,' she said, lifting a tome from the pile of books she had taken from Antoine's desk, holding it up to show Andrew. 'This is a copy of the famous Grand Grimoire, also known as The Red Dragon Grimoire.'

'I am sorry, what?' said Andrew, looking perplexed. 'What's a grimoire?'

'It is basically a collection of magic spells or incantations,' said Fiona. 'You know – if you believe in that sort of thing. This one is heavily annotated.'

'Mm-hmm,' said Andrew sceptically with one eyebrow raised. 'Where and when did something like that supposedly originate?'

'Its original provenance is a bit murky,' continued Fiona. 'The people who believe in this type of mystical stuff would tell you that it was written in the 15th century, but that it was based on what is known as the Key of Solomon.'

'You mean Solomon from the Bible?' asked Andrew.

'Yes,' replied Fiona. 'The Solomon who was the son of King David. Solomon the King of Israel who built the first temple on the Temple Mount in Jerusalem. He was supposedly also a great magus who had learnt his craft from Persian Zoroastrian mystics and magi.'

'Ok, so Antoine was reading the works of ancient magi,' said Andrew. 'But for what purpose?'

'Well,' replied Fiona, her forehead creasing. 'That's where things get a bit bizarre. This grimoire supposedly contains incantations and very detailed descriptions of items required to perform certain summoning rituals. They typically involve some sort of sacrifice. And some of them are supposedly able to summon demons. Even Lucifer himself.'

Andrew regarded Fiona for a long moment without much in the way of a facial expression.

'Please tell me you don't believe in any of this hocus-pocus,' he said flatly. 'It is ancient mysticism and superstition that was invented by illiterate goat herders in Mesopotamia at least two thousand years ago.'

'I know,' said Fiona, holding up her hands placatingly. 'I don't personally believe in it, but it doesn't really matter what you or I believe. There are plenty of people out there who take this stuff extremely seriously and who would read these texts as literal instructions on how to summon Lucifer. When you think about it, it isn't much different from when the Catholic Church performs the Eucharist for its faithful. As far as they are concerned, after the bread and wine have been consecrated, they are literally eating the flesh of Jesus Christ and drinking his blood. It's pretty macabre, really, and not unlike other rituals that most people would call pagan and primitive. And when they pray, they fully believe that someone is listening to the carefully worded address, right? But saying scripted prayers is just another form of uttering incantations.'

'I guess so, when you put it like that,' shrugged Andrew. 'Anyway – getting back to the real world here. What does that mean for us right now?'

Well,' said Fiona, placing the grimoire flat on the coffee table and carefully leafing through it. 'I guess what it means is that Antoine and his accomplices, whoever they are, are working towards performing some sort of ritual.'

Fiona suddenly stopped dead in her tracks and looked up at Andrew again.

'Oh shit,' she breathed. 'What if those rituals involve Caitlin?'

'Let's just take it easy now,' said Andrew, doing his best to come across as calm as possible. 'We don't know any of that for sure.'

'I know,' said Fiona, 'but…'

'Listen,' Andrew interrupted. 'It is important that we don't lose our heads here. We've got a lot of material we need to go through. What else in that pile of yours?'

Fiona reached for another book and picked it up, studying it for a few seconds.

'The Zohar,' she said, 'Very well known. It is regarded as the cornerstone of the ancient Jewish mystical text called the Kabbalah. They deal with the essence of what goes on in the divine realms and how they relate to the mortal realms. They were created as a way to interpret the deeper meaning of the Hebrew Bible.'

'Sounds heavy,' said Andrew. 'I suppose Antoine was studying this because it connects to the Old Testament and the whole story about Adam and Lilith.'

'Yes, most likely,' said Fiona. 'I have discovered that the Zohar actually deals with Lilith in some detail.'

Fiona put the book down and shifted a few more volumes from one side of the coffee table to the other.

'Take a look at this,' she said, holding up a large colour print of a familiar oil painting. 'Pandemonium, by John Martin. It looks like Antoine was really fascinated by that painting. And have a look here. This is quite a famous painting of Saint Peter.'

She held up another similarly-sized print of an oil painting depicting an old man with a full white beard and a white robe with three small black crucifixes on the collar. He was gazing upwards and to the side with a pious look on his face. In one hand he was holding a large black metal key, and in the other was what appeared to be a similar key but made of gold.

'It was painted by Peter Paul Rubens in the early 17th century,' she continued. 'He is holding the so-called Keys of Heaven. One for Heaven itself, and one for the Kingdom of Heaven, which symbolises the church's authority here on Earth.'

'Right,' said Andrew as he studied the painting. 'Not to be too much of a conspiracy theorist here, but what else could that painting symbolise? What does that motif remind you of?'

Fiona moved it out to one side so that both she and Andrew could see it properly.

'I don't know,' she said. 'What are you seeing?'

'Look closely,' he said. 'One gold key pointing up and one black key pointing down. Heaven and Hell. I think the implications here are pretty obvious. The gold key opens the gates of heaven. The black key opens the gates of hell. Notice the similarities between this painting and the image of Baphomet.'

'Holy crap,' exclaimed Fiona. 'I must have looked at this picture dozens of times and that never even occurred to me before. One hand pointing is up, and one hand is pointing down. It just goes to show what happens if you are conditioned to think about things in a certain way. You rarely manage to look at something with fresh eyes again.'

'Perhaps Antoine was looking for some connection between Saint Peter and Baphomet,' said Andrew. 'As strange and esoteric as that might seem. Remember, there was an inverted crucifix behind the statue of Baphomet on his houseboat.'

'You might be on to something here' said Fiona, scratching the side of her head. 'Think about it. Saint Peter, who was actually called Simon and who supposedly worked as a fisherman on the Sea of Galilee before becoming the most important follower of Jesus, was in effect the first pope of the Christian Church. And his crucifixion upside-down in Rome in 64 AD at the hands of Emperor Nero, who by the way blamed the fire of Rome in July of that year on the Jews, marks perhaps the most impactful martyrdom in history. After all, they literally built Saint Peter's Basilica in Rome on the very spot where the crucifixion took place, and Saint Peter's remains are supposedly buried inside the basilica itself. Anyway, this dichotomy between heaven and hell is mirrored in the references to the concept of balance in the depictions of Baphomet. And if you are right, then Antoine could have believed that somehow Saint Peter holds the keys to both sides of the equation. Perhaps he believed that somehow Saint Peter held the literal key to the gates of hell.'

'Maybe,' said Andrew. 'It's impossible to say. It seems to me like Antoine was all over the place in his research. I am not sure I can make head or tail of it.'

'I agree,' said Fiona. 'But I do think we need to remain extremely open-minded to make any sense of all this. However, what is clear to me is that Antoine and whoever he was working with took this whole thing very seriously.'

'No doubt,' said Andrew. 'Anyway, take a look at some of these maps here.'

He walked over and knelt next to one that he had placed on the floor.

'This is a map of the area around Roquefort-sur-Garonne in the Languedoc,' he said and pointed. 'It is on the Garonne River in the Haute-Garonne department near the border between the two regions Midi-Pyrénées and Languedoc-Roussillon. The map next to it covers the area east of the river. It is quite hilly, and on the peak of one of the highest points is an old castle by the name of Chateau La Roche. There are several maps here of that area, including one showing the layout of the castle itself, including its walls, main structures and fortifications. And on this map, there is a circle around what looks like the chapel, which sits separate from the other buildings inside the inner walls.'

'Interesting,' said Fiona. 'I wonder why he took such an interest in that place.'

'This is where things get interesting,' said Andrew, and sat back down on the sofa in front of Antoine's laptop. 'There are several research pieces here which deal with the history of Château La Roche, with several of them touching on the Knights Templar. And another thing I discovered is that Antoine has been receiving regular updates from what seems like a team of archaeologists that are in the process of carrying out some sort of dig at that castle as we speak. They have been at it for several weeks already, and it is clear from the correspondence that Antoine was pushing them to work faster to find what they are looking for. It is almost as if there is a deadline.'

'Let me see,' said Fiona, sitting down next to him.

He pushed the laptop sideways so that it was now in front of Fiona, and she immediately began sifting through the emails and research reports that had come in from the dig site. Before long, she seemed lost in the laptop's screen, reading, clicking and typing up notes in a new document.

'Would you like some coffee?' asked Andrew.

'Mmhmm,' replied Fiona, never taking her eyes off the screen. 'That would be nice.'

A couple of hours later, which Andrew spent familiarising himself with the area around the castle as well as the fortification's precise layout, Fiona leaned back in the sofa, closed her eyes and exhaled heavily.

'Right,' she finally said, sitting up again. 'I think I've got my head around this now. There's quite a lot here.'

'Ok. Let's hear it,' said Andrew, sitting down next to her once more with a fresh supply of coffee for the two of them.

'Here is a good picture of Chateau La Roche,' she said pointing to the laptop.

Its screen was displaying a full-screen, high-resolution image of a large castle sitting atop a massive sheer rock formation that itself seemed to have been forced up and out of the Earth to tower over the surrounding landscape. Far below it was the river and the town of Roquefort-sur-Garonne. Its roughly ten-metre-high outer walls wrapped around the entire castle and seemed to enclose a large area. Inside the walls was an outer courtyard with staples and some ancillary buildings. Then followed the inner walls which sported battlements throughout, and near the drawbridge were two round towers which looked to be at least twenty metres tall, also with battlements at the top stretching around their entire circumference. Within the inner walls was another courtyard with a large four-storey castle keep as well as several other buildings including a chapel that had been built right next to it. At the very back of the complex, the outer walls seemed to sit seamlessly on the very edge of the sheer rock, which meant that there was a terrifying-looking drop of several hundred metres from the top of the rear battlements to the rocky ground in the wooded valley below. The entire castle complex appeared to be in remarkably good condition.

'This château was apparently built in the decade leading up to around the year 1078,' said Fiona. 'As you can see, it sits at the top of this enormous rocky escarpment, so there is really only one way to approach it and that is up the steep hill straight towards the walls and the towers. Apparently, it has never been successfully attacked, despite having been besieged on several occasions throughout its long history.'

'It looks very impressive,' said Andrew. 'I can see why no one managed to take it. It is a fortress built on top of a much larger natural fortress. Does anyone live there now?'

'That's the interesting part,' said Fiona. 'The castle was built by a nobleman called Hugo Lafitte Rancourt, and he eventually passed it on to his two sons, Gerard and Arnaud. And both of those two brothers ended up becoming Templar Knights after taking part in the First Crusade and the conquest of Jerusalem in 1099.'

'Templars,' said Andrew, turning his head to face Fiona who nodded affirmatively.

'Exactly,' she said. 'And it gets better. Both brothers, who were known as *Les Frères de la Roche* or

'The Brothers of the Rock', returned from Jerusalem to their home three years later as full members of the Templar Order. They then went on to become important members of the organisation as it grew and became more powerful, and at least one of them had children who eventually inherited the castle. After the demise of the Templars in the early 14th century, it fell into disrepair and stood abandoned until it was sold in the mid-19th century by descendants of the Rancourt family. The buyer was another French noble family from Paris who restored it, and it then served as that family's Languedoc retreat until it was acquired 18 years ago by a French registered real estate company called Montague REIT S.à r.l.'

'Montague?' said Andrew. 'As in, Montague Solicitors? And what do REIT and S.à r.l. mean?'

'A REIT is a real estate investment trust,' replied Fiona, 'and S.à r.l. is just short for *société à responsabilité limitée*. It's the French version of a limited liability company, or what we call an LLP. It basically means that if you operate a company like that, and you do something really dangerous or stupid or both which then ends up becoming really expensive, then the creditors can come after the company, but they can't come after you the owner or your personal assets.'

'I see,' said Andrew.

'And with regards to the name Montague,' continued Fiona, 'it turns out that the Montague REIT is indeed fully owned by Montague Solicitors. It was set up 23 years ago by Cyril Montague, who is now dead. He was the father of the current CEO, Christopher Haywood Montague.'

'So, let me get this straight,' said Andrew. 'Aside from being an aficionado of the Templars and the occult, Antoine was researching a castle that is owned by the very law firm that employs Tristan Maxwell, who just happened to make silent contact with Antoine in the British Museum when he was visiting there with Caitlin.'

'Correct,' said Fiona with a look that told Andrew that she was thinking exactly what he was thinking.

'I have seen a lot of complex scenarios in my time,' he said, 'and I think I know a coincidence when I see one. And all of this is definitely *not* a coincidence.'

'I agree,' said Fiona. 'Antoine and Maxwell were both involved in Caitlin's disappearance, and I will bet you anything that this goes straight to the top of Montague Solicitors and Christopher Haywood.'

'It definitely all sounds very curious,' said Andrew, 'as well as really bizarre. Law firms are not usually in the business of owning and running real estate investment companies or operating archaeological dig sites.'

'That's what I thought too,' said Fiona.

'So, what is going on here?' he asked.

'Well, it turns out that Château La Roche is not the only castle that the Montague REIT has acquired,' she said. 'Since its inception, the company has bought a handful of other castles in the Languedoc region, all of which seemingly have some sort of familial connection all the way back to the Templars and the two Rancourt brothers. And by the looks of things, there have been archaeological excavations taking place at all of them soon after they were acquired.'

'Whatever is going on here, and whoever is ultimately in charge,' said Andrew, 'they clearly believe they are onto something important. Something significant enough that they are prepared to spend hundreds of millions of Pounds buying up old French castles and digging underneath them. They are obviously looking for something very specific.'

'Yes, and this is where things get creepy,' said Fiona. 'Firstly, all of the excavations have been headed up by someone named Fabrice Benoit. He used to be a well-respected professor of archaeology at the University of Toulouse who specialises in the late Middle Ages before he went rogue and was caught selling fake artefacts. Having trawled through most of Antoine's research and his correspondence with Benoit at the dig site, there is no doubt they appear to be looking for something that is related to a text called the Lucifer Codex.'

'Any idea what that might be?' asked Andrew, frowning slightly at the name.

'No,' said Fiona, 'I've never heard of it, but it sounds sinister.'

'Well, that much is clear,' said Andrew, looking ponderous. 'What isn't exactly clear is precisely how this Haywood character is involved. Is he the head of this particular snake, or is there someone above him?'

'If only we could get close to him somehow,' said Fiona. 'I tried looking him up online, but there is precious little to be found beyond his listing as the CEO of Montague Solicitors. On the one hand, he seems to be an important player in the City of London, yet on the other, he seems to live an extremely secluded life in the shadows with as little publicity as possible. He seems to do nothing in the open, always gets other people to do his bidding, and he never leaves a trail for anyone to follow.'

'You're saying you think he is untouchable?' said Andrew.

'More or less,' said Fiona dejectedly.

'No one is untouchable,' said Andrew. 'Trust me. There's always a chink in the armour somewhere. We just have to find it. But speaking of Montague, I found something at the bottom of the small wooden chest we lifted from Antoine's houseboat. Look at this.'

He gave Fiona a small metal item the size of her thumb. It was a cross with two horizontal bars, the top one slightly shorter than the next, and the bottom of it was connected to a horizontal figure of eight. It appeared to be made of silver, and it had a small loop at its top so it could be worn – presumably in a chain around the neck like a medallion or a talisman.

'Any idea what that is?' he asked as she turned it over in her hand studying it.

'As a matter of fact, I do,' she said. 'This is a symbol that dates back many centuries. It is called a brimstone symbol. In alchemy, it was used as the symbol for sulphur, also known as brimstone. I know that it has certain occult connotations, partly because hell supposedly smells of sulphur, but I am not sure what it means in this context.'

'It was lying inside this,' said Andrew, showing her a small envelope just big enough for the silver symbol to fit inside. 'And alongside it was a small handwritten note that simply read *'Resurget'*, signed with the initials 'C.H.' And the envelope itself was sealed with a red wax seal with the same initials. Does that make any sense to you?'

'I think so,' said Fiona, inspecting the envelope and the handwritten note. 'I am prepared to bet that C.H. is Christopher Haywood, and the word 'Resurget' is the future active indicative Latin word for 'He will rise again'.'

'Okay,' said Andrew hesitantly and with a dubious look on his face. 'I guess we can both guess who we are talking about here.'

'Lucifer,' nodded Fiona grimly.

'Ignoring the crackpot implications for a moment,' said Andrew. 'What this simply demonstrates is that Antoine clearly had direct contact with Haywood. So, somehow this bigshot solicitor is implicated in everything we have discovered so far.'

Fiona nodded glumly.

'I discovered one more thing,' she said weakly, turning to face Andrew and looking like she was struggling to hold it together. 'Remember that tattoo Antoine had on his wrist? L.D.M.? He said it had to do with a rowing club in France, but that was a lie – just like everything else. It is an anagram of a Latin phrase, and what it really means is *Lucifer Dominus Mundi*. Lucifer, Lord of the World. Andrew, these people are crazy.'

As she spoke a shiver ran visibly down her spine and she looked at Andrew with pleading eyes as if to ask him to say something, anything, to make it all better. He took both of her hands in his, squeezed them gently and looked straight at her.

'Fiona,' he said steadily. 'We will get her back. Ok? I promise you. We will move heaven and earth if we have to, but we're going to get her back. Do you hear me?'

She nodded attempting to be brave, but as she did so her eyes welled up and a single tear ran down her cheek.

'Ok,' she said, and sniffed. 'Just tell me what to do, and I'll do it.'

Fourteen

At Benoit's direction, Maurice had used the sledgehammer to smash the marble slabs that until a few minutes earlier had supported the weight of the altar. The slabs had cracked into large, sharp pieces when the sledgehammer had come down, and some of those pieces had disappeared down into whatever cavity was below. Maurice hauled some of the remaining larger pieces aside to reveal a gaping hole about a metre square. It was like a black rectangular portal down into a pitch-black dimension that was entirely invisible from above because of the complete absence of light down there.

Benoit ordered one of the other workers to bring over the nearest floodlight, and once it was positioned near the edge of the hole and the light was directed downward, Benoit stepped close to the edge and looked down. The powerful beam from the floodlight illuminated a circular hole beginning roughly half a metre below the chapel's flagstones and going straight down into what appeared to be some sort of crypt. The walls were made from large, neatly chiselled concave stone blocks, and it was a roughly three-metre drop to a dusty flagstone floor below.

Benoit ordered for a ladder to be brought, and he instructed Maurice to be the first to descend, carrying a powerful LED torch. Maurice dutifully began climbing down into the darkness, one careful step at a time. None of them had any idea what he might find down there, so he stepped gingerly onto the flagstone floor once he reached the bottom. He could hear from the way the sounds reverberated around him that he was in a relatively small space. Turning around slowly and letting the torchlight sweep across the interior of the small chamber he found himself in, he saw that he was at one end of it and that its walls were made from stone blocks similar to those in the access well. The chamber itself was empty except for a small doorway on the farthest wall. He called up to Benoit whose face he could just see poking out over the edge of the well. Holding his own torch in one hand, the bearded archaeologist then made his way down the ladder to join him.

The two men approached the doorway to discover that it led to a short passage to another chamber. Inside it at the far end was something that looked a lot like a sarcophagus of some sort. Benoit smiled. This was almost certainly it. He stopped at the doorway and directed Maurice to go first. He remembered very well reading about some of the ways in which the Templars had supposedly protected the locations where they had hidden some of their wealth shortly before the violent dissolution of their order about seven centuries ago, and so he decided that discretion was almost certainly the better part of valour on this occasion. As Maurice began to walk slowly and cautiously through the roughly three-metre-long passage towards the chamber beyond, Benoit used the opportunity to let his torchlight shine across the walls, first on one side of the passage and then the other. He saw nothing untoward. Then he lifted the cone of light up to the lintel above the doorway. In its centre was a small symbol chiselled into the stone. It was a cross with four arms of the same length that all splayed out slightly into two small separate parts at their ends. Benoit's heart began to beat harder and faster.

Les Templiers, he thought. *C'est vrai!*

Maurice proceeded cautiously along the passage, and when he reached the middle of it there was a sudden but protracted dry cracking sound as if something solid had split into several pieces. Maurice not only heard the noise, but he also felt the minute shift in the floor under his feet. He just had time to point his torch downward and look to see the large flagstone that covered the middle third of the floor in the passage quickly develop several cracks from its four corners towards its centre. A split second later, the flagstone fractured completely under his weight, and Maurice plummeted down into a black pit.

From Benoit's perspective, it looked dramatic, but he also thought it appeared vaguely comical as Maurice suddenly disappeared. It was as if a trapdoor under a medieval hanging gallows had suddenly been opened, and almost immediately, Maurice was gone amid a panicked wail. About another second later, the wail stopped abruptly and there was a surprisingly distant-sounding crunch. Then there was complete silence, and the light from Maurice's torch appeared to have disappeared entirely.

As the noise and the screaming ceased, there was a chorus of voices coming from above in the chapel, but Benoit ignored them and stepped cautiously into the passage, checking where he put his feet to make sure that he did not trigger another trap. He weighed significantly more than Maurice, so he just might trigger something that Maurice had not. Reaching the edge of the rectangular hole where the flagstone had recently been, Benoir leaned carefully over the edge and pointed his torchlight straight down. At the bottom of a dusty pit whose stone walls were covered in curtains of cobwebs was Maurice, although he was a grotesque version of his former self. The pit itself was around one by two metres in size – the same as the now disintegrated flagstone slab that had covered it, and it was roughly four metres deep. Set into its base in a grid were what looked like a dozen metre-long metal spikes pointed upwards. Maurice seemed to have landed almost perfectly on his back, and his now lifeless body had been impaled by at least six of them. Some had pierced his torso and punched up through his chest, and as Benoit's torchlight swept over them, their blood-soaked tips glistened. Several other spikes had skewered his arms and legs, and one had caught him at the base of his skull and been driven up through his brain to come straight out of his open mouth, taking several teeth with it in the process.

Benoit looked disgusted and winced as he peered down into the pit.

'*Mon dieu!*' he mumbled. '*Quel spectacle répugnant!*'

Drawing back from the edge, he shook his head and tutted. Making sure to find good purchase with his hiking boots, he then leapt across the murderous pit and landed heavily on the flagstones on the other side, relieved to find solid ground under his feet. Redirecting the torchlight ahead of himself once more and into the chamber beyond, he found himself smiling at what he was seeing. There was no doubt in his mind. This was definitely a burial chamber, and he was sure that he was now looking at a sarcophagus that had laid undisturbed since the early 14th century.

He turned his head and shouted over his shoulder for the rest of the team to come down. He didn't mention Maurice. They would find out for themselves soon enough. And anyway, the sarcophagus was sure to be one of a kind, which was more than could be said for Maurice. Then he bellowed another order at them, instructing them to bring the pneumatic jackhammer.

* * *

The next morning, after a much-needed long night's sleep, Fiona opened her eyes and stretched. She turned her head to look towards Andrew's side of the bed. It was empty. He must have got up quietly and snuck out of the bedroom, keen to allow her to catch up on her sleep. At first, she thought he might have gone for an early morning run on Hampstead Heath, but then she heard the extractor fan come on in the kitchen. He was probably frying up breakfast for the two of them.

She reached over lazily and picked up her phone from the bedside table, switching it on as she brought it back to hold it in front of her face. Several emails and other messages had arrived during the night, but much of it was unsolicited spam and the rest were things that did not need any urgent attention. She was just about to replace the phone on the bedside table when it pinged again. She looked at the screen once more and saw that there was a new email from someone called Sean Taylor. At first, the name did not ring any bells, but then she suddenly remembered Maggie from Caitlin's commune having mentioned something about a man named Sean coming around and asking questions about her sister. Could this be the same person?

She swiftly sat up in the bed and opened the email. It contained only two cryptic lines of text.

Fiona. My name is Sean. I need to speak to you urgently about Caitlin. Please call the number below.

Fiona stared at the screen for a brief moment, and then she tapped the mobile number listed in his email signature. A couple of seconds later the call was connected, and almost immediately a male voice came on the line. He sounded like a relatively young man, perhaps in his early thirties.

'Hello?'

'Is this Sean?' she asked. 'This is Fiona Keane.'

'Yes it is,' said the man. 'Thank you for calling me back so quickly. Have you got a few minutes?'

'Of course,' Fiona asked hurriedly, eager to move the conversation on to her sister. 'You said that you have information about Caitlin. What do you mean? Do you know where she is?'

'I am afraid not,' said Sean, sounding as if he knew he was the bearer of bad news. 'I don't know where she is or precisely what has happened to her, but I am calling to tell you that she is just one of many.'

'What do you mean by that?' asked Fiona confused as anxiety began to rise up inside her. 'One of many?'

Sean sighed as if he was trying to think of a way to tell Fiona exactly what was on his mind.

'My name is Sean Taylor, and I am a reporter for an online magazine called the Metro Mole. You may have heard of it?'

'Sorry,' said Fiona. 'I haven't.'

'Never mind,' said Sean. 'It's not important. What matters is that I have spent a couple of years investigating the disappearances of young women in London during the past several decades, and I believe I have discovered a pattern. They are not just random, unconnected disappearances in the way that the Metropolitan Police likes to portray them. Many of those cases have disturbing similarities, and I am convinced that they are linked.'

'Linked how?' asked Fiona. 'Are you saying my sister is one of those women?'

'I am afraid so,' replied Sean. 'I can't say for absolute certain, but she shares certain unique characteristics with a dozen other women that have gone missing, particularly in terms of her looks. And all of them seemed to have taken an interest in the occult before vanishing. I would like to ask you if the name *Baphomet* rings a bell?'

A chill instantly ran down Fiona's spine. For several days now, she had felt the gnawing sensation at the back of her mind that Caitlin's disappearance was anything but benign, and that there were sinister forces at play. Sean Taylor ringing up out of the blue and confirming her suspicion now made her skin crawl, and him mentioning Baphomet was the final straw. There was simply no hiding from it anymore. Caitlin was in serious trouble.

'How did you find me?' she asked urgently, frustrated at the voice on the phone who seemed to know more about Caitlin's disappearance than she did. 'And was that you who spoke to Maggie at Caitlin's commune?'

'Yes,' said Sean. 'That was me. Someone in Caitlin's commune must have notified the police of her disappearance, and once they added her name to the Met's list of missing persons, it was obvious to me what might have happened to her. So, I went to the commune and spoke to Maggie myself, although she wasn't really of much help. I don't think she liked me very much.'

'That sounds like Maggie,' said Fiona evenly. 'I think she just doesn't like men.'

'Anyway,' continued Sean, 'from there it wasn't too difficult to track you down.'

'What is it you want?' asked Fiona, suddenly feeling suspicious that perhaps this man calling himself Sean might not be who he said he was. 'How do I know I can trust you?'

'You don't,' replied Sean flatly. 'At least not yet. But you'll have to take that chance. I might be able to help you find Caitlin. I am tired of looking into these cases and ending up reading obituaries. Sorry if that sounds blunt, but it is the truth.'

Fiona's head began to swim at the implications of what he had just said.

'Ok,' she muttered, feeling dizzy. 'What is it you think you have discovered? Can't you at least tell me something to help me understand what is going on?'

Sean sighed again, taking his time to think carefully before he spoke.

'I have uncovered something that is going to shake the foundations of London society,' he finally said. 'Sinister things that are happening right here in this city with the involvement of some very powerful people.'

'Why haven't you gone to the police then?' asked Fiona.

'Because I have found evidence that points to at least one senior police officer being directly involved in the disappearances,' replied Sean. 'It is also the reason why I can't speak openly on the phone, so we will have to meet in person.'

At that moment, a message with an attachment pinged in on a messaging app on Fiona's phone. It was from Sean's number, and the attachment was an image file. She opened it to find herself looking at a picture of a young man leaning against a graffitied brick wall and wearing a navy-blue V-neck jumper with a white t-shirt underneath. He looked like he might be in his mid-thirties. He had a friendly smile and kind eyes behind a pair of glasses with dark brown plastic frames and oval lenses that made him look somewhat bookish. His hair was brown, medium-length and neatly combed with a side parting, and he sported a short dark beard.

'Is this you?' asked Fiona.

'Yes,' replied Sean.

'Why did you send that to me?' asked Fiona.

'Because I need you to come and meet me tonight,' replied Sean. 'Do you know a restaurant called the Feng Shang Princess?'

'Sure,' said Fiona. 'It's the one on Regent's Canal, right?'

'That's the one,' replied Sean. 'About two hundred metres to the west along the canal is a footbridge. Meet me under that bridge on the north bank at half past midnight. I'll be on the footpath by the canal waiting for you.'

'Wait,' blurted Fiona. 'I want to bring a friend.'

'Ok,' said Sean after a moment's hesitation. 'Just don't be late.'

* * *

Andrew had just finished placing the steaming hot plates of runny fried eggs, cheddar cheese sausages and crispy bacon on the breakfast table in the open-plan kitchen when Fiona emerged from the bedroom. Still wearing the white silk négligée that she liked to sleep in, her face seemed as if it was under a dark cloud, and she had an unusually worried look on her face. In her hand, she was holding her phone.

'Breakfast is served,' attempted Andrew cheerfully.

'Thanks,' she said quietly, sitting down without taking her eyes off the phone.

Andrew stepped over next to her and placed a hand gently on her shoulder.

'Are you all right?' he asked, glancing down at the phone, which was showing a picture of a young bearded man wearing glasses. 'Who's that?'

Fiona explained how she had just finished her conversation with Sean, and she outlined what he had said, as far as her memory would allow. She was still feeling knocked off balance by the sudden emergence of this man, who seemed to know a lot more about Caitlin's disappearance than she did. All she wanted to do was wind the clock forward so they could go and meet him in person immediately. As she spoke, Andrew poured them both a cup of tea and sat down across from her.

'Right,' he said pensively once she had finished relaying the call to him. 'So that's who Maggie was talking about. You're not thinking about going alone, are you?'

'Not a chance,' said Fiona. 'He sounded nice enough, but for all I know he could be one of the people involved in the disappearances he says he is investigating.'

'Fine,' said Andrew. 'I have something to tell you as well.'

Fiona swallowed her mouthful and looked at him.

'Now what?' she asked apprehensively.

'I received an email from Colonel Strickland early this morning,' he replied, picking up his phone from the table. 'He has really bent over backwards to help us out this time, despite being pretty tied up in some bureaucratic back-and-forth with the Foreign Office.'

'What did he say?' asked Fiona.

'A couple of very interesting things, actually,' said Andrew. 'He told me that on the same day that Antoine's body was recovered from the Mark Lane tube station, the Met ran a DNA test on him and sent the results to the French police. They came back last night with a positive ID.'

'So, who was he?' asked Fiona, sitting up in her chair.

'His real name was Antoine de Salignac-Rancourt,' said Andrew meaningfully.

'Rancourt?' repeated Fiona, realisation suddenly blooming in her mind like a light bulb gradually having its dimmer turned up. 'Are you saying he was a descendant of Hugo Lafitte Rancourt, the Templar knight who built Château La Roche?'

'That's how it seems,' replied Andrew. 'Apparently, he was minor French royalty because of the way his family intermarried with members of the French crown over the centuries, and his family can supposedly trace its own lineage all the way back to Hugo Rancourt and his two sons, Gerard and Arnaud.'

'Wow,' said Fiona, looking gobsmacked. 'That puts a whole new spin on things. But what does that tell us, exactly?'

'Well,' said Andrew. 'It means that somehow there is a connection from Antoine through Tristan Maxwell to the Montague family and then back to the ancestral castle of Antoine's family. But I am not sure precisely what that all means.'

Fiona had her eyes closed and was resting her elbows on the table and rubbing her fingertips against her temples in a circular motion.

'This is getting really complicated now,' she finally said. 'I can't wait to speak to Sean and find out what he has uncovered.'

'It gets even more strange,' said Andrew placing his phone on the table in front of them.

'Strickland also sent this short video through to us,' he said. 'It is only about three minutes long, and it is footage from the CCTV cameras inside Saint Katherine Marina. You're not going to believe this.'

Fiona looked down at the phone but then glanced up at Andrew with an uneasy look on her face.

'Are we in it?' she asked haltingly.

'No,' replied Andrew. 'This was recorded a couple of hours after we left the houseboat. Just watch.'

He swapped to landscape mode, rotated the phone and tapped the screen, sliding it across the desk to place it directly in front of her. She leaned in close and her eyes bored into the screen as the video began to play.

The quality was less than perfect and the footage was the usual greyscale that was used in virtually all CCTV systems because it requires significantly less storage capacity to file. The perspective indicated that it was recorded by a camera at a height of roughly five metres above the quayside pointing towards the steps leading up to Saint Katherine's Way from the marina itself. In the top right corner of the screen was a date and timestamp that ticked along as the video played. The indicated time was 04.17 a.m. The marina was deserted and all the windows in the surrounding apartments were dark. After a couple of seconds, a male figure emerged at the top of the steps and began making his way down towards the marina. He was wearing light jeans and a long-sleeved white t-shirt.

As Fiona watched, she immediately thought he looked familiar somehow. Then she suddenly froze. She was looking at a ghost. It was Antoine. There was no doubt in her mind. He had the same athletic build and the same confident walk as he made his way down the steps and strode briskly along the quayside. He had the same features and the same blond hair, although it seemed shorter now and slicked back. But his face was unmistakably that of Antoine.

'What the hell?' breathed Fiona slowly as she watched, leaning in even closer to study the screen.

The footage then switched to a different angle that showed him making his way out to the end of the short floating pier and stepping down into the houseboat in front of the main entrance. Here he suddenly stopped and seemed to be inspecting the double doors to the interior. He stood up for a brief moment and seemed to look around the marina, but then he ducked down again and disappeared inside the houseboat where the lights came on behind the dark curtains.

'He was in there for about twenty minutes,' said Andrew. 'That part has been edited out. Here he is coming out again.'

Watching the screen, Fiona saw him exit the houseboat carrying a black, heavy-looking holdall in one hand and a dark messenger bag with a strap slung over his shoulder. He stepped back onto the pier and walked swiftly back to the quayside where he seemed to hurry along towards the steps up and out of the marina. After about thirty seconds, the camera was suddenly forced to automatically adjust its aperture as the houseboat suddenly burst into flames, bathing the entire marina in bright light. It was clear from the way the fire burned that it was fuelled by significant amounts of some kind of flammable liquid. Within seconds, it was fully ablaze and after less than a minute it was an inferno that would obviously be impossible to put out without a fire truck. Then the video stopped.

'What the hell did I just watch?' said Fiona, looking deeply confused. 'That was Antoine. But he is dead. I saw him lying on that platform and he was definitely dead. Right?'

'Yes. Antoine is no longer among the living,' nodded Andrew. 'According to what Strickland was able to dig up, what you saw just now was his twin brother Laurent.'

Fiona's mouth fell open, and she looked at Andrew as if half expecting him to suddenly admit that the whole thing was made up.

'Are you serious?' she finally asked.

'Absolutely,' said Andrew. 'Antoine and Laurent de Salignac-Rancourt are identical twins. And whatever dark business Antoine was involved in, Laurent no doubt was too.'

'Oh shit,' said Fiona and placed her head in her hands. 'I just had a terrible thought.'

'What?' asked Andrew.

'What if Caitlin was dating both brothers without realising it?' she said, sounding sickened. 'What if they were playing her like that?'

Andrew winced and pressed his lips together in silent acknowledgement that she probably had a point.

'We don't know that,' he said hurriedly. 'What's important is that this Laurent character is still out there, and he realises that someone is on to them. He might even have found out that Antoine is dead. As we have already discovered, these people are connected.'

'I really don't know what to say,' mumbled Fiona whilst rubbing her eyes and shaking her head slowly. 'What are we going to do with this?'

'We are going to remain calm and keep moving forward the way we have been,' replied Andrew. 'This essentially changes nothing, except to confirm that we are dealing with some sort of conspiracy among a large group of people, some of whom wield significant power. So, we need to remain cautious, but we can't do anything now other than proceed with our meeting with your chap, Sean. He is still the best lead we have.'

'Ok,' said Fiona, sighing and nodding slowly. 'I guess you're right.'

'Your breakfast is getting cold,' said Andrew, pointing to her plate with his fork. 'Come on. Tuck in. I have a feeling you're going to need it today.'

Fifteen

When the young red-haired woman opened her eyes again, she felt much better than the last time she had woken up. But she was still inside the cell, and it had not been a nightmare. A shiver ran through her, and not just because the cell was somewhat chilly. She was a prisoner, and she had no idea where she was or why she was there.

She sat up and then quickly got to her feet. She was less unsteady than the last time she had been awake, and turning her head towards the small glass brick in the wall she realised that the light coming in seemed dull and grey as if it might be raining outside. But it was definitely daytime, so either she had fallen asleep at sunrise and now woken up later in the day, or she had passed out at sunset the night before and had slept for around eighteen hours, in which case it might now be around noon. There was no way of knowing.

She looked around the cell again and discovered that the lid on the small wooden box had been shut, and she was sure that she had left it open when she had eaten the bread and the apple. She walked over and opened it to find another piece of bread and another apple. Clearly, someone had been inside the cell, leaving her a bit more food. She picked up the jug of water and discovered that it too had been refilled. She sniffed it suspiciously. She was sure that there was a sedative in that water, but she had to drink something, so she had no choice.

She glanced back towards the bed and spotted something odd. The stonework directly beneath the glass brick seemed darker than the surrounding stone. As she walked over to it, she realised that somehow the rain from outside was collecting on the other side of the glass brick, seeping through underneath it and seemingly soaking the porous masonry.

She immediately had an idea. She picked up a small piece of straw from the bed and poked it into a tiny crevice just under the glass brick. Within less than ten seconds, a single bead of water had formed and began travelling slowly along the gently sloping piece of straw. She hurried over to the bench, picked up the metal beaker and returned to the glass brick just in time to catch the first drop of water. She placed the beaker on the floor below the brick and waited. Another bead soon formed, travelled the length of the straw, and then dropped into the beaker with a satisfying plop. She stood back to admire her handiwork. At this rate, the beaker would soon have enough water for a small mouthful, as long as it kept raining.

As she stood there, her eye suddenly caught a small pattern on some of the stone blocks that made up the wall to her left. She approached them and realised that they were not patterns, but tiny letters that had been scratched into the stonework. They were names. Female names. And there were at least twenty or thirty of them. A chill ran down her spine. Were these the names of other women like her? Women that had been held here against their will? She was sure that this cell had only ever held one woman at the time, which meant that some of these names might go back years or perhaps even much longer. The first name on the list was Lucy, and there was a tiny capital 'D' underneath it. She read through all the names from top to bottom and nearly fainted when she reached the last one. It read 'Caitlin'.

Feeling nauseous and on the verge of vomiting, she staggered to the bed and lowered herself onto it again. And then she suddenly remembered. *She* was Caitlin, and she had used a small metal nail that she had found on the floor to write her own name at the bottom of the long list of other names etched into the masonry by the other women who had been held prisoner here. Women who had never met each other, but who had somehow still managed to reach out to each other and form a bond across time. But where were all those women now? What had happened to them? And what would happen to her? She glanced at the metal jug, and then returned her gaze to the beaker.

Plop.

She was not going to drink any more water from the jug. And when whoever held her captive here returned with more food and water, she was going to pretend to be sedated out by the drugs and then try to make a run for it. It was her only chance.

★   ★   ★

The rain had begun around noon, and as the afternoon wore on, it had intensified. Andrew and Fiona had spent most of the day going over the material they had grabbed from the houseboat. Andrew studied the layout of the Château La Roche, and he had also found topographical maps of the area that highlighted just what an unassailable location the castle had been built on. Without yet knowing precisely what the French archaeologist Fabrice Benoit was looking for there, a plan was nevertheless slowly beginning to form in Andrew's mind.

'I've got it,' said Fiona, stabbing with her finger at her laptop screen. 'I've just spent the past hour accessing publicly available genealogy information about French nobility. I have managed to verify that Antoine and his twin brother Laurent are actually distant descendants of the templar knight Hugo Lafitte Rancourt. To be precise, their direct ancestor was Hugo's eldest son Gerard who eventually inherited Château La Roche when Hugo died. And it seems that both Gerard and his younger brother Arnaud continued to live there after they had become Knights Templar and had returned from the Holy Land. However, it is not clear how they managed to evade the Templar purge carried out by King Philip IV. In fact, I still haven't found any records of precisely when or how they died or where they were eventually laid to rest.'

'Either way,' said Andrew. 'If Antoine and Laurent are really descendants of Templars, how did they become involved with Christopher Haywood or Christopher Montague or whatever he calls himself?'

'Well, they clearly appear to be looking for something together,' said Fiona, 'and I think I have a theory about this.'

'Ok,' said Andrew. 'Let's hear it.'

'Well, I don't know exactly what it is,' said Fiona, 'but I am guessing it is something that was hidden by the two Templar brothers somewhere in their ancestral castle back in the 14th century. Something really important that Haywood is now trying to find with the help of the twins. And I have discovered something fascinating about that. You see, the Montague family and the Rancourt family turn out to be intimately connected.'

'Really?' said Andrew. 'How?'

'We already know that Haywood's father was Cyril Montague,' said Fiona. 'But I have discovered that Haywood's mother was a woman from French nobility by the name of Genevieve de Salignac-Rancourt.'

'You're kidding,' said Andrew incredulously. 'The terrible twins Antoine and Laurent are actually related to Christopher Haywood?'

'Yes,' replied Fiona. 'Antoine and Laurent are Haywood's much younger cousins. They are the sons of their mother Genevieve's sister, which makes Haywood their uncle.'

'Crikey,' said Andrew, scratching the back of his neck. 'It is all starting to coalesce. They are working together to find something that Haywood wants and that used to belong to Antoine and Laurent's ancestors.'

'Correct,' said Fiona. 'This is pure speculation on my part, but given how many resources the Montagues have put into this search, buying French castles left and right, I wouldn't be surprised if it turned out that Cyril only married Genevieve in order to get his hands on her ancestral castle in the Languedoc. Either way, Cyril seems to have died before he could narrow down the search and begin excavating, but Haywood has now taken over his father's mantle and is putting all of his efforts into Château La Roche with the help of this Fabrice Benoit character.'

'Wow,' said Andrew, raising his eyebrows. 'But I guess the question remains. What exactly are they searching for, and what do they want with it? And how does Caitlin fit into all of this?'

'Like you said earlier,' replied Fiona. 'All we can do is try to get answers from Sean. He is the only real lead we have at this point.'

'Right,' said Andrew and checked his wristwatch. 'How about some Chinese food?'

Fiona looked at him with a puzzled expression and her head tilted slightly to one side.

'Chinese?' she asked before it dawned on her what he meant.

'Oh,' she said. 'You want to have dinner at the Feng Shang restaurant on the canal?'

'Yes,' said Andrew. 'I figured we could kill a few hours there and go straight on to meet Sean.'

'Good idea,' said Fiona. 'The sooner the better.'

★   ★   ★

Andrew drove the two of them to Saint Mark's Square next to the church by the same name, and it was almost 9 p.m. by the time they parked up. Fiona had booked a table for them at Feng Shang for nine o'clock, so they stepped out of the car and Andrew opened up a large umbrella to shield them from the rain. They then made their way swiftly across Prince Albert Road to the pavement on the other side. There they continued for a short distance until they reached a low metal gate from where a wooden gangway covered by a green awning led across to the floating restaurant. It looked about as Chinese as anything could get. It was a three-tiered structure with a dark tiled pagoda roof, bright red and yellow painted exterior walls and dozens of large paper lanterns which cast the entire scene in a warm orange light. The whole thing looked inviting and quite unique from anything else in London, except perhaps for China Town in Soho. The canal on which the Feng Shang floated was about four metres below the level of Prince Albert Road and down a steep embankment, so the gangway extended out from the pavement and connected with the restaurant's second level.

Andrew and Fiona walked across and entered the reception area, where a smiling young Chinese lady who introduced herself as Mei checked their booking and ushered them politely towards their small circular table in the far corner on the second level. Space was clearly at a premium but the décor seemed authentic and characterful, and the leather chairs were perfectly comfortable, although they were looking well-worn.

This was obviously a busy place that benefitted from the proximity to central London and also the London Zoo located nearby at the northern end of Regent's Park.

A waiter came along swiftly and took their drinks orders, and then they spent the next twenty minutes pouring over the very extensive menu whilst trying to decide what to order. In the end, they asked for dumplings as a starter and Andrew then went for crispy duck with rice whilst Fiona ordered the crab soup. Outside, the rain was coming down relentlessly. If anything, it seemed to become heavier as darkness fell. They deliberately made sure to spin everything out in order to make their dinner last as long as possible. It was still several hours before they were due to meet Sean, so they spent the time talking over everything that had happened and ordering several more rounds of small dishes which they picked at. Fiona was beginning to sense a brewing frustration with their slow pace on the part of the staff, and there was a palpable sense of relief from Mei when they finally asked for the bill having hogged their table for an unusually long period of time whilst ordering a decent amount of food but only a very modest amount of high-margin alcoholic drinks. It was ten minutes past midnight by the time the two of them left the restaurant. They were the final guests to disembark the floating restaurant that evening. Mei bid them farewell and said she hoped to see them again, although she did not sound like she meant it.

The evening had begun relatively warm, but with the ceaseless downpour of cold rain, the temperature had now dropped appreciably. They made their way back across the gangway to the pavement and walked west along Prince Albert Road until they came to a narrow path that led down the embankment to the footpath next to the canal. The steps were slippery in the rain, and Fiona held on to Andrew's arm to steady herself.

Safely down on the path, they looked first left and then right along the canal, but all they could see was the dark rippling water and tall curtains of rain that became briefly lit up as they passed under the streetlights erected at regular intervals along the path.

'The bridge is only a few minutes this way,' said Andrew, pointing west with one hand whilst holding the umbrella with the other. 'I think I can see it already.'

'Is he there?' asked Fiona, attempting to peer through the deluge.

'I can't tell from here,' replied Andrew. 'I can't actually see anyone. Come on. Let's get over there.'

It was now twenty-five minutes past midnight, and as they peered out from under their umbrella, it was clear that there was no sign of Sean yet. Andrew looked at his wristwatch.

'We're a bit early,' he said over the noise from what was now a torrential downpour hammering onto the path and the trees and bushes lining the canal, as well as peppering the surface of the water and making it seem like it was boiling. 'Let's just get under the bridge. We will be able to see him coming.'

They hurried under the tall metal footbridge, and Andrew lowered the umbrella in front of him and shook it to get rid of the rainwater. Suddenly Fiona shrieked loudly, and in an instant, Andrew instinctively dropped the umbrella and spun around, hand inside his jacket and gripping his Glock 17. As he turned and pulled out the weapon, he saw Fiona standing with both hands covering her mouth. She looked terrified, and her eyes were wide-open and locked onto something overhead. Finally, Andrew also spotted it.

Almost directly above them and next to the concrete wall under the bridge that also served as part of its foundation, hung the body of a man. Having been huddled under the large umbrella as they approached the bridge, they had both completely failed to see it hanging up there in the darkness. As soon as he saw it, Andrew knew he was looking at a corpse.

The dead man had been secured to a metal rafter under the bridge and suspended head down with his feet tied together. His arms were splayed out horizontally to each side, causing the body to take on the appearance of an inverted cross. He had a short beard but he looked quite young, although it was difficult to tell because of the obvious head trauma he had suffered. His face was covered in blood and dirt, and his tongue was sticking partway out of his half-open mouth. A large patch of blood had soaked his jacket around the chest area where Andrew spotted two small bullet holes. He lowered his gun and flicked the safety back on as Fiona whimpered staring up at the grizzly sight above them.

'It's Sean,' she said on the verge of tears and with a trembling voice. 'It's definitely him.'

'Yes,' said Andrew. 'I think you're right.'

He put his pistol back in the holster under his left arm and stepped closer.

'I am sure he was arranged like this on purpose,' said Andrew.

'The cross of Saint Peter,' whispered Fiona.

'Yes,' said Andrew. 'Someone was keen to send a message here. Something along the lines of 'Don't mess with us.'.'

He took another couple of steps forward and stood as close to the corpse as he could without climbing over the low fence and trying to scale the concrete wall. Sean's dead body was swaying gently in the light breeze, his dead eyes staring straight ahead and across the canal. Andrew reached up and was only just able to reach his right hand. He gripped it for a few seconds and then let go.

'Still not cold,' he said. 'I am guessing he hasn't been dead for much more than twenty minutes. Thirty at the most.'

'You mean this was done to him while we were in the restaurant?' asked Fiona, looking horrified.

'Without a doubt,' replied Andrew. 'The question is whether it happened here, or whether he was killed somewhere else and brought here to be put on display. I am leaning towards the former.'

'But if he was killed here,' said Fiona, sounding increasingly nervous, 'then that means that the killer knew Sean was coming to this precise spot tonight. And that means he knows who Sean was meeting.'

They both looked around, wondering if they were being watched. The answer came within less than a second. Two loud cracks rang out from the top of the embankment near the bridge, followed by the almost instantaneous and unmistakable pinging noise of bullets ricocheting off metal. Somehow, both shots had hit the steel support structure underneath the bridge, no doubt saving the life of at least one of them. One of the bullets then smacked into the ground by Fiona's feet and the other whirred off loudly into the canal where it impacted forcefully with a sharp splash.

Andrew immediately launched himself towards Fiona and rugby tackled her out of the way and onto the ground close to the concrete wall where Sean had been strung up like dead meat. It was violent, but at least she would be out of sight of the shooter up on the pavement at the top of the embankment, and that meant that she was now out of the line of fire. She yelled in terror, but before she could utter anything else, Andrew was back on his feet with his pistol back out and pointing out under the bridge. Moving from under the cover of the bridge, he advanced swiftly but steadily, making sure to stay low and lean out to one side to line the weapon up without exposing too much of his body. Another shot rang out, and he felt the bullet whiz past his head at the same time as he spotted a figure up on the pavement above. He was wearing a black raincoat and was partially obscured by a bush. Andrew immediately fired twice in quick succession, and he felt sure that at least one of the shots found its mark. A split second later he was proven correct because he heard someone cry out in pain, and then the dark figure disappeared behind the bush amid the sound of feet running away. Andrew charged up the steep embankment, struggling for purchase on the wet soil and having to claw himself up through the bushes. By the time he emerged on the pavement of Prince Albert Road, he spotted the dark figure sprinting away from him towards the northeast corner of Regent's Park.

Andrew bolted after him, struggling to see clearly because of the heavy rain that was drenching him and blurring his eyesight. However, as he ran, he was in no doubt who the man was. In fact, he had a strange sense of déjà vu as he watched the figure running along the pavement up ahead. He moved exactly like Antoine had done, and there was no doubt in Andrew's mind that the shooter was his twin brother Laurent. He clearly wasn't much of a marksman, though. At a distance of less than fifteen metres and with two stationary targets both of his shots should have landed, but he had somehow managed to hit the bridge's steel support structure twice, and then barely miss his third shot from cover behind the bush. Laurent was obviously not a professional, but even an amateur could get lucky once in a while, and Andrew felt fortunate that neither he nor Fiona had been hit. He also felt convinced that Laurent was Sean's killer, and that he had been lying in wait to attempt to assassinate both Fiona and himself. In effect, Sean's carefully arranged corpse had been placed as a sick kind of bait, and Laurent had then loitered at the top of the embankment waiting for his chance to strike. Whether that stemmed from a desire to avenge Antoine or whether he had been ordered to do so by his masters, Andrew could only guess at. Perhaps it was both. Perhaps he had been sent to take out Andrew and Fiona, but to him, it was now also personal. And all else being equal, this made him infinitely more dangerous and unpredictable.

Andrew continued the pursuit for a few more seconds, but then he hesitated and finally stopped, watching as Laurent disappeared in the distance along Prince Albert Road in the pouring rain. He realised that even if he caught up with Laurent, it might result in a shootout in a busy area, and that could end up having unforgivable consequences. But more importantly, he simply couldn't leave Fiona by herself under the bridge. Laurent was fleeing from the scene and Antoine was now dead, but there could be others. If there was one thing that had become clear during their investigation, it was that they were dealing with serious people who had serious resources at their disposal. For that reason, he could not risk leaving Fiona by the canal while he ran off trying to catch their would-be assassin.

He tucked the gun back into the holster under his jacket, turned around and began running back towards the bridge. By then, all of his clothes were completely soaked, but he barely felt it through his anger and desire to get his hands on Laurent and wring his neck. It was one thing for himself to be shot at. That was an occupational hazard that he had long ago accepted. It was just part of the job, although he tried to avoid it. But for someone to start shooting at Fiona, that was a whole different matter and one that he was not going to let slide.

After a couple of minutes, he was back down on the footpath where he found Fiona cowering near the wall under Sean's dead corpse, trembling and looking as distressed as he had ever seen her. He hurried over and put an arm around her, leading her away from the horrific crime scene and back up the narrow path going up the embankment towards the car.

Sixteen

It didn't take long for Laurent to run north through the torrential downpour from Regent's Park through Camden and halfway along Kentish Town Road. Here he stopped next to a tall green metal gate that barred access to a narrow alley between a pair of two-storey buildings. One of them was clad in dark red tiles like many underground stations constructed in the early 20th century. On the ground floor of the building, there was now a pawnbroker, and the floor above was used by that business as a large storage room. However, underneath the building was the sealed-off and abandoned tube station of South Kentish Town, which had been opened in 1907 only to be closed down in 1924 due to low passenger numbers.

Laurent unlocked the gate, slipped through and proceeded to the back of the short alley where he unlocked and opened a door to a separate rear section of what was once the station's ground level. It provided access to a stairwell that led down about three stories to the station's now derelict platforms. Soaked through and bleeding, he made his way to another locked door that led to a small backroom that had once served as a space for the employees of the London Underground at South Kentish Station to have their lunch breaks.

The run from the canal at Prince Albert Road had been a challenge, and not because of the rain or the distance. Being extremely physically fit, he had covered the roughly one-and-a-half kilometres in less than ten minutes despite the dull yet excruciating pain in his shoulder and the burning sensation in his left ear. When the first bullet had struck, he was in no doubt that he had been hit. The projectile had missed his body armour by a hair's breadth and gone clean through his left deltoid muscle. It felt like someone had punched him in the shoulder the way he and Antoine used to do to each other when they had been playfighting as children.

He initially thought the second bullet had missed him entirely, and only later as he was running did he notice the warm, stinging sensation from his left ear. As he ran, he brought his hand up to the left side of his head, and it came away completely covered in blood. Feeling his ear as best he could whilst running along, he then realised that the entire top half of his ear was missing. He grimaced at the thought of part of his ear lying somewhere in Prince Albert Road being driven over repeatedly by cars and buses until it was ground into mincemeat and eaten by carrion birds or foxes. He found it a visceral and repugnant thought, as well as also being perversely funny in a morbid sort of way. It felt strangely appropriate that he should suffer somehow now that his twin brother had been killed. Shooting Sean Taylor in the chest and then kicking his face in and stringing him up like an animal had been a consolation of sorts, but it was nowhere near the revenge that Antoine deserved. Laurent cursed himself for having missed both of his shots. He had had all the time in the world as his two targets had stood frozen to the spot looking up at his handiwork suspended from under the bridge. But the prospect of revenge had flooded his bloodstream with so much adrenalin that his trembling hands and pounding heart had caused him to miss.

As he sat down at a table inside the cramped white-tiled but grimy windowless room, he would have given anything to find out where the two of them lived. And as he opened the bottle of vodka that he had stashed in this room months ago along with other essential supplies, he swore on his dead brother that he would do whatever it took to avenge him.

Laurent knew that he would be unable to take his gunshot injuries to a hospital without ending up in police custody, so this was something he would need to do himself. He took a big swig of the vodka, wincing as he swallowed it, and within seconds he felt the warmth of the alcohol hit his bloodstream. Then he stripped the clothes from his upper body and inspected the wound to his shoulder. Wiping his short blond blood-matted hair away from his mangled left ear, he then poured some vodka directly onto it and roared in pain as the alcohol hit the exposed nerve endings in what remained of the ear.

Panting and growling angrily, beads of sweat running down his torso, he extracted his gun, released the magazine and flicked a single cartridge out of it. Using a knife, he managed to prize the bullet off the cartridge casing and pour most of the gunpowder into the entry wound on the front of his left deltoid muscle. Much of it ended up soaked in the blood that still trickled out of the bullet hole, but this was his only option. He flicked open a Zippo lighter and took another swig of the vodka. Then he clenched his jaw tight and brought the flame up to the wound. The gunpowder ignited instantly and burned up explosively within a fraction of a second amid a rapid and violent whoosh, cauterising the wound as the flames shot out of both the front and the back of it. Laurent roared in pain and then almost collapsed in his chair whilst panting hard, barely holding on to consciousness. As he began to regain his composure, he bared his teeth and shouted every curse he could think of. He was going to find Caitlin's bitch sister and her guardian angel, and when he did, they were both going to pay for what they had done.

* * *

After arriving home in Hampstead, Andrew double-locked the front door, locked and bolted the backdoor to the garden, pulled the curtains and left his Glock 17 with a full magazine lying on the kitchen table. Then he poured them both a shot of his Glenfiddich 15-year-old single malt whiskey. They sat down next to each other on two of the tall bar stools at the white-marbled kitchen island and downed their drinks in one gulp. Then Andrew poured them another. Fiona was gradually getting back to her old self after the distress of being shot at and watching the disturbing sight of a corpse swaying above her. They were about to get up and go to bed when at exactly 2 a.m. Fiona's phone pinged. She picked it up, looked at the screen, and then stared at Andrew with her mouth partly open and the colour draining from her face.

'It's from Sean,' she said incredulously. 'How is this possible?'

'Open it,' said Andrew and leaned towards her to get a better look.

She tapped the email and read the contents out loud.

> *Hello Fiona. If you are reading this, then that means something has happened to me before we could meet. I set this email up to be sent automatically at precisely 2 a.m. in case I didn't come home. I am not usually the paranoid type, but the people I am investigating will stop at nothing to shut people like me up. And if you are reading this, then I was right to be paranoid. I have included an attachment with everything I have discovered so far. I hope you find your sister. Sean Taylor.'*

'This is insane,' said Fiona, shaking her head. 'He knew that he might not come home alive. And whilst he was being killed, you and I were just a couple of minutes away having our dinner. It makes me sick to think about it.'

'Could you forward the email to me?' asked Andrew and reached out for his laptop which was folded closed on the kitchen island's top next to them.

She did as he asked, and soon they were looking at the text document that Sean had put together. It was about five pages long and structured in a way that laid out all his findings in an easily accessible manner. One by one, the two of them read through all of the different sections together.

Sean had uncovered much of the same information that Andrew and Fiona had managed to glean from the material they had taken from Antoine's houseboat. He had investigated the Montague family as far back as possible, and he was apparently convinced that whatever Christopher Haywood was up to was part of a multi-generational endeavour that had been going on for centuries. He had also dug into the Montague REIT and its various purchases of French castles and established that Haywood seemed to have taken a deep interest in the Knights Templar over the past several years. Somehow, Sean had also managed to uncover a concerted effort by a separate corporate entity set up by Haywood to acquire dozens of ancient texts that were considered heretical and blasphemous by the Catholic Church, such as apocryphal gospels and gnostic writings from around the time of Jesus Christ. Most of them were thought to have been hunted down and destroyed by the Church, but it appeared that some remained in the hands of private collectors, and Haywood had seemingly either bought them or attempted to buy them at huge costs. Sean had not been able to work out what Haywood wanted those texts for, but it was obvious that he was investing a significant proportion of his family's wealth in the endeavour.

Sean then went on to describe something that sounded almost too far-fetched to be believable. He had become convinced that Haywood was the head of an organisation calling itself *Filii Luciferi*, or the Sons of Lucifer. This small group of powerful men, and they were all men, had been recruited from the upper echelons of a range of public institutions and private corporations, and together they operated as a sort of nefarious private members club, or a multi-sector cartel, which wielded enormous influence in the City of London and in the country at large. This allowed them to coordinate and collude behind the scenes in a way that was entirely hidden from the public and which financially benefitted them both collectively and individually to the tune of hundreds of millions of Pounds. Sean also believed that the entire organisation was set up by and for the Montague family, and that all of the other members were just a way for that family to place its hands on the levers of power.

However, Sean was certain that there was a lot more to it than that. He was convinced that amongst the inner circle of the organisation, the entire enterprise ultimately revolved around occult beliefs and sacrificial ceremonies designed to worship the Devil himself. He himself had struggled for months to get his head around the idea. It simply seemed too outrageous to be believable.

His whole investigation had begun with him trying to make sense of a series of mysterious disappearances of young women in London. Soon he had realised that the women all shared certain characteristics, and then he had discovered that several of them seemed to have been involved with a young Frenchman whose name was either Antoine or Laurent. Sean had been uncertain about his real identity. This had led him to a man called Tristan Maxwell who worked for Haywood. And when Sean had begun investigating Haywood and digging into his financial affairs and family relations, he had discovered the clear penchant for the occult, and at that point, all the pieces had suddenly begun to fall into place.

What followed was by far the most interesting and useful section in Sean's document. It related to the large temple-like building immediately west of London Bridge on the north bank, which belonged to the livery company the Worshipful Company of Jurists, which Haywood was the head of. After investigating the place for months, Sean was certain that this was where the Sons of Lucifer met and carried out their ceremonies, and he was now convinced that it involved human sacrifices – even if that sounded utterly insane. In the end, Sean had managed to infiltrate the building posing as a cleaner. This had been a complex affair in itself since he first had to work out which cleaning company serviced the building, and then he had spent many weeks pretending to be looking for a job there and waiting for an opening to come up. He had finally been signed up, and then it had taken him several more weeks to wrangle himself onto the rota for that building. Over the next several weeks he would return to the building along with the rest of the cleaning crew where he would gradually build up a detailed map of its interior, at least in the area that the crew was permitted to enter. Certain areas were completely off-limits, including Haywood's private quarters and all the subterranean levels. In fact, there were strict access procedures for the entrance and all areas of the building, and some sections were physically blocked by biometrically activated metal gates and solid doors, all of which seemed highly excessive for something as mundane as a London livery company. Sean noted that he was convinced that the sealed-off basement levels were used by the Sons of Lucifer to perform their rituals. He had been planning to attempt to force his way through the locked door from the lobby down into the bowels of the building, and he was convinced that he would find things there that would allow him to expose Haywood and his accomplices for what they really were.

He finished this section of his email by including two access codes for the electronic keypads of the building's back entrance and its internal maintenance section respectively. The latter supposedly included a boiler room and several smaller store rooms, all located near the back of the building on the ground floor. The two codes were the only ones that Sean had managed to acquire before he was killed. As Andrew and Fiona read this, they briefly took their eyes off the laptop's screen and looked at each other.

'We're going to have to get in there,' said Andrew. 'You understand that, right? It is probably the only way to get to the bottom of this.'

'I know,' said Fiona, looking anxious. 'Sean gave these codes to us so that we could use them to find out where Caitlin is. And if he is right about everything in this document, then we need to do it soon.'

The final section of the document made for chilling and disconcerting reading. Sean appeared convinced that Haywood's organisation had also infiltrated the very top of the Metropolitan Police, including the recently appointed new Police Commissioner as well as several of his predecessors. This meant that taking any of this to the police was completely out of the question. Not because it would necessarily bring with it any direct consequences from the Met, which was likely to simply ignore that sort of paranoid nonsense, but because it ran the risk of putting Caitlin in even more danger.

'Are there any other names of serving police officers in there?' asked Andrew.

'No,' replied Fiona. 'None.'

'Right,' nodded Andrew pensively. 'I guess we will have to assume that they are all compromised until proven otherwise.'

'In other words,' said Fiona. 'We're on our own.'

★ ★ ★

When Tristan Maxwell entered the offices of Montague Solicitors in the Shard early the next morning, he was already in an unforgiving mood. He knew that he had to phone Christopher Haywood with an update, and he was not looking forward to it. Being the bearer of anything other than good news was not something he was used to having to do. Come to think of it, it wasn't something he had had to do much of for a long time, except for the past few days when everything had suddenly seemed to turn to shit.

Fucking frogs, he thought as he took off his suit jacket, hung it on a coat stand and sat down at his desk inside his glass cubicle corner office.

He picked up the phone, took a deep breath and speed-dialled Haywood's office on the 66th floor just as his secretary turned up on the other side of the glass door using hand signals to ask if he would like a cup of coffee. He ignored her and swivelled in his chair so that he was facing the window.

'Sir,' he said, straightening and smoothing down his Gucci tie in a subconscious effort to look his best when addressing the boss. 'Tristan here. Do you have a moment?'

'I do,' said Haywood, managing to make it sound like a question. 'Are we encrypted?'

'Of course, Sir,' replied Maxwell.

'Right,' said Haywood flatly. 'What is the latest?'

Maxwell cleared his throat and swivelled back to face his desk. His secretary had now retreated to her own desk a couple of metres from his office door. She knew better than to disturb Maxwell when he was busy and seemed stressed.

'Firstly, the girl,' he said. 'I went and checked in on her very early this morning. Still passed out, of course, but I am sure she will be ready for the ceremony in a couple of days.'

'Good,' said Haywood evenly. 'What else? How are the excavations going?'

'I spoke to Benoit on the way to the office,' replied Maxwell. 'It looks like your theory that there was a secret crypt beneath the chapel proved correct. Benoit believes there could be a hidden burial chamber down there. And if the tomb is there, they'll find it.'

'Excellent,' said Haywood, a rare note of excitement creeping into his usually cool and restrained voice.

'I am thinking of going there myself,' said Maxwell. 'I thought I would fly down to make sure everything runs smoothly. We need everyone there to give their best and to understand how important this is.'

'I was thinking the same thing,' said Haywood, 'so I have already arranged for the jet to take you there this evening. A takeoff slot has been booked at London City Airport at 9 p.m. this evening. Make sure you're on it. My driver will pick you up from downstairs at 8 o'clock.'

'Absolutely, Sir,' nodded Maxwell whilst running his fingers through his black oiled hair. 'I'll be there.'

This was the first time Haywood had offered him the use of his Maybach and his private jet, and Maxwell felt a rush of excitement at the gesture. This was immediately followed by nervousness about what he was about to say next.

'Regarding the houseboat,' Maxwell said. 'I sent over my Romanian crew to clean it out. They stripped the interior and removed any clue to Antoine and Laurent having lived there. They left a stack of the twins' personal effects, and Laurent came by later to pick them up and torch the boat. It burnt out completely, so there's nothing left to find.'

'Very good. And Laurent?' asked Haywood calmly. 'I saw the news about Sean Taylor. That seemed to have solved that problem rather permanently, I should say.'

'Well, Sir,' said Maxwell, struggling to contain his frustration and irritation at having to help clean up that moron's mess. 'That was the other thing I needed to discuss with you. There's a slight issue there.'

Haywood initially didn't respond, but Maxwell could sense that he was still on the line, silently awaiting what Maxwell had to say. Maxwell was searching for the right words when Haywood eventually interrupted him.

'Well? What is the issue?' he asked, seemingly entirely unaffected by the news that a young man had been brutally murdered on his orders.

'Well. You see, Sir,' Maxwell stumbled on, 'Laurent seems to have taken the death of his brother rather personally, as you would expect.'

'I understand,' said Haywood without a hint of empathy in his voice. 'I too was upset, but these are the sacrifices we must make.'

'Yes. Well,' continued Maxwell apprehensively. 'It turns out that Taylor was meeting with the same people who killed Antoine.'

'What?' asked Haywood sounding puzzled. 'How do we know this?'

'Our man inside London's transport police provided Laurent with the CCTV footage from the marina,' replied Maxwell. 'And Laurent said he recognised them immediately. A man and a woman. We still don't know who they are, but we're working on that.'

'Right,' said Haywood, again making it sound like a question and clearly still waiting for Maxwell to come to the point. 'And precisely how does this present a problem for us?'

'Well,' said Maxwell. 'As soon as Laurent spotted them, he appears to have lost his composure and took it upon himself to try to kill them both. He started shooting but failed to take them out. Missed them both completely. To make matters worse, the man was carrying a weapon. So, instead, Laurent managed to get himself shot. Twice. But at least he got clear and was able to patch himself up later.'

'Shit!' swore Haywood quietly and winced. 'What a clusterfuck. Eliminating people that we already know pose a threat is unavoidable. Shooting at people we haven't even identified is reckless. I am going to need a word with him.'

'I agree, Sir,' said Maxwell. 'It is a mess. May I recommend that we contact our sources in the Met and get those two people identified ASAP? And then I will have my Romanian boys take care of it. They won't mess it up. I guarantee it.'

Maxwell could hear Haywood sigh deeply as he waited for instructions, and he sensed that his boss was furious. He could well imagine the wrathful expression on the CEO's face, and it made him feel relieved that they were not in the same room or even on the same floor of the building. Maxwell respected no one except for Haywood, who had a particular quality to him that exuded both ruthless power and a razor-sharp mind, and Maxwell admired and feared him in equal measure.

'Fine,' Haywood finally said with a steely tone in his voice. 'The gloves are already off, so make it happen. But I don't want to know the details. Just make this problem go away. Do you hear me?'

'Yes, Sir,' nodded Maxwell. 'Leave it with me. I will take care of this. What about Laurent? We already have the castle, and Benoit says we're very close.'

There was a pause before Haywood responded.

'Leave him for now,' he said eventually. 'I will deal with him. Just get your Romanians on the case, and then get yourself to France.'

'Very good, Sir,' said Maxwell. 'Sorry to…'

The line disconnected before Maxwell could finish, leaving him in no doubt that his boss was absolutely furious about the mess they suddenly found themselves in. And the timing could hardly be any worse.

'Motherfucking twins,' sneered Maxwell between gritted teeth as he put the phone down on his desk.

How often he had wished that Haywood would just get rid of those two imbeciles. Maxwell had seen nothing to justify their involvement in the project, except of course for their familial ties to the Montagues. Bloody nauseating, but at least now the job was halfway done. Perhaps he should try to speed things along without letting Haywood know. Perhaps the Romanians could deal with Laurent as well. That option always existed.

He waved a hand rapidly at his secretary, who immediately sprang up and crossed the floor to his office door with surprising speed considering the height of her stilettos. She opened the door just enough for her to be able to poke her pretty head inside.

'Sir?' she said sweetly and smiled at him. 'How may I…?'

'Coffee!' Maxwell ordered and waved her out again.

She nodded silently and closed the door as he picked up his phone once more and opened an encrypted messaging app that contained only a handful of contacts. He selected the contact simply named 'D', and began typing a message. As he did so, he thought back to how he had met the three men who were to become his fixers. His muscle – as he liked to think of them.

Almost five years ago now, Maxwell had happened to be arriving by taxi at an exclusive West End nightclub late on a Saturday night just as three doormen had been ejecting a punter. The unwanted guest was a scrawny young man sporting a ridiculous-looking designer outfit, expensive white trainers and an ego to match his clothes budget. The most senior doorman, who it later turned out went by the name Dragomir, had hauled the kid out effortlessly and pushed him along the pavement and away from the nightclub's entrance. Dragomir was tall and wide and had a full black beard that was trimmed into a short spike extending down from his chin.

The aggressive youngster had remonstrated loudly with him and had quite ridiculously threatened to kick his arse. At that point, Constantin and Radovan had appeared on Dragomir's flanks, and the unhappy customer had retreated whilst hurling yet more insults. A handsome but mean-looking Constantin, sporting a blond crewcut and runic neck tattoos was about to give chase, but the musclebound tank-like Radovan had placed one of his huge hands on his chest and held him back. He had said something in Romanian that Maxwell didn't understand, but which seemed to convey that the little dweeb wasn't worth it.

Maxwell had remained just outside the nightclub's entrance chatting up a couple of young women despite having a VIP pass because he instinctively sensed that this little *entente* wasn't quite over. Less than five minutes later, he was proven correct when the dweeb returned in a car with a group of five other young men, some of whom were wearing tracksuits and seemed significantly bulkier than their humiliated friend. From the swagger with which they exited the car and approached the three doormen, Maxwell immediately knew that these were gang members who were used to settling disputes with violence. A couple of them brandished long knives, which caused the people in the queue to panic and disperse, but it seemed to have absolutely no effect on the three Romanians.

Without a word, Dragomir had stepped forward calmly and planted himself between the newly arrived crew and the nightclub's entrance, and Constantin and Radovan had soon found their positions on his flanks. The gang members had spread out around them in the shape of a semicircle looking for their moment to attack. When it finally came, it was a glorious sight the likes of which Maxwell had never seen first-hand and up close. The only downside was that it was over after only a couple of short minutes, by which time the gang members were either bleeding from wounds inflicted with their own weapons, crying out in pain from broken arms and fingers, or trying to crawl away in agony after having their knees popped out of their sockets and dislocated.

Maxwell had watched in awe while the three men went to work as if they were a team of butchers dispatching a batch of meat. What impressed him the most was not their effortless skill at unarmed hand combat, although that was in itself remarkable. Rather, it was how calm they had been, as well as the way they seemed to be telepathically connected to each other in such a way that each of them knew instinctively where the other two were and what they were doing as the carnage and mayhem of the bloody slugfest unfolded. Seemingly without breaking a sweat, Dragomir, Constantin and Radovan had quickly annihilated their six attackers, and by the time the hapless gang members withdrew, the trio calmly stepped back towards the front door of the nightclub exchanging a few brief words in their native tongue. They seemed utterly unfazed by what had just transpired. Just another day at the office.

Spellbound by what he had just witnessed and intuitively sensing the potential of the three men, Maxwell had approached the man who he correctly suspected was the leader. Dragomir. As he walked up to them wearing his expensive tailored suit and Italian shoes, he began to appreciate just how much larger and how much more intimidating they really were up close. He also noticed that all three of them had what appeared to be prison tattoos, and he quickly surmised that they had probably established for themselves a long history with the notoriously harsh and cruel Romanian penal system before coming to the UK.

Right there on the spot, addressing them in a confident tone of voice, Maxwell had offered them a retainer for yet-to-be-specified services, and he had given them his business card and a money clip with what he guessed equated to at least a month's salary for each of them. It was evident that he was several years younger than they were, but that didn't seem to bother them in the slightest. Coming out of the

Romanian prison system, it was obvious that they understood hierarchy and they understood money, and that was all that mattered.

During their talk, they asked all the right questions, and they came across as some of the most straightforward and unapologetic people he had dealt with in a long time. And he could see from their hard eyes and mean faces that as long as he kept up his end of the bargain, he would be able to expect absolute and unquestioning loyalty from them. In other words, they were his kind of people. In the couple of years since that Saturday evening, not once had they disappointed him, and he had no doubt that they would be able to resolve the current situation very shortly after being handed their target package.

He pressed the speed dial, and after a couple of rings, the call was picked up. A slow, deep and gravelly voice with a heavy Eastern European accent came on the line.

'Dragomir speaking.'

Seventeen

It was mid-morning when Andrew and Fiona awoke to sunshine and birdsong outside their bedroom windows. The skies had cleared after the previous night's downpour, and as Andrew glanced outside to the blue sky behind the green leaves on the trees, it was difficult to reconcile the sunny and peaceful morning with the gruesome events that had unfolded just a few hours earlier. At this time, the canal by Regent's Park was probably cordoned off and crawling with police, some of whom might possibly be on the take and even directly involved in whatever this was.

His mind soon began to replay the last few moments of Laurent disappearing in the rain along Prince Albert Road and wondering where he might be now. He was sure that he had tagged him with at least one of his shots, but he was also certain that the Frenchman would not be so naïve as to take himself to a hospital. So, either he had patched himself up, or he had sought assistance from one of his co-conspirators. And this was what was beginning to weigh on Andrew's mind. Despite everything pointing in the direction of this Christopher Haywood character, who Andrew had been blissfully unaware of until a few days ago, the reality was that they had no idea precisely who or what they were up against or how many people were involved. What was clear, however, was that whoever was responsible for Caitlin's disappearance now almost certainly knew of his and Fiona's involvement, and it was probably a question of time before they managed to identify where they lived. Andrew kept his thoughts about this to himself as he got out of bed and got dressed. There was no need to drop the prospect of being hunted on Fiona. At least not quite yet.

After a late breakfast consisting of eggs, bacon and hash browns which Fiona prepared expertly, they each got on with their preparations for later that day. Fiona began studying the area around the Sons of Lucifer temple by the Thames, and Andrew made his way down into the basement level of the house, where he had commissioned a combined safe room and weapons storage room several years earlier. He unlocked the metal concertina grille across the doorway to the narrow spiral staircase that led from the corner of the large open-plan kitchen down to the basement level. At the bottom of the stairs, he used a keypad to open a heavy wooden door to the wine cellar.

He entered the temperature-controlled space whose walls were covered with wine racks containing hundreds of bottles of vintage wine from his favourite vineyards in Italy, South Africa, Australia and California. He then strode to the other end of the room where there was a large floor-to-ceiling oak wine rack with diamond-shaped cubbyholes all occupied by bottles of red wine. He reached over to the wall and pressed a small concealed button. There was a brief metallic click, and then the entire wine rack swung open on its four heavy-duty hinges to reveal the safe room.

The room was built like a bomb shelter, but an extremely comfortable one with pleasant décor, plush furniture and beds as well as entertainment systems and a small kitchenette. It also contained supplies to last two people for several weeks, and enough weaponry to start a small war. All the weapons were locked away inside solidly built wood-clad metal gun cabinets that were virtually unbreakable and could only be accessed with the correct passcode via another keypad.

Andrew unlocked them, swung the doors open, and stood back for a moment while he decided what to take with him upstairs. He wasn't expecting another firefight, but one could never be too careful, and there was no way he was going to set out that evening completely unarmed. In addition to weapons, he decided to bring along a number of electronic gadgets and other aides that were not commercially available but that he had access to due to his position inside Colonel Strickland's special SAS unit. This fact also meant that he had a license to carry all of the weapons in the safe room, including some that he normally only ever employed on covert operations abroad. He placed what he needed inside a small backpack, zipped it up and left the safe room to rejoin Fiona upstairs.

When he re-emerged into the kitchen, Fiona was busy attempting to look up all publicly available information on the building they were planning to enter. There were plenty of photos of the outside as well as the lobby area and one of the great dining halls that was used for various official functions of the livery company. However, when it came to the rest of the building, there was literally nothing to be found anywhere. There were also no publicly available floor plans or any other indications as to the precise layout of the building. All they had to go on were Sean Taylor's hand-drawn sketches of the limited sections of the building that he had managed to gain access to so far. In the end, it didn't amount to enough to put together a meaningful entry plan. They simply had to hope that the passcodes were still functional to allow them to enter the building, and then they would have to make it up as they went once they were inside.

When they arrived inside the parking garage under Lower Thames Street, it was half past eleven in the evening. They left the car and exited the parking garage, and from there it was a short walk along the dark road under London Bridge to the temple, whose front entrance faced the road. Its plain façade and varnished amber-coloured front door looked so ordinary that it was difficult to imagine anything going on in there besides excruciatingly boring meetings between groups of grey-haired solicitors, but then that was almost certainly by design.

Strolling along casually in the dark, occasionally lit up by passing cars, Andrew and Fiona stopped in front of a tall locked gate made of vertical steel bars. As soon as there was a lull in the traffic, Andrew scaled the gate adeptly and dropped down inside a narrow alley. It only took a few seconds for him to be standing on the other side of the gate, at which point he jammed his shoulder in between two of the steel bars to allow Fiona to follow him up and over. Placing one foot on Andrew's knee and then another on his shoulder, she was able to climb over the gate without too much trouble, and as soon as she was on the ground next to him the two of them continued swiftly down the alley towards the back of the building. Halfway along was a set of steps leading down to a small doorway that was set into the wall by about half a metre, which made it invisible from the road. They stepped down to stand next to the door, now completely out of sight of the sparse traffic on Lower Thames Street.

Andrew had memorised the passcodes supplied by Sean Taylor, and he swiftly flicked the transparent plastic cover away from the glowing keypad and carefully punched in the first code. The keypad produced a single long beep, and then the lock snapped open audibly. Within seconds the two of them were inside, closing the door behind them.

Standing inside a small low-ceilinged lobby with cream-coloured walls and a polished stone floor, they saw a locked door to their left and a corridor to their right.

'This is the stairwell leading up to the raised ground floor and the lobby,' said Andrew, pointing to the door on the left. 'Let's see if we can get up there.'

He tried both of the access codes, but the keypad produced an angry-sounding double-beep both times. They were not going to get through there without a breaching charge, and that was a step too far for Andrew, even in these circumstances.

'Right. The boiler room is at the back of the building,' said Andrew. 'Let's head down the corridor and see if we can find it.'

They proceeded along the corridor which ran parallel to the external wall for about five metres until it made a left turn. The corridor continued for another ten metres along what must have been the building's foundations at the rear. It was lit only by a handful of dim lamps mounted on the walls. The wall to the exterior was made from large smooth stone blocks, and halfway down the corridor was a reinforced metal door. Andrew gripped the door handle and attempted to open it, but it was locked. As he was about to continue, Fiona stepped up close to the door.

'There's a spy hole here,' she said and pointed. 'Why would there be a spyhole in a door like this?'

She stood up on her toes and put her eye to the spy hole trying to see what was on the other side.

'It's completely dark in there,' she said. 'Or perhaps it has been painted over. What if...'

'You think Caitlin might be in there?' asked Andrew.

'What if she is?' said Fiona.

She suddenly clenched her fist and banged on the door three times. It was clear from the way it absorbed the impacts and from the muffled thuds that it was extremely thick and heavy.

'Caitlin!' she called out. 'Caitlin, are you in there?'

'Shh...,' said Andrew, staring at her sternly. 'We can't make noise like that. If there is anyone else in the building, they will have heard you.'

'Sorry,' said Fiona quietly with a note of dejection in her voice. 'If she is here, we need to find her.'

'I agree,' said Andrew emphatically, 'but let's try to be quiet about it.'

He stepped over next to her and put his ear to the door, and Fiona then did the same.

'I don't hear anything,' she said.

'Same here,' said Andrew, placing a hand gently on her shoulder. 'Come on. Let's get to the boiler room. If I read Sean's sketch correctly, it is directly below Haywood's private quarters.'

'All right,' sighed Fiona. 'Let's go.'

They continued to the end of the corridor, at which point they found themselves at a T-junction. To their right were two small storage rooms and to their left was another door which had a keypad mounted next to it on the wall. At eye height in the middle of the door was a small sign saying 'Maintenance'.

He stepped up to the door entering the second of Sean's two passcodes, and the door instantly clicked open.

'Through here,' said Andrew and opened it.

As soon as the door was open, they could hear the deep hum of machinery whirring inside the dark room. Andrew found a light switch next to the door, and immediately a set of bright overhead lights mounted in the ceiling about three metres above them came on.

'Close the door,' he said and walked out into the middle of the roughly five-by-five-metre space.

In one of the corners was what looked like a gas-fired heating plant the size of a small van. Next to it was a large piece of machinery about the same size but encased in thick perforated metal plating that was painted turquoise. Several stainless steel tubes about a metre in diameter were sticking up and out of its top, after which they connected to the ceiling above and one of the walls next to it.

'That's the air-conditioning system,' said Andrew. 'That's our way up.'

'Through those?' said Fiona sceptically, pointing to the metal tubes.

'I am pretty sure they are just wide enough,' said Andrew, walking over to the machine's control panel. 'Don't worry. I'll go first.'

He quickly found the master power switch and turned the machine off. It sounded like a quiet jet turbine gradually spinning down as the air filtration and pump system inside the machine slowly reduced its RPMs until it finally stopped completely. As soon as it had fallen silent, Andrew grabbed onto a handle next to one of the outer plates and scaled the large metal shell. Within a couple of minutes, he unscrewed the series of bolts holding the main vertical air duct in place and disconnected it from the machine. Then he separated the lowest of the roughly one-metre segments from the main body of the duct. Finally, he took off his small backpack, tied it to a thin metal wire that was attached to his belt, and then he placed the backpack by his feet ready to be pulled up once he reached the top.

'There,' he said. 'That should do it. Could you come up here and hold the duct steady while I climb up?"

'But we have no idea where this leads,' she said.

'There's only one way to find out,' said Andrew, pointing to the ceiling. 'If Haywood's office is just above us, then that is where we need to go. Come on.'

Fiona did as he asked, and soon Andrew had managed to get himself up into the air duct and squeezed himself a short distance further upwards.

'Are you all right?' asked Fiona as she held on to the duct with both arms, trying to hold it steady as he climbed.

'It's a bit tight,' said Andrew, 'but if you just make sure to press hard enough against the sides you won't fall down, and you can inch your way up through it pretty easily.'

Fiona looked decidedly unenthusiastic, but she had long ago decided that she was going to do whatever it took to find Caitlin, so there was no chance of her staying behind once Andrew had reached the top of the duct.

Andrew kept climbing upwards. He had switched on his small LED headtorch, and when he looked up, the air duct seemed to continue for a lot longer than he had anticipated. It seemed to extend upwards through the ceiling level and well past what he estimated had to be Haywood's office. Had he got his bearings wrong? Were they in a different part of the building from what Sean's sketch had indicated?

As he continued upwards in the dark and confined space, he suddenly had the unnerving image pop into his mind of his clothes catching on a bolt inside the duct, pinning him in place and preventing him from moving either up or down. If it caught him near his lower back or on one of his legs, he would be unable to reach it inside the cramped metal tube. It was also becoming quite hot inside the duct, and sweat began percolating off his forehead. After another three metres of strenuous and mildly claustrophobic vertical climbing, he craned his head back and was able to see the end of the duct. For a moment he was confused and unsettled at the sight since it appeared as if the duct was a dead end, but then he noticed that it seemed to peel off horizontally to one side towards what he guessed was the interior of the building. He could only hope that the horizontal duct was large enough for him to fit through since he would not be able to turn around now.

When he finally made it to the top, he was gratified to discover that there was a larger rectangular space there from which several smaller square ducts continued further into the building. This seemed to be some sort of junction for the aircon system supplying various parts of the temple with fresh air. One of them had to lead to Haywood's office.

He extracted a rope from his backpack, tied one end to a truss inside the junction and let the rest of the rope drop down through the duct. Then he lay down on his front with his head out over the edge and called down to Fiona.

'All good up here,' he said. 'Start climbing. I will try to help pull you up.'

'Okay,' responded Fiona, feeling anything but okay.

She reached up as high as she could and gripped the rope. Then she ducked under the lower edge of the duct and placed one foot on one side whilst pushing her back against the other, wedging herself in place. Then she began to push herself up through the duct, one limb at a time whilst hanging on to the rope. As she climbed, she used her knees and feet to push against the inside of the air duct and stop herself from sliding back down through it, and she used the rope to haul herself slowly upwards. As she moved, the duct, now disconnected from the large air-conditioning unit and with no one to hold it steady, wobbled from side to side every time she moved, causing her to suffer from mild motion sickness. She looked up into the darkness above her where only a faint light from Andrew's headtorch could be seen from somewhere off to one side. It was at least four or five metres to the top. The climb required her to exert constant pressure on the inside of the duct with both arms and legs, and soon her muscles were beginning to burn with lactic acid. As she continued, she could have sworn that the duct was getting narrower and narrower, constricting her movements and threatening to trap her there. She pushed on.

Suddenly, the fabric of her left trouser leg caught on something below, and she was unable to free it. She tried to pull her left knee up under herself, but the leg was caught, and she felt her other knee that was wedged against the side of the duct beginning to slip.

'Andrew!' she called, rising panic in her voice as she gripped the rope so tightly that her knuckles turned white. 'Help!'

Immediately, Andrew's face appeared overhead, a little more than a metre away. He had been lying just out of sight with his feet against the frame of the larger duct section putting tension on the rope to help her climb. He reached down swiftly with his right arm, grabbed the back of her jacket firmly, and with a grimace he lifted her up through the last section of the duct. As he grunted from the exertion and pulled her upwards, her trouser leg finally ripped, and then she was able to grab onto the ledge and pull herself up next to him.

'Are you all right?' he asked.

'Just barely,' she nodded, panting whilst the feeling of relief at being safe flooded through her body. 'Not really a normal day at the office for me.'

'Right,' said Andrew. 'These three ducts supply different parts of the building. I am pretty sure this one is the one we want.'

He was pointing to the one on the left.

'Haywood's office,' said Fiona.

'Exactly,' he said and began moving towards it.

The three ducts were even smaller and tighter than the vertical duct they had just traversed, but at least they were horizontal, and Andrew began to crawl into the one he thought was the one they needed. The sound of his breathing and of his clothes sliding across the duct's metal interior reverberated ahead of him through what was no doubt a complex network of ducts supplying the entire building. Soon he was a couple of metres inside the duct, and he stopped next to a large ventilation grille on the side of it.

'Bingo,' he said quietly, but loud enough for Fiona to hear it. 'We can get through here.'

He reached down to his trouser leg and extracted a small set of tools which he then used to unscrew a set of bolts that held the grille in place. The grille was wedged slightly in place, so he had to punch it with his elbow in order to make it budge. It suddenly popped out of its frame and fell onto the floor inside the room. He stuck his head through and looked around. This was undoubtedly Haywood's office.

'Follow me,' he called to Fiona in hushed tones. 'We're through.'

It was tight, but Andrew managed to squeeze through the hole where the grille had been and drop down into the office. He turned and looked around. It did not look like any office he had ever been in. It was like something out of a long-gone century. When Fiona crawled through, he moved over next to the wall and let her place her feet on his shoulders, after which he lowered her to the floor.

'Quite a place,' he said.

'Wow,' said Fiona. 'Impressive.'

The dark wood panels that wrapped around the walls, and the bookcases full of old books with gold titles printed on their spines, as well as the various oil paintings, all combined to give the impression of a reading room in a gentlemen's club rather than an office. By far the most striking painting, as well as being the largest with the most impressive gilded frame, was a full-size portrait of a pompous-looking man with a severe face, grey curly wig, black bushy eyebrows, thick white sideburns, a white ruff collar and an almost black gown that had a distinctly 18th century look to it. Fiona quickly spotted the polished brass plaque at the top of the gilded frame and walked closer.

'Godfrey Montague,' she said and studied him. 'The founder of Montague Solicitors, and almost certainly also the first grand master of the Sons of Lucifer.'

'Charming,' said Andrew, walking over to stand at her side.

'He gives me the chills,' said Fiona quietly. 'There's just something really sinister about him. I wonder if this is an accurate painting, or if the artist intentionally painted him as even grimmer than he really was.'

'Or perhaps we're looking at the nice version,' said Andrew. 'Come on. Let's try the door. According to Sean, there should be a corridor on the other side.'

Andrew walked to the only visible door in the office. It sat inside a heavy doorframe and was covered in deep red tufted leather with shiny brass studs around the edges. Next to it was a small orange button that glowed faintly. The effect of old wooden décor next to modern illuminated electronics was mildly jarring.

'Let's see what's out here,' he said. 'Sean never managed to access this part of the building, so we should do a quick recon of it.'

Andrew pressed the button, which resulted in a subtle click, and then he was able to grip the handle and open the door just a crack. On the other side of the office door was a long corridor that was clearly on the first floor of the building and that seemed to stretch all the way to the other side of it. Along the length of one side of the corridor were more oil paintings, and opposite those were a set of doors to various smaller rooms. Halfway along was the landing of the wide, sweeping staircase that was accessible from both sides of the corridor, and which curved down into the lobby by the entrance on the ground floor. Andrew froze for a moment, holding up an index finger to signal to Fiona not to speak. After a couple of seconds, he opened the door fully and stepped out into the corridor.

'I am pretty sure there is no one else here,' he whispered. 'But let's not take any chances. Move quietly.'

The two of them walked along the wide corridor, glancing inside the rooms on one side where there were what appeared to be large but sparsely furnished function rooms. It was impossible to guess their purpose just by looking at them. As they continued on, Fiona noticed that on the wood-panelled wall opposite the function rooms were a number of empty spaces for paintings, preceded by a long line of portraits similar to the one in Haywood's office, although these were about a third of the size, and they seemed to be arranged chronologically. Underneath the first empty spot was a plaque with the name Edward Haywood Montague and a four-digit number. What initially struck Fiona, aside from all of these men sporting very grave facial expressions and a plaque with the name Montague, was the way in which the collection was like a multi-century exhibition of solicitor fashion. Not that the changes from painting to painting were particularly noticeable, but it gave a sense of the longevity and continuity of this family's lineage.

'Previous grand masters,' she whispered. 'These go back hundreds of years. I think I know who the first one was.'

They soon came to the end of the row of paintings, and just as she suspected it began with Godfrey Montague. But then she noticed something else.

'Have a look at this,' she said and walked closer to the painting of the first grand master. 'The plaques all have the year of their birth and death engraved on them. Look. Godfrey Montague, 1672 to 1786. He lived for 114 years. That's incredible. Particularly for that time.'

She stepped over to the next painting along and pointed at its plaque.

'Benjamin FitzAlan Montague,' she read. '1718 to 1827. That's 109 years.'

'Crikey,' said Andrew stepping closer and looking puzzled.

'Alistair Edgar Montague,' she continued after moving to the next painting. '1754 to 1872. He managed to live for 118 years.'

She turned to Andrew with her eyebrows raised and her mouth half open.

'Those sorts of lifespans are almost unheard of. Especially several hundred years ago. This is absolutely astonishing. And they all seem to follow the same pattern. They have a son very late in life who eventually becomes the next grand master, and they all ended up living unnaturally long lives.'

'Staggering,' said Andrew. 'I guess there's no reason to doubt any of these plaques. I don't see why anyone would make something like that up. But how did they manage to live that long?'

'Something in the water?' asked Fiona.

'Perhaps,' said Andrew, 'in a manner of speaking. Anyway, how old is Haywood now?'

'Eighty-four,' said Fiona, having inspected his portrait already. 'That's astounding. He doesn't look a day over sixty. This is all very creepy.'

'It does seem incredibly odd,' said Andrew. 'Anyway, let's keep moving. We have limited time.'

They walked across the wide corridor and back to the sweeping red-carpeted staircase that wound its way down to the heavy glass security gates in the lobby.

'No point in going down,' observed Andrew. 'We can't get past the gates, and even if we did, we don't want to leave yet. No sign of a way down into the sublevels up here, though.'

'I agree. There's nothing out here,' said Fiona. 'We must be missing something. Let's head back into the office.'

They walked briskly back along the wood-panelled corridor to the door to Haywood's office, which they had left open. Slipping inside, Andrew closed it behind them and took off his backpack, unzipping it and extracting what looked like a small torch.

'There has to be a secret passage from here down into where Sean thought the ceremony room is,' he said. 'And I am betting it is hidden in here somewhere and operated by a simple mechanical button. All we have to do is find it.'

He began walking methodically along the first couple of bookcases next to the door, shining the torch on the cases, their shelves and the books. As he did so, there was a purple glow along the edge of the shelves and on the top parts of many of the spines of the books where they had been handled and extracted from the shelves.

'This is a UV-A light,' he said. 'A lot of organic materials absorb this wavelength and then re-emit it as visible light. So, anything like sweat, saliva and skin cells will appear to fluoresce under this light.'

'Is that what crime scene investigators use?' asked Fiona.

'That's right,' said Andrew as he kept sweeping the light across the interior of the office, looking for anything that might stand out.

Having finished all the bookcases, he inspected the large and heavy-looking mahogany desk but found nothing except for marks on drawer handles and the edges of the desk that were closest to the office chair. These would invariably have small amounts of organic material on them, so Andrew moved on.

'I think I've worked it out,' said Fiona and nodded towards the life-size portrait of Godfrey Montague that she was standing next to. 'I'll bet you anything that if there's a way down into the basement from here, it is behind this painting.'

Andrew came over next to her and swept the torchlight over the painting's gilded frame and then along its sides. Near the top right corner, the purple glow suddenly bloomed noticeably.

'Hello,' said Andrew and stepped closer, looking up at the spot where it was clear that a lot of organic residue had been left by someone touching it repeatedly over time.

He peered at the spot and then reached up, placed a finger on that spot, and then felt a small circular section under the tip of his index finger. He pressed it, and it yielded under his touch with a barely audible click, and then the entire painting began to move aside, revealing a small compartment not much larger than a broom cupboard. On the wall at the back was a single polished chrome button with a small blue LED at its centre.

'There we go,' said Fiona. 'This must be an elevator.'

'It's barely big enough for the two of us,' said Andrew. 'We'll have to squeeze in.'

Andrew stepped in first and backed up against the back wall of the compartment. Then Fiona followed and placed herself with her back pressed against his chest.

'Watch your feet,' said Andrew. 'There's no door, so make sure to keep them well inside.'

Once they were ready, Andrew reached around to his lower back and found the button with his fingers. He pressed it and the elevator slowly began to descend, Haywood's office gradually disappearing from view. After a few seconds, they were watching the smooth concrete wall in front of them glide inexorably upwards as they descended amid the gentle hum of the elevator's electric motors. They continued descending for a surprisingly long time, which Andrew estimated equated to around ten metres before the concrete wall ended and the elevator came to a stop. In front of them was pitch-black darkness, and only when Andrew switched on his torch could they see that they were in a circular room roughly four metres in diameter constructed from light-coloured granite. They stepped out of the elevator and into the room, where Andrew allowed his torchlight to sweep across its interior.

'Where are we?' whispered Fiona, looking around the strange space.

The walls were decorated with banners containing strange symbols and the floor was made of large slabs of almost white polished marble, and there was a large black pentagram mosaic inlaid into it. On the right side of the room was a large gate with metal bars and a heavy-duty lock blocking access to a narrow stairwell that wound its way upwards. It looked well maintained, but it could easily have been down here for decades, if not considerably longer. On the left was a robust-looking wooden door painted a glossy black, and immediately across from the elevator was a doorway that seemed to be leading to a corridor or a tunnel of some kind. It was completely dark in there, and the whole place seemed like something that one would have expected to find deep beneath a medieval castle rather than in central London. It somehow managed to give the impression of having been constructed centuries ago.

Andrew gripped the handle on the metal gate, pressed it down and gave it a firm yank, but nothing happened.

'Locked,' he said. 'We're not getting through here in a hurry. I also think it might just lead up towards the lobby area.'

Then he moved over to stand in front of the black wooden door, shining his torchlight around its handle.

'Mechanical lock,' he said quietly. 'No keypad. This will take some time. Let's first see what's that way.'

He pointed at the corridor extending an unknown distance away from the circular room and into the darkness beyond. Fiona followed him through the doorway, and her eyes only just caught sight of a symbol chiselled into the lintel above it. She grabbed hold of Andrew's sleeve and he stopped and looked up to where she was pointing.

'Brimstone symbol,' she said. 'Like the one we found in Antoine's little wooden box.'

Andrew re-directed the beam of the powerful LED torch ahead of them again and they moved cautiously through what was a roughly one-metre-wide and two-metre-high granite tunnel with a vaulted ceiling. After about five metres they emerged into another circular chamber, but this one was much larger and had a distinctly ominous feel to it. It was roughly eight metres across with a ceiling that was about four metres above them, and at its centre was a raised circular stone platform with a large inverted pentagram chiselled into it. But what stood out more than anything else was the large shiny metal brimstone symbol that was placed on the platform directly opposite the entrance.

'What the hell is this place?' breathed Fiona clearly unnerved, and then she sniffed the air and frowned. 'It smells… odd in here.'

Andrew pointed his torchlight up towards the brimstone symbol, and then he focused the beam on the end of one of the two horizontal bars of the symbol. It seemed to have a leather strap attached to it that was about the same size as a belt. Shifting the beam to the other side of the symbol revealed a similar strap attached there.

'Jesus,' he said quietly. 'Are you thinking what I am thinking?'

'Is this meant for a person?' asked Fiona, dreading the reply.

'I have to say it looks like it,' said Andrew. 'Whatever goes on in here is definitely not innocent.'

'I want to get out of here,' said Fiona, taking a step backwards towards the door. 'This place is sick.'

'Hang on a second,' said Andrew, attempting to sound calm and hide his own revulsion at what this place might be for.

He walked around the circular platform to the area immediately behind the brimstone symbol. Here he found a narrow passage into a small room about two-by-two metres with various occult-looking items hanging on the walls and a desk placed against the back wall with pieces of clothing and about a dozen silver cups. Directly above the desk was a large mask of a creature that Andrew knew only too well at this point.

'Come look at this,' he said, and Fiona then wasted no time hurrying towards him and the torchlight. 'It is a chamber with what looks a lot like ceremonial paraphernalia. Almost like a sacristy in a church. And look up there.'

'Baphomet,' exclaimed Fiona before placing a hand across her mouth as if to silence herself.

'It certainly looks like it,' said Andrew, eyeing the disturbing mask suspiciously. 'Haywood and his so-called Sons of Lucifer are knee-deep in some serious occult stuff. And it doesn't really matter if any of it is real. If they are hurting people, they need to be stopped.'

'Where the hell is Caitlin?' said Fiona, looking on the verge of tears. 'We have to find her.'

'I know,' replied Andrew and wrapped an arm around her shoulders. 'And we will. 'We won't let these loonies hurt her, ok? We *will* find her.'

Fiona nodded but looked unconvinced.

'We should grab all of this stuff and go to the authorities,' said Fiona. 'This is proof!'

'No,' said Andrew, shaking his head regretfully. 'Even if they are not on Haywood's payroll, the police will take one look at this and shrug, and then they will tell us to go away. This is not tangible proof of anything, other than the fact that the patrons of this place possess the paraphernalia of crackpots who worship Lucifer. And that isn't actually illegal, even if it is ridiculous.'

Fiona's shoulders slumped as she pondered what he had said and eventually accepted that it was nowhere near enough to unravel whatever it was that was going on here in this place.

'Come on,' said Andrew. 'The clock is ticking. We can't stay in here for too long. I want to get through that black door in the other chamber.'

'But we don't have a key,' said Fiona. 'What are you planning to do? Shoot your way through it.'

'If I have to,' replied Andrew, 'But I think I can manage without using a gun.'

Soon they were back in front of the heavy wooden door. Andrew knelt in front of it and extracted what initially looked to Fiona like a pistol.

'You said you weren't…' she said, before realising what she was looking at. 'Is that a lockpick?'

'Yep,' said Andrew, holding the grip of the electric lock-picking gun and sliding the long, thin metal tip of it inside the lock. 'It's a simple tool, but it is surprisingly effective, especially against pin tumbler locks like this one. Inside these locks are a set of small pins that all have to be pushed up at the same time and by different amounts in order for the lock to turn. This gun simply vibrates this long picker rod up and down quickly and also modulates the frequency and tension as it does so. Eventually, it will hit a point where all of the pins happen to bounce upwards at exactly the same time and by the exact amount required. And then you can simply turn the lock using this little metal poker.'

'Wow,' said Fiona. 'This sounds worryingly simple. Will this work here?'

'Pretty much any lock can be picked as long as you have the right tool,' said Andrew, placing the poker at the top of the keyhole and putting a small amount of tension on it.

'But it does require a bit of practice,' he continued as he switched on the lock-picking gun and a gentle electric whirring and clacking noise started emanating from it as it began its attempt at bouncing the pins up and away from the centre of the keyhole.

Within seconds, there was an audible click as all of the pins inside the lock ended up being pushed upwards at the same time, at which point Andrew used the poker to turn the inside of the lock counter-clockwise.

'*Et voilà!*' said Andrew, pressing down on the handle and opening the door slightly. 'Simple.'

He put the lockpicking gun back in his backpack and slung it over his shoulder.

'Let's see what's in here,' he said as he rose and opened the door fully.

As soon as they entered, a set of subdued automatic lights came on along what turned out to be a long room with study tables arranged along its two sides and a narrow red carpet that lay across a dark wooden floor and stretched the length of the room to the far end. Each table had a stool in front of it, a green banker's lamp placed on it as well as a pendant light hanging above it. On each of them was a large open book with several other books placed in stacks next to it. Evidently, each table was dedicated to the study of just one tome, and whoever was carrying out the research would clearly move between tables focusing on just one at a time. Andrew switched off his torch, now that there was enough light to see.

'This must be Haywood's private research room,' he said.

Fiona stepped cautiously over to the nearest table and leaned in over it to look at the large, thick volume lying there.

'This is the Zohar,' she said. 'The Jewish mystical text that some scholars say dates back to before the time of Christ.'

She moved on to the next table.

'And here's the Torah,' she said, 'along with all of the other texts of the Tanakh, the Hebrew Bible.'

Andrew walked to the first table on the other side of the long aisle and inspected the ancient-looking book lying there.

'*Le Dragon Rouge*,' he read. 'French for the Red Dragon?'

'Yes,' replied Fiona. 'It's another name for the Grand Grimoire which was also in Antoine's houseboat. It looks like both Haywood and the twins were researching the same occult stuff, although there is lots more material here than we found on the houseboat. Some of these books look like originals, too. They could many be hundreds of years old.'

'Here's another one,' said Andrew stepping along to the next table. 'This one's called *L'Anti-Christ* by someone named Florimond de Raemond. Printed in 1597. More than four hundred years old. Wow.'

'This one is called *Adversus Haereses*,' said Fiona. 'It means 'Against Heresies', and it is quite a well-known work by a French bishop called Irenaeus. It is essentially a text created to identify and root out what the Church saw as the heretical Gnostics. You might call it the early ideological beginnings of the Inquisition.'

'Which brought so much joy into the world,' said Andrew acerbically.

'This is quite something,' said Fiona. 'These notes make reference to the *Corpus Luciferi* – the 'Body of Lucifer'.

Andrew glanced at her and shook his head.

'I am sorry,' he said caustically. 'That just sounds completely outrageous. Lucifer isn't a physical being. He is an ancient figment of people's collective imagination, designed by powerful rulers to ensure that people feared their overlords and did as they were bloody well told.'

'It isn't really meant to be taken literally,' said Fiona. 'In this context, the word 'corpus' simply means 'body', as in a body of work. And in this instance, it is the Lucifer Codex in its entirety. Perhaps that is what they are looking for.'

'Here are some recent works about the Templars,' said Andrew now standing next to yet another table. 'And a whole bunch of other books about their history. And there are dozens of maps of southern France here as well.'

'Holy crap. This looks like an original edition of Paradise Lost from 1667,' said Fiona. 'Amazing. Everything in here seems to cover the same sort of material. Lots of religious texts. Grimoires with occult rituals. Mystical writings. Gnostic texts. Templar history and maps. This definitely isn't just the harmless hobby of an eccentric. There is clearly some sort of purpose to all of this.'

'It is obvious that Haywood is trying to identify the location of something specific,' said Andrew.

Fiona walked along and stopped next to another table, where she then perched on the stool placed in front of it.

'This is interesting,' she said, leaning in over the documents laid out on the table, studying them closely.

Andrew came over and joined her.

'What is that?' he asked.

She did not reply for a few seconds as her eyes scanned the mixture of handwritten notes and printed text documents, copies of pages in various books as well as maps. It looked like a compilation of research notes.

'This has to do with something referred to as *'The Key',*' she said.

'As in, the Keys of Saint Peter?' asked Andrew. 'Actual keys to heaven and hell in the way that was depicted in that painting we found in the houseboat?'

'That's initially what I thought as well,' said Fiona. 'Antoine's interest in Saint Peter could make sense if you remember that he was also referred to as 'the Rock'. The name Peter is from the Latin *Petrus,* which means 'rock'. And La Roche literally means 'the rock'. So perhaps Hugo Rancourt named his castle after Saint Peter. But according to this, it seems like 'The Key' is actually a text that used to be part of the Lucifer Codex, which Antoine and Benoit were discussing in their email exchanges.'

'A text that is also a key,' said Andrew with a slight frown. 'What do you suppose it is exactly?'

Fiona shrugged and remained silent for a moment, staring into space.

'I am not sure,' she finally said. 'I wasn't able to find any references to it outside of Antoine's research. But it appears to be some sort of ancient mystical grimoire that is supposedly capable of summoning Lucifer himself.'

Andrew said nothing. Rather than be his usual derisive self about all things mystical and occult, he could no longer shake the dark encroaching realisation that something truly nefarious was underway, and that they had stumbled right into it in their search for Caitlin. Worst of all, the more they had discovered, the more it appeared that they were dealing with some seriously dangerous people, and there now seemed every chance that Caitlin could actually be in real danger. Fiona had been right. It didn't matter what the two of them thought of occult rituals and the prospect of dealing with demons or the Devil. All that mattered was that these crackpots seemed to believe in it, and that they were almost certainly holding Caitlin captive and were about to do her harm.

'Right. Let's focus,' said Andrew. 'What else does it say about the Lucifer Codex?'

'Well,' replied Fiona, 'If I am reading this correctly, then this Fabrice Benoit character and his team have been digging all over the south of France looking for a part of it that appears to be missing. A lost chapter. Something that they now think is the key to the main text, and which will release the full potential of the codex.'

'A lost chapter,' repeated Andrew. 'That sounds a bit spurious.'

'Or perhaps not,' said Fiona. 'Remember how Professor Kersley mentioned that the papacy was moved from Rome to Avignon by King Philip IV and the new pope Clement V in 1309?'

'Vaguely,' said Andrew.

'When that happened, it wasn't just the pope and his whole court of people that moved,' said Fiona. 'It was also the entire Vatican Archive, including the Secret Archive that only the popes themselves had access to.'

'I think I see where this is going,' said Andrew, looking intrigued.

'Now, the Avignon papacy lasted until 1378,' continued Fiona, 'when the last French head of the Catholic Church, Pope Gregory XI, finally moved it back to Rome. And of course, he arranged for the archive to be moved back to the Vatican once again. The research here seems to suggest that it was during the return of the archive to Rome that this lost chapter was either genuinely lost or perhaps intentionally removed. And from these notes, it appears that Haywood believes that the lost chapter contains the missing incantations that are required to complete the rituals laid out in the Lucifer Codex.'

'I must admit that I am finding it very difficult to take all of this nonsense seriously,' said Andrew. 'Yet at the same time, it is obvious that these people are as serious about this as they could be. Just look at the efforts they are going to. They really believe this stuff.'

'Without question,' said Fiona and pointed. 'But then look at this. Haywood seems to believe that the descendants of the two Templar brothers Gerard and Arnaud Rancourt somehow managed to get their hands on the lost chapter when the archive was in Avignon, and that they hid it somewhere under Château La Roche. From the correspondence between Antoine and Benoit, it also seemed as if Benoit is convinced that he was on the right track and very close to finding what he was looking for. They appear to believe that it was secreted away in the tomb of the younger brother Arnaud who was laid to rest in a secret crypt beneath the castle.'

'And what do you suppose they will do with it if they find it?' asked Andrew.

'I think it is pretty obvious by now that they are trying to carry out one of these ancient rituals that are supposedly described in the Lucifer Codex,' said Fiona. 'They are quite literally trying to release Lucifer from hell and bring him into this world. It sounds utterly deranged, I know, but that is what I think they believe. And I am terrified of what that might mean.'

Fiona looked meaningfully at Andrew as tears began to well up in her eyes.

'You mean Caitlin,' said Andrew, placing a hand gently on her shoulder. 'I know. But we have to stay focused now. This is our chance to find out what this whole thing is really about.'

Fiona nodded and sniffed.

'I will just take some photos of all of this,' she said bravely and extracted her phone from her jacket. 'But we should probably leave soon. Wouldn't there have been an alert sent out to whoever manages the aircon system here when we shut it down?'

'No doubt,' said Andrew calmly. 'But they won't be coming out until sometime tomorrow. First, I want to see what's behind that door.'

He gestured towards the black, solid-looking oak door at the end of the red carpet. Set into the wall next to it was a keypad that glowed a dull amber in the dimly lit research room.

'I doubt any of the codes Sean gave us will work there,' said Fiona.

'I am sure they won't,' said Andrew. 'But I've got something that just might be able to crack it.'

He walked close to it and dug into his backpack again, this time pulling out a small device about the shape and size of a marker pen, as well as a black device that looked a lot like a mobile phone. Amid a gentle whirring, he used the miniature electric screwdriver to remove the four screws holding the keypad's front panel in place. Still attached to the internal circuit board, he allowed the panel to hang down loosely next to the wall. He then plugged a set of wires into the device and attached them at the other end of the circuit board using connectors that clicked into several small ports on the board. Then he switched on the device and waited.

'What is that?' said Fiona, inspecting the device as it came alive and a flurry of numbers scrolled rapidly across the screen.

'Brute force,' said Andrew. 'This thing connects to the keypad's diagnostics interface, and then it runs through every four to eight-digit combination in a matter of seconds. Eventually, it will hit the right one.'

No sooner had he finished his sentence than the device chirped happily, and the amber panel lights turned to green. In the same moment, the lock on the door disengaged with a metallic snap.

'There,' he said. 'Easy if you have the right kit.'

'I never knew you were such an accomplished burglar,' said Fiona, raising one eyebrow.

'Just another skill they teach us at the regiment,' he replied. 'You never know when you might need those skills in the field.'

As he rose to his feet and opened the heavy door, there was a gentle hiss of air escaping.

'Hermetically sealed and climate-controlled,' he said. 'Let's see what's kept in here. It must be important.'

They walked inside and immediately another set of soft warm automatic overhead lights came on.

'Wow,' said Fiona, looking first at the polished metal-clad walls and then focusing on the only object in the room – a steel pedestal placed in the centre of the space with a glass display box resting on top of it. 'This must be Haywood's most prized possession.'

They approached it carefully, mildly surprised that no alarms had gone off. The display box appeared to have been made from thick panes of toughened glass, and above it was a single spotlight illuminating what looked like a very old book or manuscript lying open inside it.

'Holy crap,' breathed Fiona as she stood close and leaned in over the display box to study the ancient tome. 'An old vellum manuscript. It looks like another grimoire. This has got to be the Lucifer Codex. Haywood already has a copy of it. This might even be the only one in existence. Why else would it be kept in a place like this?'

Andrew moved to one side of the pedestal, inspecting the underside of the display box and the steel pedestal.

'Well, there's no way we'll be able to get this off and take it with us,' he said. 'The whole thing is welded to the floor, and there are no visible bolts anywhere on the box. And I don't see a way to open it manually. The lid must be operated by some sort of remote unit like a near-field RF card or possibly by Bluetooth via a phone. I bet only Haywood has the app installed.'

'I am not sure if it would make a difference,' said Fiona. 'Whatever is in here that Haywood deems of any value, I am sure he has memorised a long time ago, as well as taken extensive pictures of. It wouldn't change anything, except make it obvious that someone had been in here.'

'I guess you're right,' said Andrew, moving over to stand next to her and inspect the codex. 'I wonder how old it really is. And how do you suppose he acquired it, to begin with? And from where?'

'Who knows,' said Fiona, taking out her phone and snapping several pictures of the occult manuscript.

'Well, that settles it then,' she finally said, putting her phone back into her jacket pocket. 'Haywood already has the Lucifer Codex, so if they are looking for something under Château La Roche, it clearly has to be that lost chapter that was mentioned in the notes out the research room.'

Andrew stood with his hands on his hips, looking down at the codex and nodding gravely.

'I think you're probably right,' he said. 'Which really only leaves us with one option.'

'We go to Chateau La Roche and we find the lost chapter before they do,' said Fiona resolutely.

'Ok…' said Andrew, glancing at her. 'Just like that?'

'Do you have a better idea?' asked Fiona, sounding slightly vexed. 'Think about it. We've established beyond any doubt what Haywood and his people are looking for, and there is no doubt in my mind that they are already holding Caitlin captive somewhere. And if they really are as batshit crazy as they seem, then as soon as they find the lost chapter, they are going to use it to carry out a ceremony involving my sister that I don't even want to think about. The only way for us to prevent that from happening is to find the lost chapter before they do, and then trade it for Caitlin.'

'You're probably right,' said Andrew. 'These people are like all other religious fundamentalists, including the Islamist fundamentalists we were fighting in Iraq and Afghanistan. They fervently believe in the literal words of these ancient religious texts, and I have seen up close what these people are capable of. They don't care whether the codex is considered apocryphal by mainstream religion, or who wrote it or when. And they absolutely don't care what they have to do to find what they are after. All that matters to them is that they believe that what these texts say is literally true. That the gates of hell can be opened using this codex. It's obviously delusional, but a delusional person with a gun is just as dangerous as a normal person with a gun. In fact, they are probably more dangerous.'

'Exactly,' said Fiona. 'And that means that the lost chapter of the Lucifer Codex is the bargaining chip that they would give anything to possess. As you said, it really doesn't matter whether any of this lunacy is real or not. They are going to try to carry out that ceremony using my sister in the process, and I am just not letting that happen. I don't even care if I end up in prison for the rest of my life trying to stop them. I am going to France. Are you coming or not?'

Andrew was regarding Fiona as she spoke, her determination and ire growing with every word, and he had never seen her as determined and full of purpose as she looked at that moment. He briefly contemplated her plan, and then he nodded.

'Absolutely,' he said. 'It's the best shot we have at finding Caitlin right now. This whole thing is so twisted that if we try to go public or go to the authorities, chances are that no one will believe us. And it certainly won't help keep Caitlin safe or bring us any closer to actually locating her.'

'Sean Taylor was right,' said Fiona pensively. 'About all of it. And now he's dead and Haywood and his nutcases are still out there.'

'We will find Caitlin, and then we'll put a stop to this,' said Andrew with a steely expression. 'Once this is over, these people are going away for a long time.'

'Do you suppose they have killed other young women?' said Fiona. 'Just like Sean said they had.'

'It's possible,' replied Andrew. 'It's like any other cult. People are capable of the most depraved things if they end up sufficiently lost in their own delusions. As far as I am concerned, they are quite literally mentally ill, but we can't focus on that now. We need to move forward and solve this thing as soon as we can.'

'Good,' said Fiona. 'Let's just get out of here and get ourselves to France as soon as possible.'

Eighteen

Detective Inspector Graham Palmer was standing with his hands on his hips and his feet slightly apart, craning his neck to look up at the corpse dangling upside down from the underside of the bridge. The portable floodlights that had been placed around the cordoned-off crime scene reflected off the wet footpath next to the canal, and there was a strange, pungent smell surrounding the place. Palmer couldn't decide if it was because last night's downpour had caused nearby sewers to overflow into the canal, or if the body swaying gently above him had already started to decompose. Although thinking about it, the body couldn't possibly have begun to smell of death yet. The gruesome murder had happened too recently for that.

Palmer was in his mid-fifties with short, dark and curly hair that sat in an unruly mop at the top of his head and which he had long ago ceded any pretence of control over. His short-trimmed sideburns extended to the middle of his cheeks, and they had streaks of grey that reminded him every morning that life was little more than a wind-up clock inexorably ticking towards its final end. His face was slightly pudgy with the faintly rosy tint that gave away his penchant for red wine, and the dark rings under his eyes were a testament to the many late nights he spent awake when he really should be catching up on his sleep.

He was of average height and build, and as always he was wearing his long dark trench coat over a cheap grey suit, as well as a charcoal bucket hat. In his hand was a half-finished cigarette. Despite the best efforts of what was now thankfully his ex-wife, he had never even considered quitting. Smoking helped him to think, and working homicide investigations had merely had the effect of making him impervious to the gory images of blackened lungs and putrefied fingers and toes that were printed on all cigarette packets these days.

He placed the cigarette in his mouth, inhaled a big lungful of smoke and nicotine, savoured the taste and the hit for a couple of seconds, and then he looked at his wristwatch. It was now ten past five in the morning, so in all likelihood, the murder had happened less than six hours ago. The macabre sight of a corpse hanging from the trusses under a bridge in central London had been discovered by a young female insurance broker who had been out for an early morning run before going to work. Right now, she was sitting on a bench about twenty metres further along the footpath being interviewed by the patrol officers who were first on the scene. Palmer doubted that they would be able to provide anything useful. Firstly, they were just simple Bobbies, and everyone in homicide knew that those weren't the sharpest knives in the drawer. Secondly, the murder had almost certainly happened several hours before the petite blond woman had come along, so she was highly unlikely to be able to provide them with anything other than how shocked she was to find a dead body here, how she had never seen anything like this, and how this has always been such a calm and gentrified part of the city and yada-yada-yada. Most people had absolutely no idea about the sort of shit that happened every single night in London once they closed their doors and sat down in front of the TV to watch mindless entertainment. Palmer knew he was jaded by several decades of murder investigations, but in this line of work that was usually an asset rather than a liability.

He exhaled the grey lungful of carcinogenic smoke, and it drifted off in the gentle breeze. Right about now, the boys in the Met's CCTV control room should already be busy retrieving the footage from the cameras on Prince Albert Road. With any luck, they should be able to scrub through it and spot the victim coming down one of the nearby paths that led from the road down to the footpath by the canal. From there it might be possible to pin down which other individuals had been there during the night, and which one of them was likely to be the killer. They should have the results in a couple of hours. However, if this case was anything like most of the previous ones, they would end up chasing shadows and never actually manage to apprehend anyone.

Officially, Palmer was part of a special unit that had been set up to investigate the murders of young women in the capital. The number of homicides of young females had been going up steadily over the past many years, but then so had the number of murdered young males, and Palmer was often dispatched to those murders as well. However, female homicides usually received significantly more attention in the tabloids, so in an attempt to placate the media the Metropolitan Police had decided to set up Palmer's unit in order to at least be seen to address the issue. The intention had been for several more colleagues to join him, but for various reasons this had never happened. Palmer *was* the unit, and working by himself suited him just fine. He had never been particularly sociable, and he often found that colleagues and co-workers would just get in the way of his ability to do his job. Particularly the Bobbies on the beat, each of whom seemed convinced that they had a Sherlock Holmes or an Inspector Morse inside them just waiting for a chance to shine.

'Bad way to start the day,' said a voice flatly behind him. 'I guess suicide's out of the question.'

Here we bloody go again, thought Palmer wearily and turned around to see a Bobby who somehow seemed vaguely familiar.

The middle-aged officer was standing back a couple of metres with both hands inside the straps of his black stab vest, looking up at the corpse from under his police cap. In his belt was a black baton that would be about as useful against a gun-wielding killer as a flyswatter against a swarm of African killer bees. Palmer wondered whether the cop had even noticed the two bullet wounds to the victim's chest yet.

'I'm Jones,' nodded the officer in an overly familiar way that already irritated Palmer. 'I attended another one of your crime scenes about eighteen months ago. Young woman over in Kilburn. They found her in a garden shed.'

'Right,' said Palmer. 'I think I remember you now. DI Palmer.'

'Never seen one like this before,' continued the officer, looking unfazed at the sight of the dead body dangling under the bridge. 'Any idea who he was?'

'As a matter of fact, I do,' replied Palmer, despite himself.

'Really?' said Jones. 'You knew this guy?'

'Yes,' replied Palmer, looking back up at Sean Taylor's body. 'In a manner of speaking. He has been hounding me for months about a number of cases I have been working on. All of them regarding missing women. He said he had uncovered some conspiracy that explained everything. I dismissed him as just another fantasist. Now I am not so sure.'

'Well,' said Jones, making a regretful face. 'He won't be talking now.'

'No,' said Palmer evenly, pressing his lips together. 'He certainly won't.'

★ ★ ★

The black BMW pulled in by the side of the road and parked under a tree across from the house on the north edge of Finsbury Park. It had tinted windows, wide tyres and floating hubcaps that kept spinning for several seconds after the vehicle had come to a stop. The powerful engine remained on for about a minute, producing a low, throaty growl as it idled.

Eventually, the engine fell silent and the driver's side door opened, followed by the front passenger door and the passenger door behind the driver's seat. Three large body-builder types stepped out, and as they did so the car's suspension visibly relaxed and the chassis lifted a couple of centimetres further away from the road. They slammed the doors shut and straightened their clothes, and then the driver pressed the button on his key to lock the car doors. The indicator lights flashed once and the car produced a quick double-chirp.

The driver looked a few years older than his two comrades, and he was taller and wore a full but neatly trimmed black beard. The man who had sat next to him looked lean despite his bulky build, and he had short blond hair with a military-style haircut and neck tattoos. The third man was about as broad as he was tall, and as he brought up the rear of the trio he seemed to be lumbering along with his powerful muscly arms swinging at his sides like a chimpanzee.

They crossed the road and filed silently up the garden path of the handsome house directly opposite where the driver had parked their vehicle. Stepping up to the front door, the bearded man turned to say something to his two mates. Then he faced forward again, adjusted his short leather jacket and rang the doorbell. After about ten seconds, there was movement behind the door's stained-glass windows.

When the door opened, the three men remained immobile as the short elderly man regarded them suspiciously.

'Oh,' said a startled Professor Kersley, looking quite unsure of the situation. 'Erm… Good morning.'

'Good morning. May we come in?' said Dragomir in his slow and deep gravelly voice, making it plain that what he had said was in fact not a request.

★ ★ ★

The next morning, Christopher Haywood was by his desk in his home office on the 66th floor of the Shard. The skies had cleared after the deluge the previous night, and the sun was barrelling in through the floor-to-ceiling windows. It was a glorious and balmy summer morning, which ought to have made anyone start the day in a cheerful mood, but Haywood was anything but pleased. Wearing a dark pinstriped suit as he did most days, he was sitting immobile with his eyes fixed on the laptop in front of him. Its screen was showing a replay of a video recording from inside the temple building that the rest of the city knew only as the home of the Worshipful Company of Jurists. The lack of colour in the black-and-white CCTV recording was in stark contrast to the red mist that Haywood, despite his perennially unemotional demeanour felt rising inside himself as he watched.

He had replayed this several times already, but he still couldn't quite believe how the intruders had managed to enter his personal office through the ventilation system, having first gained access to the temple through a side entrance. The passcode that was required to enter the building in that way was not supposed to be given to anyone that didn't work there. But even then, it would not allow for access to areas that were off-limits to anyone without the required status within the fraternity. The codes that had been used to enter the temple and then access the boiler room could only have been divulged by one of the companies tasked with servicing the building and its internal systems. It could even have been someone from the service provider currently inside the boiler room repairing the ducts connected to the air conditioning unit. He would have to look into that further and take appropriate steps.

As he watched the replay of the ventilation grille popping out from the side of the wall just under the ceiling followed by a man emerging and dropping onto the floor, Haywood leaned forward to study him more closely, his eyes narrowing as he did so. After a few moments, a woman also appeared. She seemed familiar somehow, but he couldn't quite put his finger on why that was.

The two of them examined the office, left through the door to the corridor and walked to the other end of it, seemingly looking for something. They eventually turned around and returned to the office, having first spent a couple of minutes studying some of the portraits on the walls. Haywood had the uncomfortable feeling that the two of them were busy piecing together things about him personally.

When the two intruders returned, it didn't take them long to discover the hidden elevator to the basement level using some sort of torch that revealed where the button for the mechanism was. This was yet another disconcerting display of the degree to which the temple had turned out to be significantly less secure than he had thought it was. Once the two of them had entered the elevator and descended, he could see nothing more of what they did next, because for obvious reasons the basement level had no security cameras at all. Roughly an hour later, the trespassers re-emerged back in the office and left it the same way they had entered.

Haywood sat back in his office chair, his eyes boring through the frozen image on the laptop's screen and into the middle distance as he contemplated what had happened and what plans he might need to set in motion now. There was no doubt that these two were the same people who he had seen on the CCTV footage from Saint Katherine Marina and who had killed Antoine. And if Laurent was right, then they were also the same pair who had been intending to meet Sean Taylor and who had ended up shooting Laurent. Whoever they were, they were not just another couple of pesky journalists poking around in business they ought to stay well clear of. These were of an entirely different calibre, and so they would require a very different level of attention.

Haywood had received the footage from the marina via Maxwell in encrypted form, and it had been delivered to Maxwell by one of his paid contacts inside the Metropolitan Police. However, for some strange reason, there had been a long delay in identifying the pair. Maxwell had seemed confident that his source would be able to run them through the facial recognition system and determine who they were and where they lived fairly swiftly, but it was unclear why this was taking so long. According to Maxwell, he had also created several mugshots from the footage, which he had then sent to the Romanians. If past experience was anything to go by, once they had the exact identity of the two intruders, the trio would soon solve the problem violently and permanently.

Nineteen

Andrew and Fiona were seated on the British Airways early afternoon flight to Toulouse. It took off and broke through the low clouds up into the sunlight above. Fiona was by the window, and as the aircraft banked slightly to head south towards the English Channel and France, Andrew noticed her staring vacantly outside, seemingly lost in thought.

'I owe her my life, you know,' she said quietly whilst looking out at the white sunlit cloud cover rolling by far below them.

'What do you mean?' asked Andrew, sensing the emotion in her voice as he turned to face her.

'I mean, I wouldn't be sitting here if it wasn't for her,' replied Fiona, giving a brief shake of the head.

She paused for a moment before continuing.

'It is a long time ago now,' she said, 'but once when we were children she saved my life. I think I was twelve years old, and she would have been nine. It was winter and we had been playing in a park in Dublin called St Stephen's Green. It's just a few minutes' walk from Merion Park, but we liked to go there because it has two ponds. We always used to feed the ducks. Anyway, it was freezing cold that day, and there was a thick blanket of snow in the park. It was so pretty, and the ponds had frozen over completely, but there was no one else around. It was just me and her and the ducks. I remember them skidding around on the ice trying to be the first to get to the bread we had thrown to them. I am not sure what got into me, but I decided to step out onto the ice next to the bank to see if it would hold my weight. Maybe I was showing off, and I think I probably figured that I could get back onto the bank if the ice was too thin. It turned out to be solid on that side of the pond, and I remember walking out onto it and turning back to wave at Caitlin. She called out to me and looked worried, but I just smiled. I was so sure I knew what I was doing. But at that age, you have no idea about all the things you don't understand. I remember walking slowly towards the centre of the pond feeling like a daring explorer. But out there the pond gets a lot more sun than near the bank where Caitlin was standing, so the ice was not as thick. I suddenly heard the strange muffled sound of the ice cracking, and I even saw the white cracks appearing underneath my feet. The next thing I knew, I had gone through and disappeared under the cold water. My entire body went rigid from the shock and the cold, and my clothes immediately began pulling me down. I could barely keep my head above water, and I felt paralysed. Everyone had always told us not to go out on the ice, yet there I was. It was a stupid mistake, and I already knew I was going to die. I remember hearing Caitlin scream as my head broke back up through the surface. I was clawing frantically at the edge of the ice, but every time I tried to pull myself up, another piece of it broke off under my weight. Within a few seconds, I was completely exhausted. My body was cold and stiff and my arms and legs wouldn't do as I wanted. It was terrifying. I was about to cry out for Caitlin to come and help me, but then I realised that if she came for me, she would go through as well. So, I stayed silent and waited for a miracle, or death, whichever came first. When I looked over towards her again, I saw that she had stepped out on the ice herself and was coming towards me. I yelled at her to stay back, but she wouldn't listen. She just kept coming. When she was about five metres away, I heard the sound of the ice cracking again, and so did Caitlin. I screamed. Her eyes went wide with panic, but then she lowered herself gently onto the ice and lay down on her front with her arms and legs out to the sides to spread her weight. She crawled towards me, but at that point I was almost unable to hold on any longer. I was clinging on to the edge of the ice, but my head kept slipping under and I was swallowing water. I begged her to go back, but she wouldn't. When she was about a metre away from me, she wriggled out of her coat and flung it towards me whilst holding on to a sleeve. I grabbed onto it and then she started to pull. She was as terrified as I was. I could see it in her eyes, but somehow she held it together. She refused to give up. She was only a little girl, but she would have given her life for mine. I am sure of it. She was so small back then, but somehow she managed to hang on to the coat while I pulled myself out of the hole, spreading my weight on the ice the way I had seen her do it. We finally made it back off the ice and onto the bank, and then she took off my soaked coat, threw it on the ground and gave me hers to wear. I was rigid with cold, so she slipped inside the coat and hugged me tight, telling me to zip it up with us both inside. She told me she was going to be my hot water bottle. I couldn't believe how calm and strong she was. So, we stood there hugging each other for a while as she gave me her own body heat until I had stopped shivering. Then we hurried home through the snow. When we finally came inside, her lips were dark blue from the cold, but she just smiled at me as she stood there shivering. I think she understood what she had done, and that I would have died without her help.'

'Wow,' breathed Andrew, raising his eyebrows. 'What a story. I can see why you two are so close.'

'I would have done the same for her,' said Fiona solemnly. 'Now that she is missing, I have a chance to make it up to her. And I will give my life to find her if that's what it takes.'

★   ★   ★

They touched down at Toulouse-Blagnac Airport just after 4 p.m. local time. The former Roman town and capital of the region of Languedoc during the late Middle Ages was situated on the river Garonne – one of France's longest rivers. It runs north from the Pyrenees on the Spanish side of the border through Toulouse and then northwest past Bordeaux to the

Bay of Biscay and the Atlantic Ocean. Six hundred kilometres of waterway that has helped keep the south of France rich and fertile for centuries, and around which dozens of towns and cities such as Toulouse had sprung up.

The city, aside from being home to more than half a million people, was also the main hub for one of France's biggest employers, Airbus Industries. With more than a hundred thousand employees, it is widely known for manufacturing passenger aircraft. What is less well known is that its space division produces satellite-based navigation and intelligence-gathering systems, as well as strategic missile and defence systems. Its helicopter division produces both civilian and military helicopters, including the EC665 Tiger helicopter, which is similar to the American AH-1 Cobra and mainly used for ground attack missions.

The main Airbus assembly complex was visible from the aircraft as it taxied to the end of the runway, swung around and began to make its way to the terminal. Andrew peered out towards the buildings and reflected on his own experience with the company's military hardware. Luckily for him, he had not been on the receiving end of it. However, he had once watched a pair of Tiger helicopters lay into a large group of Jihadi fighters inside a training camp in northern Mali near the border with Algeria. Working alongside French special forces, his small team of SAS soldiers had been responsible for setting up an observation post a few hundred metres from the camp. They had remained there for several days, baking under the relentless African sun while they mapped out the movements and routines of the senior commanders. Eventually, once they deemed most of the senior leadership to be in one place, they had called in the two attack helicopters. They were armed with nose-mounted and gimbaled machine gun turrets that were slaved to the gunners' helmets. In addition, they carried wing-mounted rockets and Trigat anti-tank missiles that are similar to the US Hellfire version. While Andrew and his small team looked on, the two choppers had made short work of the jihadi fighters, their training camp and their vehicles. The helicopters had circled the camp like angry hornets letting loose with their advanced weapons systems, and they had left nothing alive when they eventually returned to base less than ten minutes after arriving. When Andrew and his team had moved into the wreckage of the training camp alongside the French special forces team half an hour later to mob up and eliminate any survivors, they had trouble finding any remains of the fighters that were much larger than a fist.

Exiting the arrivals terminal, Andrew and Fiona rented a black Audi A6 with a powerful engine and skirted around the city centre to the west through a couple of industrial suburbs until they eventually joined the *autoroute A64* going south. As they drove the approximately seventy kilometres southwest towards the foothills of the Pyrenees, they were never far from the Garonne River which meandered through the increasingly hilly countryside as they drove ever further south on their approach to the mountain range.

By the time they arrived at their destination, it was half past six in the evening and both of them were getting hungry. As it turned out, Roquefort-sur-Garonne was less of a town and more of a handful of smaller villages scattered around the river where it flowed through a wide gap in the foothills of the Pyrenees. It was warm and slightly muggy as they pulled up outside a small eatery by a large open tree-lined square near the centre of town and stepped out of the car. The sun had retreated behind a wall of clouds far to the west, and overhead were scattered grey clouds that looked like they might send a rain shower down onto the town at any minute. High up above them on a hilltop a few hundred metres to the east was a medieval tower with visible battlements just sticking up behind what looked like a small forest. A small road snaked its way up towards it from the edge of town.

'That's Château La Roche up there,' said Fiona and pointed. 'It looks even more isolated from down here than it does on the maps.'

'I guess the sheer cliff is on the other side,' said Andrew, gazing up at the château. 'But even from this side, it looks daunting. It would have been pretty much impossible to lay siege to it if the defenders had plenty of provisions.'

'Speaking of which,' said Fiona as she began to move towards the entrance to the roadside restaurant, her gaze still fixed on the castle in the distance. 'Let's get some food.'

'Yes,' said Andrew. 'Good idea. We need to get up there tonight, so we should sit down and make a plan.'

They walked inside and sat down in a booth near the back. Within fifteen minutes they both had a small basket of freshly baked bread and a steaming hot plate of omelette in front of them cooked by the resident chef with all manner of local produce.

'This is divine,' said Fiona, tucking in greedily. 'I am starving.'

'You're right. It's superb,' nodded Andrew with his mouth full of food. 'Sometimes I think countries like France and Italy eat their best produce and drink their best wine themselves, and then they sell the rest of it to people like us who don't know any better.'

'You might be right,' smiled Fiona. 'Wouldn't you do that?'

'Anyway,' said Andrew, taking a swig of his beer. 'I noticed that you were looking at those pictures you took in Haywood's research room. What did you make of them?'

Fiona had spent most of the flight and some of the drive studying the photos of Haywood's various research notes, as well as going over the texts they had found on Antoine's houseboat. As she did so, she was taking extensive notes on her phone. She had been trying to piece together what Haywood and his archaeologist Fabrice Benoit were doing and what they believed they we about to find in Château La Roche.

'In short,' said Fiona. 'They are looking for an ossuary. You know – a small container placed inside a tomb that holds ashes or skeletal remains of the deceased.'

'Ossuary,' nodded Andrew whilst chewing. 'Got it. Whose ossuary, and why are they after it? They think the so-called Key is there?'

'Precisely,' said Fiona. 'Remember the two Templar brothers Gerard and Arnaud Rancourt? As I told you,

Arnaud was supposedly buried somewhere under the castle in a secret crypt, and Haywood and Benoit seem to believe that this key was buried with him inside the ossuary containing his remains. They speculate that the older brother Gerard was concerned that it would fall into the hands of the Catholic Church. Without the key – this lost chapter – the Lucifer Codex would be ineffectual. After burying it with Arnaud's body, Gerard might have intended to retrieve it later, and it is possible that he eventually did.'

'What happened to Gerard?' asked Andrew.

'Apparently, he lived in the castle until he became an old man,' said Fiona, 'at which point he passed it to his son and moved to Paris, which was a very unusual thing to do for a land-owning knight at that time. I have been unable to find any reference to precisely when or where he died, which is equally odd. He would have been a relatively high-profile member of the aristocracy, so it is surprising that there seems to be no clue as to how he died or where his remains might have been buried. Or perhaps I just haven't been able to find it.'

'Ok,' said Andrew. 'So, Benoit is looking for a tomb containing an ossuary. Aren't there a limited number of places something like that could be?'

'You would have thought so,' said Fiona, 'but as you have seen on the maps the castle is a sprawling complex covering a pretty large area, so if you really wanted to hide something of great importance like that, you would probably put it in anything but the obvious places. So, Benoit and his team have been opening up smaller dig sites all over the castle grounds.'

'All right,' said Andrew. 'I guess we'll get the lay of the land once we get up there.'

'But we can't just pull up in front of the gates and say hello,' said Fiona.

'I know,' said Andrew, bringing out his phone to show Fiona a map of the area. 'I had a closer look at the roads around here, and there is a small forest trail that leads up near the base of the promontory that the castle is sitting on. We can drive most of the way there and then take the trail through the forest up towards the southern outer wall. If we can get up and over that, we should be able to get inside the castle unseen. But we should stay here for a couple more hours until it starts to get dark.'

They finished their meals as the sun retreated behind the hills to the west. Having polished off their omelettes, they ordered deserts and then two rounds of freshly brewed coffee while they talked over what they might find inside the castle walls. Several more hours went by during which time low clouds drew in from the east, and by the time they were ready to pay the bill, the town of Roquefort-sur-Garonne was enveloped in semi-darkness under a blanket of dark grey cloud cover.

They called over the restaurant's friendly *garçon*, paid the bill and left a generous tip, which was greeted with a smile and an '*À bientôt!*'. The two of them very much hoped that they would indeed be able to come back, but it all depended on what they would find at the castle.

From the car park, they could no longer make out the castle itself through the gloomy dusk, but the rocky promontory upon which it sat was still visible, and it seemed to loom menacingly over the town. As he looked upwards, Andrew could easily imagine how a medieval lord such as Hugo Rancourt, secluded as he was behind his high walls with a small army at his command, would have been able to dominate the entire valley and its population both physically and psychologically. The aristocracy of the Middle Ages was wealthy, not because they worked hard, but because they had managed to control the resources in their local area and force the peasants there to work for them. And the most successful of those landowners ended up becoming kings. It had been like that across all the different continents of the world and across time ever since humans stopped being hunter-gatherers and instead settled down in permanent communities relying on crops and domesticated animals to sustain them. It was a simple and brutal life where might was always right.

The two of them got into the car, but instead of driving straight up the narrow, winding road towards the castle, Andrew followed the main road that ran alongside the river for another five hundred metres. Then he made a left turn and proceeded along a dirt track that curved back towards the wooded hill from a southerly direction. He kept the headlights on short beam in order to avoid being too visible. Soon the track began snaking its way up through the small forest that consisted of various deciduous trees covering most of the large hill. As they proceeded upwards, the forest became denser and darker, and the large beech trees seemed to stand ever closer to the meandering track. After about twenty minutes they found themselves at a dead end in a small clearing where there was a picnic spot amongst the trees with wooden benches and parking spaces for three cars. It didn't look like it was used frequently.

It was now almost pitch black under the canopy of the tall trees. Only a faint, pale light from the moon managed to reach them through the cloud cover. They stepped out and stood silently for a moment, listening out for sounds of people or vehicles and allowing their eyes to adjust to the darkness. All they could hear was the light breeze that sighed through the trees above them and made their trunks sway ever so slightly. There was also the faint and far-off noise from the occasional car driving along the main road in the town.

'Ready?' asked Andrew.

'As ready as I'll ever be,' said Fiona, not looking entirely comfortable being inside a forest late at night.

Andrew got out his phone, selected his favourite hiking app and waited for the phone to triangulate its position to within a couple of metres.

'We need to head northeast,' he said and pointed up the hill and into the forest.

'There's no trail,' said Fiona, peering into the darkness where all she could see were trees and the leaf-covered forest floor.

'I know,' said Andrew. 'We want to be coming up to the castle walls from the southwest. It looks like it has rained here recently, so everything is wet. That will make the climb trickier, but it also means that we will make less noise. Try to keep that in mind as we get closer.'

Fiona looked down onto the thick carpet of leaves and the small branches and twigs strewn everywhere.

The forest was so quiet that a snapping twig would be audible from at least fifty metres away.

'Ok,' she said. 'Let's go then.'

Andrew switched his hiking app to night mode, and the screen dimmed appreciably and changed to a sepia colour scheme. Then he extracted a torch from his backpack and flicked it onto the red-light mode, which had a significantly lower lumen output, but which made the contrast between light and dark areas on the leaf-covered forest floor ahead of them seem more pronounced.

Shortly after setting off, the leaves rustling gently under their feet as they went, the ground began to rise noticeably until the trees seemed to be slanted in one direction. It continued like that for at least ten minutes, and Fiona was beginning to wonder if they were going in the right direction. However, a couple of minutes later, the forest floor gradually became increasingly rocky. There were dark moss-covered boulders scattered on the ground between the trees, and suddenly a steep grey rockface rose up in front of them. It was about ten metres high and partly overgrown, with tufts of grass and small bushes growing in the cracks and crevices that had been created by the weather over countless centuries. Andrew approached the rockface, trying to decide on the best way to scale it.

'Over here,' he said quietly after a few seconds. 'We can get up this way. It looks steep from down here, but there is plenty of purchase for our hands and feet along the way.'

Climbing up to a small ledge a couple of metres up, he stopped and waited for Fiona to join him, helping her up onto the ledge. Then he climbed up another couple of metres and waited again. They repeated the process until they were both safely at the top, and only then were they able to see the dark castle walls looming above them around ten metres away. Once upon a time, the rockface they had just climbed up would have functioned as a vertical moat that would have been impossible to scale for an attacking force.

They approached the wall quietly, and as they did so it seemed to grow taller. Andrew let the red light from his torch sweep across it looking for a place to climb over.

'It is in remarkably good condition,' he said in a hushed voice.

'Well, from what I have been able to find out,' said Fiona, 'it has been inhabited permanently since its restoration around 1850. How are we going to get up and over? We don't have a ladder.'

'We don't need one,' said Andrew, handing her his torch and backpack.

He walked back to the edge of the rockface and proceeded a short distance along the edge to where a young tree that was about five metres tall had once stood. It had germinated in the soil right on the edge of the drop, and it had survived there precariously close to the edge until it had finally grown so tall that it must have been blown over in a storm, or perhaps the crumbling rock beneath it had finally given way to its increasing weight. Now, the tree had fallen down and lay halfway out over the edge. Its demise would have happened a year or two earlier, because it was still strong and sturdy, yet relatively dry and not too difficult to pick up and carry.

Andrew tore off the remaining roots with his bare hands, separating them from the rock, and then he picked it up by the trunk and hauled it back towards Fiona. Here he lifted it up and placed it upright, leaning against the wall. The tallest branches were less than a metre from the top of the battlements.

'That should do it,' he said, looking up at his handiwork. 'I'll go first.'

'Fine by me,' said Fiona and stepped back. 'Do you want me to steady it?'

'No,' replied Andrew, donning his backpack again and then using the lower branches to begin his climb. 'It's very stable.'

Less than a minute later, he was able to reach up to grip the edge of the battlements and haul himself up and over. He dropped down and leaned back out over the edge, waiting for Fiona to follow him. Soon she had completed her own ascent, and with a helping hand from Andrew, joined him on the narrow walkway on top of the battlement of the castle's southern outer wall. It was now just after ten o'clock, and in the distance, they heard the eerie lamenting double-hoot of an owl. Down in the valley about two hundred metres below them and roughly half a kilometre away, the dim lights of the town were just visible through the tops of the trees that surrounded the castle. They crouched low and proceeded a few metres along the walkway to a spot where there was a gap in the battlements that allowed them to look down into the outer courtyard.

'Crikey,' whispered Fiona. 'It looks like a campervan convention.'

Below them were a handful of campervans of different sizes as well as tents arranged neatly off to one side near the western outer wall. The camp was complete with what appeared to be a large tent for preparing and eating meals, and a line of portaloos was arranged along the castle's outer wall at the back. Throughout the camp were small spotlights mounted on poles that illuminated the different footpaths between the various tents.

'Sean was right in saying that Haywood has thrown a lot of resources at this,' said Andrew. 'But I don't see anyone. Where are they all?'

'Sleeping,' said Fiona. 'You can't do any digging at night, and the sun comes up early, so they need to be well rested by then.'

'Unless of course they are busy excavating under the chapel,' said Andrew and pointed. 'It should be through there.'

At the far end of the outer courtyard was a gate in the inner wall with a portcullis that led through to the inner courtyard. The gate was open, and beyond it, they could just make out the keep that had once been the residence of Hugo Rancourt and then later his two sons, Gerard and Arnaud.

'The chapel is next to the keep,' he continued, 'and the crypt is under the chapel, right? We need to get down there.'

'We can't allow ourselves to get spotted,' said Fiona. 'If they realise we are here, it could put Caitlin at risk. No violence please.'

'Roger that,' said Andrew. 'I wasn't planning on it. I also couldn't bring a firearm into France, so it's best if we keep a low profile.'

'Well, we can't go through the outer courtyard,' said Fiona and pointed down below. 'Too much light. Too many people. Someone could come out of their tent or campervan at any moment.'

'We should be able to get into the inner courtyard over this way,' said Andrew, and pointed along the walkway running the length of the outer wall. 'This wall connects to the inner wall near the keep. I am sure we can climb up there and then drop down into the inner courtyard.'

A couple of minutes later they had relocated to the end of the walkway where it met the inner wall and managed to scale the final couple of metres to the top of it. Below them now was the inner courtyard with the impressive three-storey keep, what looked like stables next to it on one side and the small chapel on the other. The keep was in complete darkness, but light was flooding out of the chapel entrance with its characteristic curved gothic arch tapering up towards a tight angle at its apex. Light was also blooming out of the colourful stained-glass mosaic windows along its sides, which now seemed to glow from within.

'They might still be in there,' whispered Fiona. 'Although I don't see any movement.'

'There's only one way to find out,' replied Andrew and checked his wristwatch. 'We could wait a couple more hours before going in if you like.'

Fiona pressed her lips together and looked uncertain.

'I am not sure if I feel like sitting here for several more hours,' she said in hushed tones. 'Every minute is another minute we might get spotted. Let's do it.'

They used a set of steps near one of the round towers to descend into the inner courtyard, and then they moved cautiously around the rear of the keep. From there they made their way around the back of the chapel and finally along its side until they were by the corner near its entrance. Andrew listened out for voices or noises that might reveal the presence of some of the workers, but there was only silence apart from the owl in the distance. The moon was now peeking through a gap in the clouds, so being out in the open would instantly give their presence away.

He turned slowly and waved Fiona forward, placing an index finger in front of his lips. The two of them then slipped around the corner and stood silently for a moment by the chapel entrance where Andrew quickly peeked inside. The chapel had been cleared of pews and all other movable items, and all over the floor were tools and machinery that had been used during the excavation, along with a set of bright floodlights that lit up the centre of the space like a surgeon's table in an operating theatre.

Andrew looked past the nave towards the far end of the chapel to the apse, and there he saw a stone altar that lay broken into two jagged pieces. Where the altar had once stood was a large dark hole in the marble floor. Next to it on the left side was a small shrine of some sort, and on the right was a narrow doorway to what appeared to be a tiny vestry where the resident vicar would have prepared himself for his sermons and ceremonies.

'Come on,' whispered Andrew. 'Let's go.'

They slipped inside and moved quietly along the nave towards the broken altar. As they went, Fiona's head was on a swivel, taking in the old chapel's interior. It very plainly had a distinct theme to it, and up above their heads on the vaulted veiling was a visage that stopped her in her tracks.

'Andrew,' she whispered and pointed above.

He stopped, turned and followed her gaze upwards. Above them was a large, expansive mural depicting what was unmistakably Saint Peter. In fact, it bore an uncanny resemblance to the painting by Paul Peter Rubens that Antoine had kept in the houseboat. Saint Peter, the most influential disciple and the first pope of the Holy Roman Church was gazing upwards with a pious look on his face. In one hand he was holding a golden key, and in the other, a black key made of iron or some other metal.

'The keys to heaven and hell,' whispered Andrew.

'If Haywood is to be believed…' responded Fiona.

'Come on,' said Andrew quietly, tugging gently at her sleeve. 'We need to get down into the crypt.'

As they approached the large black hole that had been smashed down through the marble flooring where the altar had stood, they suddenly heard a voice coming from below. An instant later, a brief flash from a torch shone up through the hole, briefly illuminating the huge murals overhead.

'This way,' whispered Andrew urgently and took Fiona's hand, moving swiftly and leading her towards the doorway to the vestry.

As soon as they made it inside, a head appeared through the dark hole in the floor. It belonged to a large bearded, barrel-chested man with rolled-up sleeves and a smoking cigar in his mouth. Climbing up and out of the hole using a ladder that had been lowered into it, he was followed by a young man with slicked-back dark hair. As soon as he was out, the young man immediately began brushing dust off of his shiny charcoal-coloured business suit with an annoyed facial expression.

Andrew and Fiona were unable to see them from their hiding place, but they could hear their voices quite clearly from inside the vestry.

'Of course, I understand,' said a gruff voice with a heavy French accent and a tired and grumpy timbre to his voice. 'But *you* must understand that my men cannot work twenty-four hours a day. They need their food, and they need their rest.'

'Listen, Fabrice,' said the young man with a clipped accent, sounding agitated. 'We're not paying those lazy bastards to rest, you know. We're paying them to find the bloody tomb within the next couple of days. Otherwise, everyone's bonuses get wiped. Do you understand?'

'Monsieur Maxwell,' said the older man, now with an affronted tone. 'I know *exactement* why we are here and what we are doing. I have been involved in this project since you were a little boy. Don't forget that.'

At the mention of Tristan Maxwell's name, Andrew and Fiona exchanged a glance. The man who seemed to have helped Antoine kidnap Caitlin was right here in the chapel. Fiona's eyes quickly hardened, and Andrew could see that she was struggling to keep calm and stop herself from running out into the chapel and throttling Maxwell. He placed a hand gently on her arm and shook his head silently with a stern look on his face. Her shoulders sank back down and then she nodded. A confrontation now would risk everything.

'Mr Haywood has asked me to...,' began Maxwell.

'I do not need you in order to speak to Monsieur Haywood,' Benoit blurted out angrily. 'I speak to him directly. Not through his pet.'

'Just find the damn tomb,' said Maxwell in a menacing voice. 'You really don't was to disappoint him.'

Andrew was half-expecting another retort from the Frenchman, but after a couple of seconds, Benoit just produced a deep sigh. Then he turned on his heels and began striding along the nave towards the door to the outside, presumably heading back to his campervan.

'We need to decide what to do with Maurice,' said Benoit over his shoulder.

'Just leave him,' said Maxwell disparagingly. 'Think of it as a medieval IQ test. He failed. Let him rot.'

There was a short pause before Maxwell spoke again, this time in a challenging tone.

'Is there a problem?' he asked.

'*Bonne nuit! A demain!*' said Benoit curtly and walked off in a huff, leaving a frustrated Maxwell with his hands on his hips and shaking his head.

The young man sighed, and then he produced a noise that was a mix of a scoff and a chortle.

'Bloody lazy frogs,' he muttered quietly to himself, but loud enough for Andrew and Fiona to hear it. 'In a couple of hours, you won't be so smug.'

Soon thereafter, he followed the burly French archaeologist out of the chapel and disappeared, leaving Andrew and Fiona looking at each other.

'Lovers' tiff?' asked Fiona and shrugged.

'I am not sure exactly what to call that,' said Andrew. 'But I'm pretty certain they are not coming back any time soon.'

'I agree,' said Fiona. 'And judging by their conversation, it sounds like there is no one else down there right now. This is our chance.'

'Let's go,' said Andrew.

Twenty

As they descended the near-vertical ladder extending down into the crypt under the chapel, both Andrew and Fiona were immediately struck by just how stale and clammy the air seemed. The crypt had no doubt been sealed off for centuries until a few days ago, and whatever had been inside when the last marble block had been laid down into the floor of the chapel had remained trapped ever since. There was the distinct whiff of organic matter decomposing. Coming from the brightly lit chapel, it also seemed extraordinarily dark in the crypt.

'Wow. It smells like something died down here,' whispered Fiona, frowning. 'I hope it was just rats.'

Small pebbles and bits of dust came away from the inside of the hole in the chapel floor as they climbed down into the space below. Andrew switched on his torch to reveal that they were in a small space about two metres by one metre in size. A narrow tunnel led away through one end of it, more or less in the direction of the keep. As they approached it, they both noticed that a square section of the floor in the middle of the tunnel was missing. It was as if the flagstone that had covered it had been removed. Andrew took a couple of steps inside the tunnel and leaned cautiously out over the edge to look down into a deep pit.

'Bloody hell,' he said grimly. 'There's a dead body down here.'

Fiona joined him and had to place a hand over her own mouth to stop a yelp from escaping as she saw the gruesome sight for herself. Beneath them in the pit was the corpse of a man in his thirties who seemed to have died recently. His lifeless body was pierced by a handful of long, pointy metal spikes, and he had clearly just been left there.

'What the hell happened?' asked Fiona, looking shocked and disgusted.

'Some sort of trap,' said Andrew, now looking at the floor beneath their feet and on the other side of the pit. 'It's probably been here since this whole thing was built. I am pretty sure that was the only one, though. Both sides of this pit look solid.'

They leapt over the macabre sight to the other side and proceeded through the rest of the tunnel to emerge inside a larger chamber with evidence of excavation work having been carried out. Andrew used his torch to locate a set of battery-powered floodlights and pressed the button to switch it on. It appeared that Benoit's team had smashed through the brick walls on all three sides, finding yet another tunnel straight ahead, but something much more gruesome behind the two other walls. In the shallow spaces behind where the demolished brick walls had been, were what looked like the skeletal remains of two men. They were still attached to the chains that centuries earlier had been fixed around their necks and wrists, although some of their bones had detached themselves and fallen onto the floor below. Both of their dangling grinning skulls were still attached to their skeletons, and they also had small remnants of almost completely decomposed clothes still clinging to their shoulders and rib cages.

'Oh my word,' said Fiona, looking horrified. 'These men were walled in. Buried alive.'

'Wow,' said Andrew. 'That is a grim way to die. I wonder who they were. Seems like Benoit and his team have just left them hanging here. These men clearly weren't what they were looking for.'

'Perhaps they were enemies of the Rancourt family,' said Fiona. 'Or perhaps they were agents of the Inquisition that were caught and killed this way. Maybe as some sort of payback.'

'I guess we'll never know,' said Andrew. 'Let's press on. There seems to be another chamber past this one.'

They walked through another short but narrow passage into a larger chamber with a vaulted gothic ceiling a couple of metres above them. As with the previous chamber, Benoit's men had installed battery-operated floodlights inside it. As the lights came on, Andrew and Fiona found themselves in what had the unmistakable feel of being some sort of mausoleum. The walls were made from large and neatly chiselled granite blocks, and in the centre of the room was a square stone platform that was raised about a foot from the floor. On it was a sarcophagus whose lid had been removed and was now lying on the platform floor next to it. The two of them stepped up to it in silence and peered over the side into it.

'Empty,' said Fiona, sounding both surprised and confused at the same time. 'This looks like it could be Arnaud Rancourt's tomb,' said Fiona, 'The lid of the sarcophagus has the Rancourt family crest on it underneath the Templar Cross, but there is nothing here.'

'Either Benoit and his team have already recovered whatever was in there,' said Andrew, 'or there was nothing here to find to begin with. From the conversation we just overheard between Benoit and Maxwell, it certainly didn't sound like they had found what they were looking for.'

'Strange,' said Fiona, straightening and turning around slowly to inspect the rest of the large chamber.

'There really is nothing else in here,' she said, looking mystified. 'Although, that also means that we still have a chance of finding the lost chapter before they do.'

'Yes,' said Andrew hesitantly. 'But how? If it isn't here, then where is it? Surely this is the tomb.'

'Could this place be some sort of elaborate decoy?' asked Fiona rhetorically as she walked over to the lid of the sarcophagus and sat on her haunches beside it, studying its ornately carved imagery. 'After all, if there was one thing the Templars were good at it was keeping their most prized possessions hidden, including their gold. There are still many scholars who think that the enormous wealth they hid just before the purge of 1307 has yet to be found.'

'Perhaps,' said Andrew, glancing at the green, faintly luminous Roman numerals on the face of his Breitling wristwatch. 'It's almost midnight. There doesn't seem to be anything else here for us to find. We should head back.'

'Right,' said Fiona reluctantly and rose to her feet.

'It is still a good five hours until sunrise,' said Andrew, 'but we don't want to be down here when Benoit's men return.'

Flicking his torch back to life, Andrew switched off the floodlights and led the two of them back to the chamber with the macabre scene of the grinning skeletons, and then through the narrow tunnel to the ladder leading back up to the chapel. They paused underneath it to make sure there were no sounds of movement coming from inside. Satisfied that there was no one in the chapel, Andrew was about to climb up when Fiona suddenly placed a hand on his arm.

'Wait,' she whispered, her eyes gleaming in the reflected light coming down through the hole from the chapel. 'The light.'

'I switched them all off,' said Andrew.

'Not those lights,' said Fiona in a hushed voice. 'The light of Lucifer.'

'What?' said Andrew, looking perplexed.

'You said the sun comes up in five hours,' she said, her eyes blinking as the cogs in her head began clicking together and whirring in the way that Andrew had seen so many times before.

'Closer to four and half hours now, actually,' he replied.

'Listen. I was studying the photos I took of Haywood's research,' said Fiona, 'and in one of them was a note that contained a handful of cryptic phrases. One of them said, "To enter the tomb, let the Light of Lucifer shine upon you". And another one said, "When he appears, let us worship him".'

'Right?' said Andrew, waiting for her to explain. 'Sounds like your box-standard religious grovelling in front of a deity.'

'Well, in a Gnostic context,' she continued, 'light equates to knowledge. So, it can be interpreted as a way of saying that whoever enters the tomb will receive deep knowledge of some sort. You must have heard the phrase 'The light of the Lord' in Christian theology, right? It's exactly the same thing. And up there in the chapel is a giant mural of Saint Peter holding the two keys. I am sure this is why Benoit and Haywood are digging under it. They think it is all part of a secret message hidden in plain sight, saying that this special key that they are looking for is hidden in the tomb underneath the chapel.'

'Well, they did find a tomb,' said Andrew.

'And I would probably have come to the same conclusions as them,' said Fiona. 'Except the tomb was empty.'

'So, what's your point?' asked Andrew, glancing up towards the top of the ladder and looking vaguely impatient.

'I am suddenly not so sure that this is how that particular phrase is meant to be understood,' she replied. 'I'll bet you anything that it is nowhere near as cryptic as it seems. I think it should be taken literally.'

'How do you mean?' asked Andrew.

'It is probably true that the phrase is a clue to the location of the tomb,' she said, 'but I bet the light it mentions is simply light from the sun. The sun is the light-bringer, which is what the word Lucifer literally means in Latin.'

'Ok, that makes sense,' said Andrew. 'But I still don't think I follow.'

'The sun appears first in the east,' said Fiona, 'and the only part of this castle that is illuminated by the morning sun is the sheer cliff on which the eastern walls were built.'

The jigsaw pieces suddenly snapped together inside Andrew's mind.

'So, the entrance to the real tomb must be somewhere on that cliff face,' he said, 'perhaps inside a natural cave of some sort.'

'Exactly,' said Fiona emphatically whilst trying to keep her voice down.

'So, basically what you're saying is…' began Andrew, gesturing with one hand back towards the underground chambers they had just left as Fiona looked at him with gleaming eyes, nodding enthusiastically.

'Yes,' she said. 'They are digging in the wrong place!'

★   ★   ★

When Caitlin awoke, she once again felt the now unpleasantly familiar sense of disorientation induced by the drugs that she was sure were being mixed into her drinking water. She had decided to drink from the jug nonetheless since the beaker under the window was only half full of rainwater. She had decided to only drink from the beaker when it was full to the brim. That also meant waiting for more rain, but if her plan was going to work, then she needed to have collected enough water in the beaker to not need to drink any of the water in the jug for about one whole day.

She sat up in her bed and rubbed her eyes, and then her dream suddenly rushed back into her mind as clearly as if it had actually happened. She felt the tears well up in her eyes as she replayed it in her mind. It was a strange dream in that she did not remember seeing anything at all during it. All she remembered was a strange yet familiar soundscape that seemed to be far off in the distance. A muffled metallic banging noise. And a voice calling out to her. It had been Fiona, calling her name. She wiped a tear from her cheek.

Am I finally going crazy? she thought to herself.

She got up from the bed and walked into the middle of the cell. The dim light in the ceiling was on as usual, but through the glass brick in the exterior wall, she could see that it was dark outside. She moved to the corner next to the metal door and crouched next to the area where the previous captives had left their names. She looked again at the first name on the list, placing her fingertips on the letters and feeling the contours of them. Then she realised that all the names had either a capital 'D' or a capital 'J' underneath them. And the two letters alternated throughout the long sequence. It was a pattern that seemed to have developed after the first name had been etched into the stone block by 'Lucy' long ago, whoever she had been.

It took Caitlin a few moments to realise what they meant. 'J' meant June, and 'D' meant December. Every six months going back decades, someone had been held here against their will. But for what purpose? And why did it only ever happen during June and December? She suddenly realised that it had to be related to summer and winter solstice, and a chill ran down her spine when she reflected on everything that she had read about Wicca and other ancient pagan solstice ceremonies, which were remarkably similar across the world. In countless locations and cultures across continents and millennia, human beings had venerated the sun and worshipped it at altars that were aligned in a way that produced a unique visual display on those two days of the year. And there was almost invariably some type of sacrifice involved, sometimes of the human kind.

As her fingers moved gently across the names etched into the stone blocks, they left faintly darker trails of moisture from her sweaty fingertips. She suddenly felt dizzy again. Off to one side of the main body of names, she spotted a separate set of letters, and when she wiped the dust from them to be able to read them, she could see that it was a brief sentence in French.

'*Mon Dieu. Aidez-moi.*'
'My God. Help me.'

★ ★ ★

DI Graham Palmer was sitting in his cubicle inside the Metropolitan Police's homicide section, officially known as the HMCC – the Homicide and Major

Crime Command. Residing inside the Met's headquarters building on Victoria Embankment called New Scotland Yard, the unit had a couple of hundred staff in total, although only a few those bore the title Detective Inspector. Palmer had been a DI for a little over a decade now, but he still did not have his own office. Apparently, at some point in the past, some management consultancy firm had been invited in by one of the well-meaning but ultimately inept senior managers, and by the time they had left the entire unit had been reorganised. They had left virtually everyone asking the question: 'Who is now going to be doing what, and why not?' It had also resulted in everyone working in an open-plan office which Palmer had never liked. It felt like the floor of a tabloid newspaper, and it was in no way conducive to his own ability to focus. Now, however, at half past midnight, he was able to concentrate fully on what he was doing. It had already been a long day, but he had decided to stay on for a bit longer. He usually found that the later it got, the more productive he was, as long as he had a steady supply of caffeine.

He was wearing a dull brown suit with an off-white shirt and a mottled tie. He only had this and one other suit, five almost identical shirts and three similar-looking ties, all of which he alternated between. However, no one had ever seemed to notice. He could probably get away with wearing the same clothes every single day without anyone ever realising it, except perhaps for when they would inevitably begin to smell.

He had just come back from the coffee machine and was now sipping his sixth or seventh cup of heavily sugar-laden coffee since most of his colleagues had gone home to their families. Only a couple of other officers with tenuous personal relations with other people were still there with him, but everyone kept to themselves. There seemed to be an unspoken agreement amongst them that no one would bother anyone else after regular office hours.

Placing the disposable paper cup next to his grubby keyboard, he placed his hand on the mouse and clicked on the icon for the Met's CCTV systems. The application fired up, and he quickly found the footage he had clipped earlier from the cameras near Sean Taylor's murder scene. He also retrieved the still image from Tower Hill tube station and from inside Saint Katherine Marina that showed several groups of people in the vicinity of the houseboat that had later been set on fire. He selected a group of images, all showing the female and the gun-wielding male that had been at all three locations. The male looked to be in his mid-thirties with a handsome chiselled face, the physique of an athlete and the self-confident demeanour of someone who was ex-military. The attractive female was probably slightly younger, and she did not look to Palmer like someone who was used to much else than sitting in an office. He finally opened the Met's facial recognition system and fed the images into it.

The computer screen dimmed slightly and a white box with the word 'Searching...' appeared in blue text in the middle of it along with a small animated hourglass. Palmer picked up his cup and slurped some more coffee. After about twenty seconds, the message box winked out and the application reappeared with a message saying 'Match found.' The system had been unable to match the female with anyone already known to the police, but it had been able to identify the male.

'Let's see who you are,' he said.

He clicked on the search result box that would normally have opened a complete file of whoever the system had identified. However, that was not what happened now. Instead of the file image and all the available information being presented neatly on a single page with links to all additional relevant sources, the application simply threw up a small white box in the middle of the screen with a message in red.

> *Error. Unable to display results.*
> *Commissioner-level clearance required.*

A deep frown spread across Palmer's face as he tilted his head slightly to one side and eyed the message box suspiciously.

'What the bloody…' he mumbled to himself.

He tried again, half-expecting this to be a glitch in the notoriously rickety Metropolitan Police IT system, but once again he was denied access. He leaned back in his chair and involuntarily looked around the office as if somehow the answer to this mystery might lie there. Then he returned his gaze to the screen and took another sip of his coffee. There was definitely something fishy going on here.

'Who the hell *are* you?' he said quietly, staring intently at the grainy image of the man on the screen.

Twenty-One

About an hour later Andrew and Fiona had exited the chapel the way they had come in and retraced their steps behind the keep, up onto the inner wall and then climbed down using the tree Andrew had positioned there a couple of hours earlier. He dragged the tree away from the castle wall and put it where he had found it. Instead of returning to their car, the two of them followed the outer wall all the way to the point at the back of the castle where it met the sheer cliff face down to the valley to the east.

Standing on the edge of the towering promontory and looking out along the eastern outer wall of Château La Roche above the terrifying drop, it was suddenly clear what a feat of medieval engineering it had been to build a fortification of such magnitude in this location. The outer wall was about four metres tall, but the cliff face below extended at least another fifty metres to the valley floor below, and the drop was almost vertical. Climbing up from down there was as dangerous and foolhardy now as it would have been centuries ago, and that was why Andrew had decided that the only way to explore the cliff face was to make their way along the outside of the wall to the middle of the cliff face and then rappel down using a thin black carbon fibre rope that he had brought in his backpack.

They proceeded along the precarious edge of the cliff that the outer wall rested upon until they were more or less at the centre of the cliff face. Here, Andrew began securing one end of the rope to a small rocky outcropping. Once it was tied firmly, he yanked it hard several times to make sure that the rock would not be pulled over the edge once he put his full weight on it.

'You should stay here for now,' he said in hushed tones. 'I am going to go down and see what I can see. If there is anything down there, I reckon it won't be too far down, since anything close to the valley floor would be easily visible.'

'Fine,' said Fiona, feeling both relieved that she wouldn't have to attempt the perilous descent just yet, but at the same time envious of what Andrew might discover. 'I will make sure this end of the rope stays secure.'

Andrew put on a small but strong climbing harness and used a black metal carabiner to secure the rope. He wrapped it around his right hand and gripped the other end with his left. Then he stepped out to the edge of the drop and began leaning out until he was at a forty-five-degree angle with his back towards the valley floor below. Loosening his grip on the rope slightly and feeding it slowly through the carabiner, he took the first step downwards. Gradually feeding ever more rope through the carabiner, he soon began stepping his way backwards down the cliff face one foot at a time. The rope now lay across a sharp rocky edge that suddenly looked uncomfortably fragile to Fiona. Several small pebbles came loose from the rocks as Andrew descended, and they fell past him and bounced off the cliff face below, after which they continued their long, silent fall to the wooded valley floor below. Fiona was unable to hear them hit the ground.

'Are you ok?' she whispered, standing on the edge and looking down towards Andrew whilst attempting to fight off a creeping sense of vertigo.

'Yup,' he replied. 'All good. I don't see anything yet, though. I'll keep going. There's plenty of rope.'

After about ten metres, Andrew paused to orientate himself. He looked to the left and to the right along the cliff face, searching for anything that might indicate a hidden cave, but he could see nothing. The entire cliff face seemed remarkably smooth, except for a few long but narrow cracks that had gradually formed in the promontory over many long centuries. He fed some more rope through the carabiner and continued for another five metres until he had to push off from the cliff face and bounce sideways past a jagged-looking outcropping with multiple small fissures that might have got his rope tangled or damaged. Continuing down past it, he then realised that the outcropping hung over a larger fissure into the cliff face. Bouncing sideways and back over towards it, he was amazed to discover that the fissure had a flat lower section that was wide enough for one person to stand inside. It also seemed to stretch further into the cliff face, although access looked very narrow indeed.

He let himself drop onto the flat surface, loosened the rope and took a step inside, turning his head-mounted LED torch on as he did so. The fissure seemed to constrict itself to an impassable endpoint just a couple of metres further in, but when he produced a brief whistle, the multiple echoes reverberating back to him made it clear that there was a sizeable cavity in there somewhere.

He stepped back out to the edge and leaned out just far enough to be able to see Fiona above, signalling for her to come down and join him.

'There's something here,' he said in a hushed voice that was just loud enough for her to hear.

Up on the ledge by the outer wall, Fiona swallowed hard and strapped on her own climbing harness and attached another carabiner. After a few moments of hesitation, peering over the edge and trying to decide whether she was really up for this, she finally gritted her teeth, gripped the rope tightly and began leaning out into the void. Once she had taken the first couple of steps and got used to the feel of the rope in her hands and the way she could adjust her centre of gravity based on her angle and the bend in her knees, she quickly became more confident, and soon she was walking slowly but assuredly down the cliff face toward the fissure. After a couple of minutes, she was down and Andrew grabbed onto her harness and pulled her inside the fissure.

'That wasn't so bad,' she beamed, clearly on a high from the danger and excitement of the hazardous descent. 'What did you find?'

'A deep fissure extending into the cliff face,' he replied. 'There is some sort of large cavity in there.'

'Really?' said Fiona, instantly intrigued and craning her neck to look into the darkness. 'It doesn't look like much.'

'Which is what makes it a great hiding place,' observed Andrew. 'And look. This is an amazing location. Step back just a bit from the edge, and you suddenly can't see the valley floor below. This also means that this place is completely hidden from view from down there. It just looks like a large crevice in the cliff face.'

'I wonder how they originally found it,' said Fiona. 'How far do you suppose we are from the wall?'

'At least twenty metres,' replied Andrew, 'so there is no way they could have discovered it by digging down from the castle. Whatever this is, it is part of the bedrock that was lifted up above the surrounding landscape aeons ago, and they couldn't possibly have dug their way down to it from up there.'

'In other words,' said Fiona. 'Someone went to quite a lot of effort to find this place to begin with. Whoever that was clearly wanted to make sure that whatever they were hiding remained hidden.'

'Let's have a look inside and see if anyone has actually ever been here,' said Andrew. 'I reckon the chances are pretty good, but it might have been a while ago.'

Andrew began to move further into the fissure, illuminating the way ahead with his head torch, and he soon discovered that what had appeared like a small short crevice into the cliff face was in fact just the beginning of a narrow path leading much deeper into it. They had to walk sideways to squeeze through, and the path turned at sharp angles several times before suddenly widening dramatically into a large natural cave with a ceiling above that was full of stalactites.

'Wow,' said Fiona, using her torch to inspect the cone-shaped mineral formations hanging from the ceiling above. 'Judging by the size of these things, this cave must be thousands of years old.'

'But that over there isn't,' said Andrew, pointing his torchlight at an arched doorway deeper into the cave. 'This was built by human hands, and there is bound to be something important on the other side of it. Something the builders didn't want anyone to find.'

The two of them approached the doorway, and when Fiona stepped close she noticed something carved beautifully into the lintel above it.

'Look,' she said and pointed to three neat relief symbols carved into the stone. 'A Templar Cross, with a fleur-de-lis on either side.'

'Templars and Lilith,' said Andrew pensively. 'We are definitely on the right track here.'

'The fleur-de-lis is also a French royal symbol,' said Fiona, 'as well as being a more universal symbol of perfection and light.'

'Light, as in Lucifer?' said Andrew.

'Almost certainly,' replied Fiona.

'Ready to go on?' he asked.

Fiona nodded and directed her torchlight through the doorway and into the tunnel beyond. Once again, Andrew led the way, and the two of them had to crouch slightly to make it through. When the tunnel ended after about three metres, they found themselves in a square chamber the size of an average living room that seemed to have been carved from the bedrock.

'This is incredible,' said Fiona, looking astounded. 'It must have taken ages to excavate this. We're deep inside the very bedrock Château La Roche is sitting on.'

'What the hell are those things,' said Andrew, his torchlight now pointing at another doorway on the other side of the room.

This doorway was about twice as wide as the one they had just passed through, and it was also much taller. But what really caught their eye were the architraves which were carved directly from the bedrock and seemed to depict large bulky, semi-naked and brutish-looking men. They were muscular and formidable-looking, with deep-set eyes and full beards. Each of them had a large hand pushing up against the lintel above them, whilst the other was gripping the neck of an ox. The two oxen were like small toy animals in their powerful hands. On the lintel itself was carved another Templar Cross.

'Look at the scale,' said Fiona, intrigued. 'These oxen are tiny, or rather, these men are enormous. Giants. These must be the Nephilim.'

'The giants mentioned by Friar Cormac,' said Andrew, looking up at them.

'The spawn of the Watchers after they had mated with human females,' nodded Fiona. 'The giants who devoured everything.'

'Well,' said Andrew. 'If this isn't a direct reference to the First Book of Enoch, I don't know what is.'

'I agree,' said Fiona. 'This proves that at least some Templars believed the stories described in that particular apocryphal text. And it seems pretty clear from this that the Templar brothers Gerard and Arnaud were fully invested in the idea of Lilith being the true wife of Adam.'

'So, the connections to Gnosticism and to Lucifer seem to be there,' said Andrew.

'Exactly,' nodded Fiona. 'Let's head in deeper and see what we find. Watch out for traps.'

'Don't worry. I already have my eyes peeled,' said Andrew. 'I don't want to end up like Benoit's chap down in that pit.'

They advanced through the doorway and into yet another chamber, which looked similar to the one they had found in the crypt under the chapel. The walls were smooth, and the chamber was carved out from the bedrock in a near-perfect cube shape with a ceiling roughly a metre above their heads. However, on a raised platform in the centre of the room was something other than a sarcophagus. It was an ornate stone altar roughly the size of a sofa with a square box sitting atop it that was about a metre long and half a metre wide as well as tall. The box was similarly decorated with intricate patterns of writhing vines and fleur-de-lis symbols, and on its lid was a prominently positioned Templar Cross.

'The ossuary,' exclaimed Fiona excitedly as she stepped forward towards the platform. 'Which of the two Rancourt brothers could it be?'

'Be careful,' said Andrew. 'There could be more traps here.'

Fiona proceeded to place her feet gingerly on the platform and then slowly approached the altar, shining her bright torchlight at the small ossuary. Upon reaching it, she lowered herself onto one knee and stretched out her hand to grip the lid.

'Ready?' she asked, as Andrew drew level with her and crouched.

'Yes,' he said. 'Let's see what's inside.'

Fiona lifted the lid and the two of them leaned in to peer down inside. On the bottom of the ossuary was a human skull placed on top of a pile of bones. It was a disturbing sight, but leaning against the skull was something even more intriguing. A small stone tablet. It was about the size of a large book and seemed to have been made from a perfectly rectangular slab of pale grey limestone. Across its front were several lines of text which seemed to have been chiselled into it, and which were now covered in dust. Fiona picked up the tablet as gingerly as she could, held it in front of her face and blew away the dust. Then she ran her fingers across the text, reading out loud somewhat unsteadily as she went.

La clé des portes infernales
Aux pieds de la Vierge sous la rose
Où le Dieu du ciel et du tonnerre habitait
Et où les druides dansaient autrefois

'Sorry,' said Andrew, peering at the tablet. 'I took some French in school once, but that is many moons ago. What does it mean?'

'Let me see,' said Fiona, clearing her throat.

'The whole thing roughly translates to, "The key to the infernal gates. At the feet of the Virgin under the rose. Where the God of the sky and the thunder once dwelt. And where the druids once danced.".'

'Any idea what that is supposed to mean?' asked Andrew, 'aside from the fact that it sounds a lot like clues to the location of the lost chapter.'

Fiona read it once more, whispering the words to herself as she did so. Then she sat immobile for a few moments, trying to make sense of it.

'I can only think of one place it could be,' she said. 'Notice how the words "Virgin" and "God" are capitalised. That means that this is referring to specific entities. In the case of the virgin, it can't be anyone other than the Virgin Mary, the mother of Jesus Christ. Although it is not clear to me what is meant by "under the rose." And as for the god of the sky and the thunder, because of the gnostic strains that clearly ran deep through these Templars, I am sure it is not the Christian god or the Hebrew god Yahweh. And I don't think it is the Greek god, Zeus, although he was also thought to dwell in the skies above, wielding lightning.'

'And it couldn't possibly be Thor, could it?' asked Andrew. 'After all, he was the Norse god of thunder.'

'No,' said Fiona, shaking her head. 'I think this refers to Jupiter. Remember how he is often depicted with lightning in one hand and a staff in the other? And he was also the Roman god of the sky.'

'Okay. So, what does all this mean then?' asked Andrew.

'Well,' said Fiona as the pieces began falling into place inside her mind. 'There is a city which has a large and famous cathedral dedicated to the Virgin Mary. It was constructed around the 12th century on the former site of a Roman temple built for the worship of Jupiter. And that temple was itself built on a site where druids used to perform their pagan rituals, centuries before Christianity was even invented.'

'And where is that?' asked Andrew.

'*Notre Dame de Paris*,' she replied, looking up at him, her eyes now gleaming with excitement. 'Our Lady of Paris. One of the greatest medieval cathedrals ever built.'

A proud smile began to spread across Andrew's face as he watched Fiona's delight at having solved the riddle.

'You're a genius,' he said.

'No,' she said, returning his smile bashfully. 'But I *am* pretty good at working things out once I have the right clues.'

'What do you suppose is meant by the reference to the key being at the feet of the Virgin Mary?' he asked.

'Well, if I am not mistaken,' she replied, 'there is a statue of the Virgin Mary on the main façade of Notre Dame in front of the huge stained-glass rose there. I bet that is where the Key is hidden.'

Andrew nodded, allowing the powerful beam from his torch to sweep over the interior of the otherwise empty chamber.

'Right,' he said. 'I guess we should get ourselves to Paris then. Let's get out of here before dawn arrives. We don't want to be spotted by the municipal police dangling halfway down the cliff face under Château La Roche. That is bound to create problems for us.'

'I agree,' nodded Fiona. 'Let's go.'

Twenty-Two

A woman's scent. There was no question in his mind. Standing under the dimly lit vaulted ceilings deep beneath the Temple of the Sons of Lucifer, it was not just the faint trace of perfume that Christopher Haywood could smell. It was the unmistakable lingering scent of the warm skin of a young female that still remained in the air inside his personal research library. It was especially pronounced near the table that had many of his handwritten notes spread out across it, and it answered the question he had been wondering about ever since he watched the CCTV footage from his private quarters upstairs in the Temple. Had they found this place? The answer was most certainly 'Yes'.

The female, who quite maddeningly was yet to be identified, had undoubtedly sat in this very chair by this table and perused his private research notes as if she had been in a public library. The thought of that made his blood boil. This place was sacred to him. Inviolable. Only he and his late father had ever entered it up until yesterday, and now it had been sullied by the presence of these two interlopers. The notion that this meddling bitch and her male companion had made it into the Temple and all the way into this most hallowed place was abhorrent. What was worse still was that they had somehow managed to hack their way through the electronic locks on the door to the sealed inner chamber which held the only known copy of the Lucifer Codex. Thankfully, the display box in the climate-controlled chamber had been constructed so that it was impossible to remove the codex without destroying it, and the two intruders had wisely chosen not to attempt this.

Haywood glanced towards the door to the chamber. For the first time ever, he did not immediately experience an urge to enter and behold once more the ancient and powerful codex. It had now been tainted by the very presence of the intruders, and until they had been eliminated he would not be able to bring himself to enter again.

He exited the research library and walked along the short corridor into the ceremonial chamber, where the raised circular platform and the enormous metal brimstone symbol loomed above him. As he stood there by himself, he felt the creeping impatience that always arrived deep within him around this time. In another two days, it would be the summer solstice once more, and yet another sacrifice would be made. But this time would be different, as long as Benoit and his team were able to find the lost chapter of the codex. Every indication he had received from the Frenchman and now also Maxwell pointed to them being very close.

Once it had been recovered, after several centuries of being secreted away under the château in the Languedoc, the Sons of Lucifer would then finally possess the complete ritual that would allow them to wrench open the gates of hell and summon Lucifer himself. The death of the young woman would be a small price to pay. An irrelevance really. She was just one of many that had come before her – cut and bled dry for the glory of the Lord.

He understood now that in a way all of those deaths had been for nothing. Yet they had not been entirely in vain, because they had finally caused both Haywood and his father to realise that there was something missing. Some incantation that was required to complete the ceremony.

Haywood closed his eyes and briefly allowed himself to reminisce about the most recent ceremony. The surge of power he had felt. The low murmur of the incantations. The final moments of the young woman. There was an undeniable and incomparable rush that he felt from taking another life, and anyone that had ever killed another human being would be lying if they claimed anything different. The feeling of absolute power over life and death was exhilarating, and something ordinary people living inside their carefully constructed delusions about the world could never even begin to comprehend.

Haywood did not care at all whether they thought he was the delusional one, or whether they saw people like him as believers in archaic superstitious nonsense.

None of it mattered. He *knew* that it was all true. He had seen it. He had felt it. It was real.

★ ★ ★

When Andrew and Fiona returned through the darkness down the long slope through the forest to the picnic spot where they had left their car, they discovered that another vehicle had parked on the other side of the small clearing. It was a minivan.

It was now about an hour before sunrise and the skies to the east were taking on a weak pale orange hue. However, it was still very dark on the forest floor, and because the vehicle was painted a dark metallic grey they only saw it through the trees when they were close. Only when they were within fifteen metres did they spot it when the moon was reflected in its windshield. The rest of the vehicle seemed to absorb almost all of what little moonlight managed to penetrate the canopies of the tall trees. From the distinctive silver logo on the front grille, they could see that it was a Mercedes that had a decidedly muscly look to it, and its windows were tinted so dark that it was impossible to see if anyone was inside. The distance to their Audi rental was less than ten metres.

'Stop,' whispered Andrew as soon as he spotted the van, instantly alert to the fact that this vehicle was almost certainly here because of them.

Fiona stopped next to him, and as he took another few cautious steps forward, he instinctively reached up and over with his right hand to where his Glock 17 should have been. He winced as his intuition was screaming at him to get the hell out of there. Glancing back at Fiona, he was about to tell her to turn around and run back up the hill, when suddenly the van's powerful headlights came on, flooding the forest floor with white light. At the same time, its large side door unlocked and slid swiftly open as a light came on inside.

Before either of them could react, two large musclebound men wearing short leather jackets stepped out from inside, and another man emerged from the driver's side door. The bearded driver who also wore a leather jacket was heavier and meaner-looking than the two others, none of whom looked like the sort of people anyone would want to bump into late at night in a dark alley.

All three men were carrying weapons. The bearded man had drawn a black and bulky-looking handgun that looked to Andrew like a Beretta 92 semi-automatic. His two comrades held what appeared to be small submachine guns across their torsos. Andrew instantly clocked them as Czech-made 9 mm Scorpion EVO 3s. They were powerful modern weapons that were capable of spewing out more than a thousand rounds per minute, and they were only meant to be available to the military, mainly in Eastern Europe. It was certainly not a weapon that was supposed to find its way into the hands of civilians, which these men clearly were. In short, Andrew and Fiona were in trouble.

'Raise your hands,' said the bearded man in a slow, gruff voice with a heavy eastern European accent.

Andrew and Fiona did as he asked. After all, neither of them had any weapons. They were simply hopelessly outgunned and outnumbered. A couple of seconds later, the front passenger door on the far side of the van opened and a tall and slender man stepped out and walked casually around the front of the Mercedes. He was wearing a smart suit and a smug smile that Andrew and Fiona both knew only too well by now. It was Tristan Maxwell.

'Well, if it isn't our two meddlesome friends,' said Maxwell in his clipped accent, positively radiating the power he felt he now held over them. 'Finally, we meet in person. Frankly, you two have been a real pain in the groin lately, and we still haven't even been able to work out who you are. Care to introduce yourselves?'

'Fuck you,' snarled Andrew icily.

'How very uncivilised,' scoffed Maxwell derisively.

'Where's my sister, you creep?' shouted Fiona, suddenly overcome with fury now that Maxwell was right in front of her.

Tristan frowned, looking vaguely surprised and not a little irritated by the antagonism. He stopped about five metres away from the two of them and pressed his lips together whilst regarding them as if they were two lab rats he was trying to decide how to dispose of.

'Sister?' he then said, suddenly looking intrigued. 'Oh, that does explain quite a lot, doesn't it? And you?'

He looked at Andrew who remained silent and whose brain was now racing to try to assess risks, evaluate options and decide on a course of action – preferably one that would not result in the deaths of Fiona and himself.

Maxwell studied him for a few more moments, seemingly surprised and perhaps even slightly unnerved by the stone-faced man in front of him. Maxwell was like a shark in a small ocean usually full of defenceless fish, but he knew intuitively when he had met another shark, and he suddenly understood that he was looking at one right now.

'You're probably wondering what happened, aren't you?' he asked with a smirk. 'So, let me enlighten you. When you two thought you were sneaking out of the chapel unseen, I was watching you from the shadows the whole time. And when you headed up onto the wall, it wasn't too difficult to work out where you were going. And it just so happened that my best three Romanian friends here were arriving from London and were just a couple of minutes away. So, here we are.'

Maxwell splayed out his hands and looked highly pleased with himself, but neither Andrew nor Fiona reacted to his self-congratulatory missive. After a couple of seconds of waiting, seemingly hoping for a response, Maxwell gave a resigned shrug.

'Dragomir,' he said in an arrogant voice, snapping his fingers. 'I'm so pleased you three managed to get here just in time. Would you be so kind as to deal with our two friends? They've caused quite enough trouble. I want them in the pit with Maurice. I'd say that would be a fitting end. You can kill them before or after. I don't really mind as long as they end up dead.'

Dragomir produced a sly smile as he advanced towards Andrew and Fiona flanked by his two compatriots Constantin and Radovan, all three of them looking like they were relishing the prospect of inflicting deadly violence. Raising his Beretta and pointing it straight at Andrew's head, Dragomir came to within a metre of him, but then he stopped, waiting for his two colleagues to come around his flanks and grab the soon-to-be prisoners. From the way Dragomir held the gun – slightly tilted to one side the way he had probably seen street gangsters do it in the movies – Andrew knew that for all his intimidating physical presence, this man was not experienced in weapons handling. A pistol like the Beretta 92 will always want to recoil back and up, which is why it should be held in the normal vertical position when fired. Otherwise, it will kick out to the side and throw the shooter's aim off immediately after firing the first bullet. And if that bullet failed to find its mark, the shooter would then suddenly be highly vulnerable with his gun pointing away from the target.

Andrew knew that he would only have a couple of seconds before the tall blond man with the neck tattoos and the steroid-filled neanderthal with the enormous arms were on them. It was now or never. Concealed in the palm of his hand, he was holding what he hoped would quite literally be the key for them to get out of this situation in one piece. It wasn't a weapon, but he hoped it would provide enough of a distraction to buy them the few seconds they needed. He just had to hope that Fiona would be sufficiently alert and quick on her feet for the plan to work.

Shifting his thumb onto the remote starter button on the car key, he slowly turned his head to one side and looked meaningfully at Fiona. From that brief glance, she instantly caught the intent in his eyes, and her body tensed visibly. Then he pressed the button. Immediately, the engine of their Audi A6 rental sprang to life with a roar and revved loudly, and at the same time, its powerful headlights came on. Their four adversaries instantly and instinctively turned their heads to face the car. Constantin and Radovan immediately swung their automatic weapons around towards it, startled by the noise and the light. Dragomir did not move his pistol, but he turned his head slightly towards the car as his eyes darted briefly in that direction. It was all the opportunity Andrew needed.

Using a weapon disarm technique that was so embedded in his brain and his muscle memory that he could have done it in his sleep, his hands shot out towards Dragomir as he took half a step towards him. It all happened in a flash. Almost too quick to see for the untrained eye. With his left hand he gripped the top of the gun and twisted the barrel away from his head, and in the same instant, his right hand came in hard from the side and impacted on Dragomir's wrist. Before the Romanian knew what had happened, Andrew had slapped his arm away, rotated the gun out of his grip and turned it around whilst releasing the safety and aiming the Beretta at his torso. A split-second later, Andrew fired three rounds in quick succession directly into the musclebound chest of the huge Romanian. They impacted instantly, slapping into the leather jacket and punching through the big man's lungs and heart, exploding out the other side and spraying blood out into the air and onto the leaf-covered forest floor.

Andrew was about to shout something to Fiona, but when he spun around to start sprinting for their car, he saw that she was already moving, scrambling to get to the passenger seat as fast as possible. Near the van, Maxwell yelled out in terror and threw himself on the ground behind the vehicle. Before Dragomir's bulky corpse had even hit the ground with a heavy thud, Andrew and Fiona were halfway to the car. Only then did his two compatriots realise precisely what had happened. Seeing their leader fall to the ground dead must have left them momentarily stunned because neither of them moved for a couple of seconds. However, it was long enough for Andrew and Fiona to open the doors of the Audi and launch themselves inside. When Constantin and Dragomir finally snapped out of their shock and regained their composure, their response was ferocious. They both opened up with their Scorpions, firing badly aimed but still deadly bursts of gunfire towards the Audi. Their bullets smacked into the bodywork of the car and shredded the bark of a tree behind the vehicle. But by then, Andrew had put the car in gear and floored the accelerator whilst wrenching the wheel all the way to one side, making the car leap forward and causing its rear end to lurch out to one side and swing around in a wide arc so that the car did a 180-degree turn in mere seconds.

The two enraged Romanians had to leap out of the way to avoid being struck by the vehicle's rear, and by the time they got to their feet again and were able to open fire once more, the Audi was racing down the forest track towards the main road and the town.

'Are you all right?' shouted Andrew as he gripped the wheel and floored it through the forest whilst glancing briefly up into the rear-view mirror to realise that the car's rear window had been shattered.

'I think so,' panted Fiona, her body's instinctive fight-or-flight response making her tremble.

'Are you hurt?' he shouted, this time more urgent.

She frantically checked her body whilst being thrown from side to side as Andrew navigated the narrow and twisting forest track.

'I'm ok,' she finally said, out of breath as they reached the end of the track and swung onto the road back towards the village.

'They're coming,' said Andrew, looking past Fiona and out of the passenger side window to the forest where a set of headlights were racing along the track in their direction.

'This car is faster,' said Fiona, sounding hopeful but frightened.

'Not for long,' said Andrew, glancing down at the instruments. 'One of the bullets must have taken out the radiator. The engine is already overheating. I reckon we have a couple of minutes before it seizes up completely.'

He changed gears and accelerated north along the road towards the centre of Roquefort-sur-Garonne, and as he did so he pressed the magazine release button on the Beretta, let the magazine drop into his lap and then he handed it to Fiona.

'Look at the side of the mag and tell me how many bullets are left,' he said, changing gears again and glancing up into the rear-view mirror once more to see the van just reaching the main road behind them.

'Twelve,' she replied after a couple of seconds.

'Good,' said Andrew. 'At least the big guy came prepared with a full mag.'

'He's dead, right?' asked Fiona, glancing at him with an uncomfortable look on her face.

'Very,' responded Andrew evenly. 'It was him or us. You understand that, right?'

She nodded.

'What do we do now?' she said and twisted around in her seat to see the headlights of the Mercedes van chasing after them.

'I'm not sure,' said Andrew. 'Twelve bullets are better than nothing, but in a straight firefight against two submachine guns it's a losing battle every time.'

The Audi's engine was beginning to sound severely strained, even though Andrew was trying to keep the revs down. He looked at the temperature gauge again. The needle was now well into the red, and he felt as if the engine was beginning to lose power. Then out of the corner of his eye, he spotted something moving alongside them in the distance. It was a series of lights that seemed to be gliding smoothly across the field just on the other side of the river about two hundred metres away.

'The train,' he said. 'Northbound. I bet it is the early morning regional to Toulouse.'

'I think there's a train station in town,' said Fiona, pointing ahead.

'We need to get to that station and get onboard before those goons catch up with us,' said Andrew. 'They won't be very happy now that their boss is dead in the dirt.'

'It looked like Maxwell was their boss,' said Fiona.

'Maxwell is Haywood's lapdog,' said Andrew. 'All bark and no bite.'

'But probably a real psychopath,' said Fiona darkly, again glancing back at the van behind them in the distance. 'He seemed to get a real kick out of telling his three goons to kill us.'

Andrew didn't slow down as they entered the town but raced across the square with the restaurant they had dined at only hours earlier. From there a road led towards a bridge that crossed the river, which he figured would take them across to the train station on the other side. They accelerated along the bridge, made it across, and took a sharp right after a couple of hundred metres to drive alongside the train track towards the station a few hundred metres up ahead. Their vehicle was now producing a disconcerting grinding noise, and it left a white trail of steam and smoke behind it as it barrelled down the road. The inside of the car was beginning to smell like burning oil.

'The train is already at the platform,' exclaimed Fiona anxiously and pointed out of the windshield. 'Go faster.'

'I can't,' said Andrew. 'The engine is almost dead.'

Squeezing the last life out of what until that evening had been a prime example of high-quality German precision engineering, Andrew depressed the accelerator as far as it would go as they covered the final stretch to the train station. The speedometer showed 90 kilometres per hour. The engine was now screaming as its pistons began to melt, and the camshaft finally broke and disconnected from the drivetrain, leaving the car a coasting hunk of metal that was unlikely to ever see a road again. But by then, they had made it to the front of the station. Andrew slammed the brakes and the two of them jumped out and raced inside, leaving the smoking wreck outside.

They sprinted through the station and out onto the platform just as the last passengers were boarding. The train was painted a metallic grey and blue, and both the front and the rear carriages were slanted at one end to improve the aerodynamics of the train. The doors were still open, but at the front of the train, a conductor was waving a small flag to indicate to his colleagues that the train was now about to depart. Running to the nearest set of doors, they hurried inside the almost empty carriage just as they folded shut, but then nothing happened for several seconds.

'Let's go, damn it,' said Andrew between gritted teeth.

They heard the high-pitched whine from the electric capacitors as the train prepared to depart, and then it finally started to inch painfully slowly along the tracks and away from the station. As it began to pick up speed, Andrew stepped over to the doors and looked back out of the window along the platform. Just then, the doors to the ticket hall burst open and a black-clad juggernaut of a man came running out. He didn't stop, but immediately veered off and made a beeline for the train. It was the short, musclebound neanderthal, and he was moving surprisingly fast as he chased after the train. With his powerful arms and legs pumping like pistons, he was now sprinting along the platform, clipping other commuters as he went and sending them flying as if they weren't even there. He barely seemed to notice them, his speed and seemingly unstoppable momentum throwing them aside like toys.

Out of sight of Andrew and the other passengers, and with gritted teeth and sweat pouring off his brow, Radovan, was drawing level with the back of the train which had a driver's cockpit identical to the one at the front. However, it was empty so neither passengers nor train staff saw him sprint the final distance to the back of the train, leap onto the small footrest and grip one of the long vertical handlebars that were inset into the body of the train on either side of the cockpit door. He had ditched the submachine gun but was still carrying a pistol strapped to his chest in a shoulder holster.

'Shit,' said Andrew. 'We've got company. The short steroid addict is about to catch up with us.'

'But he can't get inside, can he?' asked Fiona incredulously.

'He doesn't need to,' said Andrew. 'All he has to do is attach himself to the train and stay there until the next station. The town of Cazeres if I remember correctly from the trip down here. It's probably only about ten minutes away. And I'd say it's another thirty minutes from there to Toulouse.'

'So, what do we do?' said Fiona in hushed tones, suddenly aware that some of the other passengers were glancing at the two foreigners suspiciously. 'Get out at the next station and run? Or try to take him on?'

Andrew pressed his lips together and gave a small shake of the head.

'I would fancy my chances against that guy any day of the week,' he said, 'But if we give him half a chance he will spray down the platform in Cazeres with bullets until his magazine is empty. Even if I manage to take him down, he will end up killing innocent people. We just can't risk that.'

'So, what do you suggest?' said Fiona, now looking worried.

'An ambush,' said Andrew. 'We let him come to us.'

Twenty-Three

As Andrew and Fiona moved through the carriage towards the front of the train, Andrew looked out of the window and spotted a dark Mercedes van through the trees in the early morning gloom. It was racing along on the road next to the train with its headlights lighting up the road about fifty metres away.

'Looks like the blond tattooed guy hasn't given up either,' he said, jerking his head towards the outside.

Fiona followed his gaze and peered at the van which soon disappeared behind a set of houses and some trees.

'Shit,' she said. 'Who the hell are those people?'

'I doubt he will be able to catch up,' said Andrew. 'We're moving fast now, and he has to negotiate traffic and winding roads next to the river. By the time we get to Cazeres, he will still be a couple of minutes away. But I am sure they have worked out where this train is going. Come on. Let's get to the front.'

They continued through the carriages where a small number of commuters were reclining on the blue velvet seats reading their books, sleeping or doing things on their phones. None of them even looked up as Andrew and Fiona walked along the centre aisle. Eventually, they came to the gangway connection point where the bulk of the carriages met the front carriage, which also contained the driver's cockpit. They crossed into the final carriage where there was an open area next to a set of doors as well as a narrow aisle with a sliding door to a toilet.

'When we get to Cazeres,' said Andrew, placing himself directly in front of the door to the toilet, 'I need you to walk to the far end of this carriage and sit down somewhere out of sight but where you can still see this spot right here. Now, here's what I need you to do.'

*   *   *

When the train pulled into *Gare de Cazeres* in the sleepy town from which it had received its name, Radovan waited until the train had almost come to a stop before jumping off the back of it and onto the platform. His hands were sweaty and slippery from the effort of gripping the handlebars while the train had been moving at speed. However, he had been determined to hang on, not least because falling off would be a guaranteed way of ending up in hospital. The three people standing near the middle of the platform did not notice his presence, and soon the train had come to a complete stop, its doors swinging open amid an electronic-sounding trill. No passengers disembarked, but the three commuters on the platform stepped up and onto the train in the lazy tempo of people who until half an hour ago had been asleep in their beds.

Radovan hurried up to the nearest set of doors and slipped inside. Then he adjusted his clothes and wiped the sweat from his face, reaching inside his leather jacket to grip his holstered Beretta 92. He glanced along the virtually empty carriage, and when he saw no familiar faces he began walking calmly towards the far end of it, checking all the seats as he went. When he came to the other end, he slid the door to the gangway connection aside and passed through it into the next carriage. Here he repeated the exercise, making his way along the centre aisle whilst checking all the passengers in front of him, his hand ready to pull out the weapon.

Eventually, he came to what was quite obviously the front carriage, because at the far end of it was not a gangway connection but a door to what he assumed was the driver's cockpit. He tensed slightly since he knew that this was the only place the two fugitives who had killed Dragomir could be. He pulled out the gun and flicked the safety to Off. It was time for revenge.

In that instant, the sliding door to the toilet right next to him flew aside and Andrew barged out and into him. As soon as he made contact, Andrew knew he might have miscalculated. He had decided that a gunfight onboard the train was out of the question, so he had to attempt to overwhelm the man instead. The musclebound brute was shorter than him, however, he was easily fifty percent heavier. Using his momentum,

Andrew managed to ram his opponent up against the wall opposite the sliding door, but he was immediately aware of the man's significant heft. With surprising agility, Radovan twisted around and gripped Andrew by the throat with his huge left hand, while his right hand reached for the gun strapped to his chest. The Romanian grimaced furiously as his brain struggled to process both actions at once.

Andrew saw the move coming and reached for the weapon himself, just managing to snatch it out of the holster ahead of the Romanian. However, before he could fire it, the brute used his left hand to grip Andrew's right wrist and twist the gun up and away from himself. Then he stepped forward and shoved Andrew forcefully back into the restroom, at which point the automatic sliding door closed, sealing the two combatants inside in what they both realised was now a fight to the death.

Pinned against the frosted window to the outside, Andrew attempted to wrestle himself free, but the Romanian held his throat and his right hand in vice-like grips. Andrew was unable to breathe, and his attacker snarled angrily as he squeezed as hard as he could around his neck. Using his left hand, Andrew landed two powerful punches in Radovan's gut, but to no avail. His muscular physique worked as a set of armour, and he stood his ground, seemingly relishing Andrew's frantic attempts at inflicting damage.

Pulling his head back slightly, Andrew managed to headbutt him on the bridge of his nose. He was unable to put as much force into it as he would have liked, but it was enough for it to result in a wet crunch as Radovan's nose broke and blood immediately began running down over his mouth and his chin. However, he did not let go, and if anything, his expression became maniacal as he grimaced showing his blood-stained teeth.

Now almost out of options, Andrew raised his right foot and stomped down on Radovan's right knee as hard as he could, and that finally elicited a response. The knee seemed to buckle, and the Romanian produced a shrill cry, but he still did not let go of his prey. He did, however, stagger back slightly as the pain shot up through his leg, and this left him slightly off balance. Andrew exploited the brief window of opportunity to twist his body to one side, and with the gun still held pointing uselessly at the ceiling, he managed to sidestep the Romanian and rotate the two of them so that his opponent was now the one standing with his back against the window. Outside, Andrew could see that they seemed to be driving along a stretch of rail track that had several train signals positioned along it. The black shapes flashed past the window in an instant every few seconds, and this was the opportunity Andrew had been waiting for.

With the powerful hand of the Romanian still around his throat, Andrew began twisting the gun inward towards the man's head as far as it would go, but it was nowhere near enough to fire and hit him. The brute realised this, slanted his head slightly to one side and looked mockingly into Andrew's eyes as he panted and grinned menacingly. He knew that his grip on Andrew's wrist was strong enough to prevent him from aiming the gun directly at him, and all he had to do now was wait for him to pass out. Then he could get his gun back and shoot the bastard in the head.

Radovan was right, except shooting him had never been Andrew's plan. When he finally did pull the trigger, the toughened glass window behind Radovan's back instantly shattered into a thousand pieces as the bullet ripped through it. As the fresh air from the outside rushed violently into the space, Andrew immediately thrust himself forward with everything he had. His effort, combined with the fact that Radovan no longer had the support of the window behind his back and was now off balance, resulted in the Romanian's entire upper body ending up leaning backwards out of the empty window frame. Andrew let go of the gun and used all of his remaining strength to fix the brute in place as the wind rushed past him.

Only too late did the Romanian realise what was happening. He only had time to turn his head in the direction of travel, his eyes widening in horror. A split second later the train reached another signal post which, amid a sickening thud and a metallic clang, instantly decapitated the Romanian and sent his head flying into the air and rolling along the rail tracks before it came to a stop in a ditch.

After the initial violent jerk as the head separated from the body, Andrew released his grip on the headless corpse, which then slumped heavily down onto the floor in an expanding pool of dark red blood. He stepped back from the open window, clutching his throat and heaving for air. At that moment, there was banging on the sliding door and the sound of Fiona's panicked voice.

'Andrew,' she shouted. 'Are you all right?'

Andrew yanked the sliding door open, and before Fiona could say anything more, he pulled her inside and closed the door behind her. It was all she could do to not scream at the sight of the dismembered body on the floor in front of her. The Romanian's head had been separated from his body in what was evidently an extremely violent fashion. Unlike the movies where a head might be cut off neatly by a guillotine and drop into a basket, here there was no head. And the head that used to be there had not so much been cut off as ripped off, leaving odd strands of tissue and veins that still oozed blood.

Fiona clasped a hand in front of her mouth just in time to suppress a yelp, and then she involuntarily turned away, closing her eyes as she attempted to control her gagging reflex.

'Oh my god,' she finally said, looking up at Andrew, the swirling wind inside the toilet wafting her hair around. 'What the hell happened?'

'It was him or me,' said Andrew grimly, rubbing his throat.

Fiona just looked at him aghast, shifted her gaze to the mangled corpse and then back to Andrew again.

'We need to stay in here until we reach Toulouse,' he said.

'What?' exclaimed Fiona, horrified by the idea.

'We can't let anyone come in here and see this,' he said, gesturing to the dead body. 'I reckon it's another fifteen minutes until we arrive at the central station. If we leave calmly, we should be able to get away. And then we need to catch the first TGV to Paris and Notre Dame.'

Fiona stared in horror at what was left of Radovan, but then she nodded.

'OK,' she said, swallowing hard as she mobilised all of her strength to remain calm. 'Whatever it takes.'

*   *   *

Detective Inspector Palmer had managed to catch a brief nap on a sofa in a meeting room and had just come back to his cubicle when his mobile phone rang.

'DI Palmer,' he said gruffly. 'Who the hell is calling me at five o'clock in the morning.'

'Oh shit,' said a male voice. 'Sorry mate. This is Peter Vickery. I didn't realise what time it is. The sun comes up so early now.'

Vickery was another homicide investigator that Palmer had worked with on a couple of occasions in the past. A bright guy who, like Palmer, spent too much time in the office and too little time being a normal person with healthy interests such as relationships.

'Good morning Pete,' said Palmer, still sounding grumpy. 'It's all right. I am actually still at the office. How are you this glorious morning?'

'I am fine, thanks,' replied Vickery. 'I decided to call you because I have come across something that I think might help with your investigation into those missing young women.'

It was widely known within the Met's HMCC that Palmer had been working on a large number of missing persons cases over the past several years, and that several of those had turned out to be murders just as he had suspected. However, when it came to the dozen or so cases of missing young women, neither he nor his colleagues had managed to make any progress on quite a few of them. Eventually, the cases had come to be known as 'Palmer's girls', and for years now he had spent more time on those than on anything else.

'Really?' said Palmer, sounding tired and as if he was expecting Vickery to give him information of precisely no value whatsoever.

'Yes,' replied Vickery. 'For months these cases have been percolating at the back of my mind, and I haven't been able to figure out why I couldn't put them down. But now I know. I looked into all of them again, and there are definitely similarities between many of them.'

'Similarities?' asked Palmer, now sounding more interested.

'Yes,' said Vickery. 'When looked at in isolation, these young women seem to have nothing in common, but when looked at as a whole it becomes clear that they share a whole bunch of characteristics that might seem trivial. Especially with regard to their looks. And I don't think that is a coincidence.'

'You're saying you think you've discovered a pattern?' asked Palmer.

'Precisely,' replied Vickery.

'Well, what is it then?' asked Palmer. 'Spit it out, man.'

Vickery sighed, and then there was a long pause during which Palmer thought he could hear the sound of Vickery scratching his stubble.

'Listen,' said Vickery finally. 'I won't go into details, but I have reason to believe that there are people inside the Met who are involved in this.'

Palmer frowned but did not respond.

'I can't tell you how I know this,' continued Vickery, 'At least, I am not prepared to discuss this in any detail over the phone.'

'You think your calls are being recorded?' asked Palmer with a sigh, sounding sceptical.

'Let's just say that if I am right about this,' said Vickery, 'then this thing goes right to the top, and there are some powerful people who will think nothing of removing someone like me from the chess board, ok?'

'Right…,' said Palmer, waiting for Vickery to speak again.

'Can we meet?' asked the other man hesitantly. 'Somewhere quiet.'

'All right. Sure,' said Palmer reluctantly. 'Just tell me where and when. I'll be there.'

Twenty-Four

The departure of the first TGV of the day from the Toulouse-Matabiau central station to Paris had been scheduled so that connecting early morning trains from other cities in the south of the country would arrive close to that time. As the high-speed train finally began moving at exactly 6:28 a.m., Andrew and Fiona both drew a sigh of relief. About fifteen minutes earlier, they had slipped out of the toilet on their regional train to Toulouse, leaving the headless Romanian inside. As they had left, Andrew had used raw strength to break off the flimsy aluminium door handle so that no one would be able to open the door to the inside – at least not for a few minutes until a member of staff realised that the door had been vandalised. By then, the two of them were seated comfortably inside a first-class carriage of the TGV as the electrically powered train was pulling away from the platform.

Ahead of them was an almost six-hundred-kilometre journey to Paris' Gare Montparnasse where the southern TGV services terminated. The average speed would be around 300 kilometres per hour, so the entire trip, including three short stops, was scheduled to take just over four hours.

As the train streaked across central France at the speed of a high-performance car going full throttle, Andrew and Fiona sat in a corner of the carriage wearing the black linen caps Andrew had picked up inside the central station in Toulouse. Pulling them down low to obscure their faces, they leaned back in their seats and managed to catch a couple of hours of sleep. They spent the rest of the time trying to pin down precisely what the tablet under Château La Roche had been referring to. There was no doubt that it pointed to the Notre Dame Cathedral on the artificial island of Île de la Cité in the middle of the river Seine in Paris.

'If what the tablet said is correct, and the lost chapter is hidden somewhere under the stained glass rose on the west façade of the cathedral,' said Andrew, 'then where could it possibly be? If I am not mistaken, that is the main entrance to the cathedral, and thousands of visitors pass that point every single day. It somehow seems unlikely.'

'That's a good point,' said Fiona. 'It almost seems too straightforward. Perhaps there is another clue hidden in plain sight there, only obvious if you know what to look for.'

'It is such a huge building, though,' said Andrew. 'It would take weeks for us to search the whole place, and there is no way we could do that without looking highly suspicious. Plus, we don't have that sort of time.'

'I know,' said Fiona. 'We will just have to wait until we get there.'

'Were you able to find out anything else that might be useful to us?' asked Andrew.

'I was, actually,' replied Fiona. 'It turns out that the cathedral itself is riddled with references to ancient alchemy. And this means it is steeped in Gnosticism.'

'Really?' said Andrew. 'Such as?'

'Have a look,' she said, showing him an image on her phone of the façade of the cathedral with its two square thirty-metre-tall towers above the three portals into the interior. 'Let's begin with the design and orientation of the cathedral. With its twin towers facing west, it resembles the Temple of Solomon in Jerusalem, where the Knights Templar order was founded. There is even a statue of King Solomon above one of the portals. And here on the central pillar of the main entrance, known as the Portal of Judgement, is a bas relief of a woman on a throne. Her head reached up into the clouds above, and she is holding a sceptre in her left hand and two books in her right hand. One of the books is open, symbolising public knowledge, and the other is closed, symbolising esoteric or occult knowledge. In front of her is a seven-rung ladder that symbolises the seven steps alchemists would follow in their quest to transform ordinary metals into gold. And it is obvious that this alchemical quest always represented the pursuit of purity and the divine. Alchemy has always been inextricably linked to the pursuit of the sort of deep knowledge and divine insights that is central to Gnosticism.'

'Interesting,' said Andrew, studying the image.

'And look at this,' said Fiona, swiping to show another image. 'Here's a photo of a figure positioned high above the ground on the external gallery. It is a small sculpture of an old bearded man with a distinctive Phrygian cap, which identifies him as an alchemical initiate of that time. He is sitting amongst the gargoyles, and he is the only human up there. He is known as the Alchemist of Notre Dame.'

She swiped again to show another photo of the façade, zoomed in on the porch where there were six sets of bas-reliefs on either side of the portal

'The top row here is depicting various stages of the alchemical process,' she said, 'and the bottom row is depicting the result of those processes.'

'Those references seem to be everywhere,' said Andrew, sounding intrigued.

'That's right,' said Fiona, 'and there are many scholars who believe that the entire cathedral is one big open book for those initiated in the secrets of alchemy and the occult.'

She swiped again to show a bas relief of a knight in heavy armour wielding a lance and a shield.

'Look at this,' she said. 'He is fighting off some intruding creature somewhere outside of the image, and he is clearly protecting the alchemy furnace called an 'athanor' which is sitting on the ground behind him.

'So, what does all this mean for us?' asked Andrew.

'Well,' replied Fiona. 'It means that there is a clear connection between alchemy, Gnosticism, the Knights

Templar, and the cathedral of Notre Dame. And that in turn means that the idea that the cryptic text on the tablet under Château La Roche is pointing to something real inside the cathedral suddenly doesn't seem so far-fetched.'

'All we have to do is find it,' said Andrew pensively. 'We should be able to get to the cathedral by around 1 p.m., and I think it closes at six o'clock. That gives us plenty of time to look around inside.'

'Yes,' said Fiona. 'I just did some research, and it seems like there are several statues of the Virgin Mary in the cathedral, so it might not be as simple as I first thought.'

'When did that ever put you off,' asked Andrew, giving her a sideways smile.

'Never,' she acknowledged. 'Complex things are interesting. But let's not forget what we are here for. Leaving Paris without a solid clue to the location of the lost chapter is just not an option.'

★ ★ ★

When the TGV train pulled into the enormous modernist Gare Montparnasse in Paris, which had the dubious honour of having once been voted the 2nd ugliest building in the world by international travellers, Andrew and Fiona left swiftly and made their way outside. The one redeeming quality of the station was that upon exiting onto the dramatically named *Place des Cinq Martyrs du Lycée Buffon*, they were treated to a view across the city towards the northwest with the Eiffel Tower in the distance sitting just in front of the Seine and the Palais de Chaillot.

They quickly hailed a cab and got in. At the wheel was a surly driver who seemed to become noticeably less amicable when he realised that his two passengers were speaking English. Fiona made a valiant attempt at switching to French, but by then the damage was done, and the rest of the journey took place in a silence that Andrew welcomed.

Soon they were well underway, and the less-than-friendly driver could not take away from the beauty of the city as they drove past handsome buildings situated along wide tree-lined boulevards. It was already turning out to be a warm sunny day, and the City of Lights seemed to effortlessly present itself from its most enticing side as they drove through it. They cut through the 14th arrondissement towards the east, passing the enormous cemetery Cimetière du Montparnasse where such luminaries as Jean-Paul Sartre lay buried. They then turned north along Boulevard Saint-Michel past the Palais du Luxembourg where the French Senate resides, and after about fifteen minutes they made their way along the final stretch of Rue Saint-Jacque and across the short Pont Petit bridge over the river to Île de la Cité and Notre-Dame Cathedral.

Stepping out of the taxi and paying the seemingly indifferent driver who took their money and sped off without so much as *a Salut* or an *Adieu*, they found themselves in a sea of people who were milling around the front of the cathedral taking photos of the façade and padding their social media accounts with excited holiday snaps.

'Busy,' observed Andrew, putting his cap back on and pulling it down low. 'Suits us fine, though.'

Fiona did the same and pointed to a nondescript set of concrete walls about as tall as a person on the edge of the large open square in front of the cathedral. It appeared to be an entrance of some sort.

'That's the entrance to the *Crypte Archéologique*,' she said. 'It's an archaeological exhibition that displays all sorts of things discovered during excavation here on the island. The oldest finds go back more than two thousand years to around 300 BCE when this place was called Lutetia and was the home of a Gaulish tribe called the Parisii. So, this is a very old city.'

Andrew looked up at the two tall rectangular towers of the cathedral and the giant stained glass rose directly above the main entrance.

'It's an amazing building,' he said, his eyes remaining fixed on the huge structure for several moments, 'regardless of what you might think of the mythology behind it.'

'Shall we make our way inside,' asked Fiona. 'We might as well get going.'

'Sure,' he replied, and then the two of them began making their way casually through the crowds of tourists and across the square towards the three wide portals at the bottom of the imposing gothic façade.

As they approached the façade, Fiona pointed to the various bas reliefs that she had shown Andrew pictures of on the TGV. Taking them all in at once, it was difficult to escape the sense that the builders of this place had embedded messages into the structure that were decidedly non-Christian, and that there was a lot more here than met the eye.

'Up there just in front of the stained-glass rose,' said Fiona and pointed up to the balustrade above them, 'is the statue called the 'Virgin Mary with Child' that I showed you a picture of.'

'Well,' said Andrew. 'She is clearly standing under the rose, but below her is a massive entranceway and hundreds of people, so I fail to see how the lost chapter could be hidden there.'

'I agree,' said Fiona. 'And I just discovered that this particular statue was placed there around 1850, so it can't possibly be that one. I feel like we're missing something. Let's get inside.'

After paying the entrance fee, which was roughly equivalent to the price of a cup of coffee and a piece of pastry from one of the nearby pâtisseries, Andrew took a visitor's guide from the ticket desk. They entered the spectacular cathedral and spent the first few minutes marvelling at the gravity-defying gothic arches stretching away overhead to their apexes more than thirty metres above them. The fact that this place had been built almost a thousand years earlier when most people in Europe lived in rickety wooden houses with thatched roofs, was astonishing to both of them. Turning around to face the inside of the façade, they marvelled at the enormous nineteen-metre wide eighty-four-panel stained-glass rose that depicted a plethora of scenes from the Bible.

They proceeded along the centre of the more than one-hundred-metre-long nave to the transept near the middle of the cathedral, at which point there were two more portals with stained-glass roses above them on either side facing north and south respectively. The former was the *Portail du Cloître*, also known as the Portal of the Cloister, and the latter was the *Portail du Saint Etienne,* or Portal of Saint Stephen. Fiona tugged at Andrew's sleeve and moved towards one of the massive load-bearing pillars that seemed to reach up effortlessly to the vaulted ceiling high above. In front of the pillar was a statue of a young woman with a baby, placed atop a roughly three-metre-tall cylindrical plinth.

'This statue is also of the Virgin Mary,' she said. 'It is the main representation of Mary in this cathedral. And this one is holding a child too. But notice how the child looks less like a baby and more like a miniature adult. This was done deliberately to hint at him being Jesus Christ, both God and future saviour incarnate all in one. And he is holding a globe in his hand to signify dominion over the Earth.'

'A virgin,' said Andrew pensively, looking up at the statue. 'In fact, a supposed virgin holding her *own* child. It is difficult not to grasp the notion of the divine in the form of immaculate conception here. It's certainly very clever if nothing else. But according to the stone tablet at La Roche, shouldn't the lost chapter be at her feet?'

They both moved closer to inspect the statue that towered above them. It was surrounded by a crescent of tourists, all gazing up at the cathedral's iconic and eponymous statue and taking pictures and videos with their cameras and phones.

'This can't be right either,' said Fiona, inspecting the feet of the statue and looking down onto the floor beneath the plinth. 'Unless the lost chapter is actually inside the statue or the plinth, but I seriously doubt that is the case.'

'I agree,' said Andrew, taking out his visitor's guide, folding it open on the page showing a map of the cathedral's interior.

They both studied it for a few moments, and then Fiona pointed to the spot on the map where they were standing.

'Look here,' she said. 'This description says that the statue in front of us is of the Virgin Mary, and that it is from the 14th century.'

'Right,' nodded Andrew.

'But now look over there,' she continued, shifting her index finger to another location about fifteen metres away near the *Portail du Cloître*. 'There is yet another statue of the Virgin Mary over there which is supposedly from the 13th century.'

They both looked up and turned their gaze towards the north, but they were unable to see the north portal behind the massive pillars at the intersection of the nave and the transept. Extracting themselves from the throng of people by the main statue of the woman in whose honour the cathedral had been named, they soon found themselves just a few metres from the north portal that served as the exit out onto the street called *Rue du Cloitre-Notre-Dame*.

Near the eastern wall in a dark and easily missed corner next to the massive oak doors out to the street, there was another statue that was almost identical to the one they had just inspected. However, this one was smaller and seemed much less impressive. It had much less detail and appeared almost plain by comparison. It stood on a square pedestal about a metre off the ground, and the pedestal was sitting on flagstones very similar to those under the previous statues' plinth. Above it on a cylindrical stone column was a small circular bas relief of a rose about the size of a hand. If they hadn't been looking for it, they could easily have missed it.

'Look up there. This one has a rose above it,' said Andrew, glancing sideways at Fiona.

'Wait a minute,' said Fiona suddenly. 'When I was looking into this on the train to Paris, I came across a map of the crypts below the cathedral. And I am sure that the crypts extended all the way from the crypt's entrance out on the square to right under the cathedral itself.'

'You're saying you think the ossuary is somewhere underground?' asked Andrew.

'It has to be,' said Fiona.

'So, what do you suggest?' he asked.

'We wait until just before the crypt closes,' she said, 'and then we find a place to hide down there. Once it is closed off and everyone has left for the day, we can look for the lost chapter. They close at 4 p.m.'

Andrew considered the idea for a moment, but he had nothing better to offer, so he eventually nodded.

'All right,' he said. 'That means we need to kill a few more hours before we can make our move. Let's head outside.'

★   ★   ★

She knew was being watched. Someone somewhere was observing her through the camera mounted above the metal door. It was the only thing in the prison cell that hinted at this being the modern age rather than medieval times. She still couldn't work out why her captors had designed it this way, but what she was sure of was that there was a purpose to everything that had happened. Her surroundings were not accidental, and her presence in this place was part of some larger scheme that was hidden from her, although she now feared the worst.

The evening before, there had been another one of those warm late afternoon rain showers that often happened in London during the early summer. For this reason, her metal beaker placed on the floor behind the bed and thus out of sight of the camera had finally become full to the brim, and so she had decided that today was going to be the day she would attempt to escape. Judging by the light coming through the glass brick in the exterior wall, she had woken up more or less at the same time as usual, and she had consumed the remaining contents of the wooden box that seemed to magically refill once a day. It was enough to keep her going, but she was still aware of a constant gnawing hunger which told her that she was not getting the amount of nourishment and energy that her body needed. The lack of food and water had left her weakened and lethargic, but she could not let that stop her now.

After finishing the last morsels, she then drank all the rainwater collected in the beaker, leaving the metal jug on the floor full of the water. Water she was sure had been laced with a strong sedative that caused her to fall into a deep sleep after every meal. Not today, however. Today she was well rested and free of the drug. Now she was lying on the austere-looking bed pretending to be asleep and waiting to find out what would happen next. She assumed that someone would eventually enter the cell, check on her, and leave more food. She was soon proven correct.

Still pretending to be in a deep drug-induced sleep bordering on unconsciousness, she heard the faint noise from what sounded like a metal gate being unlocked, opened and then closed again. It seemed to squeak slightly on its hinges, and there was a muffled clang as it closed again. Then she heard footsteps approaching and stopping outside the cell door. After a couple of seconds, there was the metallic snap of an electronic door unlocking, and then she heard the door open and someone step inside the cell.

There was a brief moment of silence, during which time she could hear breathing. Having been isolated from the outside world for days, the presence of another human being near her felt decidedly strange. It was as if her psyche had already adjusted to being completely alone in the world, which is what it had felt like for however many days she had been here. She had simply lost track.

Still lying on her side with her back towards the door, she heard a rustling sound by the bench and then the strangely and eerily familiar sound of a male voice mumbling something to himself. Whoever was inside the cell with her now had clearly noticed how none of the water in the jug had been drunk. Clenching her jaw, she silently cursed herself for not having poured out some of the water to make it look like she had consumed at least a small amount of it. Was her plan unravelling already? She felt the panic rising inside her. She had to move. It was now or never.

Spinning around and leaping from her bed, she jumped to her feet and barged into the man whose body and face was covered by a long black silk robe with a red hood. They both crashed into the wall, and he grunted in shock and pain as his head made contact with the stone wall. Once again, something deep inside her recoiled at the sound of his voice. But all she could think about was to try to use this brief moment to get out of this dreadful place and attempt to escape. Before the man could recover from the impact, she pushed off from him. On unsteady legs, she bolted through the door, swinging it shut behind her. She knew she would not be able to lock her captor inside, but it might buy her another few seconds.

Confused, she found herself in a modern-looking corridor with concrete walls and a slippery tiled floor, which seemed almost alien to her after her long confinement in a medieval-looking prison cell. One end of the corridor was dark and seemed to extend for a long distance before turning at a right angle. At the other end was what appeared to be daylight coming from a window above. For some reason, she found it difficult to focus her eyes, and through her blurry vision she was unable to see exactly what was there, but the light was enough for her to run towards it.

She quickly reached the end of the corridor only to find it locked by the metal gate she had heard open when she was lying inside the cell a few minutes earlier. As she gripped the black-painted metal bars, she heard the cell door fly open and slam into the wall behind her. Then she heard the sound of heavy footsteps approaching her. She pulled and yanked frantically at the bars, but she only managed to produce a loud metallic rattling sound. The footsteps came inexorably closer, and her captor was now almost upon her.

Panic-stricken and hyperventilating, she spun around with her back pressed against the metal gate, and her legs almost gave way beneath her when she saw the face of the man coming towards her. It was Antoine. Her head was spinning, and she blinked several times through her tears, trying to make sense of what she was seeing. It was Antoine, except he seemed to have changed his hairstyle and he had a small bandage on his right ear. His eyes were like burning embers filled with disdain as he moved closer, and in his hand was a small medical jet injector.

'Antoine,' she yelled out in terror, her voice trembling and almost breaking. 'Please. No. What is happening? Why are you doing this?'

Upon hearing her speak, he seemed to visibly react with a pained expression on his face. But he kept coming, now with a snarl and real menace written across his face. And was there something else in his eyes? Something more primeval and disturbing? Her knees began to buckle under her, and with her last ounce of strength, she turned around once more to try one last desperate attempt at forcing her way through the metal gate. She pulled at the gate and screamed, but her efforts were in vain. As soon as she turned around, he was on her, pinning her body against the metal gate and pressing the injector against the side of her neck. It felt cold against her skin, and in the next instant, there was a quick, sharp click as the sedative shot out of the injector and into her bloodstream.

Confused and distraught, she called out Antoine's name one more time, but there was no reply. She managed to fill her lungs with air for one final scream for help, but then she felt herself slipping down into a dark well once again until all sounds disappeared and the world constricted into a tiny pinprick of light that finally winked out and she lost consciousness.

Twenty-Five

Directly opposite the Notre Dame cathedral's north portal, the *Portail du Cloitre* was a small creperie imaginatively named *Crêperie du Cloître*. They waved at a friendly waiter who placed them at the only available table on the pavement under a deep red awning with the name of the eatery emblazoned across it in gold lettering. The temperature was now in the high twenties even in the shade of the cathedral, and they made themselves comfortable, ordered crepes and cold drinks and settled in to watch the world go by.

Surprisingly, cars were allowed to drive along the street just metres away from the almost millennium-old cathedral. Observing it with disquiet, Fiona was convinced that it would reduce the life expectancy of the exterior walls significantly due to the tremors generated by the moving vehicles, and as a result of the acidity of their exhaust.

At one point, Andrew spotted a black Mercedes with dark tinted windows approaching them. It was driving along the street and passed them very slowly, and he immediately found himself on high alert, reaching instinctively for the Beretta 92 that he had kept in his belt under his jacket. However, he then spotted the car's diplomatic plates and realised that there were probably hundreds of vehicles just like this one driving around central Paris all day ferrying diplomats back and forth between meetings.

About half an hour before the *Crypte Archéologique* was scheduled to close, the two of them paid the waiter, got up and walked casually across the square in front of the cathedral and down the steps into the underground museum. The transition from the light and the busy, noisy square above to the darkness and the quiet below was abrupt, and it felt like stepping back in time. In front of them was a huge, low-ceilinged space that stretched away in the direction of the cathedral. The entire complex went on for almost a hundred metres under the square towards the cathedral. It was about thirty metres in width, and in certain places, it reached up to ten metres down into the buried history of the city. Everything was bathed in the warm glow from the many floodlights that had been arranged throughout the subterranean museum, and many of the structures were little more than sharply defined silhouettes unless viewed up close from the correct angle.

They began moving along the walkways, looking to the sides and down onto the many different ruins and excavated remnants of buildings and foundations. Instead of remaining buried here for eternity with new buildings placed on top of them, they were now on display for all the world to see after their accidental discovery during the now-abandoned construction of an underground car park several decades earlier.

There were ruins covering the entire period from Roman times to the 18th century, and everything that was on display was in the exact places where they had originally been discovered and excavated. Because cities tend to be built in layers one after another on top of what was there before, digging down meant going back in time, and so the most ancient remnants of the Roman city of Lutetia were in the lowest sections.

There were exposed ruins of walls and several ancient dwellings, remains of a 4th-century rampart from the Gallo-Roman period, Roman baths with remnants of tile mosaics, and a small Roman quay for transport along the Seine. There were also the vestiges of roman fortifications that had been built almost two thousand years earlier to defend the island from Germanic invaders. They also passed a medieval cellar that had been opened up and put on display, as well as the foundations of residential houses built through the ages.

'This is amazing,' said Fiona. 'We're looking at almost two millennia of human settlements in this tiny spot on this island in the middle of the river. I am glad they decided to leave it all here and turn it into a museum.'

'Let's move towards the back,' said Andrew, looking around furtively. 'They will be closing soon, and we need to be well out of sight when that happens.'

They pushed deeper into the underground complex until they reached the far end of the large main space. Here there were a set of narrow stairs leading down into a separate section which had a section of the foundation of the Merovingian Church of Saint Étienne on display. This church had stood on the island of Île de la Cité from around the 6th century until it was replaced with the cathedral of Notre Dame around seven centuries later.

As they entered, a pre-recorded female voice on a hidden PA system announced that the museum was now closing, and asked that all visitors begin to make their way towards the exit. The last of the other visitors were coming up the stairs as Andrew and Fiona entered, and soon they found themselves alone inside the roughly twenty by ten metres large space.

'This will do,' said Andrew and pointed down to a section of the ruins about three metres below the walkway they were standing on. 'Come one.'

They quickly slipped over the side and squeezed under a stone arch that had once supported part of a building. Here they bunched up at the very back so that they could not be seen from the walkways circling the ruins in the room. After about ten minutes they heard the sound of a single person walking along the walkway at a pace that indicated that this was not a visitor but one of the staff members doing the end-of-the-day rounds to make sure everyone had left. Soon the staff member had disappeared, and everything fell eerily quiet. Then all the lights went out.

'Stay here,' said Andrew in hushed tones. 'We need to wait at least another fifteen minutes before moving.'

In the pitch black, Fiona felt his hand finding hers, and he gave it a quick squeeze and held it. She couldn't see a thing, and to test it, she brought her other hand up right in front of her face. She turned it from side to side, but her eyes registered nothing but blackness. There was not a single source of light anywhere in the room, and along with the complete absence of any noises apart from the sounds of their own breathing, it was like having been buried alive. Up on the square in the late afternoon sun, it was bright and warm, but down here the temperature was probably as low as eighteen degrees, yet Fiona soon felt small beads of sweat meandering down her forehead. The creeping sense of claustrophobia was beginning to worm its way inexorably into her mind.

Finally, Andrew shifted slightly and spoke again.

'Okay,' he said quietly. 'I think we're good to move out.'

He switched on his phone light and Fiona quickly did the same. Rarely had she felt such relief at seeing light, and after being plunged into perfect darkness for that long, their two small torches somehow seemed able to illuminate the entire large space. They climbed back up onto the walkway and made their way back up the stairs into the large main room. It was equally dark, except there was a faint red light at the far end, which looked to be some sort of emergency first aid station.

Moving to the opposite corner of the main room, they found a wooden door to a sealed-off area in the direction of the northwestern corner of the cathedral.

'This must lead closer to where we want to go,' said Andrew, gripping the door handle but finding that it was securely locked. 'I'll be right back. Stay here, please.'

Less than a minute later, during which time Fiona heard the sound of glass breaking near the entrance, Andrew returned with a large red fireman's axe. Waiting a moment for Fiona to stand clear, he gripped the handle, flipped the axe around so that the murderous-looking spike at the back of the axe head was pointing forward, and then he swung it forcefully in a slightly tilted overhead arc. When the steel spike hit the wooden door just next to the door handle and the lock, it embedded itself deeply. Using all of his might, Andrew was then able to wrench it to one side so that the wood near the handle splintered and broke open. After repeating the exercise one more time, the entire lock came free and clonked onto the floor. The door then swung open to reveal a long concrete corridor that seemed to have been built relatively recently. Bringing the axe with them, they proceeded through the corridor to emerge into what was evidently an active excavation area. The room was about ten by ten metres, and at the far end was a doorway with a gothic arch leading to a dark area beyond.

'This looks like late medieval structures,' said Fiona, inspecting the masonry. 'I reckon we are now well under the northern part of the cathedral itself. This might even be part of its foundations.'

'Could that be the way into the cathedral's own crypt?' asked Andrew, pointing at the doorway.

'It might be,' said Fiona. 'There could even be a way up into the cathedral itself from here.'

Pushing onwards through the doorway, they discovered a winding stone stairway, but it did not go up towards the enormous medieval church above them. Instead, it led further down into the bowels of the underground complex.

'This looks like it has been discovered quite recently,' said Fiona as they descended the stairway. 'Everything is covered in dust and I don't see any evidence of any actual excavations having been done yet. This place might have laid completely untouched for centuries.'

Holding the fireman's axe in two hands, Andrew continued down the final turn of the stairway to emerge in a space that seemed strangely familiar.

'Wow,' said Fiona as she emerged behind him, shining her torchlight around the musty-smelling subterranean chamber. 'This looks almost identical to the chamber under Chateau La Roche.'

'You're right,' said Andrew, stepping forward with an astonished look on his face. 'Same proportions. Same architectural style.'

'Be careful,' said Fiona, placing a hand on his shoulder. 'Look down and make sure you don't step on a trap.'

'Good point,' said Andrew, shifting his light down onto the flagstone floor in front of them.

Fiona walked along slowly next to him as they proceeded out into the middle of the seemingly empty room.

'At Chateau La Roche, these two walls were the ones that had people walled in behind them,' said Andrew, pointing to the walls on either side. 'So, if there is anything to be found down here, it has to be through that wall straight ahead.'

Fiona directed her light forward to the ancient-looking brick wall directly ahead of them as Andrew shifted the fireman's axe in his hand. She sighed, suddenly looking hesitant.

'I don't have a problem with smashing through a mass-produced wooden door like the one back there,' she finally said, jerking her head back towards the archaeological crypt's main room. 'But I can't help but feel that wrecking a medieval wall with a giant axe just to see what is on the other side somehow feels like vandalism.'

'Remember why we are here,' said Andrew, fixing her with a firm but sympathetic look. 'Everything we're doing here is for Caitlin.'

Glancing at the wall in front of them, Fiona nodded silently, and after a few seconds she looked up at him again.

'Do your worst,' she said.

Andrew stepped up next to the wall, gripped the large red axe tightly and swung it as hard as he could at the masonry around chest height. The axe slammed into one of the stone blocks with a loud clang, and for a brief instant, bright golden sparks flew as the hardened steel of the axe head connected with the granite. The brick cracked into several pieces, but the wall held. However, for a brief moment after the impact, they could hear distinct reverberations from some sort of cavity behind it. The wall was definitely not as solid as it looked, and from the sounds permeating the confined space it was obvious that there was air rather than soil on the other side of it.

After another couple of swings, Andrew's axe finally crashed through the wall and several bricks fell onto the floor on the other side with dull clonks that echoed slightly, hinting at the size of the cavity beyond. Less than a minute later, Andrew had created a hole through the wall that was big enough for the two of them to squeeze through. Andrew stuck his head through first and shone his torch around. Then he climbed through the opening and pulled the axe with him to the other side.

'Another short tunnel,' he said. 'Exactly like under Chateau La Roche. Checking for traps.'

Fiona soon joined him, and together they carefully stepped through the tunnel and into a room that seemed like an exact copy of the final chamber under the castle in the Languedoc. The air was cool and damp.

'It's so cold in here,' said Fiona, hugging herself.

'We're probably about fifteen metres below the cathedral now,' said Andrew. 'I am guessing it is this temperature all year round.'

In the centre of the chamber was another altar with an ossuary very similar to the one in which they had discovered the first stone tablet.

They stepped up to the ossuary and carefully removed its lid. It was adorned with a *fleur-de-lis* and a Templar Cross. Inside was a skull and a pile of bones much like the one they had found under Chateau La Roche, and leaning against the skull was another stone tablet.

'Look,' said Fiona. 'This must be the final resting place of the older Rancourt brother, Gerard.'

'Let's see what the tablet says,' said Andrew.

Fiona picked it up and wiped small amounts of dust from the text that had been chiselled neatly into its front. Then she slowly began to read it out loud.

Où le trésor de Lucifer repose
Veillé par le premier Templier qui a souffert
Sous le château des loups
Ses murs arrêtaient les hommes du nord
La pierre angulaire vous guidera

She took another moment to read it again before turning it towards Andrew so that he could see it properly, tracing the lines of text with her index finger as she translated the words.

'It says, "Where the treasure of Lucifer rests. Watched over by the first Templar who suffered. Under the castle of the wolves. Its walls stopped the men of the north. The cornerstone will guide you".'

'Cryptic,' said Andrew. 'Any ideas?'

Fiona shook her head pensively, a small frown gradually spreading across her face.

'I am not sure,' she said. 'Except, of course, the treasure of Lucifer has to be the lost chapter.'

'Could the first knight who suffered be the first Templar knight?' asked Andrew. 'Could it be its founder, Hugues de Payens.'

'It could, I suppose,' said Fiona, 'except Hugues de Payens died peacefully of old age in Jerusalem at the beginning of the 12th century. Unless…'

'What?' asked Andrew.

'Unless what is referred to here is not the first but the last Templar,' she said, her eyes like two small almond-shaped windows into the machine that was now busily whirring inside her head.

'What do you mean?' asked Andrew. 'The tablet specifically says "the first Templar", right?'

'Yes,' she replied, 'But what if the word 'first' refers not to the first in a timeline but to the first among equals? In other words, the leader of the Templars.'

'But there were dozens of those, weren't there?' asked Andrew.

'There were,' nodded Fiona, 'but the last of them was the one who suffered, to put it mildly. He was burnt at the stake right here in the middle of Paris on the western tip of this island of Île de la Cité.'

'It's Jacques de Molay,' said Andrew, finally grasping what she meant. 'The last grand master of the Knights Templar.'

'Correct,' said Fiona.

'All right,' said Andrew. 'So far so good. But what did Jacques de Molay watch over?'

'I think I've got it now,' Fiona smiled. 'As he burned to death, Jacques de Molay would have faced roughly north, and he would have been able to see what was just on the opposite bank of the Seine at that time.'

'Which was what?' asked Andrew.

'The Louvre,' replied Fiona.

'Do you mean *the* Louvre?' asked Andrew sceptically. 'One of the biggest museums in the world?'

'Yes,' nodded Fiona. 'That huge complex, which is now also known as *le Palais du Louvre*. The Palace of Louvre.'

'I don't understand,' said Andrew. 'The lost chapter can't possibly be in the museum. It wasn't even built until several centuries after the Rancourt brothers died.'

'That's right,' said Fiona, 'but before the Palace of Louvre existed, there was something else on that site called *Le Chateau fort du Louvre*, or the Louvre Fort. It was built by King Philip II around the year 1200 to protect the city against attack from the Normans in the west of France. And the first Normans were Norse Viking settlers who began intermarrying in north-western France and eventually became the powerful nation that conquered Britain and many other parts of Europe. These are the men of the north.'

'Its walls stopped the men of the north,' said Andrew, reciting the fourth line of the riddle. 'Right. Ok. But what about the reference to wolves?'

'In Latin, *Lupa* means wolf,' said Fiona. 'And in modern French, it is called *Louve*. It is believed the fort was named this way because of the many wolves that roamed the area in those days.'

'All right,' said Andrew. 'So, we're definitely talking about the Louvre, in one form or another. That leaves the reference to the cornerstone. What do you suppose that means?'

'I think it should be taken literally,' she replied confidently. 'It is a reference to the actual cornerstone in the foundations of the Louvre Fort.'

'But surely that no longer exists,' said Andrew. 'The Louvre Palace was built on top of the fort over the course of many centuries. There's nothing left now, is there?'

'There is,' said Fiona. 'Part of the foundations of the 12th-century fort have been excavated. They are actually a part of the Louvre Museum's exhibitions.'

'I did not know that,' said Andrew. 'Well, I would say we should just leave and head for the museum. But what exactly are we looking for there? The tablet doesn't say.'

'We will just have to hope that it becomes clear once we get there,' she said. 'But it has to be the lost chapter. The key that Haywood is after. And we need to get to it before he does. Let's get out of here.'

★ ★ ★

Peter Vickery had chosen the spot for his meeting with DI Palmer carefully. It was by a couple of benches near the centre of Tower Hamlets Cemetery where several footpaths crossed each other. After everything he had discovered, he would not be surprised if the ringleaders of the operation had connections in the Metropolitan Police itself, which they would be able to exploit to monitor his movements. He had long been convinced that he was being watched, but this was the first time he had shared his concerns with anyone else, and he wasn't about to take any chances. He had picked that location because he knew the cemetery had no CCTV cameras, and because his great-great-great-grandfather lay buried there. His ancestor had himself been a chief constable of what was then the local parish police force before the Met was founded in 1829. Vickery figured that even if someone with access to all the CCTV cameras in the Greater London area decided to track his movements, a visit to this cemetery was unlikely to make anyone look twice.

Vickery's home was in a small cottage near Epping Forest that he had bought two decades earlier. Located on a small plot backing onto the edge of the forest itself, it was small but perfectly comfortable for someone like him who lived by himself. In many ways, it felt as if it was hundreds of miles from the bustling capital, but it was only a five-minute drive from Buckhurst Hill tube station and the Central Line, from where he could be in central London within 35 minutes. A short commute by London standards.

The house also had the additional benefit of having an unusually large double garage in a separate timber structure next to the main house. This allowed Vickery to indulge his passion for vintage cars. The garage was big enough to house his Ford Fiesta on one side, and his pride and joy – the silver 1967 Austin Healey 3000 MKIII on the other. With its throaty six-cylinder engine, burgundy leather seats and rich amber-coloured mahogany dashboard panelling, it was a thing of beauty. The vehicle had been in a sorry state when he had bought it just over six years ago at an auction, but he had always been good with his hands, and once upon a time he had imagined himself becoming an engineer. Life had played out differently, but upon seeing the classic car listed online, he had taken the leap and bought it. Within weeks, he had carefully taken it apart, placing the hundreds of different components and parts neatly on the concrete floor of the garage.

He had found the restoration work immensely soothing – therapeutic even. He had also discovered that it enabled him to switch off from his otherwise near-obsessive focus on his often-grim job at the Met, to focus entirely on lovingly restoring a piece of British motor history. Those of his colleagues that he had made the mistake of mentioning the project to had joked that the vehicle was a substitute for a real woman. Perhaps they were correct. But that didn't take away from the joy of the meticulous restoration work. Not in the slightest. He spent hours out in the garage all through the year, and it was very obvious to him that the project was beneficial both to his body and his soul.

Vickery had taken a day off so that he could focus on his afternoon meeting with DI Palmer, and he was in his living room looking at the diagrams he had been drawing on sheets of paper to try to make sense of the connections between the various missing young women he had been looking into. They were all laid out neatly on the floor. He was hoping that Palmer would also be able to spot the pattern he believed he had discovered, and that the detective inspector could provide insights that would allow the two of them to piece together what had happened to these women and who the perpetrators might be.

Emptying his glass of water, he got up and went to the front door where he put on his shoes and jacket. Then he left the house and walked across to the garage under the tall elm trees. Low dark clouds were now hanging immobile overhead and there was a light drizzle. However, the fresh air was warm and pleasant and a world away from the toxic pollution of London. Somewhere deep inside Epping Forest, a deer was making its characteristic drawn-out grunting call.

He walked across the gravelled drive, pulled the left garage door open and walked to the driver's side door of the white Ford Fiesta. He was about to enter, but then he turned to look at the Austin Healey that had now been almost completely reassembled. All it needed was the bodywork. It was currently at a specialist body shop. The owner had promised him they would be able to replicate the original silver paint job from when the car had first rolled off the production line at Jensen Motors Limited in West Bromwich not long after Vickery had been born. What a beauty she was.

He smiled and opened the Ford Fiesta's door, folded his tall frame inside, closed the door and reached for the seatbelt with his left hand. At that moment he sensed movement behind him, and an instant later in the rear-view mirror he spotted a balaclava-clad man immediately behind him in the backseat. Before he even had time to turn his head, the man had reached forward past Vickery's headrest with his right hand pinning his head in place, and a split second later the attacker's left hand came around in front of him holding a long kitchen knife. In the blink of an eye, the blade scythed across Vickery's neck, slicing open a wide gash from which blood immediately spurted violently as both carotid arteries were severed. The knife also cut straight through Vickery's windpipe, instantly silencing him.

In a blind panic, Vickery's arms and legs flailed wildly as the blood gushed from his neck, but the balaclava-clad attacker held him in place with his strong arms. The struggle only lasted a few seconds before Vickery's brain was starved of blood and its oxygen supply was depleted. Soon his movements were reduced to a feeble and entirely ineffectual clawing at his attacker's bloodstained hands. Finally, it was all over. Vickery's head slumped forward and the flow of blood abated as his heart ceased to beat.

The balaclava-clad man stepped out of the car, removed the headpiece, his blood-covered denim overalls and the wellies he had brought along for the job. He threw them all onto the backseat of the car. There was so much blood sprayed and smeared all over the inside of the windshield and the driver's side window that it looked like a grenade had gone off in there. Then he walked over to a large petrol can that he had placed there earlier, popped the lid off and began pouring out the petrol inside the car and all around the inside of the double garage.

Finally, he stepped outside and looked around. The small leafy plot was secluded, sitting as it did around a bend in the private road leading to it and overlooked by no other nearby buildings. Satisfied that he was not being observed, he placed an old rolled-up cleaning towel that was full of dirt and motor oil on the ground so that it just reached the nearest puddle of petrol on the concrete floor. Then he bent down and lit one end of it with his lighter. Within a couple of seconds, the towel was burning helped along by the motor oil. He rose, exited the garage and made his way to the back of the property where he pushed through the hedge to the forest beyond. He stood there and waited for about half a minute until there was an audible whoosh as the petrol inside the garage suddenly and violently ignited. Soon, the timber structure was fully ablaze. After observing it for a few seconds, he turned his back on the conflagration and headed deeper into the forest where he disappeared.

Twenty-Six

The door from the *Crypte Archéologique* to the steps leading back up to the square above it was easily unlocked and opened from the inside, so Andrew left the fireman's axe on the floor before they exited. The walk to the Louvre Museum was about ten minutes, and as the two of them made their way along *Quai des Orfèvres* on the south side of Île de la Cité next to the Seine, the golden early evening sunshine was glinting off the black-tiled mansard roofs of the elegant light-coloured five-storey residential buildings on both sides of the river. With their impressive facades, large dormer windows and ornate black metal balustrades in front of narrow balconies, they looked just as exclusive and expensive as they no doubt were. Built in the distinctive 19th-century style of the main Paris architect at the time, Baron Georges-Eugène Haussmann during his revamp of the city centre on behalf of Emperor Napoleon III, they lent an effortless sophistication to the city. Spanning the period from around 1850 to 1870, the enormous and costly project transformed much of the city by removing around twelve thousand medieval structures and replacing them with tall, graceful and much more uniform buildings. Along with the new broad tree-lined avenues, they gave the French capital a refinement and grandeur that had subsequently been emulated the world over.

'I have to say,' said Andrew, looking along the river at the buildings on both sides. 'You can probably say a lot about the French and Paris, but I will admit that it is an exceptionally attractive city. The architecture here is quite something.'

'And there is just as much history hidden in plain sight here as there is in London,' said Fiona. 'We're just about to reach the bridge called *Pont Neuf*. There is a piece of history there that is very relevant to what we are here for.'

She pointed ahead of them to where the street running along the quayside ended and a bridge crossed over from the south bank across Île de la Cité to the north bank.

'You mean that statue of a guy on a horse?' asked Andrew and pointed.

'That *guy* is Henri IV,' said Fiona. 'He was the king during the time when France established its colonies in Canada in the 16th century. Interestingly, he was forced to convert from Protestantism to Catholicism in order to wear the crown.'

'Needs must…' said Andrew evenly.

'Anyway, that's not what I was referring to,' said Fiona as they crossed to the opposite side of the road. 'We need to head down here.'

She led them past the equestrian statue and down through the huge foundations of the monument on a set of narrow steps that emerged on the very tip of Île de la Cité on the edge of a tiny park by the name *Square du Vert-Galant*. There were a handful of trees lining the small lawned area and a couple of benches on either side where the two sections of the Seine meet at a narrow point at the northern tip of the island.

'A park?' said Andrew as they stopped halfway down the steps.

'Turn around,' said Fiona, and pointed to a plaque on the wall behind them.

The plaque was roughly forty by fifty centimetres in size and was covered in the thin dark-green patina of corrosion called Verdigris that literally means *'green of Greece'*, indicating that it was made of copper but quite heavily weathered. At its centre were five brief lines of text.

> *A CET ENDROIT*
> *JACQUES DE MOLAY*
> *DERNTER GRAND MAÎTRE*
> *D'ORDRE DU TEMPLE*
> *A ÉTÉ BRÛLÉ 18 MARS 1314*

Fiona stepped closer and translated.

'At this location, Jacques de Molay, grand master of the Order of the Temple, was burned on March 18, 1314.'

'At this very spot?' asked Andrew.

'Yes,' said Fiona, gesturing to the ground in front of them. 'Both de Molay and his second in command Geoffroy de Charnay. Their pyres and stakes would have been right here where we are standing now.'

'A grim way to go,' said Andrew.

'And they were just two out of hundreds of Templars that were put to death that way,' she said. 'But look over there.'

She pointed northwest across the widest part of the river to where a long ostentatious renaissance building stretched away along the north bank of the river past *Pont des Arts* and several hundred metres further towards the west.

'That's the Louvre,' she said, 'and that section over there that is closest to us is the site of the original Louvre Fort.'

'The castle of the wolves,' said Andrew, peering across the Seine.

'So, as it said on the second stone tablet,' continued Fiona, 'Jacques de Molay would have been able to see the castle as he died.'

'Speaking of which,' said Andrew. 'When does the museum close?'

'Seven o'clock,' replied Fiona. 'We have enough time to get inside.'

'It is probably also better if we arrive nearer to closing time when the museum is emptying,' said Andrew. 'Fewer eyeballs.'

They proceeded across Pont Neuf where Fiona stopped and turned around to point back across the Seine to the north-facing *Quai de l'Horloge* which runs along the edge of Île de la Cité on its northern side.

'See that building over there with the battlements, the round towers and the cone-shaped roofs?' she said. 'That is the *Palais de la Cité*, and it is very similar to how the Louvre Fort once looked. Walls built out of large neatly-cut square blocks of stone and round towers with curved foundations. You'll recognise some of that in a few minutes.'

They continued on to the sprawling museum complex and through the portal to the large and impressive rectangular square called *Cour Carrée*. The square lay almost exactly where the Louvre Fort had once stood until its partial demolition in the early 16th century when it was gutted to make way for a new palace. Walking across the square and through another portal, they emerged on *Cour du Louvre* with the now iconic modern glass pyramid. Erected in the 1980s, it had initially been a controversial departure from the surrounding classical architecture, but it had eventually become a globally recognised hallmark of the museum, symbolising a capital city that was rich in history but also modern and forward-looking.

They joined the short queue next to the 21-metre-tall glass pyramid that gleamed in the early-evening sunlight. The sun now seemed to hover perfectly above the centre of the elongated and almost one-kilometre-long *Jardin des Tuileries* park that stretched away from the museum towards the northwest. The 180-tonne glass pyramid was constructed from 673 individual panes of glass, and as the two of them filed inside and headed down to the floor of the large atrium below, it still felt very much as if they were outside because of the clear glass and the deep blue sky above.

They quickly found themselves moving against the main current of visitors, most of whom were heading for the exits now that it was approaching closing time. Hundreds of people were moving slowly towards the escalators, but as soon as they were being transported upwards to the exit, hundreds more appeared from the many hallways and corridors that converged on the large subterranean atrium.

With its almost thirteen kilometres of exhibits and thirty-five thousand items on display, the museum was truly vast. Anyone who desired to see the entire collection and who wanted to spend only ten seconds in front of each item would still need almost one hundred hours, or more than four full days and nights to do so. With annual visitor numbers approaching ten million, an average of about thirty thousand people passed through the museum every single day.

'The Louvre Fort's foundations are straight ahead,' said Fiona, 'but I want to see something else first. It's important.'

'All right,' said Andrew. 'What it is? And where?'

'You'll see,' said Fiona. 'It's better if I just show you. I want you to see it with fresh eyes.'

As they walked south through the wide underground tunnel to the *Denon* wing and back up to Level 1, they passed the largest exhibition room in the museum, *La Salle des États*. Also known as Room 711, it contained some truly enormous paintings as well as a small dark portrait on one wall around which a huge gaggle of visitors had gathered in a dense permanent crowd that was busily taking pictures and gawping at the famous oil painting.

'What's in there?' asked Andrew, jerking his head as they passed it walking along the adjacent corridor.

'Oh, that's just the Mona Lisa,' said Fiona, waving her hand dismissively. 'Except it is almost certainly a replica. The original was stolen in 1911 by an Italian museum worker, and ever since there have been rumours that the real Mona Lisa is being kept safe in one of the vaults under the building.'

'Interesting,' said Andrew, raising his eyebrows.

'What we really want to see is in here,' she said and led them into Room 713, also in the Denon Wing.

The room was relatively small by Louvre standards, but it was still about the size of six average living rooms. It was painted a deep ochre red colour, had a shiny amber herringbone wood floor and black wood panelling up to around waist height, and on its walls hung famous works of British and American painters. In the middle of one of the walls was the largest painting in the room, drawing visitors in with its dark moody greys and blacks, accentuated by the smouldering reds and orange near its centre. It was contained within a large, wide and ornate gilded frame, and underneath was a sign that read: *Le Pandemonium, 1841. Martin, John; Grande-Bretagne.*

'Here it is,' said Fiona, sounding apprehensive. 'The original of the painting in Caitlin's room.'

They both stepped up in front of the huge painting and took it in. It was somehow much more impactful in its full size and with the brush strokes in the oil paint clearly visible up close. The image was already seared into Fiona's memory, but standing in front of the original was chilling. She studied the dramatic scene closely. The tall, caped and helmeted figure on the right stretching up his arm whilst holding a golden shield and a lance. The terrified-looking cowering figure at his feet. Searing hot lava roiling up from the fissures in the rocks in front of them, and the grand but menacing city of Pandemonium towering over them in the distance.

'It's a disturbing painting,' said Fiona. 'But I am still a bit disappointed. I think I was hoping to spot something that we might have missed before. Something that could give us a clue as to exactly what has happened to Caitlin or where she might be. But I don't see anything. Except perhaps that the whole façade of the city of Pandemonium reminds me a lot of the buildings on the north bank of the Thames.'

Andrew stood close to her and took her hand in his.

'It's just a painting,' he said gently. 'Just because those lunatics think it is all real doesn't mean that it can help us find Caitlin. Only *we* can do that. Come on. Let's find those castle foundations. The cornerstone must be there somewhere.'

They turned around and went down the stairs, returning to the atrium by the entrance under the pyramid. From there they continued straight ahead towards the east until they came to a broad stairwell that went down two levels to where the ground level had been several hundred years earlier. This was now approximately five metres below the *Cour du Louvre* square. Here, a roughly fifty-metre section of the original foundations of the Louvre Fort had been excavated and presented for the viewing public. It was about four metres high, tapering in slightly as it extended upwards, and it even had two complete semi-circular tower foundations that were around ten metres in diameter. Of the hundreds of large stone blocks that it had been built from, virtually all of them were in almost pristine condition.

When Andrew and Fiona arrived in the long wide corridor running alongside the excavated section of the foundation, there were only a couple of other visitors left and they looked as if they were getting themselves ready to leave. They were taking the final snaps with their phones and marvelling at the impressive stonework as they slowly meandered ever closer to the two stairwells at either end of the corridor.

'Just look at this masonry,' said Fiona, stepping closer and placing a hand on one of the cold pale grey stone blocks. 'Each one of them is perfectly cut to size, and look here. They all have small marks chiselled into them near their corners. This one has a heart. And the one next to it has an asterisk. Here's one with a square.'

'Late medieval graffiti?' asked Andrew as he came over and inspected the many different symbols chiselled into each of the stone blocks.

'No,' replied Fiona. 'Each of these symbols belonged to one of the many stone masons who supplied the blocks for the construction of this foundation and this wall. The symbols were just put there by the masons so that they could demonstrate to the royal treasury how many they had supplied and were due payment for.'

'Simple but clever,' said Andrew, letting his fingertips run across a few of them.

As they walked further along the towering masonry, they began to get a sense of the true scale of the chateau during its heyday. The foundations alone comprised hundreds of stone blocks just on this short fifty-metre section, and the castle walls that had once extended around twenty metres up from there would have needed many thousands of such blocks for their construction.

When they reached the middle of the masonry section between the foundations of what had once been two towers, they saw that there was a small, low passage that led into the foundation itself. It was only about a metre high and barely half a metre wide, but it was obvious from the way it had been built into the foundation that this passage had been part of the original construction. However, its purpose was unclear, and there were none of the small descriptive signs that were otherwise found in their tens of thousands throughout the museum.

Placed almost inside the passage and blocking access to it was a metal bollard that had clearly been put there to prevent visitors from entering, but it immediately drew Fiona's attention as she approached the passage and knelt next to it. It was completely dark inside, but it was as clean and dry as out in the corridor. Looking up at the lintel that stretched across the narrow opening, she spotted another one of the small chiselled symbols. However, instead of it being placed in the lower corner of the stone block, it was positioned exactly in the middle near its lower edge.

'What have we here?' she whispered to herself.

'What?' said Andrew and joined her. 'What is this?'

'I don't know,' said Fiona, 'but I do know what *that* is.'

She was pointing to the small symbol which was much more intricate than any of the others, and which she immediately recognised as having truly ancient origins. It was essentially three simple symbols joined together. A semi-circle with the opening facing upwards at the top, attached to a full circle underneath, which was then finally joined with a cross at the bottom.

'This is the ancient alchemical symbol for Mercury also known as quicksilver,' she said. 'The only metal that is liquid at room temperature.'

'And highly toxic,' said Andrew.

'Yes,' replied Fiona, 'but that was not understood until fairly recently, by historical standards. The alchemists in ancient Mesopotamia treated it as a magical substance and attempted to use it along with other metals to make gold.'

'Needless to say,' observed Andrew, 'it never worked. Otherwise, everyone would be making gold in their garages.'

'No,' said Fiona, 'but in ancient times before modern empirical sciences like chemistry and physics, people took a mystical approach to most things. It was quite natural for them to perceive that there was something spiritual or even divine in the alchemical transformation of one metal into another. And these metallurgical methods, which do resemble religious rituals, were obviously closely guarded secrets amongst the Zoroastrians of Mesopotamia.'

'So, what does this symbol mean?' asked Andrew. 'Why is it here? It seems like quite a complex symbol for a stone mason to chisel into every block of stone.'

'Exactly,' said Fiona. 'There must be some other purpose to it.'

At that moment, one of the Louvre Museum's uniformed guards came around the corner at the end of the corridor, having just descended the stairs from the ground level. He was clearly doing his last round before closing time to gently encourage visitors to wrap up their visit and leave. As he came closer, he shot them a smile and gave them the five-minute warning that he had no doubt given thousands of times before.

'*Cinq minutes, s'il vous plaît,*' he said, pointing to his wristwatch just in case the two laggards in front of him didn't speak French.

'*Merci beaucoup,*' smiled Fiona apologetically.

The guard didn't slow down, but simply nodded and continued walking past them towards the other end of the corridor, clearly satisfied that the two respectable-looking visitors would be on their way back to the exit any moment now. As soon as he had disappeared from view, Andrew ducked down, swiftly squeezed past the metal bollard and disappeared into the passage. A second later, his arm shot out and tugged at Fiona's sleeve.

'Get in,' he said urgently. 'We don't have long.'

Twenty-Seven

Fiona joined Andrew inside the tight low-ceilinged passage, and they then moved a couple of metres further inside where the light quickly began to fade. However, Andrew was reluctant to turn on the torch on his phone in case it was visible from the corridor. Sitting in the relative darkness and out of view, Andrew placed his index finger in front of his lips. After a couple of minutes of not moving or speaking, his concerns were proven justified as they both heard the distinct sound of approaching footsteps reverberating along the corridor from one end to the other. They were unable to see who it was, but during the brief glimpse afforded to them out through the end of the passage, they could see that it was a guard. Continuing on without stopping, the guard soon reached the other end of the corridor, and then they heard the faint, fading sound of feet walking back up the stone stairwell.

Andrew turned around and switched on the torch. Ahead of them was a neatly constructed corridor which extended around five metres towards the west where it ended in a small square chamber. Only when they moved all the way inside did it become apparent that there was a circular opening in the floor. It was about a metre in diameter and seemed to reach down roughly three metres to a stone floor below. The walls of the circular pit were built from the same type of stone as the rest of the castle's foundations, but there seemed to be nothing down there.

Andrew shone his torch down into it, moving it around in an attempt to get a better view of what they were looking at. However, there were no discernible features, aside from the relatively smooth walls. The air smelt old but dry, and it looked as if the pit had been excavated but then left to its own devices, possibly because the archaeologists had been unsure of its purpose.

'Hold this, please,' Andrew whispered and handed Fiona his phone. 'I am going down there.'

'Will you be able to get out?' asked Fiona quietly.

'There are plenty of gaps between the stone blocks,' he replied. 'I can climb out again quite easily.'

He gripped the edge of the pit with both hands and let himself slip into it, feet first. A brief moment later, his feet landed with a thud on the stone floor below, and Fiona let his phone drop down to him. He caught it and began turning slowly to examine the inside of the pit.

'Hang on. There's another symbol down here,' he said in hushed tones, inspecting something on a stone block near the bottom of the pit that was much larger and heavier than the others. 'It's the mercury symbol again. Come down and have a look.'

Fiona hesitated for a moment, but then let herself slide over the edge and down along the curved wall of the pit where Andrew grabbed her around the waist and helped her down safely.

'Look there,' he said and pointed.

Fiona knelt and inspected the symbol, which was the same size and seemed to have been chiselled by the same person who had made the one on the lintel in the corridor above.

'What do you suppose this means?' said Andrew.

'Two identical symbols inside this place,' she said. 'Almost like signposts.'

'Let me try something,' he said, pulling out the Beretta 92 from his belt.

'Wait,' hissed Fiona nervously. 'What are you going to do?'

Andrew flipped the weapon around in his hand so that he was holding the barrel with the pistol grip sticking out like a hammerhead.

'Relax,' he said calmly. 'I am not going to shoot it. I want to know what this sounds like.'

He gently tapped the bottom of the pistol grip on the stone, and the effect was instant and unmistakable. Instead of a brief dull clonk, there was a much more extended and hollow-sounding reverberation.

The two of them looked at each other.

'Holy crap,' whispered Fiona. 'It sounds like there's some sort of cavity behind this stone.'

'I think you're right,' said Andrew. 'How do we get through, though? I wish I still had that fire axe.'

'Wait a second,' said Fiona. 'I don't think we need to break anything. I am pretty sure that sort of destructiveness would have been beneath the alchemists who built this place. They would have come up with a much more elegant solution.'

'Such as?' asked Andrew, replacing the Beretta.

'I think I have an idea,' said Fiona, suddenly looking excited. 'Aristotle referred to mercury as *Hydro-Argyros* – which translates literally as 'Liquid-silver' or 'Water-silver'. The ancients attempted all sorts of uses for it, but one that has been employed many times over the ages is lubrication. Mercury is such a viscous metal that it is ideal for making things slide across each other, and because it doesn't corrode or degrade like other metals it maintains that quality virtually indefinitely.'

'So, what are you saying?' asked Andrew.

'Try pushing it,' she replied, pointing at the large stone block with the mercury symbol.

Andrew did as she suggested and placed both hands on the block, but it didn't budge. Then he shifted his body so that he was sitting on the floor with both feet on the stone block and his back against the wall on the opposite side of the pit. He then began pushing, and it didn't take more than a couple of seconds before the brittle mortar around the edges of the stone block cracked and crumbled like dry clay, and almost immediately the entire stone block began moving inward amid a strange low grinding and rumbling noise. The further Andrew pushed it in, the easier it became as the block seemed to begin picking up a tiny bit of momentum, and within five seconds his legs were completely outstretched and the block had disappeared into the side of the pit. In its place was a short tunnel, only about half a metre on both sides, but what really caught their eyes was what the stone block had revealed underneath itself. It was a series of small, expertly chiselled channels into the rock underneath where the stone block had been, and they stretched across the width of the tunnel from one side to the other. Inside each channel were what appeared to be iron cylinders that were now floating on top of silvery mercury.

'Wow,' said Andrew. 'A roller system. I can't believe how easy it was to move this huge block of stone. It must weigh about half a tonne.'

'Look at the rollers,' said Fiona. 'Iron is heavy, but it is only about half the weight of mercury, so they actually float. But when the stone block was in place, the rollers would have been submerged in mercury. This would have prevented them from rusting, and it would have kept them perfectly lubricated. It's an absolutely ingenious system. If we came back here again in a thousand years, it would probably still work.'

'How on Earth could the archaeologists who excavated this place not have realised this?' asked Andrew.

'They probably thought this was just some sort of well,' shrugged Fiona. 'And to them, this was just another stone block. If you don't know what you're looking for, then you won't spot something like this. And archaeologists are not exactly known for their use of brute force. They would rather dig through a giant pile of dirt with a tiny brush than use a bulldozer.

They simply never realised that this stone was any different from the surrounding stones.'

'Let's see what is in here,' said Andrew, and got down on his hands and knees to begin crawling through the newly revealed passage.

'Try not to get the mercury on you,' said Fiona. 'It is not exactly known for its health benefits.'

When he reached the movable stone block, Andrew was able to push it further forward without too much effort, and within about a minute he emerged inside a chamber with walls and a ceiling built exactly like the rest of the castle's foundations.

'Come through,' he called to Fiona. 'There is some sort of chamber in here.'

She joined him, and the two of them soon found themselves facing a gothic doorway leading into another chamber. Above the doorway was a bas relief of a Templar cross above an inverted pentagram.

'Andrew,' said Fiona, her voice trembling. 'Look up there.'

'The pentagram,' said Andrew, realising what she was thinking.

'The lost chapter,' she said. 'It's here. I know it. I can feel it.'

As they were about to pass through the doorway, Fiona noticed a single line of text chiselled into the stonework directly above the apex of the Gothic arch.

'Wait,' she said and stopped just underneath it. 'There is some sort of inscription up here.'

'What does it say?' asked Andrew and joined her.

She craned her neck, wiped the dust from the indents and shone her torchlight at the inscription from an angle in order to accentuate the letters and make them more legible.

'It's an inscription in French,' she replied, taking a moment to study it. 'It reads *"Cumulus d'infinie mord"*. How strange.'

'What does it mean?' asked Andrew.

'It sounds rather cryptic,' replied Fiona without taking her eyes off the inscription. 'But it translates roughly into "an accumulation of infinite bites".'

'How bizarre,' said Andrew, peering through the dark tunnel ahead. 'What could that mean?'

'No idea,' said Fiona, shaking her head. 'Something along the lines of 'keep out', I suppose.'

'Well, we're not turning back now,' said Andrew, directing his torchlight through the narrow tunnel. 'We have to go on.'

Using the torches on their phones to light the way, they passed through the doorway into the tunnel, which was about two metres high and perhaps ten metres long. Its sides were decorated with bas reliefs of more Templar crosses that looked as if they had once been painted red. As they neared the end of it, they could see that the tunnel emerged into some sort of chamber, and Andrew was just about to pass over the threshold and through another gothic doorway when Fiona suddenly called out to him.

'Stop!' she exclaimed, pointing to the ground in front of him. 'Don't move.'

Andrew froze and slowly turned his head to look at her over his shoulder.

'What?' he said.

'There. On that flagstone in front of you,' she said.

He turned his head back to look ahead and down to where Fiona had now directed her torch beam. Barely visible to the unwary, but now quite obvious in the light from their two torches, was a symbol depicting what appeared to be a cross-section of a bulbous drinking vessel like a chalice, but with the mouth turned downwards.

'What is that?' asked Andrew.

'It is another ancient alchemical symbol,' replied Fiona. 'The symbol for life is a drinking vessel just like that one, but this is upside down, which means death. So do *not* step on that flagstone. I am sure it is some sort of trap to catch out the uninitiated.'

'Right,' said Andrew, peering down at the flagstone. 'I'm glad you're here.'

He walked carefully to the edge of the flagstone and then took a long step over it and inside the room beyond. Shortly thereafter, Fiona did the same, and soon they were safely on the other side.

They found themselves in a large circular space that was instantly recognisable. In its centre was a raised platform with an inverted pentagram chiselled into its surface, and near the edge on one side was a human-sized brimstone symbol made of metal. On the far side of the chamber was what appeared to be a now walled-up stairwell that once upon a time would have led up into the medieval castle itself. It looked like it had been deliberately blocked, perhaps in order to hide this place from intruders.

'This is exactly like the ceremonial chamber under the temple in London,' said Andrew. 'Or rather, the temple in London is probably a replica of one like this.'

As she made her way slowly around the platform, Fiona looked up at the brimstone symbol with a dismayed look on her face, shaking her head in disgust.

'Look,' said Andrew, pointing near the base of the brimstone symbol. 'Is that what I think it is?'

Fiona directed her torch beam to where he was pointing and stopped dead in her tracks.

'Another ossuary,' she said haltingly. 'Could this really be…'

'Let's find out,' said Andrew and climbed up onto the platform, followed closely by Fiona.

They both went down on one knee and each gripped one end of the stone ossuary's lid. Lifting it gently amid a faint grating noise as the stone lid scraped against the lip of the container, they raised it up and then placed it gently on the platform next to it. Leaning forward and using their torches to shine inside the ossuary, they found no skulls or bones, but instead, there was a tablet similar to the two others they had already discovered. It was roughly thirty by forty centimetres in size, with a thickness of perhaps three centimetres. However, this one was very obviously not made of stone. It gleamed and shone golden in the light from the two torches, emitting a warm glow that bloomed up and out of the ossuary and onto the faces of the two of them. Several lines of text had been stamped into the front of the malleable precious metal, but they were shorter and somehow looked different from what they had seen before.

'A gold tablet,' said Fiona. 'And it looks like it is in immaculate condition. The ultimate goal of alchemy. A metal virtually immune to entropy.'

'Well, pick it up and read it,' said Andrew.

Fiona put down her phone and reached inside the ossuary to grip the tablet and begin gently lifting it out.

'It's so heavy for such a thin piece of metal,' she said. 'It must weigh at least ten kilos.'

'What does it say,' asked Andrew, leaning forward to peer at it.

'I am not sure,' said Fiona as she studied it. 'It's not in French. It looks like it might be in Aramaic.'

'Aramaic?' said Andrew puzzled. 'That means that it is old, right?'

'Yes,' replied Fiona. 'Probably very old indeed. Not that you can tell just from looking at it. Even if it had been made thousands of years ago, it would still have looked exactly like this. It's no wonder that it was seen by the ancient alchemists as a divine metal.'

'But why Aramaic?' asked Andrew.

'I can't be sure,' said Fiona. 'Either it is genuinely so old that it stems from a time when that was the *lingua franca* of the Levant, and perhaps the Templars brought this back from the holy land. Or perhaps the Templars made this tablet themselves and simply decided to use it for this specific purpose. It would make sense since they would have been familiar with Aramaic from their many years on the Temple Mount in Jerusalem. And of course, Aramaic was the language of Jesus Christ, but also of the Bible's first humans – Adam and Lilith. At least according to the First Book of Enoch. And it was also the language in which the Babylonian Talmud was written around 500 BCE.'

Suddenly they heard movement from behind them, followed by the unmistakable sound of a pistol being cocked. In the next instant, a powerful torchlight came on, bathing the circular chamber in white light, and then they heard a familiar voice.

'What a fascinating bit of speculation that was,' said the man in a clipped and arrogant tone of voice.

The two of them spun around to see Tristan Maxwell standing inside the ten-metre-long tunnel near the doorway holding a powerful torch in one hand and a silver revolver in the other. Behind him was the towering blond neck-tattooed figure of the remaining Romanian thug. He was holding the Scorpion EVO 3 that Andrew and Fiona had already been on the receiving end of near Chateau La Roche. With a menacing scowl and eyes that gleamed with hatred, he was pointing it past Maxwell and straight at Andrew and Fiona.

'You two really are exceptionally persistent,' continued Maxwell. 'But I must commend you. You managed to do in a couple of days what our useless team of French so-called archaeologists have failed to achieve over several years. Well done. Oh, and allow me to introduce Constantin. He's very upset about his two dead friends. Now hand over the tablet.'

'How the hell did you find us?' seethed Fiona.

Maxwell tutted, tilted his head slightly to one side and looked at her condescendingly.

'You really ought to have understood by now,' he said, glancing briefly over his shoulder. 'We have friends in low places. And in high places, for that matter. You two were never going to walk away with that tablet.'

'You fucking sociopath,' said Andrew icily.

'Says the trained killer,' replied Maxwell mockingly before fixing them with a hard stare. 'Now, hand over the damn tablet.'

'Where is my sister, damn you?' shouted Fiona.

Maxwell sighed and hesitated for a moment whilst looking briefly up at the ceiling as if pondering how to phrase his next sentence.

'How shall I put this,' he finally said rhetorically. 'Your bitch sister is going to be bled dry like the sacrificial goat that she is. Apparently, that's all she was ever good for, according to the late Antoine. Anyway, you'll be interested to know that you two walked right past her when you made your little excursion inside our Temple in London. I was surprised that dear Caitlin didn't wake up when Fiona was banging on the door. Needless to say, all the access codes have now been changed.'

At the mention of Caitlin's location, Fiona's body tensed visibly. The thought of having been so close to her was torturous, and tears began to well up in her eyes.

'But,' continued Maxwell in his affected and self-congratulatory manner. 'She is safe and sound and in the hands of Laurent, whom I believe you have already met. I am sure he will take *very* good care of her if you know what I mean.'

Having listened to the barrage of taunts and insults from Maxwell, and now having to lay ear to the insinuation that Laurent would take advantage of Caitlin, Andrew was on the cusp of giving in to his basic impulses to rip out his gun and empty the magazine in Maxwell's direction. There was only so much rage his military discipline was able to suppress. His hand moved a hair's breadth closer to his weapon, but Fiona immediately sensed what he was thinking and fixed him with a stare and shook her head almost imperceptibly. Then her eyes darted towards Maxwell and down to his feet. Andrew instantly understood what she was trying to say.

'Anyway,' said Maxwell now sounding both bored and frustrated. 'Enough of this chitchat. Give me the *fucking* tablet!'

Neither Andrew nor Fiona moved a muscle, but just remained where they were, watching the increasingly impatient public schoolboy work himself into a state of rage. Drunk on his own sense of power over the two of them, Maxwell finally lost his patience and took a step forward whilst holding the revolver up in his outstretched arm and pointing it directly at the two of them.

When it happened, there was hardly any advance warning. The soft metallic click from under the flagstone with the alchemical symbol for death was barely audible, but the slight shift of the flagstone underfoot was enough for Maxwell to notice it. However, he would never have time to get out of the way. With staggering speed, almost too quick for the naked eye to register, two sets of long needle-like iron spikes shot out with huge force from both sides of the tunnel right where Maxwell was standing. Amid a sickening meaty slicing and skewering sound, a dozen spikes lanced out of their small circular recesses with incredible speed and force to impale Maxwell's body through multiple limbs. Two of them pierced his torso, one punched straight through his heart, one stabbed into his abdomen and another punched through his right thigh. One of the spikes higher up caught his neck at the base of his skull separating his spinal cord and dislocating his jaw to leave his mouth twisted open with his tongue sticking out. The final spike entered his brain through his right temple and pushed violently forward in such a way as to fracture the eye socket and cause the right eye to pop out, leaving it hanging down onto his cheek, attached only by the optic nerve. His mutilated body twitched several times, and he somehow remained standing in an unnatural contorted posture, held up by the diabolical spikes that in an instant had turned his strong athletic body into a lifeless yet erect corpse.

During those first few seconds after the trap had sprung, Constantin had been too shocked to do anything other than watch the macabre scene playing out in front of him. But then he suddenly seemed to regain his composure and leaned over to one side trying to get a clean shot with his submachine gun at the people who had killed his two mates. Andrew and Fiona immediately scrambled off the raised platform and out to the sides of the chamber where Constantin did not have a line of sight.

Seeing them begin to move, the Romanian decided that his opportunity to fire was fast disappearing, so he pressed the trigger and held it down, spraying bullets through the gap between the spikes. However, many of them caught Maxwell's dead body, and it twitched and jerked as the bullets impacted, as if it had suddenly come alive again. Those of the bullets that managed to get through slammed into the wall behind Andrew and Fiona, and some hit the large brimstone symbol, ricocheting off it and bouncing around the room. Blinded by rage and frustration, Constantin made the fatal mistake of emptying his magazine, and suddenly he was trapped behind Maxwell's barely recognisable body and the roughly eight metres to the other end of the tunnel.

Realising his mistake, he spun around and bolted for the far end of the tunnel, but Andrew had heard the distinctive click of the submachine gun magazine running dry. He moved quickly to the doorway, raised what had once been Dragomir's Beretta 92, aimed past Maxwell's corpse and between the metal spikes and fired three times in rapid succession. All three bullets slammed into the back of Constantin as he ran, tore through the dense layer of muscle and bone between his shoulder blades and punched out through his chest. The force of the impacts sent him toppling forward and falling heavily onto his front on the dusty floor, his head hitting the flagstones with an audible crack as several bones in his nose and skull broke. But by then, his heart had already stopped beating, and a few seconds later he exhaled for the final time with a protracted liquid-sounding gurgle.

Andrew, who had been on one knee in standard firing position, rose and looked past Maxwell at the immobile body of the last of the three Romanians.

'I don't usually shoot people in the back,' he said frostily, 'but in this case, I am prepared to make an exception.'

Fiona came over and stood next to him. Her breathing was much more rapid than Andrew's as she shifted her gaze from Constantin to Maxwell. Blood was escaping from the body of Haywood's protege where it had been pierced by the metal spikes, and it ran languidly along the underside of the spikes and dripped audibly onto the flagstones below.

'Gross,' she whispered.

'Nothing less than they deserved,' said Andrew flatly. 'These people think nothing of killing anyone who gets in their way, so if this is what it takes to stop them, then good riddance. I certainly won't lose any sleep over it.'

Fiona had sat down on the edge of the raised circular platform, staring blankly into the wall. In her mind's eye, she could see small glowing letters dancing around on the stone blocks, re-arranging themselves in different sequences as her brain attempted to make sense of the cryptic inscription above the doorway to the ceremonial chamber.

'Holy crap,' she said suddenly. 'I think I have just worked out what that inscription above the doorway meant. It's an anagram.'

'Really?' said Andrew.

'Yes,' she replied. 'If you rearrange the letters, *'Cumulus d'infinie mord'* becomes *'Lucifer Dominus Mundi'*. Lucifer, Lord of the World.'

'L.D.M.,' said Andrew.

'That's right,' said Fiona. 'That phrase wasn't something Antoine and Laurent came up with themselves. It is hundreds of years old, and it is clearly tied to the history of their family. It is almost as if that entire clan is steeped in this type of mythology going back all the way to the two Templar brothers Gerard and Arnaud.'

'What a lovely way to grow up,' said Andrew deadpan, once more looking at Maxwell's grotesque upright corpse. 'Anyway, I think that's what they call poetic justice. One of the Sons of Lucifer killed by a contraption of so-called infinite bites made by the very people who laid down the foundation of this madness that he adhered to. It serves him right.'

'So, what do we do now?' said Fiona, looking back at the ossuary with the golden tablet that Haywood and his father had been seeking for decades.

'Well,' said Andrew. 'We have the lost chapter, so we now possess the ultimate bargaining chip. But I am suddenly not sure if we actually need it.'

'What?' said Fiona flabbergasted. 'Why not?'

'Well,' said Andrew, 'Haywood has no idea that Maxwell is dead, and he might not even know that all of the three Romanians are now also pushing up daisies.'

'I guess,' said Fiona hesitantly. 'So?'

'And access to the Temple in London is controlled by a biometric ID system, right?' asked Andrew. 'Wasn't that what Sean told us?'

'Yes, and?' she asked.

Andrew shifted his gaze from her to the mutilated corpse of Tristan Maxwell, studying it for a moment. Then he looked at Fiona once more.

'You probably won't like this,' he finally said, 'but I think I might have an idea.'

Twenty-Eight

It was nighttime. That was all she knew. There was no light coming in through the opaque glass brick in the exterior wall, although the small and weak overhead light in the apex of the vaulted ceiling was on as usual. She assumed that the light was left on all the time so that she could always be monitored by the small camera above the door, but this also meant that if there was a power cut she would be plunged into complete darkness. She reflected ruefully on how that was gradually becoming a fitting analogy to her state of mind and increasingly brittle psychological state.

Her failed attempt at escaping had left her with a sense of hopelessness and despair, as well as a small but painful bruise on her neck where the drug injector had penetrated her skin and flooded her body with a powerful sedative.

Sitting on the edge of the bed with her head down, her long auburn hair spilling down in front of her face, she suddenly heard the distinct sound of the metal gate at the end of the corridor outside open. The noise was faint, but it jolted her nonetheless in the way an animal might react to the sound of its abuser's cane being picked up, or the way in which a victim of domestic violence might react to the sound of the key in the front door late at night. She steeled herself for what was to come.

During the past several hours, she had sat on the floor by the names that had been etched into the wall, trying to work out how long she might have been locked in this cell. Her memory was blurred and her sense of time was warped by the drugs, but she had eventually arrived at the terrifying conclusion that tonight was almost certainly summer solstice.

She listened as the sound of footsteps approached. It sounded like two people. The sound stopped and there was a brief moment of complete silence. Then she thought she heard a man's voice. It sounded familiar somehow. Or was she finally losing her mind?

Suddenly filled with determination, she decided that as soon as the door opened she was going to hurl herself at whoever came in, punching, clawing and biting with all of her remaining strength. Despite her weakened state, she was prepared to do anything to try to escape one final time before it was too late. Even to kill if she had to. The lock on the metal door produced a sharp metallic snap, and then the door swung open.

★ ★ ★

The Eurostar trip from Paris' *Gare du Nord* to London's St Pancras International had taken two hours and fifteen minutes. Before catching the last departure for the British capital on that day, Andrew and Fiona had retraced their steps up and out of the subterranean ceremonial chamber. They had been carrying the gold tablet containing the lost chapter of the Lucifer Codex, as well as two other items which Andrew had wrapped in a piece of cloth he had torn from Constantin's clothes.

They had been disappointed to find that Tristan Maxwell's phone had not survived the spike trap, as one of the sharp, pointy metal spikes had punched clean through the phone before piercing his torso. It was quite possible that the phone's memory bank was still retrievable somehow, but they did not have the time to find a technically skilled data recovery specialist to do the job. They had finally found the lost chapter, and they now also had a way to access the Sons of Lucifer temple back in London, and that was all that mattered. Unless something unforeseen happened, they would be able to find Caitlin and free her at last.

By the time the blue, yellow and grey bullet-shaped train slid the final distance to the platform at St Pancras, it was a quarter past eleven at night. They disembarked and rushed to King's Cross tube station and took the first Northern Line train south to Monument Station. Sitting quietly inside the carriage surrounded by commuters and clutching her bag containing their golden cargo, Fiona felt as if everyone could see right through her. She spent the next ten minutes staring down at the floor and avoiding eye contact with anyone. Andrew stood in the aisle next to her, looking as calm as ever despite the unusual items he was carrying inside his jacket pocket.

The journey took only ten minutes, but to Fiona, it felt more like half an hour. Exiting Monument tube station, they hurried the short distance south to Upper Thames Street. It had only been a couple of days since the last time they had been there, but it felt like several weeks had passed. As had been the case during their previous visit, the dark street was moderately busy, with cabs and other cars zooming past every few seconds. This time they walked straight up to the front door and pushed inside into the large lobby that was divided into two sections separated by the glass wall with the elaborate security gates. Andrew walked up to one of the biometric scanners and initiated the identification procedure. The first set of heavy glass doors swung open, and they both moved forward to squeeze inside a space only designed to be big enough for one person. The door swung shut behind them, and the small panel in front of them came alive with a blue glow, presenting them with a short piece of text requesting biometric ID.

Andrew extracted a piece of cloth from his inside jacket pocket and gently folded it open. As Fiona looked on, her face was a picture of revulsion. Peeling back the slightly damp and sticky final corner of the cloth, Andrew then used the thumb and index finger on his right hand to pick up Tristan Maxwell's severed right eyeball by its optic nerve. It was beginning to smell distinctly putrid. As he shifted his fingers to hold the eyeball using all five fingertips, the slippery and slightly squishy sphere almost slipped out of his hand. He caught it and held it up in front of the biometric scanner. As soon as the scanner detected something in front of itself, it directed a low-powered beam of light to sweep across the eyeball, mapping out the intricate structure of blood vessels and performing a search of its database to find a match. Within less than a second, the panel turned green. Immediately thereafter a small finger-sized glass shelf shot out from underneath it, and the panel once again turned blue asking the occupant to place his or her right thumb there. Having remembered the contents of Sean Taylor's notes, Andrew opened another cloth parcel and extracted Maxwell's thumb, placing it carefully in the middle of the shelf. The scanner swept a red light across the severed digit, reading the fingerprint. Shortly thereafter the ID panel turned green once more and then the second set of glass gates opened allowing them inside.

'Well, that was easy,' whispered Fiona, looking somewhat suspicious. 'We need to move fast in case there is someone else here.'

They took a sharp right turn and proceeded down the winding staircase towards the underground levels. Knowing their way around from their previous visit, they quickly found the corridor with the door behind which Maxwell had claimed Caitlin was held. Andrew pressed the button next to the metal gate, and soon they were inside the corridor. Fiona suddenly rushed ahead, forcing him to hurry to keep up.

'Here it is,' she said in a hushed but tense voice.

'Hang on a second,' said Andrew, once again extracting the eyeball and placing it in front of the scanner. It produced a brief beep, and then a green light lit up the control panel.

Andrew quickly pulled out his gun and placed himself next to the door on the opposite side from the hinges, ready to move into the room with his pistol up and engaged in case someone had set up an ambush for them inside.

'Ok,' he said. 'Ready?'

Fiona nodded.

'Open it,' he said, and she immediately pressed the button to disengage the lock.

It snapped loudly, and Andrew then yanked the door open and moved inside with his pistol out in front of himself, ready to fire.

'Shit,' he said, as Fiona cautiously peeked around the door frame. 'It's empty.'

'What?' said Fiona, sounding like she was on the verge of tears as she pushed inside and past him.

They looked around the medieval prison cell, barely able to comprehend what they were seeing.

'What the hell is this sick place?' exclaimed Fiona. 'Where's Caitlin?'

'They must have moved her,' said Andrew, turning to inspect the room and immediately clocking the CCTV camera that was embedded in the wall above the door. 'And I think we're being watched.'

'Look here,' said Fiona, moving towards the far end of the cell where there was a small wooden bed with blankets made from coarse grey fabric. 'There is a phone over here.'

Andrew turned and joined her by the bed. Placed neatly on the grey blanket was a cheap-looking black mobile phone.

'Is that Caitlin's?' he asked.

'No,' said Fiona. 'Her phone is pink, and this thing looks old and battered.'

At that moment, the phone's screen lit up and it began to ring, producing a chirpy melody that sounded decidedly strange inside the prison cell. The two of them looked at each other, and then Andrew picked it up, took the call and turned around to face the camera. He suddenly had the distinct and unpleasant feeling they had been outmanoeuvred.

★ ★ ★

Sitting inside his 66th-floor office in the Shard, Christopher Haywood was watching the live feed from inside the prison underneath the temple. His new plan was built on certain assumptions and had been somewhat risky, but he felt confident that he had deduced what had transpired over the past few days. As a consequence, and in order to maintain the upper hand and acquire what he had spent years and countless millions attempting to find, he had been forced to adjust.

Next to him was Tom, who stood immobile with his feet slightly apart and his hands in front of himself, one hand clasping the wrist of the other arm. A small bulge on the left side of his jacket hinted at the concealed weapon he was carrying in his capacity as both driver and private close protection staff.

Watching the man and the familiar-looking woman on the screen in front of him, Haywood picked up his mobile phone and dialled a number that Tom had recently entered into the contacts list under the name 'Lilith'. The phone rang once before it was picked up, and Haywood watched as the tall, powerfully built man placed it next to his right ear and turned around to look directly at the camera with an icy stare.

'Who is this?' said the man coldly.

'Let's finally introduce ourselves,' said Haywood in a calm and confident baritone voice. 'My name is Christopher Haywood. I think I can guess who the young lady is, but I have yet to discover who you are. Would you care to…'

'My name is Andrew Sterling,' interrupted Andrew, his voice cutting and his eyes seeming to bore into the CCTV camera, 'and if you touch so much as a hair on Caitlin's head, I swear I will hunt you down, nail you to the fucking wall and flay you alive. And then I will send the pictures of your rotting corpse to your two kids.'

To Haywood's right, Tom shifted slightly at the vicious threat to his paymaster, but he made no sound.

'Now, now, Mister Sterling,' said Haywood superciliously, seemingly entirely unaffected by Andrew's attempt at intimidation. 'There'll be no need for that, my dear chap. Am I safe in assuming that you managed to find the lost chapter?'

'Yes. We found it,' replied Andrew curtly. 'And we will trade it for Caitlin.'

'You have it?' asked Haywood, now leaning forward in his chair, sounding captivated by the notion of the item he had been seeking for so long finally being within his grasp.

'We have it right here,' said Andrew as Fiona dug into her bag and extracted the tablet, showing it briefly to the CCTV camera.

'It's the real thing,' she said before putting it away again.

'My word...' breathed Haywood. 'You really managed to find it.'

'What about Laurent?' asked Andrew curtly. 'Is he there with you?'

'He seems to have made himself scarce,' Haywood said, sounding slightly perplexed and looking up at Tom, who nodded once. 'I think he finally realised that he wasn't quite the man he thought he was. Especially after you killed Antoine, and he almost got himself shot dead trying to get revenge. The truth is, I never really fully trusted those two boys to live up to my expectations. But you might say that they were a necessary evil for acquiring Chateau La Roche, which I gather you are now quite familiar with. Anyway, I couldn't have predicted just how incompetent those twins would turn out to be when it really mattered. I suppose that's a lesson learnt.'

'Yes. Lightweights both of them,' said Andrew derisively. 'Same with Maxwell. You really can pick them.'

'Ah,' said Haywood. 'Regarding young Maxwell, I must say I was rather disappointed that he also failed. I gather you got the better of him too? Would you care to tell me what happened?'

'Let's just say hubris got the better of him, and that he decided to stick around under the Louvre,' replied

Andrew, sounding increasingly impatient. 'Listen, we don't have time to stand here and talk to you all night. Where the hell is Caitlin? And are you ready to make the trade or not?'

'Of course,' replied Haywood, glancing across his large office to a sofa where Caitlin was lying tied up and knocked out by a powerful sedative. 'She's right here with me. If you bring me the tablet right now, Fiona can have her little sister back. I take it you know where to find me?'

'Yes,' said Andrew, turning to look at Fiona. 'We will be there in fifteen minutes.'

Fiona nodded her agreement to the plan.

'Use the private lift from the parking garage under the Shard,' said Haywood. 'I will unlock access for you once I can see you on the CCTV.'

'Don't even think about pulling some stunt on us,' said Andrew. 'It will end very badly for you.'

'Come now,' said Haywood. 'You may not like me or my methods very much, but I am a man of my word.'

'We will see about that,' said Andrew coldly.

'As long as I get the lost chapter, Caitlin will be safe,' continued Haywood, a hint of menace now suddenly creeping into his voice. 'But understand this. Any subsequent attempt by you or Fiona to go public about the private affairs of my family or my business will be met with swift and brutal consequences for you and everyone you know. You should doubt neither my capacity nor my willingness to follow through on this warning.'

'Oh, I am sure you mean it,' said Andrew. 'One thing at a time, though. Let's just get this thing over with. Every second I spend talking to you makes me want to vomit a little bit more.'

'I do like you,' chuckled Haywood humourlessly. 'People like you are a rare commodity. I would offer you a job, but I somehow sense that is not an option for you.'

'You sense correctly,' said Andrew tersely. 'There's not a chance in hell of that ever happening. See you in fifteen minutes.'

Twenty-Nine

When the elevator doors opened after the extraordinarily long ride from the parking garage beneath the towering Shard, Andrew and Fiona found themselves in a large lobby. It was tastefully decorated in muted earthy colours with Italian-designed sofas around a glass coffee table. On the walls were oil paintings in gilded frames, and the soft, warm downlights in the coffered ceiling gave the space the ambience of a swanky member's club or a quiet bar area in an upmarket hotel. However, that illusion was soon shattered when they spotted a tall and broad, dark-haired man on the other side of the lobby and down a short corridor. He was standing in front of a wide mahogany door with brass trim around the edges, and he was wearing a black suit and tie. In his right hand was a pistol, which he held low in front of himself, his left hand clasping his right wrist.

Their appearance as the elevator doors opened seemed to neither surprise nor disturb him. He stood immobile and simply regarded them cooly as they emerged. Andrew's attention immediately zoomed in on the weapon. It was a SIG Sauer P320, which was extremely difficult to come by in the UK. Having been designed in a modular fashion that allowed it to use different barrel lengths and types of ammunition, it was a highly flexible firearm. It had also been designed to be ambidextrous in its handling. In other words, it was a weapon which indicated that the man holding it knew how his way around firearms. His calm demeanour and the quiet confidence with which he observed Andrew and Fiona as they walked towards him further hinted at the fact that he was almost certainly ex-military and very capable of squeezing the most out of the weapon he was holding. He might even have some sort of special forces background.

'You already know who we are,' said Andrew frostily as he and Fiona stopped a couple of metres from the tall, well-groomed man. 'Just open the door.'

The man narrowed his eyes momentarily, and there was a look of acknowledgement on his face as he regarded Andrew. Then he nodded silently and gave a wry smile, seemingly recognising that he was dealing with a fellow warrior.

'SAS?' he asked.

'That's right,' replied Andrew.

'I was SBS myself,' said Tom.

'I really don't care, mate,' said Andrew. 'We're not here to make friends. Let's just get on with this.'

'Suit yourself,' shrugged Tom. 'Are you armed?'

Andrew opened the left side of his jacket to show the big man the Beretta 92.

'I am going to have to take that off you,' said Tom, taking half a step towards Andrew.

'Negative,' said Andrew in a tone of voice that made it clear that his position was non-negotiable. 'We don't trust any of you people, so if you have a gun, I have a gun. Otherwise, we walk away.'

Once again, Tom shrugged, and then he extracted a small clamshell phone from inside his suit jacket and pressed the speed dial. A few seconds later, Andrew and Fiona could hear the faint but familiar voice of Christopher Haywood, and after a couple of brief exchanges, Tom snapped the phone shut and slipped it back into his pocket.

'You're good to go in,' said Tom. 'But leave the gun in the holster. I will be watching you.'

'No problem,' replied Andrew.

Fiona had been watching the exchange between the two men, feeling tense and uncomfortable. On the one hand, it felt like a typical male pissing contest, but on the other hand, there was clearly also more to it. The idea of weapons being brought to the meeting was deeply unsettling to her, but she trusted Andrew to make the right decision at this moment. It was also clear from the interaction between him and the tall man in the suit that there was a certain level of grudging mutual respect between the two of them because of their similar backgrounds. She just hoped that the exchange could happen without anyone losing their heads and resorting to violence. Deep down, she was very sceptical about Haywood simply handing over her sister in exchange for the golden tablet, but she had to believe that he was going to stay true to his word. After all, the tablet was what he and his father had been after for all these years. What was to come later on was something they would have to deal with at that point. All that mattered now was getting Caitlin back.

Tom opened the heavy front door to Haywood's apartment and led them inside. They soon stood in the middle of a much larger lobby that looked very similar to the one they had just left, except here open doorways led off in three directions to different parts of the enormous home. Judging by the size of the tapering tower here on the 66th floor, the floorplate was easily twenty thousand square feet in size, and most of that was taken up by Haywood's private residence.

As Tom led them through the western side of the apartment towards Haywood's office in the far north-western corner, Andrew and Fiona were treated to a view of the opulence with which Haywood surrounded himself. There was expensive furniture, Italian marble flooring, wood panelling and countless pieces of art in the form of sculptures and oil paintings throughout the place, and each room was more or less the size of most normal houses.

When they arrived at Haywood's office door, Tom knocked, opened it, stepped inside and then turned around to walk another few steps backwards and to the side while pulling the slide on the SIG Sauer to chamber a round. He was clearly keen to signal that he would be ready in case the SAS soldier tried anything stupid.

Andrew and Fiona calmly walked inside to see Haywood sitting behind his desk on the opposite side of the room with his back to the tall floor-to-ceiling windows. Outside, darkness was enveloping the towering building they were now inside, but from below they could see the yellow glow of the lights of central London blooming up into the sky and lighting up the underside of the grey cloud layer.

Once Tom had closed the door behind them, Haywood rose and regarded them silently for a few moments while he adjusted his suit, tie and cufflinks.

'So,' he said, as Tom, still holding his gun and ready to fire, walked over to stand next to him. 'We finally meet.'

'Where's Caitlin?' said Fiona with barely contained venom as she stepped forward to face the man who for days now had put her sister as well as herself through an unspeakable nightmare.

Haywood produced a cold, thin smile as he walked slowly to stand next to the desk about ten metres from his two visitors.

'Show me the tablet,' he said, 'and then I will bring your sister to you.'

Fiona looked at Andrew who nodded, and she then extracted the gold tablet from her bag. It gleamed under the spotlights in the ceiling, and Haywood's gaze was now firmly fixed on it. His face was a picture of enchantment, and he seemed utterly mesmerized by the artefact and the idea of what he might be able to do with it.

'No more delays,' ordered Andrew. 'Show us Caitlin.'

Haywood allowed himself another brief moment to admire the tablet before he tore himself away and turned to look at Tom who had not moved a muscle throughout the exchange. The former SBS soldier then left the office through a doorway into an adjacent room, returning a few seconds later with a gaunt-looking Caitlin. Her hair was the same rich auburn colour it had always been, but her face looked emaciated, and her eyes appeared sunken and vacant. As Tom gripped her arms and led her roughly into the office, she seemed to stagger along in a daze and appeared wobbly on her feet. She was obviously exhausted, but clearly also under the influence of some sort of drug.

Upon finally seeing her sister again, it was all Fiona could do not to immediately run towards her, and Andrew sensed her impulse to do so. He placed a hand on her lower arm, hoping it would be enough for her to maintain control of herself.

'You fucking arseholes,' Fiona seethed, tears of anger mixed with relief welling up in her eyes as she struggled to resist the impulse to launch herself at Haywood. 'What the hell have you done to her?'

'And now the tablet,' said Haywood, ignoring Fiona's outburst and sounding slightly impatient.

At the sound of her sister's voice, Caitlin seemed to partly regain her senses and suddenly notice her surroundings. She raised her head and looked up, suddenly seeing Fiona for the first time.

'Fiona?' she said weakly, sounding as if she didn't quite dare believe that her sister was really there.

'Caitlin, it's me,' said Fiona, her voice almost breaking. 'I'm here to take you home.'

'Hand over the bloody tablet!' shouted Haywood, in a rare and sudden burst of anger, seemingly oblivious or simply indifferent to the drama playing out between the two reunited sisters.

Fiona's gaze snapped to Haywood, and she regarded him for a brief moment with unadulterated venom in her eyes. Then she held up the tablet next to her head.

'Listen, you pompous prick,' she said spitefully. 'I will throw this onto the floor between us if you tell your rabid dog over there to get his hands off my sister and let her walk to us.'

Haywood winced at the insult, which was no doubt something he was not used to.

'Calm yourself, young lady,' he said ominously, glancing at Tom and making a clenched fist with his left hand. 'You don't want your dear sister to be hurt, do you?'

At Haywood's signal, Tom gripped Caitlin's arm tight and jolted her violently, which made her cry out in pain. Watching the building tension, Andrew was becoming concerned that the entire situation was about to spin out of control and descend into chaos. His right hand was itching to reach inside his jacket for the Beretta and just finish this the old-fashioned way.

'I will fucking bury you,' seethed Fiona menacingly, her eyes burning with fury as she looked from Haywood to Tom and back again. 'Once this is over, you two and everyone in your sick circle of delusional freaks are going down. I am not going to let you do this to anyone ever again.'

'Oh, will you just shut up, you stupid little bitch,' roared Haywood. 'We both know that you wouldn't get anywhere with your tittle-tattle. No one would believe a word of it. It would be my word against yours. Who do you think would come out on top? Especially since mental illness clearly runs in your family.'

He gestured crassly towards Caitlin.

'Just look at her!' he continued contemptuously. 'Paranoid delusions. Even if you shouted it from the rooftops, no one would ever consider it anything but slander. And my firm would have a field day with such an attempt at character assassination.'

Andrew sensed that things were now about to boil over. Haywood's composure was slowly but surely eroding, and he could tell from the tension in Tom's body that he was instinctively readying himself for violence. Like a coiled spring about to be released.

'Character?' scoffed Fiona disdainfully, pinning Haywood with a hard stare and continuing in a voice as cold as ice. 'Christopher. Your so-called character committed suicide a long time ago when you boarded this looney train. You and your whole sick lineage have caused more than enough harm already chasing after your deranged ideas. If anyone here is delusional, it is you. Tell me, does delusion run in *your* family? Is your son already as batshit crazy as you are, or are you still working on screwing him up the way old Cyril did you?'

Haywood finally looked rattled, his eyes darting between Fiona and the golden tablet. Being this close to his goal and finding himself having to deal with insults from this nuisance of a woman was becoming too much for him. He had tried to do this the civilised way, but it was clearly becoming intractable, and his deep-seated impulse to do what he did best and simply impose his will using brute force finally won out. Without turning his head, he shifted his gaze to Tom and nodded almost imperceptibly – but not quite. Andrew spotted the signal, and he heard the subtle but unmistakable click of the SIG Sauer's safety being flicked to Off. His right hand was darting inside his jacket before Tom could begin to raise his gun.

As his weapon arm came up, Tom took half a step away from Caitlin whilst shoving her in the direction of Haywood. In a single fast and fluid movement, Andrew had already pulled out the Beretta and dropped to one knee with the pistol held in two hands, aiming at Tom. Fiona stood frozen to the spot as the entire scene unfolded in less than a second. In the next instant, two loud shots rang out almost simultaneously, and she screamed as the gold tablet next to her head was ripped from her grasp with a clang as if hit by a metal baseball bat. In the same moment, the 9 mm bullet fired from Andrew's Beretta slammed into Tom's left shoulder, making his torso twist slightly to one side and throwing off his aim so that when he squeezed the trigger again the shot went up into the ceiling above Fiona's head. A split-second later, Andrew's pistol barked angrily twice more in quick succession. One of the bullets punched into Tom's solar plexus while the other smacked into his throat with a wet slap and exploded out of the back of his neck, taking blood, tissue and fragments of vertebrae with it. It then covered the distance to the large floor-to-ceiling window directly behind

Haywood in an instant and shattered the huge glass pane into thousands of tiny pieces. Almost instantly, hundreds of kilos of glass dropped heavily onto the floor in a loud crystalline cacophony, leaving a pile of white glistening fragments right on the edge of what looked like a black void outside.

Tom's body slumped down onto the expensive wood flooring like a sack of wet laundry, and almost immediately the cool wind from outside whirled into the office, suddenly reminding them all that they were on the 66th floor near a roughly 230-metre drop to the ground below.

Haywood seemed to take no notice but darted forward with surprising speed and agility for a man of his age, grabbed the petrified Caitlin roughly by her auburn hair and suddenly produced a short but vicious-looking silver dagger with a curved blade. He pulled Caitlin towards himself and quickly backed up to stand next to his desk again. Andrew shifted his aim to the grand master, who then violently yanked Caitlin's head backwards and brought the razor-sharp blade up to her exposed throat. As he moved almost fully behind his hostage, making it a reckless endeavour for Andrew to try to shoot him, his eyes were ablaze with fury and his breathing was fast and heavy.

'Seems your hired gun wasn't such a good shot after all,' said Andrew coldly, attempting to stall for time whilst frantically trying to come up with a way to get to Haywood without putting Caitlin at risk. 'I guess they don't call them the Shaky Boat Service for nothing.'

'You bloody vermin!' Haywood sneered through gritted teeth, seemingly unaffected by the violent death of his long-time bodyguard as he pressed the blade visibly against Caitlin's neck. 'Enough of this bloody waste of time. This is your last chance. Hand over the fucking tablet, or I will slit this little lamb's throat and bleed her dry.'

'That's won't be necessary,' said a calm male voice from the direction of the office door. 'I'll take it from here. I need everyone to put down your weapons immediately.'

Andrew and Fiona turned their heads to see a man with a pudgy-looking face and short, dark, curly hair and sideburns. He appeared to be in his fifties, and he was wearing a beige trench coat over a badly-fitted brown suit and a charcoal bucket hat. In his hand was a Glock 17, which was the standard handgun for the tiny number of Metropolitan Police officers who had firearms licenses, and it was pointing straight at Andrew.

Without taking his aim off Haywood, Andrew turned his head just enough to be able to see the new arrival. Fiona instinctively raised her hands above her head.

'Who the hell are you?' asked Andrew.

'My name is Detective Inspector Graham Palmer,' said the man, whilst taking a couple of steps into the room, fishing out his police ID and holding it up for Andrew to see. 'I work homicide and missing persons cases at the Met. Please, sir. Put your gun on the floor and take a step away from it.'

'Arrest him!' blurted Fiona in an agitated voice, pointing at Haywood. 'He is a psychopath. He has been kidnapping and killing young women. That's my sister.'

Palmer jerked his head towards Haywood and Caitlin who were standing just a couple of metres from the precipitous drop.

'I know what this man is,' continued Palmer placatingly. 'I will sort this out. More officers are on their way here as we speak. Please, sir. Lower the weapon and place it on the floor.'

Reluctantly, Andrew flicked the Beretta's safety to On and bent down slowly to place the weapon on the floor in front of him.

Palmer moved forward in an arc that kept him several metres from Andrew and Fiona whilst shifting his aim to Haywood.

'Please step away from your weapon,' he said whilst looking at Andrew. 'I will take care of this.'

Andrew did as he was asked and took a step back whilst still looking at Palmer. He then shifted his gaze to Haywood, who was still holding a whimpering Caitlin by the hair and pressing the silver blade against her throat. A small red line of blood had now formed on the side of it where the dagger had grazed open her soft skin. As Andrew looked at Haywood's face, he thought he saw a subtle change wash over it. The grand master suddenly seemed calm and cold as ice again, with the look of a serpent carefully studying its prey and simply waiting for its opportunity to strike. When Andrew's eyes met Haywood's, his intuition was suddenly screaming at him that something was terribly wrong. A cold chill ran down his spine. Haywood turned his head slightly to look straight at Palmer.

'*Sit mundus ardeat*,' said the grand master.

Andrew's grasp of Latin was shaky at best, but he understood enough to be able to translate what Haywood had just said. 'Let the world burn.'.

The reaction from Palmer was almost instantaneous. Turning his body and shifting his aim, he was now pointing the Glock directly at Andrew.

'No…' breathed Fiona as she suddenly realised to her horror what was playing out in front of them.

She fell to her knees where she stood, keeping her hands above her head. Andrew began to raise his hands slowly, realising that he had no counter to the situation that was now unfolding. Haywood had outplayed them, and the chances of them seeing the next sunrise were suddenly looking extremely slim.

'You corrupt bastard,' he said icily, his eyes shooting daggers at the police officer. 'How much is he paying you?'

'He doesn't have to pay me,' replied Palmer with a strangely unemotional sigh. 'My reward is coming.'

'So, you're another one of those superstitious cranks,' said Andrew, shaking his head in disgust. 'I can't seem to go a single day lately without running into more of you people.'

Palmer fished out a set of handcuffs from a pocket in his trench coat and took a step towards Andrew.

'Put these on,' he ordered, tossing them towards a spot on the floor next to Andrew whilst still pointing his gun at him.

As the handcuffs sailed through the air, Palmer caught movement down low and to his side. It was Fiona who was suddenly holding a weapon with both hands. In the next instant, the loud dry crack of what had until recently been Constantin's Beretta 92 rang out inside the office, and an instant later the bullet slammed into the side of Palmer's head. It tore through his skull and exploded out the other side in a misty cloud of blood, hair and cerebral matter. Immediately, his body seemed to concertina downwards, slumping heavily onto the floor like a ragdoll suddenly having had all of its strings cut.

With her hands now trembling violently from the shock of what she had just done, Fiona shifted her aim towards Haywood who immediately pulled his head behind Caitlin's. Suddenly terrified that she might accidentally shoot her own sister, Fiona splayed out her fingers on both hands, letting the Beretta drop to the floor as if it had been red hot. In the same moment, Andrew dove for his own weapon, and in a flash, he was back up and pointing it at Haywood. From this angle, he now had a clear shot at Haywood's head. However, before he could aim and fire, Caitlin's bound hands suddenly shot up to grab Haywood's wrist. Like a vicious predator, she bared her teeth and bit down as hard as she could on Haywood's hand, eliciting a shrill cry of pain from the grand master and causing him to relinquish his grip on the dagger. As it clattered to the floor, Caitlin brought her head back with as much speed and power as she could muster, and as the back of her head connected forcefully with the bridge of Haywood's nose, there was a sharp crunch as it broke.

Instinctively, Haywood staggered back a couple of steps and suddenly found himself teetering on the edge of where until a few minutes ago the floor-to-ceiling window had been. His expensive flat-soled

Italian leather shoes slid on the glass fragments and he lost his balance, tipping backwards. His right hand shot out in a flash and gripped into the wide painted-steel window frame, where razor-sharp pieces of glass were still embedded. They cut deep into his fingers and blood immediately began to ooze out, but he held on as his entire body now leaned precariously out over the lethal drop. His face was an image of terror.

Moving quickly, Caitlin turned around and took a step forward. Bracing herself against the frame with her left hand, she extended her right hand so that Haywood could grab onto it. He quickly did so, but when he tried to pull himself back to safety, Caitlin held his hand in place. His shoes were now right on the edge, slipping ever so slightly to one side and threatening to make him lose his footing and plunge to the street below.

'Help me,' he pleaded in a whisper, looking imploringly at Caitlin.

As the sweat on Haywood's hand began to cause his grip on hers to slip, she regarded him for a moment. Inside herself, she felt the deep-seated and instinctive impulse to help another human being and save them from certain death, but as she looked into his eyes, hers suddenly narrowed and hardened. Then she spoke.

'Burn in hell,' she breathed icily.

Then she let go.

★   ★   ★

The last sound Christopher Haywood made came from a sharp intake of breath as his hand slipped, and he began his long fall towards the ground below. As his body began to accelerate towards the ground, the enormity of what was happening to him sank in. He closed his eyes and began to recite incantations.

The fall took just under seven seconds, during which time his body clipped the slanted side of the building once, which sent him into a rapid spin, arms and legs flailing. When his body finally hit the street below, it was travelling at just over 230 kilometres per hour, or roughly the average speed of a Formula One car going around a track. His frail body slammed into the concrete pavement slabs with such force that it broke practically all the roughly two hundred bones in his body and shattered his skull as if it had been an egg. His brain matter exploded from his disintegrating skull like a watermelon hit by a shotgun at close range, and it shot out onto the concrete in all directions with a wet slap. He had fallen onto an area that was already covered with fragments of glass from the shattered window above. What was left of him was now barely recognisable, and the macabre spectacle, as well as the loud noise of the violent impact, sent the few remaining pedestrians in the area scurrying for cover.

★   ★   ★

Up on the 66th floor, Fiona broke away from Andrew and darted towards Caitlin, who stood frozen to the spot, stunned by what had happened and by what she had just done. Her face was an image of confusion mixed with relief, but she realised that she felt no sense of regret about what she had just done. Seeing Fiona rush towards her, she launched herself at her big sister, and then the two of them were locked in a tight embrace. They clung to each other for a long time. Whimpers of relief escaping from their lips. Tears running down their cheeks. The nightmare was finally over.

Epilogue

Père Lachaise Cemetery, Paris – One year later

It was just after daybreak and the early morning sun was casting its first rays across the large and leafy cemetery located northeast of the centre of Paris in the 20th *Arrondissement* of the city. The cemetery, which is the largest in Paris, dates back to 1804 which was the year when Napoleon Bonaparte was given the title of Emperor by the French Senate. It was also the year when the new Napoleonic Code entered into force, allowing freedom of religion, forbidding any privileges based merely on birth, and specifying that all government positions should be filled by the most qualified. In many ways, it set the standard for civil legal codes throughout Europe from then on.

More than one million people have been buried in the cemetery since it opened, and roughly sixty-nine thousand elaborately decorated stone tombs sit on the forty-five-hectare plot, often shaped in the gothic style that originated in this capital city from around the 12th century. After its opening, it quickly became the fashionable place for prominent Parisians to be buried, and it is now home to the tombs of such illustrious names as Polish composer Frédéric Chopin, French actress Édith Piaf, Paris architect and city-planner Georges-Eugene Haussmann, Ettore Bugatti who was the founder of the eponymous car manufacturer, the American musician Jim Morrison and many more.

Close to its eastern edge near the *Avenue Circulaire* which wraps around the entirety of the cemetery just inside its borders is the tomb of Oscar Wilde. It is a large cuboid shape which was seemingly created from a single large block of stone without much consideration given to its ultimate destination amongst the smaller and mostly gothic-inspired tombs in the cemetery. The sculptor made clear efforts to incorporate imagery onto its sides that reflected Wilde's most famous poems, including a winged human-shaped creature with a sphinx-like head that seemed to be in mid-flight. A tradition quickly emerged on the part of certain female visitors of kissing the tomb whilst wearing red lipstick. As a consequence, the tomb was for years virtually covered in red imprints from the lips of poetry pilgrims, until the local authority erected a tall glass barrier around it after it was discovered that the lipstick was seeping into the stone and eroding it.

Standing on the footpath by himself in front of the tomb of the Irish poet as the golden morning sunlight cut through the trees and began to caress the writer's final resting place, Andrew extracted his phone and checked the time. The cemetery would officially open in ten minutes, so he needed to get moving.

As he walked south along another one of the many gravel-covered footpaths towards a separate section of the cemetery reserved for the French aristocracy, he reflected on the aftermath of the events that had transpired here in Paris and in London over the course of just a few days, almost exactly one year earlier.

He remembered watching the news on TV carrying the story about the shocking suicide of one of London's most preeminent solicitors, who had inexplicably decided to end his own life and had plunged to his death from his apartment in the Shard. It later turned out that he had been at the head of a cartel that had manipulated everything from the property markets to the currency markets. A special investigative unit operating under parliamentary scrutiny had subsequently been set up, and it was in the process of concluding that several cabinet members were intimately connected to the dead CEO and the now-defunct Montague Solicitors. As for the ancient gold tablet with the Aramaic text, Fiona had retrieved it and handed it in to the British Museum. Initially, she had been tempted to melt down the diabolical tablet, sell the gold and give the money to charity. However, the historian and archaeologist in her had been unable to go through with it. Regardless of its sinister connotations and origins, it was still the case that the tablet was an ancient historical artefact and as such not something she could allow herself to destroy. With regards to Professor Kersley, it had turned out that the old man had been on Christopher Haywood's payroll as a scholar helping him to make sense of some of the ancient texts and thereby unwittingly assisting the Sons of Lucifer in their sinister quest. However, it had subsequently been established beyond doubt that he had been unaware of the fraternity's agenda and of its history of abducting and killing young women during their evil rituals at the Temple.

Arriving in the secluded area inside the cemetery where only members of the French upper classes lay buried, Andrew veered off the gravel path and stood in between a group of bushes. The path he was watching dipped down a couple of metres and curved slightly, giving anyone walking along it the sense of descending into a mausoleum, with dozens of tombs arranged on either side. This was where members of the Rancourt family had been buried since the cemetery's opening more than two centuries earlier. From Andrew's vantage point, he was able to see the most recent tomb, and if he was right in what he had been suspecting, then all he had to do now was wait and arm himself with patience.

After about an hour, his patience was rewarded as a man with a familiar gait came walking along the curved path and down into the dip. Wearing a short grey jacket and blue jeans, he stopped by the tomb, approached it slowly and knelt beside it. Moving silently, Andrew approached him to stand about five metres away before he spoke.

'Stand up and turn around slowly,' he said cooly as he pulled back the hammer on the suppressed Glock 19. 'And keep your hands where I can see them.'

From the way Laurent Rancourt's posture stiffened, it was plain that he instantly recognised Andrew's voice.

'I figured I might find you here,' said Andrew calmly, in a voice devoid of emotion. 'Almost a year to the day from when I sent your sick brother off to meet his maker, I thought you might show up right here.'

'How did you find this place?' said Laurent, his voice and accent almost identical to that of his dead twin.

'The funeral ledgers of Paris are publicly available,' replied Andrew. 'Not exactly a job that requires Hercules Poirot to show up.'

'What do you want?' asked Laurent. 'Everyone is dead already.'

'Almost everyone,' said Andrew stonily.

'So, you've come to kill me?' asked Laurent, a cold and quiet acceptance creeping into his voice as he turned slowly to face his stalker.

'I came to make things right,' said Andrew. 'You and your brother put a lot of young women through hell, and almost all of them lost their lives because of what you two did. Did you really think you would be able to get away with that without paying the price one day?'

'Just get on with it then,' said Laurent, placing himself so that he faced Andrew directly, and then raising his chin and clenching his jaw briefly. 'I know where I am going.'

'Any last words?' said Andrew dispassionately.

'I guess I will see you in hell,' said Laurent with a snarling scowl. 'And when I do, the Lord Lucifer will surely…'

The recoil of the suppressed Glock 19 made the weapon twitch in Andrew's hand. A split second later the 9 mm bullet smacked into Laurent's forehead and removed a palm-sized section of the back of his skull, taking a large chunk of brain matter with it and sending a spray of blood splattering onto the leaves of nearby bushes with the sound of heavy rain drops.

'I very much doubt that,' said Andrew coldly as Laurent's dead body slumped ungracefully to the ground in a heap.

He lowered the weapon and quickly unscrewed the suppressor, took out the magazine, released the slide from the body of the gun, extracted the barrel and stuffed the components into his jacket pocket. About half an hour later, as he was walking across the Seine along Pont de Sully on his way back to catch the next Eurostar departure back to London, he casually tossed each component over the stone barrier. No one noticed as the small metal parts sailed over the side one by one and plunged into the murky grey water with barely audible splashes.

Three hours later, the Eurostar train pulled into London St Pancras and shortly thereafter Andrew was back in the house in Hampstead where Fiona was waiting for him.

NOTE FROM THE AUTHOR.

Thank you very much for reading this book. I really hope you enjoyed it. If you did, I would be very grateful if you would give it a star rating on Amazon and perhaps even write a review.

I am always trying to improve my writing, and the best way to do that is to receive feedback from my readers. Reviews really do help me a lot. They are an excellent way for me to understand the reader's experience, and they will also help me to write better books in the future.

Thank you.

Lex Faulkner

Printed in Great Britain
by Amazon